"It can't work, Nick. Can't you see? You're part of this."

Laura waved her arms around her. "The house, the history, all of your family. All of it. It's massive. And you're trying to pretend it doesn't matter, but it does, Nick."

He folded her hands into his, like he always did. "Laura. If I can't have a normal life outside of it, I'm doomed. Of course all this is important to me. But there are other things, too," he said, and he leaned forward and kissed her.

She pulled away from him.

Nick looked at her in disbelief. "You're actually going to throw this all away, because you're an inverted snob," he said angrily. "You're a coward," he said, his voice harsh.

"If you like," said Laura. Her hands were shaking as she unlocked the car door.

"You know, I actually thought I might be falling in love with you," he said quietly. He turned and walked toward the house, and didn't turn back once.

Turn the page to read rave reviews for
A Hopeless Romantic *by Harriet Evans!*

"Where's all the passion, romance, and comedy we love gone? Enter Harriet Evans and not before time."
—Heat

Praise for Harriet Evans and *A HOPELESS ROMANTIC*

"A delicious romcom, surprisingly believable."
—Marie Claire

"Hard to resist."
—Elle

"Harriet Evans has scored another winner with her second novel . . . will warm you up like brandy on a winter's night. . . . Witty, entertaining, self-reflective, and full of characters you'll grow to love."
—Heat

"An entertaining page-turner."
—Closer

"Superior romcom with heart and soul."
—Bella

GOING HOME

"Fabulous. . . . I loved it."
—Sophie Kinsella

"A joy from start to finish—sharp, funny, and modern as well as warm, cuddly, and nostalgic."
—Fiona Walker

"A brilliant debut novel. . . . A delightful romantic comedy with self-effacing humor and witty dialogue."
—*Romantic Times*

"A lovely, funny heart-warmer. . . . Evans's heightened comic style and lovable characters make it effortlessly readable."
—*Marie Claire*

"An engaging first-person recounting of a watershed six months in one young woman's life."
—*Booklist*

Also by Harriet Evans

going home

Harriet Evans

a hopeless romantic

DOWNTOWN PRESS

New York London Toronto Sydney

DOWNTOWN PRESS
A Division of Simon & Schuster, Inc.
1230 Avenue of the Americas
New York, NY 10020

This book is a work of fiction. Names, characters, places, and incidents either are products of the author's imagination or are used fictitiously. Any resemblance to actual events or locales or persons, living or dead, is entirely coincidental.

Originally published in Great Britain in 2006 by HarperCollins*Publishers*

First Downtown Press trade paperback edition October 2007

Designed by Mary Austin Speaker

Manufactured in the United States of America

10 9 8 7 6

Library of Congress Cataloging-in-Publication Data

Evans, Harriet, 1974-
A hopeless romantic / Harriet Evans.
p. cm.
ISBN-13: 978-1-4165-5068-6
ISBN-10: 1-4165-5068-2
1. Single women—Fiction. 2. Vacations—England—Norfolk—Fiction.
3. Truthfulness and falsehood—Fiction. I. Title.
PR6105.V347H67 2007
823'.92—dc22

2007015142

For the magnificent specimen,
my mother, Linda. With all my love.

acknowledgments

With many thanks to Kim Witherspoon, David Forner, Beth Davey, and all at Inkwell. No thanks to David for revealing the *Desperate Housewives* finale secret, though. And a huge thank-you to Louise Burke and all my friends at Pocket, especially Maggie Crawford.

How to understand it all! How to understand the deceptions she had been thus practicing on herself, and living under!—The blunders, the blindness of her own head and heart!—she sat still, she walked about, she tried her own room, she tried the shrubbery—in every place, every posture, she perceived that she had acted most weakly.

—*Emma,* Jane Austen

part one

chapter one

Laura Foster was a hopeless romantic. Her best friend, Jo, said it was her greatest flaw, and at the same time her most endearing trait, because it was the thing that most frequently got her into trouble, and yet falling in love was like a drug to her. Having a crush, daydreaming about someone, feeling her heart race when she saw a certain man walk toward her—she thrived on all of it, and was disastrously, helplessly, hopelessly incapable of seeing when it was wrong. Everyone has a blind spot. With Laura, it was as if she had a blind heart.

Anyone with a less romantic upbringing would be hard to find. She wasn't a runaway nun, or the daughter of an Italian count, or a mysterious orphan. She was the daughter of George and Angela Foster, of Harrow, in the suburbs of London. She had one younger brother, Simon, who was perfectly normal, not a secret duke, or a spy, or a soldier. George was a computer engineer, and Angela was a part-time translator. As Jo once said to her, about a year after they met at university, "Laura, why do you go around pretending to be Julie Andrews, when you're actually Hyacinth Bucket?"

But Laura never allowed reality to get in the way of fantasy. By the time she was eighteen, she had fallen for: a runny-nosed, milk-bottle-glasses–wearing, primary-school outcast called Kevin (in her mind, Indiana Jones with glasses); her oboe teacher, Mr. Wallace, a thin, spotty youth, over whom she developed a raging obsession and calluses on her fingers, so ferociously did she practice; and about fifteen different boys at the boys' school around the corner from hers in Harrow.

When she went to university, the scope was even greater, the potential for romance limitless. She wasn't interested in a random pickup at a club. No, Laura wanted someone to stand underneath her window and recite poetry to her. She was almost always disappointed. There was Gideon, the budding theater director who hadn't quite come out of the closet. Juan, the Colombian student who spoke no English. And the rowing captain who was much more obsessed with the treadmill at the gym than with her; her dentist, who charged her far too much and then made her pay for dinner; and the lecturer in her humanities seminar whom she never spoke to, and who didn't know her name, whom she wasted two terms staring at in a heartfelt manner.

For all of these, Laura followed the same pattern. She stopped eating, she mooned around, she was acutely conscious of where they were in any room, thought she saw them around every corner—was that the back of his curly head going into the newsagents? She became a big, dumb idiot whenever any of them spoke to her; so fairly often they walked away, bemused that this nice girl with dark blond hair, a sweet smile, and a dirty laugh who'd seemed to like them then behaved like a tourist in a strange land, eyes downcast, virtually mute. Or they'd ask her out—and then Laura, for her part, usually came tumbling down to earth with a bang when she realized they weren't perfect, weren't this demigod she'd turned them into in her mind. It wasn't that she was particularly picky, either. She was just a really *bad* picker.

She believed in The One. And every man she met, for the first five minutes, two weeks, four months, had the potential in her eyes to be The One—until she reluctantly realized he was gay (Gideon from the Drama Society), psychopathic (Adam, her boyfriend for several months, who eventually gave up on his MA in the Romantic poets and joined the Special Air Service to become a killing machine), against the law (Juan, the illegal immigrant from Colombia), or Josh (her most recent boyfriend, whom she'd met at a volunteer reading program seminar at work—she worked for the local council—decided was The One after five minutes, and dated for over a year, before realizing that, really, all they had in common was a love of local council literacy initiatives).

It's fine for girls to grow up believing in something like The One; but the generally received wisdom by the time Laura was out of university, as she moved into her midtwenties, as her friends started to settle down, was that it didn't really exist—well, it did, but with variations. Not for Laura. She was going to wait till she found him. To her flatmate and childhood friend Yorky's complaints that he was sick of sharing his flat with a lovesick teenager all the time, as well as a succession of totally disparate, odd men, Laura said firmly that he was being mean and judgmental. To Jo's pragmatic suggestions that she should join a dating agency, or simply ask out that bloke over there, Laura said no. It would happen the way she wanted it to happen, she said—you couldn't force it. And that would be it—until five minutes later when a waiter in a restaurant would smile at her, and Laura would gaze happily up at him, imagining herself and him moving back to Italy, opening a small café in a market square, having lots of beautiful babies called Francesca and Giacomo. Jo could only shake her head at this, as

Laura laughed with her, aware of how hopeless she was, compared to her pragmatic, realistic best friend.

Until, one evening about eighteen months ago, Jo came round to supper at Yorky and Laura's flat. She was very quiet; Laura often worried that Jo worked too hard. As Laura was trying to digest a mouthful of chickpeas that Yorky had marvelously undercooked, trying not to choke on them, Jo wiped her mouth with a piece of paper towel and looked up.

"Um . . . hey."

Laura looked at her suspiciously. Jo's eyes were sparkling, her heart-shaped little face was flushed, and she leaned across the table and said, "I've met someone."

"Where?" Yorky had said stupidly.

But Laura understood what that statement meant, of course she did, and she said, "Who is he?"

"He's called Chris," Jo said, and she smiled, rather girlishly, which was even more unusual for her. "I met him at work." Jo was a real estate solicitor. "He was buying a house. He yelled at me."

And then—and this was when Laura realized it was serious—Jo twisted a tendril of her hair and then put it in her mouth. Since this was a breach of social behavior in Jo's eyes tantamount to not sending a thank-you card after a dinner party, Laura put her hand out across the table and said, "Wow! How exciting."

"I know," said Jo, unable to stop herself smiling. "I know!"

Laura knew, as she looked at Jo, she just knew, she didn't know why. Here was someone in love, who had found The One, and that was all there was to it.

Chris and Jo moved into the house she'd helped him buy after six months; four months after that, he proposed. The following December, a couple of weeks before Christmas, he and Jo were to be married, in a London hotel. Jo had eschewed grown-up bridesmaids, saying they were deeply, humiliatingly tacky, much to Laura's disappointment—she was rather looking forward to donning a nice dress, and sharing with her best friend the happiest day of her life. Instead, she was going to be best woman, and Yorky an usher.

It seemed as if Jo and Chris had been together forever, and Laura could barely remember when he hadn't been on the scene. He fitted right in, with his North London pub ways, his easy, uncomplicated personality, so laid-back and friendly compared to Jo's dry, rather controlled outlook on life. He had friends who lived nearby—some lovely friends. They were all a gang now, him and Jo, his friends, Yorky and Laura, sometimes Laura's brother, Simon, when he wasn't off somewhere being worthy and making girls swoon (where Laura was always falling in love, Simon was always falling into bed with a complete stranger, usually by dint of lulling her into a false sense of security by telling her he worked for a charity). And Hilary, also from university and christened Scary Hilary—because she was—and her brother, Hamish, their other friends from work or university, and so on. Laura's easy, happy, uncomplicated life went on its way. She had a brief, intense affair with a playwright she thought was very possibly the new John Osborne, until Yorky pointed out that he was, in fact, just an idiot who liked shouting a lot. Yorky grew a mustache for the autumn. Laura got a raise at work. They bought a PlayStation to celebrate—games for him, karaoke for her. Yes, everything was well within its usual frame, except that Laura began to feel, more and more, as she looked at Jo and Chris so in love and looked at the landscape of her own dull life, that she was taking the path of least resistance, that her world was small and pathetic compared to Jo's. That she was missing out on what she most wanted in the world.

Under these circumstances, it was hardly surprising that the next time Laura fell, she fell hard. Because one day, quite without meaning to, she woke up, got dressed, and went to work, and everything was normal, and by the next day, she had fallen in love again. But this time, she knew it was for real. And that was when everything started to go wrong.

chapter two

Laura's grandmother, Mary Fielding, was the person Laura loved most in the world (apart from whomever it was she was in love with at that moment), even more so perhaps than her parents, than her brother. Mary was a widow. She had lost her husband, Xan, eight years before, and she lived on her own, in a small but perfectly formed flat in Marylebone. There were various reasons why Laura idolized Mary, wanted to be just like her, found her much more seductive than her own parents. Mary was stylish—even at eighty-four, she was always the best-dressed person in a room. Mary was funny—her face lit up when she was telling a joke, and she could make anyone roar with laughter, young or old. But the main reason was that Mary had found true love. Her husband, Xan, was the love of her life to an extent Laura had never seen before or since. They had met when each was widowed, in Cairo after the Second World War. Mary had a daughter, Angela, Laura's mother. Xan also had a daughter, Annabel, whom Laura and Simon called aunt, even though she wasn't really related to them, and neither was Xan.

Because of her mother's natural reserve, it was Mary whom Laura told about her love life, her latest disaster, the person she was in love with. Because she lived in central London, and so not far from Laura on her way into and out of work, it was Mary Laura called in to see, to talk to, to listen to. And it was Mary whom Laura learned from, when it came to true love. She did not learn it from her own unemotional parents. No, she learned that true love was epic stuff, as told by Mary.

One of Laura's favorite stories was how Mary and Xan had realized they were in love, on a trip out to the pyramids to see the sun rise. It had been pitch black as they rode out, crammed in a jeep with the other members of their club in Cairo. And as the sun rose, Xan had turned to Mary and said, "You know I can't live without you, don't you?" And Mary had said, "I know."

And that was that. They were married six months later.

George and Angela, by contrast, had met at a choral society function off the Tottenham Court Road, when they were both at university. Somehow, Laura felt this wasn't quite the same.

"You are the love of my life. The woman I want to grow old with. I love you."

He was staring at her intensely, his eyes boring into hers. Laura raised her hand to his chest and said breathlessly, "I love you, too."

Beyond them, the sun was rising, flooding the vast desert landscape with pink and orange color. Sand whipped her face, the silk of her headscarf caught in the breeze. She could feel the cold smoothness of the material of his dinner jacket against her skin as he caught her and pulled her toward him.

"Tell me again," Laura whispered in his ear. "Tell me again that you love me."

Suddenly, a microphone crackled loudly, jerking Laura back to reality, as someone cleared his throat and said, "To my beautiful wife, Jo!"

"Aah," the wedding guests murmured in approval, as Laura came back down to earth with a bump. There was some sniffing, especially from Jo's mother up at the top table, as Chris raised a glass to his new bride, kissed her, and then sat down, to a welter of applause and chair shuffling.

"Aah," Laura whispered to herself, leaving her daydream behind with a sigh. She looked at Jo, her best friend, so beautiful and happy-looking, and found tears were brimming in her eyes. She turned to her flatmate, Yorky, who was sitting next to her, and sniffed loudly.

"Look at her," she said. "Can you believe it?"

"No," said Yorky, raising an eye at Chris's cousin Mia. Yorky had recently begun to teach himself how to raise one eyebrow, in a "come to me, pretty laydee" way. This had involved several hours of grimacing into Laura's hand mirror in the sitting room of their flat, whilst Laura was trying to watch TV. She got very irritated when he did this, and frequently told him that being able to raise one eyebrow was not the key to scoring big with the ladies. Wearing matching socks was. As was having a tidy room. And not acting like a crazy stalker when some girl said no after you asked her out. These were the things that Laura frequently told Yorky he should be concentrating on; yet, much to her deep chagrin, he ignored her every time. For Yorky's retort was always that what Laura knew about dating was worthless.

What a perfect, happy day, Laura thought as she gazed around the room, clapping now that the speeches were over. She was gripping her glass, searching for someone she couldn't see. Suddenly her eye fell on Jo and she watched her for a moment, truly radiant, happy and serene in an antique lace dress, her hand resting lightly on her new husband's as they sat at the top table. Laura couldn't help but feel a tiny pang of something sad. It wasn't just any bride sitting there in the white dress with the flowers and the black suits around her. It was Jo, Jo with whom she had danced all night in various Greek nightclubs, with whom she had spent hours in Topshop changing rooms, with whom she had stayed up all night when she sobbed her heart out after her last boyfriend, Noel, dumped her. It was her best friend, and it was weird.

She blinked and caught Jo's eye, suddenly overcome with emotion. Jo smiled at her, winked, and mouthed something. Laura couldn't tell what it was, but by the jerking of her head toward the best man, Chris's newly single brother, Jason, Laura thought she could guess what Jo meant. Laura followed her gaze, shaking herself out of her mood. Jason was nice, yes. Definitely. But he wasn't . . . Damn it, where *was* he?

"Who are you looking for?" said Yorky suspiciously, as Laura cast her eyes around the room.

"Me?"

"Yes, you. Who is it? You keep looking round like you're expecting to see someone."

"No one," said Laura rather huffily. "Just looking, that's all."

"There's Dan," said Yorky.

"Who?" said Laura.

"Dan. Dan Floyd. He's raising his glass. He's talking to Chris."

"Right," said Laura calmly. "Ah, there's Hilary. And her mum. I should go and say—"

"Laura!" said Jo, coming up behind her, dragging someone by the hand. "Don't go! Here's Jason! Jason, you remember Laura?"

"Hey. Of course," said Jason, who was an elongated, blonder version of Chris. "Hi, Laura."

"Er," said Laura. "Hi, Jason, how are you?"

There is nothing more likely to induce embarrassment in a single girl than the obvious setup at a wedding in front of friends. Laura smiled at Jason, and once more cast a fleeting glance around the room. Where was he?

"Good, thanks, good," said Jason, as Jo nudged Yorky and grinned, much to Laura's annoyance.

"See the match on Wednesday?" Yorky asked Jason, in an attempt at bloke-ish comradeship.

"What match?" said Jason.

"Oh . . ." Yorky said vaguely. "You know. The match. The big game."

"What, mate?" Jason repeated, scratching his head.

"Anyway, great to see you, mate," said Yorky, changing tack and banging Jason hard on the shoulder, so that he nearly doubled up. "So, Laura was just saying— Laura? Help me out here."

Jason gazed at Yorky, perplexed. Laura looked wildly around her, seeking an escape, and then someone over Jason's shoulder caught her eye.

"Jason split up with Cath two months ago," Jo hissed in her ear, in a totally unconvincing stage whisper, as Laura gazed into the distance. It was him, of course it was him, she would know him anywhere. "You know he's living in Highbury now? Laura, you should—"

But Laura was no longer standing next to her; she had turned around to say hello to their friend Dan, who had appeared by her side. Vaguely she heard Jo's tut-tutting; vaguely she was aware that she should be making an effort.

For Jo hadn't seen the look on Laura's face after Dan tapped her on the shoulder. In fact, Jo and Yorky hadn't been seeing quite a lot of things lately, and if they had, they would have been worried. Especially knowing Laura as they did.

"You had a good evening, then?" Dan was saying to Laura, smiling wickedly at her.

"Yes, thanks," she replied, looking up at him, into his eyes. "Good speeches."

"Great," he said, shifting his weight so that he was exactly facing her. It was a tiny movement, almost imperceptible to Jo, Yorky, or any of the other hundred and fifty people in that room, but it enclosed the two of them together as tightly as if they were in a phone box.

Dan smiled at her again as Laura pulled her shawl over her shoulders, and she smiled back, helplessly, feeling her stomach turn over at his sheer perfectness. His dark blond hair, the boyish crop that curled over his collar. His tanned, strong face, wide cheekbones, blue eyes, lazy smile. He reminded her of a cowboy, a farmhand from the Wild West. He was so relaxed, so easy to be with, so easy to be happy with, and Laura glowed as she gazed up at him, simply exhilarated at the prospect of a whole evening in his company—a whole evening, during which anything could happen. Suddenly she could barely remember whose wedding it was, why those rich people were there—she didn't care.

He was here. She was here with Dan, and he was hers for the rest of the evening, and for those hours only, she could indulge herself with the secret fantasy that they were a couple who'd been going out for years. Perhaps they were married already. Perhaps Jo and Chris had been the only witnesses at their beach wedding in Barbados two years ago. Dan in a sarong—a sarong would suit him, unlike most men. She in a silk sundress, raspberry pink, her dark blond hair falling loose down her back. Some spontaneous locals and other couples gathered at the seashore, crying with joy at how perfect, how in love they obviously were, totally poleaxed by the strength of their emotion, the purity of their love. Laura and Dan, Dan and Laura. Perhaps—

"Laura!" a voice said sharply. "Listen!"

Laura realized she was being prodded in the ribs. The lovely bubble of daydream in her head burst, and she tore herself away from Dan and looked around to see Yorky glaring at her.

"I was talking to you!" he said, affronted. "I asked you a question four times!"

"I'll see you later," Dan murmured, shifting away from her. "Come and find me, yeah?" And he very lightly ran his hand over her bare arm, a tiny gesture, unnoticeable to anyone else, but Laura shuddered, and looked up at him fleetingly, even more sure than ever. As Dan moved off, he raised his glass to her and smiled a regretful smile. Laura screamed inwardly, and turned away from him toward Yorky. "Sorry, love," she said. "What was it?"

"Is this fob watch too much?" said Yorky, fingering the watch hanging from his waistcoat. "I think it is. I'm not sure, but perhaps it overloads the outfit. What do you think?"

"Ladies 'n' gentlemen," came a bored-sounding voice from a loudspeaker in the back of the room. "Please make your way back into the ballroom. Mr. and Mrs. Lambert are about to perform their first dance. Ah-thann yew, verrimuch."

Laura looked wildly around, as if trying to prioritize the many tasks on her mind. She glared at Yorky, who was still waiting for an answer.

"Yes, it is. Far too much. I totally agree. In fact, it's *hideous,*" she said crossly. "You'd better take it off and throw it away. I'm going to the loo, see you in a minute," she finished, and hurried away.

* * *

Dan, Dan, Dan. Dan Floyd. Even saying his name made her feel funny. She muttered it on her way to the loo, feeling sick with nerves, but totally exhilarated. Laura had got it bad. She *knew* it was bad, and she knew if any of her friends knew they'd tell her it was futile, that she should get over it, but she couldn't help it. It was meant to be. She was powerless in the face of it, much as she'd tried not to be. Dan, Dan Floyd, looking like a ranger or an extra from *Oklahoma!*, calm, funny, and so sexy she couldn't imagine ever finding any other man remotely attractive. Laura wanted him, plain and simple.

She had constructed a whole imaginary life for them, based around (because of the *Oklahoma!* theme) a small house in the Wild West with a porch, a rocking chair—for Laura's granny, Mary—corn growing in the fields as high as an elephant's eye, and a golden-pink sunset every night. Mary would drink gins on the porch and dispense wise advice, and would sit there looking elegant. Dan would farm, obviously, but he would also do the sports PR job thing that he did. Perhaps by computer. Laura would—well, she hadn't thought that far. How could she do her job on the prairie? Perhaps there were some dyslexic farmhands who'd never learned to read properly, yes.

Her friend Hilary was in the loos when she got there, washing her hands. "Oi," she said. "Hi."

Laura jumped. "Oh. Hi!" she said brightly. "Hey. Great speech, wasn't it."

"Not bad," said Hilary, who didn't much like public displays of affection, verbal or physical. She ran her hands through her hair. "That idiot Jason's here, did you see?"

"Yeah," said Laura. "He's quite nice, isn't he?"

"Well," said Hilary in a flat tone. "He's okay. If you like that kind of thing."

"He's split up with Cath," Laura said encouragingly.

"Yeah, I know," Hilary said coolly. "Hm. I might go and find him."

"'Kay. See you later," said Laura, and shut the door of the cubicle. She rested her pounding head against the cool of the white tiles. She was stressing out, and she didn't know what to do. Dan had got to her. The worst bit of all was, she didn't just fancy him something rotten. She really *liked* him, too.

She liked the way he was always first to buy a round, that the corners of his blue eyes crinkled when he laughed, the rangy, almost bowlegged way he walked, his strong hands. She liked the way he rolled his eyes with gentle amusement when Yorky said something particularly Yorky-ish. She liked him. She couldn't help it. And she knew he liked her, that was the funny thing. She just knew, in the way you know. She had also come to know, in the last couple of months, that there was something going on between her and Dan. She just didn't know what it was. But somehow, she knew tonight was the night.

Dan was a friend of Chris's from university. He'd moved about five minutes away from Laura, round the corner from Jo and Chris toward Highbury, about six months ago—though she'd known of him vaguely since Jo and Chris had got together. In July, Dan had started a new job, and more often than not Laura found herself on the Tube platform with him in the morning. The first couple of times, it was mere coincidence. By the end of summer, it was almost a routine. They would buy a coffee from the stall on the platform and sit together in the second-to-last carriage, deserted in the dusty dog days of August, and go down the Northern Line together till they got to Bank. And they would read *Metro* together and chat, and it was all perfectly innocent—"Dan? Oh, yeah, we're Tube buddies," Laura would say nonchalantly, her heart thumping in her chest. "They're transport pals," Chris and Jo would joke at lunch on Sundays. "Like an old married couple on the seafront at

Clacton." "Ha-ha-ha," Laura would mutter, and blush furiously, biting her lip and shaking her hair forward over her face, burying herself in a newspaper. Not that they ever noticed—it's extraordinary what people don't notice right under their noses.

But to Laura, it was obvious, straightforward. From the first time she'd recognized him on the Tube platform that sunny summer day, and he had smiled at her, his face genuinely lighting up with pleasure—"Laura!" he'd said, warmth in his voice. "What a nice surprise. Come and sit next to me"—through the sun and rain of September and October, her running down the steps to the Tube platform, not knowing what was going on, knowing it was completely strange but not wanting to know any more. They had built up a whole lexicon of information. Just little things that you tell the people you see each day. She knew when his watch was being mended, what big meeting he had that day, and he knew when Rachel, her boss, was being annoying, and asked how her grandmother had been the previous day. Out of these little things, woven over and under each other, grew a web of knowledge, of intimacy, and one day Laura had woken up and known, with a clarity that was shocking, that this was *not* just another one of her crushes, or another failed relationship that she couldn't understand. She and Dan had something. And she was in love with him.

Oh, the level of denial about the whole thing *was* extraordinary, because you could explain it away in a heartbeat if you had to: "We go to work together, because we live round the corner from each other. It's great—nice start to the day, you know." Whereas the truth was a little more complicated. The truth was that both of them had started getting to the station earlier and earlier, so they could sit on the bench together with their coffees and chat for ten minutes before they got on the Tube. And that was weird. Laura knew that. Yes, she was in denial about the whole thing. She knew that, too. It had got to the stage when something had to give—and she couldn't wait.

Laura collected herself, breathed deeply, smoothed the material of her dress down, and came out of the loo to put on more lip gloss. She realized as she looked in the mirror that she was already wearing enough lip gloss to cause an oil slick—it was a nervous reflex of hers, to apply more and more when in doubt. She blotted some on the back of her hand, and strolled out the door nonchalantly, looking for Yorky, or Hilary, someone to chat to. It was strange, wasn't it, she mused, that at her best friend's wedding, knowing virtually everyone in the room, she could feel so exposed, so alone. That on such a happy day, she could feel so sad. She shook her head, feeling silly. Look over there, she told herself, as Jo and Chris walked through the tables of the big ballroom, hand in hand, smiling at each other, at their friends and family. It was lovely. It was a privilege to see. Out of the corner of her eye, she saw Hilary pinning Jason against a wall, yelling at him about something, her long, elegant hands waving in the air. Jason looked scared, but transfixed. Another man scared into snogging Hil, she thought. Well done, girl.

Someone handed her a glass of champagne, and she accepted it gratefully and turned to see who it was.

"Sorry," whispered Dan casually, though he didn't bend toward her. He said it softly, intimately, and clinked his glass with hers. "I thought I'd better leave you to deal with Yorky's sartorial crisis by yourself. Where did you go?"

"Loo," said Laura, trying to stay calm, but it came out, much to her and Dan's surprise, as a low, oddly pitched growl. He smiled. Laura smiled back, and ran her hand through her hair in a casual, groomed manner. But she'd forgotten the lipstick mark of gloss adhering to the back of her hand; her hair stuck to the gloss, and her fingers got tangled in her hair as she flailed wildly around with her hand in the air.

"Arrgh," said Laura, despair washing over her. Her hand was stuck in her hair. Dan took the champagne glass out of her other hand and put it on a table, then held her wrist and slid her fingers slowly out of her hair. He smoothed it down and swiftly dropped a kiss on the crown of her head in a sweet, intimate gesture, then put his palm on the small of her back as she picked up her glass and guided her through the room onto the terrace.

"Thanks," whispered Laura, trying to walk upright and not cower with embarrassment. "I should go back in, to see the first dance, look—"

"No problem," said Dan calmly. "In a minute. I just want to do this." And he slid his hand round her waist, drew her toward him, and kissed her. No one else was watching; they were all turned toward the dance floor where Mr. and Mrs. Lambert were dancing. They were alone on the terrace, just the two of them. Dan pulled her toward him, his hands pressing on her spine, his lips gentle but firm on hers. He made a strange, sad sound in his throat, somewhere between a cry of something and a moan. Laura slid one arm around his neck and drew him farther toward her. Her other hand, by her side, was still holding the champagne glass. It tilted and the champagne spilled; neither of them noticed.

After a short while, they broke apart slowly, and said nothing. There was nothing to say, really. Laura drained the meager contents of her glass and leaned into Dan. They stood there together as the music died away and applause rippled out toward them, aware of nothing but themselves, alone in their bubble.

"Well," Dan said eventually. "I didn't know *that* was going to happen tonight," and he put his arm around her.

Laura twisted round, looked up at him. "Oh, yes you did," she said, smiling into his eyes. "Of course you did."

That was Laura's second glass of champagne; shortly afterward, she found Yorky and Scary Hilary on another terrace having a cigarette, so she joined them. After her third glass, thirty minutes later, she was a bit tired. After her fourth, she felt better again—and she'd eaten from the buffet as well. After her fifth and sixth, she danced for an hour with Jo and Chris and their other friends. And after her seventh glass, she didn't know how it happened, but she found herself in a taxi going home with Dan Floyd, and they were kissing so hard that her lips were bruised the next day. And that was when it really started, and Laura went from knowing lots of things about Dan and how she felt about him and her place in the world in general to knowing nothing. At all.

At one point during the night, she propped herself up on her elbow and leaned over him and kissed him again, and he kissed her back and they rolled over together, and Laura pulled back and said, "So . . . what does this mean, then?" It just came out. And Dan's face clouded over and he said, "Oh, gorgeous, let's not do this now, not when I want you so much," and he carried on kissing her. Something should have made Laura pull away and say, "No, actually, what *does* this mean? Are you going to tell your girlfriend? When will you leave your girlfriend? Do you like me? Are we together?" But *of course* she didn't. . . .

chapter three

Yes, Dan had a girlfriend, Amy. Just a tiny detail, nothing much. They were as good as living together, too—although she still had her own place. Another detail Laura tried to forget about. She had *almost* managed to convince herself that if she didn't tell anyone about her—well, what was it? A "thing"? A "fling"? A fully formed relationship just waiting to move into the sunlight of acceptance?—her liaison with Dan, then perhaps the outside world didn't matter so much. And it didn't, when she was with him. Because he was The One, she was sure of it. So it became surprisingly easy for Laura, who was basically a good girl, who never ever thought she could do something like this, to turn into a person who was sleeping with someone else's boyfriend.

After Jo and Chris's wedding, she told herself—and Dan—that it wasn't going to happen again. She bit her nails to the quick about it because, much as Laura might be clueless about some things, she was clear about other things, and one of those was:

Don't sleep with someone who has a girlfriend. She'd already tried going cold turkey from him, as autumn gave way to winter and she realized she was falling for him, badly. She tried avoiding him at the Tube station—but she couldn't. She tried to forget him—but she couldn't. When she thought about him, it was as if he were talking to her, pleading with her, communicating with her directly. Laura, it's you I want, not Amy. Laura, please let me see you, his eyes and his voice would say in her head, until the noise got so loud it was all she could hear. Every time was the last time. Every time was the first time.

Laura knew it was wrong to be thinking like this. But she assuaged her secret guilt with the knowledge that Dan and Amy weren't getting on well. Dan himself had told her it wasn't working out. Well, he had in so many words, with a sigh and a shake of the head, in the early days of their coffee mornings together on the Tube platform. And she knew from Jo that Dan was going out with Chris and his other mates more, playing more football, watching more football, in the pub more, working harder. Added to which, no one in their group ever really saw Amy. She and Dan were together, but they were never actually together. She was completely offstage, like a mystery character in a soap opera whom people refer to but who never appears. You know when a couple are happy together—mainly because you don't see either of them as much, and when you do, they're either together or they talk about each other. Or they're just happy. You know. Laura knew—as did everyone else—that Dan wasn't happy with Amy. Dan wanted out, he just didn't know how to get out.

And, actually, Amy wasn't really her friend. They occasionally all went out for drinks, Jo and Chris, Dan and Amy, Hilary, Yorky, and Laura, and so on, especially now that Dan had moved nearby. But Amy rarely came along, and in any case, Laura had long ago realized she couldn't stand her. Never had been able to, in fact. Because not only was Amy a quasi-friend of hers, they had also been at school together, many moons ago, and there is no more mutually suspicious relationship than that of two ex-schoolmates who are thrown together several years later. Added to which, Amy had been one of the mean girls who had teased Laura relentlessly about her love for Mr. Wallace, the oboe teacher, and the subsequent rumors surrounding Laura's giving up the oboe. She'd even told Laura's mother about it at a school concert, all wide-eyed concern. Angela Foster had got the wrong end of the stick, and assumed Laura was being pestered by Mr. Wallace. She'd complained. He'd nearly been fired. The whole thing had been deeply embarrassing. So Laura's dislike of Amy was historical, rather than based upon the fact that Amy was with the man Laura felt quite sure she loved. It made her feel better, in some obscure way.

Amy ate nothing, exercised obsessively, talked about shoes and handbags the entire time (like, the *entire time*), and played with her beautiful red hair—nonstop. It was her thing. She always had, even when she and Laura had been eight-year-olds in plaits and kneesocks at school. Twenty years later, the same soft white hand would smooth down the crown of its owner's hair as Amy softened her voice to tell a sad story—about a friend's mother's death, or something bad in the news. Or said something deeply meaningful at the pub, which made Laura want to gag childishly on her drink, and then made her hate herself even more.

The thing was, Laura knew Amy was the kind of girl men fell for, even though she led them on a merry chase. Laura wasn't. She was nice, she was funny, but she knew she was ordinary, nothing special. She knew that. It perplexed her, as much as it exhilarated her. Why would anyone, especially Dan, choose her when they could be with Amy? Why did he understand her so well, laugh at her jokes? What amazing thing had led him to think of her as this perfect person for him, just as she felt the same way, knew that he was her Mr. Right? It was extraordinary, it was magical; and so, even though it was underhanded and stressful, she carried on doing it.

"So, then she said I should know why she was pissed off. And I'm thinking, well, God, woman, you're pissed off the entire time, how the hell am I supposed to tell the difference between you being annoyed because I was late back from football or annoyed because I didn't notice your new haircut? Is that for me? Hey, thanks so much. Toast, too. Wow."

"Thank you," said Laura, setting down a tray on her bed. She peered out the window. It was two months after Jo and Chris's wedding, a cold, gray Saturday morning in February. Dan shifted up in bed, crossed his legs, and pulled the tray toward him.

"This is great," he said, pouring some tea. "Come on, get back into bed."

Laura hopped back in beside him. He handed her a cup of tea and kissed her. "Mmm. Thank you," she said.

Dan and Amy had had another huge row the night before, and Amy had stormed back to her own flat. Laura cleared her throat.

"So, what did she say next?" she asked, desperate for more details, but not wanting them, too, fearing what he might say or not say.

Dan frowned momentarily, as if thinking something through. He put his mug down on the tray and took her hand, looking serious. "Forget about it," he said. "I'm sorry." He looked down. "It's crap of me. I'm so crap, boring you with all this stuff. It's . . . I've got to sort it out."

"Yes," said Laura, her heart beating fast.

"Not just for me," said Dan, looking intently at her. "For . . . for Amy as well, you know?"

"Yes, of course," Laura said, less urgently. "Amy." She picked up a slice of toast and bit into it. "Mmuh."

Dan smiled, and picked up another bit. "So, I'm pretty much free today now. Do you want to . . . you know, spend the day together? I know it's last-minute, but we might as well make the most of it." He leaned forward and kissed her.

"Er . . ." Laura said, swallowing fast. She had a lunch date with Yorky and her brother, but she supposed she could cancel. And instead, she and Dan could go to Kenwood House, muffled up in scarves and hats. Drink hot chocolate and walk through the grounds hand in hand. Kiss in the lanes of yew trees that led away to the Heath. Her eyes sparkled. She'd cancel Yorky and Simon—they were boys, they didn't mind that sort of thing. Although—gah. Simon, more a graduate of the love 'em and leave 'em school, was *always* making fun of her about her love life. Saying she was a romance addict, that she'd ditch her own brother at the last minute if there was a chance of a red rose heading her way. And she'd done it to him a couple of weeks ago, as well . . . the cinema, shit. She bit her lip. He was going away soon. She was a bad sister.

"Don't cancel anything special for me," Dan said, as if reading her mind. "It was just a suggestion." He stroked her knee. "God, it's so nice to be here, sweetheart."

"I think I was supposed to be having lunch, but it's quite a vague thing," said Laura, trying not to choke on her toast. "I'd . . . of course I'd prefer it if . . ." His hand was lying on the duvet. She hooked her little finger around his and said, "Yes, I'd love to spend the day with you. We should talk, anyway."

Laura was always doing this, trying to stage moments when she and Dan "talked." But it never seemed to work. She desperately wanted there to be some kind of agenda to their relationship, instead of Dan turning up when he could, secretively texting or e-mailing, having hurried, passionate, mind-blowing sex at one in the morning when he would drop by unannounced on the way back from the pub, wake her up, shag her senseless, and then go home—to what, Laura didn't know. Every time they tried to talk, something else would get in the way; Dan would tell her a funny story, or kiss her neck, or have to leave because Amy was calling. They'd tried not seeing each other, but the truth was it was so easy to have this relationship, it was so full of pleasure and excitement that, three months after they'd first got together, nothing had really changed. Dan was still with Amy, trying to sort it out or break it off gently. And Laura—Laura was so wildly happy with the whole thing that she would no more have irrevocably ended it than she would have moved south of the river.

When she looked at the facts of the relationship, the bare facts, only then did she get depressed. Nothing had changed. He was still with his girlfriend. And while he and Laura got along really well, she also had to admit that what they spent most of their time doing was not having a laugh and enjoying each other's company, but—having sex. And, God, the sex was great, but that was part of the problem—it had obscured the actual facts of the relationship, or whatever it was, for some time now.

On New Year's Eve, Laura and Yorky had gone round to the newly married couple's house for a party, along with lots of other people, but Dan wasn't there. He was on holiday with Amy, in Prague. Laura stood on Jo and Chris's balcony with Yorky and watched the fireworks over London. It was a clear night, sharp and cold, and for once the fireworks from the Thames were visible. They fizzed in the distance, tiny and indistinct, and around them, across the rest of London, streets and parks and houses were lit up by similar flashes and bangs, stretching as far as they could see. Simon had been next to her, and as he hugged her tightly, he asked, "So, sis. What's your New Year's resolution, then? Tell me."

"Ha," said Laura despairingly. She gave him a squeeze back. "You wouldn't believe me if I told you."

"Oh, really," said Simon, not actually listening, as his eye had fallen upon an attractive brunette in the corner of the room. "Love life?"

"Yes," said Laura honestly.

Simon looked at her briefly. "Who is it this time, then?" he said.

Laura resented the tone in his voice. "It's . . . not like that."

"Oh," said Simon, not believing her for a second. "Right," he added vaguely. "You should do something about it."

"Thanks," said Laura. "I am."

Simon smiled. "Really?" She nodded. "Well, good luck, then," he said. "Who is it this time? Someone at work? Ken Livingstone?"

"Go away," said Laura. "You're no help."

"Well, don't just stand there," Simon said. "I mean it. Do something about it." And he shrugged apologetically, as if admitting this wasn't helpful, and moved across the room in search of his prey.

Laura watched him go. He was right, though, wasn't he? This was going to be the thing that she did this year. She'd been searching for true love for as long as she could remember. This year, it was going to happen. She just had to make it happen.

So, shivering on that cold balcony on New Year's Eve, as Jo and Chris kissed each other, and Yorky danced crazily inappropriately with a scared-looking cousin of Chris's, and Simon charmed the pants off the brunette—literally—Laura clenched her fist, and she went to bed that night with a new resolve of iron. Three weeks after her "thing" with Dan had begun, but months after she had realized that he was the one for her, she knew she was the one who had to do something about it. Even now, nearly two months later, she remembered it clearly; it kept coming back into her head like a drumbeat.

She had to know, she had to sort this thing out, because somewhere in her lovesick, crazy brain was a small voice telling her that this wasn't how normal people behaved, fell in love, lived together; and that small voice had been getting louder and louder since before Christmas till now it was like a foghorn in her ear. She and Dan had to take the next step. Well, Dan had to take the next step and finish with Amy; then Laura and Dan had to take the step after that, which was to work out if they could be together.

So they would go to Kenwood House on this cold February Saturday, with the hot chocolate/ gloves/yew trees, and during that time they would talk, and Laura would explain, calmly and clearly, that Dan had to sort out his situation, otherwise they couldn't be together anymore.

"Talk," Dan said. "Yes, talk." He looked at her, their fingers still entwined. Laura smiled at him, took the toast out of his mouth, put the tray down on the floor, and reached for him, and they crawled back under the duvet, muffling their laughter and then, a while later, their moans as they came together again and any further discussion was put aside for the moment.

An hour later, Laura emerged from her room carrying the teapot and padded into the kitchen in her bare feet. Yorky was sitting at the little table by the French windows, gazing out at the view. Their flat was in a slightly cramped, dodgy Victorian mansion and had interesting design features—the French windows, for example, opened not onto a charming balcony with pots of geraniums and basil, but onto a sheer drop down four floors. The boiler was in Yorky's bedroom, and the sitting room had three electrical sockets, but all right next to each other by the door, nowhere near anywhere helpful like underneath the bay window where the television was. It was Yorky's flat, bought with some help from his elderly parents, since he was a teacher at a school nearby and earned in a year what most bankers earn in a month; and he and Laura were very happy there, though the water frequently turned itself off, the windows rattled, and the linoleum was curling, because they had laid it themselves, not very well. Added to which, Yorky had a mania for collecting interesting things from around the world, so the flat was stuffed with: a) painted gypsy floral watering cans, buckets, etc.; b) elephants made of wicker he'd picked up traveling through Africa; and c) comic books.

Yorky didn't look up as Laura came into the kitchen, humming to herself. "Morning," she said brightly. "How are you today, love?"

"Fine," muttered Yorky bitterly. "Oh, just fine."

"Oh, right," said Laura, nonplussed. "Er. Are you, though?"

"Oh, don't worry about me," Yorky spluttered into his tea. "I'll survive." He stared moodily out the window. Since he spent quite a lot of his leisure time doing this, Laura ignored him and put the mugs down on the counter.

"What are you eating?" she asked curiously.

"I made scrambled eggs with tomatoes," said Yorky shortly. He gestured to the plate, which looked like pink brains. Yorky was an enthusiastic but disconcerting chef.

"Oh. It looks nice," Laura lied. She ran the mugs under the tap.

"It's not enough that Mia hasn't answered any of my texts," Yorky said, picking up the thread after a few moments' silence. Laura obediently swiveled round to listen. "I've texted her four times—why hasn't she replied? Oh, no. I have to sit in solitary silence, with the TV my only companion, and listen to my flatmate who I've known since she was five screaming with pleasure as some git rogers her senseless at eleven A.M. for about the fifteenth time this morning."

Laura bit her lip to stop herself grinning. "Sorry." She went over and patted him on the shoulder. "I'll make you some tea. Why don't we all go into the sitting room and have some tea?"

"No, thanks a bundle," said Yorky, pulling his tattered paisley dressing gown about him with an attempt at dignity. "I prefer to watch *Saturday Kitchen* on my own, thanks very much, not squashed up on the sofa with you and Mr. Playaway while he tries to molest you under my very nose."

"Okay, okay," said Laura. This was going to be tricky. She'd had to tell Yorky about Dan, and she hated making him a party to it, making him lie. It wasn't for long, and so far he'd been great, but . . . She filled the kettle and affected a tone of nonchalance. "Er . . . any plans for today?"

Yorky looked up suspiciously. "Yes," he said. "You know I have. We're going out to lunch with Simon."

"Simon?" Laura said blankly. She pulled a mug off one of the hooks above the sink and examined it. "Urgh, this is dirty."

"Your brother, Simon, who's about to go to Peru for four months."

Laura winced. Simon worked for a charity. He was taking time off to travel to Peru, but since he was going to be volunteering for some other charity, it didn't really seem like time off to Laura.

"And then you know perfectly well we're going round to Jo's because Chris is away and she wants a hand with painting the kitchen," Yorky said, glaring at her. "Oh, my God, you're bailing out. I can't believe it."

"What?" said Laura. "I don't know what you're talking about."

"You lying bitch," said Yorky. "Go back in that bedroom, ease those chafed thighs onto the bed, and tell Dan you're not spending the day with him or whatever it is he's suggested you do. You're coming out to lunch."

"Honestly, Yorky, I had no idea," Laura pleaded with him, aware of how weak she sounded. "Sure, Jo mentioned coming round to me, but it was ages ago—I didn't think it was a proper plan. . . . No one e-mailed me about it this week—I thought it was a casual arrangement."

"Casual arrangement," Yorky repeated.

"Yep," Laura said. "And lunch—hey, you'll have a much better time without me there. You never see Simon on his own, you can really catch up. And stuff."

Yorky looked at her, and Laura realized the atmosphere in the kitchen was no longer one of grumpy, amusing sniping. It was suddenly more tense than that.

"No, Laura," he said quietly. "That—that thing you've got going on next door with Dan. *That's* a casual arrangement."

"No, it's not," said Laura in a small voice.

"Oh, God, you stupid girl." Yorky slapped his hand to his cheek. "I don't care. Just don't try to lie to me. It's not a big deal, Laura, honestly. But"—he held up his hand as Laura made to speak—"don't lie to me. You know it was arranged ages ago. You, of all people."

"What do you mean?" said Laura, feeling her chest tighten.

"I mean, I've always thought you were a good person, someone I could trust, someone I could rely on. Thick and thin, all that."

"Oh, for God's sake, Yorky," Laura said, her face reddening, feeling cross all of a sudden. "That's such crap. It's only lunch, get over it! I am—I am a good person. Dan—I—you *know* how I feel about him, don't do this."

Yorky turned his back on her and looked out the window, as if he was counting to five. Then he turned around again.

"Hey, love," he said in a gentle voice. "I know how you feel about him. But it's never going to happen. He's never going to leave Amy. Can't you see that? He's a wanker, and he's using you."

"How dare you say that," Laura said, her voice rising. "How dare you! That's bullshit. He's not like that, it's not like that. It's just . . . complicated. He can't just dump her, I don't want him to do that. We have to wait before we can be together . . . we . . . oh."

She slumped down into a chair, tears in her eyes. "It sounds so fucking clichéd," she whispered. "I'm so stupid."

"You're really not, darling," Yorky said, patting her hand across the table. "You're just mad about him, and what's wrong with that? Eh? You've got to . . . you've got to sort it out, that's all. You know what you're like."

Laura stood up again and went over to make the tea. "I have to, I know," she said. "It's just . . . it's just—I can't think of anyone I'm ever going to like more than I like him." Hot tears ran down her cheeks and she rubbed her eyes, feeling like a little girl on the playground at school.

It was true, that was the awful thing. She knew all this; she thought she was a sensible girl. But some kind of love had taken hold of her and refused to let her go, and it wasn't a happy, easy, joyful thing; it had her in a viselike grip.

She looked up at Yorky and smiled, trying to be brave. His face contorted with sympathy, and he walked over and gave her a big hug. "Do something about it, darling," he said, his voice muffled against Laura's shoulder. "Give him an ultimatum. Or give yourself an ultimatum. Get pregnant. No"—he stood back and shook her—"forget I said that. Really, don't get pregnant."

"I won't," Laura said, touched, for Yorky really did look alarmed. "Don't be stupid." She picked up the mugs. "I'll do something about it, honestly."

"Deadline. You need a deadline," Yorky said, sitting back down and picking up the newspaper that was lying on the table. "Ooh, travel. Book a holiday." He threw the travel section at her. It flapped through the air and Laura caught it, scrunching it in her hand and wedging it under her arm. "Book a holiday to somewhere fantastic, and then you have to go," Yorky said. "You know, in a few months' time, when everything's sorted out. God, I'm brilliant. As you were, young woman. Go off and shag that worthless young man in there. I'll make your excuses to Jo, but she's not going to be happy. You know she's not—you blew her off last week."

It was true. Laura had arranged to go to the cinema with Jo, but something else had come up—a Dan-shaped something else.

"It's her birthday in a couple of weeks. I'll make it up to her then," Laura said gratefully.

"Honestly. The things I do," Yorky said.

"Thanks, Yorky." Laura paused, as if she might say something else, gazing at the back of his head as Yorky picked up his tea and turned a page of the newspaper. "Thanks a lot. I . . . well."

A watery ray of pale sunshine was shining weakly through the window. Laura turned and left, with the fresh pot of tea, her head bowed in thought.

"I've canceled lunch," she said as she came back into her room.

Dan sat up in bed and spread his arms wide. "Great, great news, my gorgeous darling girl," he said. His hands slid inside her ratty old dressing gown and slipped open the tie, and he pulled her toward him. Laura laughed.

"Let me put the pot down," she said as he started kissing her. She crouched to put the paper and the teapot on the floor, then stood up again and said, as Dan flung the duvet to one side, "So, what do you want to do today?"

"You," Dan said, jumping on her with the kind of alacrity usually shown by sailors on shore leave. "God, I could be with you all day, you are so fucking gorgeous. Mmm."

"No," Laura said, laughing as he pulled off her dressing gown. "I mean later. I've canceled lunch. We could go out, you know. Maybe . . . er, Kenwood House for . . . er, hot chocolate."

Dan didn't answer, but carried on doing what he was doing. Laura sighed and pushed him away. "Dan, listen."

"Yes, yes," Dan said. "Hot chocolate."

"No," she said. "I mean, we go out to get hot chocolate, at Kenwood."

"What are you talking about?" Dan said, looking down at her. "Why do you want to go and get hot chocolate at Kenwood? Is there a festival there or something?"

"No, I mean—what shall we do today, then? We should do something. Go out, you know, make the most of it. The sun's just come out."

Dan cupped her breast in his hand and bent over to kiss her again. "I can't, darling," he said. "We can't. Someone might see us. Imagine if they did." He looked up, his expression anguished. "I'm sorry."

"But," Laura said, trying to be patient, "who are we going to bump into in the yew trees at Kenwood?"

"The what?" Dan said. Laura watched him intently. "No, we just can't. We should . . . we have to stay here. Not for much longer, I promise. But things might be tricky for the next couple of months."

"Why?" said Laura, not understanding, and reluctantly waving good-bye to her winter-wonderland dream of laughing and joking in a Missoni print cape as she and Dan carelessly drank hot chocolate and held hands amidst the frosty trees.

"I mean," said Dan, "if I'm going to split up with Amy, you and I won't be able to see each other for a time while it's going on. I mean, on our own—not the usual in the pub with everyone else there. Right?"

"Oh, right," said Laura, not daring to hope he was saying what he was saying. "So . . ."

"So," said Dan, bending over her nipple and kissing it gently, "this might be the last time we get to do this for a long time. So—we should—make the most of it. . . ."

"Yes," gasped Laura suddenly, understanding him, pulling him down. "Yes, I see. . . ."

As Dan moved down her body, Laura closed her eyes, and the last thing she saw was the crumpled cover of the *Guardian*'s travel section. ROAD TRIP: FLORIDA'S HIDDEN TREASURES, the front page declaimed. A road trip, she thought, and abandoned herself to something more immediate.

chapter four

Laura worked for an inner-city London council as a schools and business coordinator. She loved her job, contacting local businesses, trying to get them to support their nearby schools, arranging volunteer reading programs—in which employees would go into the local schools and read with children—or school sponsorships, which arranged for companies or individuals to sponsor a school, donate money, and feel good about themselves. She loved it because she could see how it made a tangible difference, how much disillusioned company secretaries enjoyed reading with a six-year-old once a week, or how much it benefited a school to have a thousand pounds for new computers that some corporation or anonymous donor could easily spare. She had been there for nearly four years now, and the previous year had been put in charge of the council's new fund-raising scheme and the volunteer reading program, which meant a lot more work, but she loved it.

At least, she used to love it. Like everything these days, it seemed to have lost a little of its allure.

If Laura had stepped back from her situation, chances were she would have seen that she was behaving badly. The trouble was, her lack of perspective meant she couldn't see the main reason why she was in thrall to Dan, would do anything for him, no matter how degrading: He made her feel gorgeous. He made her feel devastatingly attractive, that she was so powerful to him that he had to have her, he couldn't control it. It made her feel just marvelous, and a little bit dirty, too. It was dangerous, because Dan was like all the others in that Laura had fallen for him hook, line, and sinker, without really stopping to think about it—only this time it was harder and deeper than with anyone before, and she had no control over the situation she'd got herself into, and there was no endgame in sight. It's a very powerful thing, to know you have that effect on someone—and having always thought of herself in the bottom half of the class in terms of looks, attractiveness, and intelligence, not to mention sporting prowess, Laura still couldn't quite believe that she affected him this way.

Laura knew she wasn't working as hard as she should; she knew her boss, Rachel, was on her case about things. She knew she wasn't being a good friend, or daughter, or sister, since Dan had come along. She forgot birthdays; she was late for work; her mind wandered. But she consoled herself with the knowledge that this was a temporary situation and in a few short months—by the summer—they would have sorted it out and could be together. And then she would make everything all right.

He just needed a little push, that was all. Just a little something to let him know she wasn't going to wait around forever, that she had deadlines of her own. She had another life apart from him and she was neglecting it, he had to see that. But so did she.

* * *

The following Wednesday afternoon, Laura was in the office when the phone rang. It was pelting rain, which rattled on the windows of the shabby, drafty Victorian building where the education authority was housed in Holborn.

Laura looked up wearily from her e-mails and glanced suspiciously at the caller ID panel. A teacher from a primary school nearby, St. Catherine's, had said she would be calling to discuss a problem with the latest batch of teaching volunteers who'd just started at the school, once a week, helping individual children with their reading. The volunteers were from a firm of financial advisers, pretty big, called Linley Munroe, and it was something of a coup to have them involved—perhaps they might be induced to get involved in other ways. Laura didn't particularly like Mrs. McGregor, though she could see how devoted she was to the school and the children. She knew from experience that Mrs. McGregor was the kind of person who had her own worldview and couldn't be persuaded that anyone else's was admissible. Laura knew why she was ringing—she made the same complaint, along different lines, every year. Laura picked up the phone with a heavy heart.

"Hello?" she said tentatively.

"Laura? Laura Foster?" came a slightly husky voice down the phone.

"Yes," said Laura, resigned.

"Oh, Laura, I really must talk to you. I'm afraid this is a very bad situation, very bad indeed. Something's going to have to be done, it's a disaster. Catastrophe."

"Yes, hello, Mrs. McGregor," said Laura.

"Well, Laura . . ." And she was off.

". . . I've told him," the voice was saying five minutes later, " 'You may think you can come here and think you're doing something marvelous, helping these kids so you can sleep easy at night in your big banker's flat. Well, you can't behave like that and get away with it.' I'm not putting up with it anymore, really I'm not."

"I explained the guidelines to him and all his colleagues, back in October," Laura repeated. "I'm sure this Marcus bloke's just got his wires crossed. I'll talk to Clare at Linley Munroe, tell her to have a gentle word with Marcus. But I really don't think he should be banned, Mrs. McGregor. He's obviously enjoying it, and—well, let's face it, all he did was tell this boy to shut it? They call each other the most horrific things on the playground, don't they?"

Her e-mail alert beeped and her eyes flicked instantly to the screen. She opened the message and read, her heart pounding.

"Do they?" Mrs. McGregor said. "Not in my experience, Laura. Sure, there are rude words, but—"

Laura wanted to reread and reply to this e-mail she'd just got. She said shortly, "Oh, come on, Mrs. McGregor. You know what I mean. Fuck, bum, willy, vag. And . . ." She paused, realizing what she'd just said. "Er. Well, we used to, anyway. That sort of thing."

Mrs. McGregor was silent. Then she said, "Well, I must say. Honestly, Laura."

"It's an illustration," said Laura briskly, marshaling all her inner resources and kicking herself ferociously on the ankle, while her coworkers Nasrin and Shana gaped openmouthed at her and started laughing. Laura flapped her arms at them to shut them up, and said, with what she hoped was an air of finality in her voice, "I'm sure if Marcus Sussman used inappropriate language, he was doing so to try to communicate with them. But I totally understand what you mean, and I'll make sure it doesn't happen again."

Mrs. McGregor droned on, but Laura didn't listen, only vaguely registering she had to get rid of her, reply to this e-mail.

". . . have to speak to Rachel about this, Laura, yes, I will. Nasty man. Smooth young prat with cuff links who thinks he can treat these kids like dirt because he went to university and they didn't. It's vile. And I'm surprised at you for not seeing it."

"Fine," Laura said, finally losing her patience. "Talk to Rachel, but I'm surprised you're being so blinkered. I always knew you were an inverted snob, but I didn't think you'd let it derail the volunteer program like this."

"Oh!" Mrs. McGregor inhaled sharply. "Laura Foster. You'll regret this, I promise you. Yes, you will." And she slammed the phone down.

"Laura!" said Shana, her eyes sparkling with the unexpected office excitement. "Fuck, bum, willy, vag? What the hell . . . ?"

Laura put her head in her hands and moaned softly to herself.

"It was brilliant," said Shana joyfully. "Best thing I've heard in ages."

"Oh dear," said Laura, finally looking up at Nasrin, who put her magazine down and gazed at her. "St. Catherine's again. Mrs. McGregor. Stupid old bitch, I hate her," she said defiantly. "I'm going to get in trouble, aren't I?"

"She always makes a fuss, every year," Nasrin said placidly, picking up *Pick Me Up* again. "Rachel knows that, don't worry. She's just a sad old rebel without a cause."

Laura turned back to her e-mail. Now that she was free to read it properly, she didn't want to. Mrs. McGregor had spoiled her afternoon.

A holiday is a great idea. You and me, nothing else. Imagine what we could do all week. Why don't you start thinking about where to go. July is best for me, by then everything'll be sorted. We can celebrate properly. I want you.

Dxx

And the rest of the day passed much more pleasantly than she'd expected.

The next day it was still raining, and Mrs. McGregor wrote a letter of complaint about Laura to the local education authority. She faxed it to Laura's boss, Rachel, who gave her a formal warning. She had no choice, she said, looking firmly at Laura, who still wondered what all the fuss was about. Marcus Sussman was a bit hearty over the phone, but he seemed to be a nice man; all he'd done was tell a kid who called him a fucking cunt to shut the fuck up—well, was that so bad? No, not in her book.

"I won't say I'm not disappointed," said Rachel, leaning over her desk toward Laura. "I thought that was one of your strengths, people management. You've always been so good at it, Laura. They love you at St. Catherine's, too. What happened?"

Laura looked at her and felt tears start in her eyes. She was being stupid, she knew it, behaving so irresponsibly, but she didn't know how to start to explain. So she just said, "Oh, you know. I just—she really was so vile. I just couldn't take it anymore. I'm really sorry, Rachel. You know it won't happen again. Can I ring Mrs. McGregor and apologize?"

Rachel smiled at her, slightly more warmly than before. "Of course. Thanks a lot."

"So, darling," said Angela Foster that evening, smoothing the sofa cushion with her hand. "How's work?"

She glanced around the sitting room as if she expected a troupe of tiny tap-dancing mice to cancan out from a hole in the skirting board and pirouette off with her handbag.

"Fine, fine," Laura said hastily. "Today was . . . er, fine. Thanks for these, so much. They'll look great." She gestured to the pastel-spotted blinds her mother had bought her from John Lewis as a belated birthday present. "It's so nice of you to bring them round, Mum, you shouldn't have."

"Not at all, darling," said Angela. "And I wanted to see my girl. We haven't seen you for such a long time, you know. You're so busy these days."

Laura changed the subject quickly. "So, Mum. Have you got time for a cup of tea, or do you have to go, then?"

Angela looked at her. "I can see you're longing for me to stay," she said drily.

"No, of course I am," Laura said. "Of course. Do stay. I've got some biscuits, too. Sit down, Mum. I'll put the kettle on. Sit down, make yourself at home."

"I'll try," said Angela, lowering herself gingerly onto the blue sofa with its tea-stained arms and cigarette holes in the cushions.

Laura sighed and hurried into the kitchen, glancing anxiously at her watch. Dan had said he'd come round later, and she didn't want the two to collide. Not that it was likely they would—he only ever turned up after the pubs shut, whereas her mum was usually in bed and fast asleep by the time the pubs shut.

When Laura returned with the tea, Angela said, "The flat's looking nice." Laura gritted her teeth. Her mother was a grand master at the art of faking it. Laura knew she didn't do it on purpose, but her superbly repressed nature meant that whenever an unkind or negative thought crossed her mind, she felt she had to atone for it by saying the opposite of what she thought. It was quite a good barometer, actually. "What a lovely short skirt, darling!" meant "I am embarrassed to go with you dressed like that to the Hunts' anniversary party, you look like a common prostitute." Or "Your friend Hilary is very lively, isn't she? Dad loved talking to her" meant "Your friend Hilary drinks more than is socially acceptable at a barbecue buffet lunch in Harrow and is nothing more than a jailbait husband stealer."

"Thanks, Mum. It's a bit of a tip at the moment. Yorky's been on half-term break from school and he just lazes round reading newspapers all day in his dressing gown."

"Ahh," said Angela fondly. She had more than a soft spot for Yorky. "How is James?" She always called him by his given name. It was strange, Laura mused, that Yorky could read mothers—and his female friends—like open books, yet be so disastrously out of sync with the opposite sex the rest of the time. Half-term break had been notable for Yorky's attempts to catch the attention of the girl in the flat downstairs, which involved hanging around the stairwell for half the day and smiling mysteriously, raising the eyebrow he'd now learned to raise, and generally looking like an unemployed spy. The girl in the flat downstairs—whom Laura had met; she was called Becky and seemed really nice—simply cast him looks of something amounting to concern for his mental state every time she saw him. He was despondent about it, because he actually did really like her. And before he'd decided he fancied her and had started acting like a lunatic, they'd actually got on quite well, the few times they'd chatted. Added to which, Mr. Kenzo from the flat opposite now thought Yorky was a delinquent or else some kind of dodgy sex practitioner, and spent a lot of time watching him watching Becky, which all contributed to the atmosphere of light comedy pervading the stairwell of the building.

"Yorky's fine. Bit gloomy at the moment."

"Any girls on the horizon?" asked Angela hopefully.

Laura didn't want to get into Yorky's love life with her mother. She cast around for something else to say about him. "He's giving me a hard time—" Laura stopped and cursed herself. "—for not tidying up more," she finished, inwardly hugging herself for her own ingenuity.

"Well, I'm sure he's right," said Angela. "You are a bit messy. Still, it's nice to live with someone who is, too, isn't it? You're only young once, it does no one any harm to leave the Sunday papers strewn about once in a while."

"True, very true, Mum," Laura agreed with a grin.

After they chatted about her aunt Annabel, Angela's stepsister, her mother said, "I should be on my way soon, you know. Dad's coming back from Norway tonight and I ought to have something ready for him, poor thing." She drained the last of her tea and stood up. "Right, darling, I'll be off."

"Oh, okay," said Laura. "Thanks so much for the blinds, Mum. They're great. I love them."

"I'm glad, darling," said Angela, kissing her on the cheek. "Your granny picked them out with me. She said they were very *you.* And—oh, my goodness, that reminds me. I nearly forgot. Honestly, where am I these days?"

"What?" said Laura, handing her mother her coat.

"Granny. You know it's her eighty-fifth birthday in July? Well, we want to have a little party for her at Seavale. With Aunt Annabel and Uncle Robert, and Lulu and Fran." Laura groaned, but Angela ignored her and carried on. "I think Simon will still be away traveling, so it's even more important you're there. I just wanted to check—you're around in July, aren't you, darling? No holiday plans or anything?"

"Well . . ." Laura said.

Angela looked at her.

"I'm not sure," said Laura.

"The whole of July? You're *not sure*?" said Angela.

"Of course not," said Laura, collecting herself. Good God, she was being stupid. "Any time's good. I was thinking . . . thinking I might be on holiday in July sometime, but I'll wait till you tell me a date and then plan round it. Of course I'll be there. And do tell Granny thanks for the blinds, too. I love them."

"You could ring her up and tell her, she'd be over the moon.

She'd love to hear from you. Maybe you could meet for lunch—she was saying she hadn't seen you for a while." Angela wrapped her scarf carefully around her neck.

It was true. Mary was not usually offstage. Laura usually saw her about every other week, even if it was just to pop in for a drink after work or to meet for a coffee. But Laura hadn't seen her for a while. She pushed the thought from her head, and the associated guilt, and said, "Yes, I must call her. I must. Just been quite busy. Now, safe journey. Yorky will be disappointed he missed you, you know how much he loves you."

Angela blushed. "Go on," she said. "Thanks for the tea, darling. And call Granny. I'll let you know when we decide on a date for the party."

"Yep," said Laura, standing at the doorway. She waved as her mother disappeared down the curving staircase, and wandered back into the flat, kicking a stray football out of the way. As she stood in the hallway, she realized it had been ages since she'd seen her grandmother. In fact, since Christmas. That was ridiculous. It wasn't as if she could say she lived in the middle of nowhere, either. Mary lived behind Baker Street—"within walking distance of Selfridges, good for the soul, my dear"—in Crecy Court, a 1930s apartment building that Laura absolutely loved.

She went to pick up her mobile, to call her grandmother. There was a text from Dan.

> *Can I come over? Have told Amy I'll be late tonight. I really need to see you and I want you. I miss you so much, beautiful girl. Please say yes. D*

As Laura stood holding the phone, the doorbell rang, and she started. She dropped the phone and went over to the intercom. "Hello?"

"Did you get my text?" said the voice. "Is Yorky there? Can I come up?"

"Dan?" Laura said shakily.

"Yes, it's Dan," the voice said, amused. "Who else sends you text messages saying they want to come over and give you a good seeing-to? Am I one in a long line, should I join a queue?"

"Aaagh," said Laura. "I was just confused, I was about to call someone and I was just—oh, come up, sorry, I'm just being thick."

"Are you sure?" Dan lowered his voice. "I can't stay long. I just wanted to see you."

Laura's legs wobbled a bit and she smiled into the intercom. And then, out of nowhere, she found herself saying, "I'd love you to come up. But not if you can't stay. Oh, Dan, I'm sorry."

"What?" said Dan.

"I mean, you're not just coming up for a quick fuck and then scooting off again. Not that that wouldn't be nice. It would . . ." Laura wavered, then checked herself. "Hm. I want you, too, but no, that's not going to happen. I'm really sorry. Night, darling."

"Okay," said Dan. He paused. "I'm sorry," he went on. "You're right. Shit, oh well. I deserve it. Soon, soon, you know? Can you do me a favor?"

"Depends," Laura said cautiously, dreading him asking her to come outside and do it on the porch.

"Can you look out the window and wave, just so I can see you tonight? Right, I'm off then. Bye, my darling. I wish . . ."

"Bye, Dan," Laura said softly. "I love you."

The intercom went dead as she stuffed her fist into her mouth. I love you? Why? Why had she said that? Damn. She ran over to the window and gazed out over the quiet surburban North London street. The rain had stopped and the night was clear, and on the street below she could see a tall figure staring up at her. She opened the window and looked down, and there he was, his gorgeous face turned up toward her.

"I love you, too," he shouted, and his voice echoed in the silence of the street. "I love you."

Laura stood there, her eyes filled with tears. And then she blew him a kiss and shut the window.

chapter five

In May, Amy, who had been very much in the background, suddenly came out fighting. She started making plans for her thirtieth birthday in September. She let it be known that she wanted to hire a villa in Spain for two weeks, she and Dan, and have various friends fly out at different times, all gathering together on the middle Saturday for a huge party in the garden of the villa, which Dan was going to organize. She was back in the game. She even made an appearance at the pub.

Laura hadn't seen Amy for about six months. She had become, in Laura's mind, this vast, beauteous Amazonian woman, with tiny stick-thin wrists and a huge expensive handbag and matching shoes. She was dazzlingly beautiful, terrifyingly confident, and she knew something was up with Laura and Dan. In Laura's nightmares, Amy walked up to Laura and dragged her by the hair out of the pub, pulled all her hair out, then kicked her into the road.

The trouble was, in these nightmares, Laura kind of sided with Amy, not with herself. If she'd heard just the facts without knowing the details of it, she'd side with Amy, too. But, she kept telling herself, just a little longer, and then it'd be over. And when she and Dan had been together for twenty-five years and were as happy as ever, no one would remember the slightly murky beginnings of their relationship. It would be lost in the mists of time, and Amy would be off married to a billionaire banker—it wasn't even as if she and Dan were happy, after all. Laura was doing her a favor, in the long run.

So when Laura walked into the Cavendish and saw Amy, as tall and beautiful and stick-thin as ever, sitting on the sofa laughing girlishly with Jo, and realized that she *was* the terrifying Amazonian beauty of her nightmares, and that she, Laura, was still—well, normal, normal height, normal hair, normal *everything*—it was all she could do not to walk out. Amy gave her a lizardlike, thin-lipped smile, which meant nothing, as Amy pretty much hated all girls except her own, incredibly similar friends, who were kind of like the Pussycat Dolls mixed with the clique in *Mean Girls*.

"Hey, Dan," said Chris as Laura came over to the bar. "There's your Tube buddy!"

"Hey, Tube buddy," said Dan, bending over to kiss Laura. How could he be so nonchalant, Laura wondered, as his hand squeezed her shoulder fleetingly and he kissed her on the cheek. "Can I get you a drink?"

"Oh, a beer, thanks, Tube buddy!" said Laura. "Hi, Jon. Hey, Chris. How was Morocco?"

"Haven't seen you since then, have we? Can't believe it. It was great," said Chris, hugging her. "Got some great photos to show you! The girls are over there, go and say hi."

The girls. Laura went over to where Amy and Jo were sitting. Jo jumped up immediately. "Laura, hi!" she said, her eyes sparkling. "God, it's so good to see you, babe! How long's it been? How long? This is crap, we mustn't leave it that long next time."

"Hi, Laura!" said Amy. She looked down at Laura—both actually and metaphorically, thought Laura—and all three sat down again. Whoa, what an evening of direness lies ahead of me, she thought. Dan put her beer on the table and smiled at her. Amy leaned back and caught his hand. He smiled mechanically at her and released himself, walking back over to the bar to rejoin Chris. Laura didn't know whether to laugh or cry.

"I know we've had our problems over the past year," Amy confided to Jo and Laura, an hour and a couple of drinks later. "But lately, he's been . . . so different. I think he's realized."

"Realized what?" asked Jo.

"Oh, I really hope he's realized . . . Gosh, it's awful saying it out loud, isn't it?"

"Oh, honey," said Jo. She patted her hand. "I know. . . ."

Jo was no fan of Amy's either, but was a far more tolerant person than Laura.

"Well . . ." Amy blinked slowly, her huge eyes gazing at Jo with intensity. "That, you know. He'll lose me. I'm going to finish with him if he doesn't shape up, and I've told him that."

Laura looked round to see if Dan could hear any of this conversation. Chris and his brother were at the bar, talking to Hilary, but she couldn't see Dan anywhere. She turned back and looked at Amy, and suddenly felt the old hot flush of guilt wash over her.

"Well, that's great, Amy," said Jo kindly. "I hope it works out, if that's what you want."

Laura flashed her a look as if to say, "We hate Amy, what are you doing?" But Jo only glanced at her briefly in return.

"I really think it will," said Amy, smoothing down her hair and smiling. "I hope by then . . . well, I'm going to drop some gentle hints about what I'd like more than anything else for my thirtieth. If you know what I mean!"

"Great," said Jo, taking a sip of her drink. "Well, we'll just have to wait and see!"

"What?" Laura asked stupidly, thinking, What does she want? Some new shoes, probably, knowing Amy.

"Oh, Laura . . . !" Amy looked at Laura as if she were a little alien, or a Mexican peasant unfamiliar with her ways. Amy delicately ate an olive, and licked one of her fingers. She smiled at Laura pityingly. "An engagement ring, of course."

A pit from the lemon slice in Laura's gin and tonic wedged itself in her throat and she nearly choked. "Right," she gasped, determined not to lose control. "Right. Aaah. Aaaaah. Loo. Excuse me." And she got up and stumbled outside, to the clear fresh air of the spring night. She stood there taking big gulps of air, one hand clutching her throat, the other rubbing her stomach, a habit she had had since she was little. Right, indeed. She looked in through the big glass windows of the Cavendish, over to the squashy leather sofas where her friends sat, and wondered how things had come so far, got so out of control, so ridiculous. She looked at Jo, methodically folding up her cardigan, neatly stowing it in her bag, and felt helpless. She felt a million miles away from her best friend, from those she thought she knew.

As if by magic, Dan appeared around the corner. He had been to get some cigarettes. He jumped when he saw Laura standing outside, and she nearly screamed.

"What the—what are you doing out here?" Dan said testily.

"Having a breather," Laura said, suddenly furious at him, especially at his tone. "Listening to your girlfriend talking about her thirtieth birthday in September, how she wants all of us to fly out to Valencia and watch while you *propose* to her in front of all of us—oh, Dan, *Dan* . . ."

She started sobbing, great heaving sobs that shook her, and Dan pushed her away from the window and against the shop next door. He put his arms around her, holding her so tightly she thought she might not be able to breathe.

"Now, listen," Dan said, putting a thumb up to her cheek to wipe away a tear. "I have been such a shit to you. And to her, but this is about you. I promise you, that is not going to happen. I promise you I'm going to talk to her in the next couple of weeks. This has to end. I can't be with her anymore, I just can't stand it. And I want to be with you."

He held her tighter and kissed her. She could feel him growing hard against her leg.

"I want to be with you, do you understand me?"

"Yes," Laura whispered. "So . . . it's over with her, then?"

"Yes," Dan said solemnly. "Shit. I'm going to have to do something about it now, aren't I?"

"Yes, you are," Laura said, hiccupping.

"Good. Now"—Dan bent down and kissed her again—"I'm so sorry I've been so useless. It's not fair to her, or me, and especially you. We will be together, I promise."

"You really promise?" Laura said, wanting a final reassurance.

Dan gripped her wrists and pressed himself against her. "Shit, Laura, I don't know what else I can say." He looked around, shaking his head. "I want you to believe it, I really do, but until I've talked to her, I can't . . . if only there was some way."

Laura said slowly, "How about that holiday? In July? The Florida road trip we talked about. Ending up in Miami. Two weeks, just us."

She looked into his eyes and could see the glimmer of uncertainty, of something else—what was it?—there. He looked back at her, trying to bridge that final gap between them. Laura started to turn away, feeling powerful for the first time, and Dan grabbed her again and said, "No, fuck it. Book it. I'm just scared. But I'm being weak and crap. Book it."

"Seriously?" Laura said, trying to stay calm, though a big smile broke out across her face.

Dan laughed. "Seriously." He kissed her again. "I mean it."

He walked back into the pub without looking behind him once, and Laura hung back for a few seconds. This was their usual routine. If someone she knew appeared, she'd just get out her phone and pretend to be texting. She turned toward the door, but as she was pushing it open, someone caught her elbow. She spun round, half with shock, and saw Jo behind her, standing on the pavement. Her face was pinched, her eyes huge.

"Laura . . . ?" she said. "Laura?"

"What?" Laura said, completely calm. Nearly six months of this had made her a professional. She was certain Jo hadn't seen anything. She held up her phone. "I was just texting someone, reception's terrible in there." She gestured inside.

"What's going on?" Jo said, not reacting.

"Nothing, what do you mean?" said Laura, slightly on edge.

"You're screwing Dan, aren't you?"

"What?" Laura said. "*What?* I wish. Come on, let's get back inside."

"I saw you," said Jo, advancing slowly toward her. "I saw him kiss you, I saw you both just now. Laura, *Laura*!" The words were tumbling out of her; she looked distraught. "What the—what the fuck are you doing? How long has this been going on? Does Amy know?"

"It's nothing," said Laura, her self-preservation gene kicking in. "Completely the wrong end of the stick. You know how matey we've become."

Part of her wanted more than anything else to tell Jo, to confess all, to ask her best friend's advice. But she couldn't. She'd chosen it this way, and soon it would all be sorted out.

"I know what I saw," Jo said. "Oh, Jesus. All this crap about you two being friends on the Tube platform, that's how it started, isn't it? I *knew* you were up to something. Chris said he could tell you were getting it from somewhere, and I told him he was wrong. But . . . Dan! Laura, I know you're a screwup when it comes to relationships, but . . . not again! What the fuck are you doing?"

"Whatever I'm doing," Laura said, feeling really angry, "it's none of your business, so why don't you just butt out, okay?"

"Oh, no," Jo said, coming right up to her, her blue eyes enormous in her pale face. "It *is* my business, love. It's my business when my supposed best friend starts shagging our best friend Dan behind everyone's backs, and then sits there in the pub pretending to be all matey-matey with his *girlfriend.* It's my business when my best friend lies to me all the time, and I never know where she is, and it turns out that's because she's having an affair with one of our best friends. It's my business when I send you an e-mail saying I'm taking Chris to Morocco for a surprise to cheer him up because of his granddad, and you send a long reply going on about how *fat* you think you are! And you never even call, you don't remember I've even gone!"

"I didn't—" Laura said, putting out her hands.

"You're not interested," said Jo, her eyes filling with tears. Laura was horrified. "You just weren't interested in anything but yourself. And normally I wouldn't care, because you've done it before, but like I say—it's started being my business." She took a deep breath. "One more thing, Laura. It's my *business* when my *best friend* forgets my fucking birthday and Dan Floyd fucking drops a birthday card round from her that she's obviously bought at some *corner shop* when the two of you took a break from shagging each other senseless! You selfish cow. I can't believe it. Well, that's the awful thing. Actually, I can." She stepped back again, collecting herself. "I'm sorry," she said. Screeching, Italian-style emotion was not Jo's normal mode of behavior. She coughed. "Yes. I'm sorry."

"That's okay," Laura said, shaking her head. "Look, Jo—"

"No, let me finish," Jo said politely. "Look, Laura. I hate this. I'm sorry, but I always end up having this conversation with you! You're always doing this. Some guy, you think he's totally right for you, and you can't see what everyone else can see, because you're off in Laura Land making up some fantasy about it."

"Shut up," said Laura. She was furious. "It's not how you think. You don't understand. It's complicated."

"Listen to yourself," Jo said. She pulled her handbag over her shoulder and folded her arms. "You sound like every cliché. You're *not* Julie Andrews, Laura! And Dan's not fucking Captain von Trapp! Don't you ever learn? Don't, *don't* treat me like I'm stupid! God, Laura, what—what's going to happen?"

"Don't worry," Laura said urgently. "Look, Jo, I know it looks bad, but it's really not. We're in love. He loves me and I love him. He's leaving Amy, in about two weeks, he's just got to sort some stuff out. We're going on holiday. To Miami."

There was nothing she could say to convince Jo, and she didn't even want to try that much. She didn't know what was going to happen, or even what to do. So she just said, "Look, let's go inside. Don't tell anyone, will you?"

Jo stared at her. "Of course I won't," she said eventually.

"Not even Chris," Laura said anxiously. "He really mustn't know, no one can know. Dan's really paranoid about it."

"I'm sure he is," said Jo. She opened the door. "Fine, then. We won't talk about it."

"Fine, then," Laura echoed.

Amy was standing at the wide bar next to Dan, flinging her hair over her shoulder. She looked up as Jo and Laura walked in, both silent. "Danny's getting some more drinks, girlies," she called. "Laura, Jo, what do you want?"

Jo didn't answer; she went over to Chris, bent over, and whispered in his ear. Chris immediately got up.

"Actually," Jo said, "me and Chris have to go, got to shoot off. Really sorry. See you all soon."

"Yeah, bye," Chris called out.

No one else seemed to notice this remarkably hasty exit except Laura, who stood at the bar feeling sick.

"Okay?" Dan said, nudging her absentmindedly, his arm still round Amy's waist. "Do you want another drink?"

"I'm fine," said Laura. "I'm fine."

Laura didn't talk to Jo about their conversation outside the Cavendish. In fact, they didn't really talk at all after that night. Over the next few weeks, they met with the others, sat next to each other, had funny conversations, but the intimacy of their friendship vanished, completely overnight. Laura didn't worry about it—well, she did, but she knew she could put it right at some point.

Besides, Laura was busy booking the Miami holiday online. She extended her credit card limit and took out a loan, not wanting to ask Dan for money. So when she should have been writing her review of the year for her boss, Rachel, she was spending the days sorting out cars and flights and hotels, e-mailing Dan to get his opinion, waiting in desperation for his replies, soothed and cheered when he would sign off "I can't wait, I can't wait." The holiday in July became their secret focus, and as the days lengthened and May shifted into June, Laura didn't ask what was happening with Amy, with them, to her. And then one day, without warning, the axe fell.

chapter six

"Laura, can you come in here for a second?" Rachel called from her office.

Laura finished the e-mail she was typing, stood up, and smoothed down her skirt. It was nearly the end of the day and she was in a good mood. It was Yorky's birthday, and that evening a whole bunch of them were going to an amazing steak house in Stoke Newington called Jean Michel's.

Laura poked her head around Rachel's door. "Hi," she said.

"Hi, Laura," Rachel said. "Come in. Shut the door a moment, will you?"

Laura froze, knowing from long experience that the shut-the-door request meant either a promotion or something really bad. Usually something bad. She racked her brains, running through a list of options about what this could be, as she slowly pushed the door shut. She'd done something wrong. Again. Someone had complained. She turned around, genuinely mystified, and then she saw a pile of letters on the desk in front of Rachel. Of course! It was pay review time. They'd had an e-mail about it yesterday. Laura sat down gratefully, sweating slightly, and promised God that when she got back to her desk she'd work extra hard, finish that report for Rachel she should have done two weeks ago, instead of finding a hotel near the Kennedy Space Center for her and Dan (Dan was obsessed with outer space, and wanted to spend at least a whole day there).

"Laura," Rachel said, smiling kindly at her. "You okay?"

"Yes, sorry," Laura said, slightly breathlessly. "Just thinking about something. How can I help you?"

"I need to talk to you," Rachel said. She fiddled with one of the buttons on her cardigan. She was normally very much in control; this was odd. "I've—I've been worried about you."

"Oh?" said Laura. She crossed her legs and shifted forward in her seat, leaning attentively toward Rachel. "What do you mean?"

"Is everything okay, Laura? At home?"

Laura felt as if she were in an episode of some teen drama on TV. "Eh? You mean—with my mum and dad? Yes, of course it is."

"No, I mean with you," Rachel said, her smile remaining fixed. "In your life. Is everything okay? No . . . problems?"

"No, of course not," said Laura automatically. "What do you mean?"

"Your behavior . . ." Rachel trailed off, then gathered herself for the full attack. "I'm afraid we are all rather concerned about your behavior and the deterioration of your performance in the last few months. Laura, I have to ask you. Are you using drugs, or alcohol, in any way that might affect your work life or home life?"

Laura's jaw dropped. The first thing that flitted through her mind, unbidden, was, How can you say that to me! I'm George and Angela Foster's daughter! I'm from Harrow!

She looked at Rachel, whom up until this point she had always thought of as a reasonably sane person, and blinked. "No, of course I'm not," she said. "Of course I'm not."

She assumed Rachel meant using alcohol in a *seriously* bad way, not the four white wine spritzers she'd had the previous night with Hilary.

"This . . . this isn't about the pay reviews, is it?" she said weakly.

Rachel looked bewildered. "No, of course not. This is what I mean about you, Laura. It's absolutely not about the pay review. Laura," Rachel said quietly, putting her hand out toward her over the desk. "We're suspending you."

There was a silence, broken only by the sound of the printer whirring outside the door. Someone coughed, far away.

"Laura?" Rachel said.

"What?" said Laura. "Are you serious? I mean—are you—What?"

"Laura, I'm so sorry. I don't know what else to do. I think you're a great person to have on the team, and I've loved working with you—at least, I used to. But I'm afraid you—your—well, over the past six months or so, your performance has deteriorated so much that I'd—I'd—" Rachel looked down at her notes.

"Just say it," said Laura, sitting bolt upright in her chair.

"I'd call you a liability." Rachel looked up at her again, and that was when Laura knew this was for real. Rachel was composed. Cold, even.

"You're late. And I don't mean ten minutes late now and then. You're consistently late, and you never explain why, even though I warned you formally about it three months ago."

"But—" Laura said. It was true, she'd been getting in a bit later, but that was because Dan was working on a project at the moment that was nearer than before so he was getting a later train, so she'd wait on the platform to go with him. . . .

"It's not acceptable, Laura. You take long lunches every day. You leave at five on the dot. Your absence report is staggering—do you realize you've been off sick for twenty-five days over the past year?"

"I was sick!" Laura gasped.

"No, you weren't, Laura," Rachel said. "You just couldn't be bothered to come in. They were all on Fridays or Mondays. What were you doing?"

Laura remembered the Friday morning in January when she and Dan had been on the train platform, and Amy had rung him to say her father wasn't well and she was taking the day off and going down to Dorset for the weekend. They'd looked at each other, there on the bench in the winter gloom, and Dan had grabbed Laura's hand, walked briskly out of the train station with her, taken her back to her flat, and basically ravished her all day, all night, and for the rest of the weekend. She smiled at the memory.

"Things . . ." she said carefully, trying not to smile again. Then she rushed on, "I know, I know. I know I've been a bit crap. But—it's all going to be fine. When I get back from holiday—you know—oh, I wish I could say more than that, but I can't. I'm sorry, Rachel. I know I've been useless."

"That's exactly it," Rachel said, looking grave. "Laura, look, the problem is you *don't* know you've been useless. You've had three formal warnings—this is your third." She leaned forward, her dark brown eyes huge, full of concern. "That's why I have to suspend you. You're lucky you're getting that, you know. I should just be firing you, but, oh, Laura, I think you're so good. I just—I just don't understand it!"

A tear rolled down her cheek. Laura watched it as it splashed onto her personnel file.

Rachel went on, "You're rude to the volunteers, you're hopelessly disorganized, nothing ever seems to get done. Four schools didn't have any reading programs in place for the new year just because you hadn't got the forms and police checks sorted out. And you know how desperate those schools were for help."

"They—"

"And the fund-raising," Rachel said. "You know we're looking for a big cash injection. You know how crap funding is this year. You were in charge of it, and you've done nothing about it, have you?"

"Well . . ." said Laura. "Linley Munroe—Marcus Sussman—I was going to contact them for the . . . but then he . . ."

"Oh, Laura," said Rachel softly. She swallowed. "It's just—I just don't understand why you, of all people . . . why you've lost interest, why you don't even seem to care."

"I do care!" Laura said. "I do. It's just . . . I've been crap."

As she said it, she realized how inadequate the words were. How she was someone who'd always prided herself on getting the job done, not letting people down; how she'd scorned others for their blinkered approach, their inability to get off their arses and do something to make a difference in their lives, other people's lives. More than a hundred children, the ones who most needed some individual attention, had been let down by her. Money that could really make a positive difference in someone's life, perhaps permanently—not there, just because she never got round to it. Because she was thinking about herself. About her and Dan. And Amy. She was the blinkered one. She heard Jo's voice clearly in her head: *"Don't you ever learn?"*

"And the holiday," Rachel was saying. "You've never cleared it with me, never asked for time off. You know we have to clear it with each other. Everyone else in the office will be away, I couldn't have let you go then in any case."

"Well, I'm going," Laura said stubbornly.

"I know you are, love," Rachel said. She smiled sadly. "It

doesn't matter what you do anymore. I'm suspending you, effective immediately. You'll be on thirty percent of your pay, and we're getting someone in from Lambeth to cover your job. Our school programs finish next week. I want you to take at least two weeks to think about things. A fortnight, okay? And then we'll call you back in after the school term is over and see where we are."

"See where we are?"

Rachel shuffled the papers on her desk. "Well. Where we are with a view to reinstating you. Or whether we have to . . . make this permanent."

Surely this wasn't really happening. Surely they were just threatening her. It was a bad dream and she'd wake up in a minute. She was a responsible person, a working girl, like all her friends. How would she explain it to them? To her parents? To her grandmother? She didn't get . . . suspended, it was ridiculous!

"But what will I tell everyone?" Laura said angrily. "You can't do this to me. You really can't, seriously. This is fucking ridiculous."

"No, it's not," Rachel said. Her voice was distant, unfamiliar, suddenly. "I just don't get it, honestly I don't, Laura. I'd always thought you were one of the best, the brightest of all of us. I hoped one day you'd run the program, or become an adviser, a consultant, perhaps even working with the government. I honestly thought you could do whatever you wanted. Be someone who made a real difference . . ."

Laura stood up and held the handle of the door, in tears. She shook her head at Rachel, wordlessly. Rachel sighed.

"There's a boy somewhere at the bottom of all this, isn't there?" Laura heard her say as she ran out. "There always is. . . ."

chapter seven

Laura didn't go to Yorky's birthday dinner. She didn't tell him the truth. She lied and said she'd been sick and come home from work early. She looked so forlorn and pale in the heat that Yorky obviously believed her, as he stood there fiddling with his keys, looking down at Laura as she lay on the sofa.

"Are you sure you're going to be all right on your own?" he said anxiously.

Bile flooded Laura's stomach at her deception, at how she was deceiving and lying to those who loved her the most. How could she do it? She clutched her stomach and winced with real pain, and Yorky looked at her with compassion.

"Oh, babe," he said. "Poor thing. Look, call me any time and I'll come home early if you want."

"It's your birthday," Laura said grimly, clenching her teeth. "Go away. Have a great evening. Give the others my love. I'll see you later."

"Okay," said Yorky. "Really sorry, babe." He tightened the thin, patterned tie he was wearing and shook his head. "Well, I'm off. Ladies, watch out. The birthday boy's a-comin'!"

He yelped and tried to moonwalk out of the sitting room. Laura heard him yelp again as he crashed into the hall table, and then the door shut behind him and the flat was silent again. She lay staring up at the ceiling, quite still, for a long time. At last she reached down to the floor and picked up the phone and dialed.

"Dan," she said. "Yes, I know. . . . Yes, I know. . . . Listen! Can we meet tomorrow? . . . I know. . . . Yes, me too. . . . No, not for that. Yorky's in. . . . No, he's in tomorrow, we can't. I want to talk to you. About the holiday. And things. . . . Oh, okay, then. Is it on Rathbone Street? . . . Yep. Okay, see you—yes, see you there."

The following evening, the heat of the day hung over the city. It was inescapable, both in Laura's flat, which was airless and oppressive, and out on the street, which was dirty and smelled stale.

Laura stood against the upholstered pad by the stairs of the bus as it lurched its way from the cooler, leafier roads of North London down into the heart of the city. The bus was sweltering, crowded, uncomfortable, and she grew angrier and crosser as it jolted down Oxford Street.

She was late to meet Dan—even though she'd had nothing to do all day, even though no one knew she wasn't at work, not even Yorky. No one had called; no one had noticed her absence from e-mail or the phone. She had sat in the flat all day, talking to no one, eating nothing, smoking a lot, and thinking about this evening with an increasing sense of dread. There was no one she could talk to, anyway. No one who knew how badly she'd fucked up, and she'd wanted it to stay that way. No, she'd sort this situation out first, and if it worked out—a big if, but she knew it would, it had to this time—then at least, no matter what else happened, she and Dan Floyd would finally be able to tell everyone they were in love, they were a couple, Amy was history, and everything in the garden was finally fantastically rosy.

The Newman Pie Room was above a pub, the Newman Arms, tucked away off Oxford Street on Rathbone Street. It was one room, decked out in old-man's-pub traditional style, with a few tables and a board on the wall announcing what pies were on offer that particular day. It was one of Laura's favorite places—Dan had taken her there on one of their first evenings out together. It was a great hidden secret, and certainly not the kind of place you'd ever catch Amy in, more to the point.

Laura's legs shook slightly as she climbed the rickety twisted stairs, but she reminded herself once again that this choice of location for their summit meeting must be a good thing. Dan was reading the paper, but as he caught sight of her he leaped to his feet, folded it up, and shoved it into his back pocket. He smiled at her, his eyes huge, then drew her into his arms, kissed her, and hugged her tightly for a long time.

"Hello, babe," he said, resting his forehead against hers. "How are you?" He smoothed the hair away from her face and tucked it behind her ear.

"I'm fine," Laura said, smiling back at him. She wound her arms round his neck. "I'm okay. Yeah, fine."

"Good," said Dan, looking over her shoulder. "Sorry, I thought that was . . . no, it's fine. So you're really okay? I missed you, baby. I really missed you."

He pulled her down onto the bench next to him, and casually put her hand over his crotch. Laura smiled at his cheek, still the same Dan, and looked at the menu board.

"Yep, I'm really okay," she said, pretending to ignore him but moving a little closer.

The couple at the next table looked at them with distaste.

"Perhaps I should move there," said Laura, pointing at the chair on the opposite side of the table.

"No," Dan said, and kissed her ear gently. He whispered, "Please, I want you near me. Who knows when we might be together next?"

"Well," said Laura weakly, "that's what we need to talk about, kind of, isn't it?"

Dan was looking at the menu board and didn't answer. He snaked his arm around Laura and gently cupped one of her breasts. Laura wriggled with pleasure and nerves. This wasn't going the way she'd anticipated. She leaned into him, gave into it.

"I missed you, too."

"Hm?" Dan said. "I'm having the lamb and mint pie, what about you?"

Food. A day spent at home mulling over her problems and failing to come up with solutions had not calmed Laura down one jot. It was sweltering outside, even hotter inside, and she was feeling fairly emotionally fraught. She had eaten very little that day, and had actually been sick before she came out, in a kind of wretched, stressed way. A lamb and mint pie was not really what she was in the mood for.

"Um," she began, knotting and unknotting her hands in her lap. "I'm not that hungry, you know. I feel a bit funny. I might just have a salad."

"Really?" Dan looked at her as if she were insane. "You're okay, aren't you?"

"Yes," Laura said, beginning to be slightly irritated that the question kept being asked yet not followed through on. She steeled herself and put her hand on Dan's wrist. "Look at me," she said.

He turned to face her.

"I am fine," she said. "I'm really fine, in fact. But we need to talk. There's . . . things we need to discuss. Tonight."

Dan looked slightly alarmed. "Right. Why aren't you hungry?" he said after a pause.

"Well, I was a bit sick today, but that's normal . . . nothing. Look—"

Dan's reaction to this news was unexpected. His jaw dropped and he gaped at her, then gasped several times as if short of breath. "You were sick?" he said. "Why?"

Laura wanted to be touched by his concern, but he was looking genuinely horrified. She found it a little off-putting. How could she explain everything to him? Why couldn't he understand? "I . . . well. I haven't been feeling too good lately."

"Are you . . . ill?" Dan said, his jaw muscles clenching. "Have you been off work?"

"Well . . . actually, I have. Something's happened. That's what . . ." She swallowed. "Things are going to be difficult over the next couple of months, Dan," she said softly. "That's why I have to know what's going on with us. I have to know, I can't do it anymore."

She sat back in her seat, shaking with adrenaline, and reached out to take his hand, but Dan put his head in his hands and was silent. Laura watched him, a growing sense of unease welling within her.

"Fuck . . ." Dan said eventually. "Oh, fuck." He looked up again, and then, strangely, ran his eyes up and down her body. "Just tell me. Tell me the truth. You're . . . fuck, you're *pregnant*, aren't you?"

A waitress had materialized beside them during this sentence. She let out an involuntary gasp. "Shall I come back?" she said, glancing from one to the other and looking ultracurious.

"No," said Laura, slightly maliciously, though it was only afterward that she recognized the emotion for what it was.

Dan was sitting stock-still, staring into space. "Fuck," he repeated.

"I think we're ready to order here," Laura said calmly. "Can I just have the Greek salad, please? And, Dan—you want the lamb and mint pie, don't you?" No response was forthcoming, so she nodded to the waitress. "Yes, he'll have that, and some broccoli, too, please."

"Another beer?" said the waitress, gesturing to Dan's pint.

"I think so," said Laura briskly, "and can I have a bottle of house white, please?"

"One bottle?" said the waitress incredulously. "For you?"

"Yes, please," said Laura airily. "I've got a bit of a wine head on, you see. When you need a drink, you just need a drink, don't you!"

"Hm," said the waitress, looking appalled, and she strode off toward the bar, beckoning the barman over to her and instantly engaging him in whispered conversation, which involved blatant staring at the happy couple and rolling of eyes.

Dan awoke from his reverie with a start. He stared at Laura and rubbed his chin. Laura stared back at him, and her heart melted again. He was so gorgeous, with the day or two's growth of beard, the tanned, chiseled face. Their children would be beautiful, if they took after their father, there was no doubting that. However . . .

"How . . . when?" said Dan hoarsely. "Not you . . . fuck, this is . . . Laura, you swore you were on the pill. Have you told . . . why did you . . ."

Laura looked at his face again. The questions, the accusations, the problems ahead. And she was glad, glad it wasn't true, glad she wasn't giving Dan this news, if that was his reaction. She put her finger on his lips.

"Why the fuck would you think that?" she said, half laughing.

Dan didn't smile. He looked even worse, if anything.

"You stupid man," she said, laughing a little, as the waitress returned with the drinks. "I'm not pregnant, did I ever say I was?"

"She's not . . ." the waitress hissed over their heads to the barman, gesturing wildly at both of them and shaking her head.

"You're not?" Dan said. "Really?"

"Really," said Laura drily.

Dan licked his upper lip, which was dewy with sweat, and said hoarsely, "Thank God for that." He slumped back into his seat and took his drink, almost sullenly. "Thank God. Sorry, Laura love, but you had me there for a moment. The timing . . . not good."

"I didn't say—" Laura began, then broke off. She patted his arm. "Calm down, Dan. I wouldn't do that, I'm not stupid."

Dan took a huge swig of his drink. "No, you're not," he said simply, and gazed around him. Laura breathed again, feeling almost light-headed. Dan said suddenly, "That's one of the things I've always loved best about you, you know."

"Me?" Laura said, taken aback. "Really?"

"Yeah," Dan said, fiddling with a beer mat. "You know. You're so . . . just smart. You know? You make things better. You're organized. You do that job, you know. Help all these kids, give them a better start and shit. And the way you organize things, remember everyone's birthdays, all that stuff. It's . . . it's . . ."

He put his pint down and turned to her, and Laura was astounded to see he had tears in his eyes.

"It's . . . it's just always better when you're in the room."

Laura had often wondered—ever since the fifth day of bumping into each other at the station and chatting away till they missed two trains, when Dan had said, "This is ridiculous. Let's meet fifteen minutes earlier. We can have a coffee. Yes?" and she had trotted down onto the Tube platform the next day to find him waiting for her, a smile of welcome on his face, holding a coffee he'd bought from the stall for her—what exactly it was about her that he apparently liked so much that he was willing to risk so much for her, for himself. And now she knew. She was dependable, she was nice. She was organized. She got the job done. A more prosaic—no, *boring*—set of qualities would be difficult to find, she thought, and had she been displaying any of those qualities lately? No, absolutely not.

She swallowed, trying to look on the bright side, and immediately an image flashed into her head of Amy, stunning, slim Amy, reclining at home, flicking through a magazine, gingerly blowing nail varnish dry on one fingernail. Wearing some exquisite lace and silk nightgown, specifically for lounging around in, probably. Why? Why was Dan . . . why was he *here*, with her, then?

She looked at him, swallowed again, and gripped the side of the table. She knew the moment was coming; she could feel it creeping inexorably toward the conversation, like a marching beat. It couldn't be avoided anymore.

"Thank you," she said.

"I mean it," Dan said. "When you're around . . . I just feel better. You look after me. The way you make breakfast, for instance, and remember I like to put the Marmite on myself." He ran his hands through his hair. "That sounds crap, but you know what I mean. You listen to me if I've had a bad day."

And how many times have you ever asked me about my day? Laura suddenly thought. It was a straightforward question, but suddenly she couldn't think why she hadn't thought it before, six, seven months before, ever. How many times? She didn't want to be a boring nice person! She wanted him to see her as the unattainable, the alluring woman of mystery who drove him to the edge of distraction, not . . . not this. Pleasant. Kind. Ugh.

"And you . . . I don't know. You care about me, I can tell you stuff. And Amy, she never . . . Well, to be honest, I just think that's why we don't—" He stopped suddenly. "Oh, God."

"You don't what?" Laura said sharply. "She never what?"

"I shouldn't complain about her to you," Dan said. There was a pause, and then he said again, "It's really good to see you." He stared at her almost hungrily. "Oh, Laura. I know we need to talk, but . . . can't we just leave? Go back to yours? You know—"

"No!" said Laura, much more loudly than she'd meant to. Dan jumped, as did the middle-aged American couple at the table next to them.

"Right, then," Dan said, smiling at the couple, who obviously thought Dan and Laura were mad. He handed them a napkin to mop up the beer that the husband had spilt, and gave them a charming smile. Laura did, too, and found herself thinking, What a great couple we make.

"No!" she said again, more to herself, and the wife jumped again.

Dan stared at her and said, slightly impatiently, "Laura, what's going on with you? I'm trying to . . . to talk to you, to tell you stuff, and—well, you're behaving like a schoolgirl who's afraid she'll be caught for bunking off or something, darling. What's up?"

Laura took a deep breath, and another draught of wine. "Right. We do need to talk, you're right. What's going on, Dan? What's going on with us? I want . . . er . . . I want some answers," Laura said, holding her nerve.

"Well," Dan said. He ran his hands through his hair again. "Darling, I've told you. Well . . . God, you know how I feel about you—"

"It's not enough," Laura said gently. "It's not enough anymore. Dan, we're going on holiday in two weeks' time, for God's sake! And you're supposed to be leaving Amy before that. You—you know how I feel about you. This has been going on for—how long is it now—seven months? And we're nowhere nearer than we were at the beginning of it. It's not enough. We have to sort it out. I'm—I'm in love with you. It's killing me, this is. We have to sort it out. Otherwise . . ."

Laura trailed off. She didn't know what the otherwise was—or, at least, it was too terrifying for her to come out with.

"Otherwise . . ." she repeated softly, and lowered her head.

Dan took her head in his hands, lifted her face up, and looked at her. He looked serious, more serious than she'd ever seen him.

"Laura . . ." he said. "There's something I have to tell you. I didn't want to, but you're going to know sooner or later. God . . . I can't believe I'm doing this to you."

"Wait a minute," Laura said.

"No, let me finish." Dan's hands were clammy against her cheeks. "I didn't want to tell you tonight; I just wanted to see you, for us to have a nice evening, one last night."

Laura's stomach clenched and she felt sick again. "What?" she said quietly. "Dan, what is it?"

"Amy's pregnant, Laura."

Dan released her, and Laura could feel the dampness his hands left on the sides of her face. He was quite sweaty, she thought, as if watching this scene idly from another room, another life.

"Laura, are you listening?" Dan said sharply.

"Yes . . ." Laura cleared her throat. "You . . ."

Her eyes filled with tears, and one ran down her cheek. She

gave a tiny cough, almost a gasp, and sat up straight. No, she wouldn't cry. She would *not* cry.

"Laura . . . I wanted to tell you, I've been trying to—"

"How pregnant?" Laura said calmly. "When's it due? It's yours, I presume?"

"Yes, of course," Dan said. "Of course it's mine." He wiped his hair off his forehead. "It's . . . it's due in January."

"Three months," Laura said, calmer still. "She's three months pregnant. How long have you known?"

"About a month. Laura, I've been trying to find a way of telling you. I couldn't . . ." Dan punched his fist into his thigh. "I—fuck. Look, she did it on purpose, I—I didn't want her to get pregnant. I don't know what to do, but I've got to—we're going to make a go of it, I have to. Of course I have to."

Amy. Of course it wasn't a mistake, Laura thought. Amy was as likely to accidentally get pregnant as hippogriffs and unicorns were to be found wandering in Hyde Park. She had planned this down to the last letter, and Dan—oh, God, Dan was the sacrificial lamb, and she, Laura . . . she had to leave. She had to leave, or else break down completely.

Dan was wringing his hands, quite literally clutching them in an agony of inaction. He touched her arm. "Laura, I know you must hate me. But believe me, I hate myself more. I can't—I've completely screwed this up, my whole life, and hers. And yours, and that's—that's worst of all, because—oh, God—" He broke off, and buried his head in his elbow.

"I'm going to go," Laura said, and again she had the sensation of watching herself from another room, from afar, and that other person was cheering her on, saying, *Well done, girl, you're doing well.*

Dan grabbed her arm as she reached for her bag. "Listen, Laura. Listen to me, just one thing before you go. Please."

Laura turned to face him, and looking at him nearly broke her composure, but she steeled herself.

"Look, Laura," Dan said. "I realize . . . it's over now, you and me."

"Well, I kind of assume so now," Laura said, repressing all emotion and taking refuge in heavy sarcasm. She removed his hand from her arm, shaking slightly. "It's one of my rules. Practically the last one left I haven't broken, actually." She laughed bitterly, feeling the breath catch painfully in her throat. "Don't carry on shagging someone who tells you he's in love with you and that he's going to leave his girlfriend, then gets his girlfriend whom he was supposed to be dumping six months ago pregnant, and makes you realize the whole fucking thing was a pack of fucking lies."

She stood up and pulled her bag slowly up onto her shoulder. "Bye, Dan," she said. "Bye."

"It wasn't a pack of lies," Dan said as she turned to go. "If you want to punish me, you've got your punishment. I love you. I always will. I never lied to you, Laura."

She tried to think of something to say back, something grand, something great, something worthy of Carrie Bradshaw in *Sex and the City* or Barbra Streisand in *The Way We Were*. But there was nothing to say, and the moment was nothing, it wasn't about that anymore. There was nothing for her to do but leave. As she stood in the door frame, she half waved at him, then turned and quietly walked down the stairs.

chapter eight

As Laura marched briskly out of the pub, she paused for a split second at the door, clutching the old brass handle, her hand smearing the metal with perspiration. Her vision blurred as her eyes filled with heavy, painful tears. She knew Dan would be watching out the window as she left. She had to hold her head up high. She couldn't let him see how hurt she was. This wasn't Mary and Xan and their early-morning moment at the pyramids, this wasn't it at all. It was all a lie.

Legs shaking, eyes still filled with tears, Laura walked into the street, up Conville Place, past the cafés where people were sitting and enjoying the evening's warmth. A man at a table on the corner raised his espresso cup to her and nodded as she turned left down Mortimer Street. He raised his eyebrows as Laura stopped, put the ball of her hand against her lips and cheek, and breathed deeply, expecting the tears to flow.

But they didn't. She couldn't cry. It was as if she were in a shock so sudden she didn't know how to react. The clarity of her mind startled her. It was over with Dan, there was no question that it wasn't. There could be no reconciliation, no "I've changed my mind," no "I'm leaving her." Amy was *pregnant,* and whatever happened between them, Laura had to be out of it. She was surprised, she noted with detached interest, that she could see it with such clarity, that it wasn't mired in a welter of excuses and what-might-have-beens. No. It was over.

Laura carried on walking down Mortimer Street, welcoming the cool breeze that played around her shoulders and the back of her neck, after the unbearable heat of the restaurant. Ahead of her stretched the city, unfurling into relaxation, gently welcoming, quiet and warm and beautiful. She passed the wide dark driveway of the ornate Royal Marsden Hospital and kept walking.

How would she feel about everything, how did she feel about it now? She probed her feelings delicately, like a child touching the cavity of a newly lost tooth to see how it hurts, where it hurts, how much. It was strange, foreign to her; she didn't know how to deal with it, so she kept on walking, into the night, along the wide street, the branches of the trees that lined it gracefully dipping and framing her in the quiet breeze.

She had lost her job. She had lost her best friend. She had lost—she winced suddenly as she thought of it—nearly all the money she had in the world on a holiday she now wouldn't be going on. For what? For a golden dream, a sweet, stupid boy with a beautiful smile. For that. For someone who had never even given her any definite idea of his commitment to her. He loved her, she knew that. He was going to leave his girlfriend, she knew that. But how and when and what would happen after that—she had never had any idea.

Laura had reached Regent Street. She looked about her, bewildered, at the purr of sudden, slow-moving traffic. Down to her left lay the lights of Oxford Circus, the permanent chaos and snaking crowds of people visible to her even now. To her right loomed the ascetic outline of All Souls Church and Broadcasting House behind it. Ahead lay the white-faced, formal squares behind Oxford Street. Where was she going? She didn't know. She couldn't face Yorky or being at home just yet. She just wanted to walk.

So she did. She crossed the road and carried on walking, through the impersonal grandness of Cavendish Square, past Coutts, past the Wigmore Hall, along the jumble of shops and converted mansions on Wigmore Street. She kept a steady pace, neither swerving nor stopping, just walking, looking ahead, pounding the streets, trying to walk herself back into sanity.

She walked until she could see the vast space of Portman Square and the back of Selfridges looming up ahead of her. She didn't know what to do then—didn't want to go toward the roaring hustle of a main road. She could go and see Mary, she thought suddenly, and then her heart sank; no, of course she couldn't. This wasn't the kind of situation her grandmother had ever found herself in. Better to keep on walking. So she ducked right, up Duke Street to gracious, leafy Manchester Square, past the Wallace Collection, its windows black and unblinking. She walked up Manchester Street and crossed the road.

Suddenly a car swerved around the corner and nearly smashed into her. It missed her by a hairbreadth, and the driver swore at her and sped on, not even pausing. Laura fell against a car, and ricocheted herself slowly off it so she was sitting on the edge of the curb in between two parked cars.

Then she cried at the shock, the loneliness, the feeling of terror that had flashed through her. She cried, silent heaving sobs, fat tears spilling out of her, dropping between her legs into the gutter. She felt totally alone, powerless; with nowhere to turn, she was bone-weary, flattened. And most of all, she felt stupid.

Amy was *pregnant.* She and Dan were going to have a baby, an actual live baby. *This* was reality, not the dreamworld she, Laura, had invented for herself about it all. How could she have been so naïve, so stupid? What was she doing?

Laura ran her hands through her hair, riding out the jerking sobs that racked her. As they subsided, she breathed out, and a juddering, blubbery sound escaped her that even she, in her darkest hour, found strangely funny. It made her smile to herself, a wobbly smile. She chewed her lip and sat motionless on the curb for a moment. When was the last time she'd actually had a relationship based on reality, instead of some completely invented fantasy she'd written in her head? In her stupid, silly, romantic head.

The calm after her crying was cathartic. Laura stood up slowly, her legs shaking. Suddenly she was tired, dog tired, and when a black cab swung into view a few seconds later, she hailed it gratefully and sat huddled in the back, staring blankly out the window, for the journey home.

chapter nine

Laura couldn't remember going to bed. She didn't remember much, and when she woke up, it was early Saturday afternoon. Which meant that she had slept for around twelve hours. She had no job to go to on Monday, no friends, no money, no Dan. . . . She rolled over and closed her eyes again. Her pajamas were sweaty, and so was she. She tried to think about the previous night, reached for her phone to check for messages, and then swallowed and gripped her hands into fists. She wasn't going to. She felt nothing, nothing at all, and she closed her eyes again and sank back into an exhausted, defeated sleep.

When Laura woke up again, it was later in the afternoon, and she realized she was starving. Without really thinking, she pulled on her jeans and, zombielike, went downstairs to go to the shops round the corner. She was stumbling back, clutching in her arms a paper, some crisps, a soda, a bottle of wine, some chocolate, and a DVD, when she felt dizzy and thought she was going to collapse.

When she reached home, she leaned against the wall of the building's entryway, unsure how she was going to get up the stairs again, feeling so totally alone and sad she didn't even know how to respond to her own feelings. Should she cry? Scream? Yell? Smile bravely? She didn't know; she was simply sick of the treadmill in her head going round the same old thoughts over and over again. What was she going to do now? What *could* she do now?

What she really wanted to do was curl up under the mailboxes and go to sleep for a year. Would anyone notice, would they care? No. And she deserved it. More than anything, Laura realized helplessly, she wanted a shoulder to cry on, and the reason she had none was entirely her own fault.

Laura gritted her teeth. She would go upstairs. She would.

Back on the third floor at last, she fumbled for her keys, and the door behind her opened. It was Mr. Kenzo, who lived in the flat opposite Laura.

"Laura!" he cried at her back, as Laura gathered up her haul from the shops in one scooping motion and tried to turn the key in the lock. The paper and the can of Coke slid out of her hand, and the sections of newspaper feathered across the floor.

Laura stared at them and tried not to cry. She bent down as Mr. Kenzo also bent over, tut-tutting, and deftly folded them up.

"My dear, my dear," he said, handing the newspaper and the can back to her. "Are you okay? You look not well, let me tell you."

"Thanks," said Laura blankly. "I'm going in now." And she turned away and tried to unlock the door.

"Do you need some help?" said Mr. Kenzo, unfazed by her rudeness. He stepped forward and took the key from her. As he turned it in the lock, the door was pulled open from inside, and Mr. Kenzo nearly fell forward into Yorky's arms. Yorky gazed at them both with bemusement, his hands in the pockets of his dressing gown.

"Sorry, Mr. Kenzo!" he said. "How are you? Helping Laura out there, are you?"

"Yes, yes," said Mr. Kenzo, eyeing Yorky's dressing gown curiously. He gave Yorky a packet of crisps. "She dropped these, take them please."

A voice on the stairs said cautiously, "Er—James? Laura?"

Not really caring who it was, Laura turned toward the door again, but the expression on Yorky's face stopped her. He was smiling in a dazed, stupid fashion and running his hands through his hair.

"Becky!" he said. "Hi! Hi-ya!"

Becky-from-Downstairs, who was still very much the object of Yorky's affections, appeared on the landing. "Hello, Mr. Kenzo," she said, not at all ruffled by the strangeness of the scene in front of her. She shifted her bag on her shoulder. "Hi. James—er, someone's signed for this delivery, and they pushed it through my door, and I think it's for you." She held out an envelope bearing the legend "Ticketmaster" on it.

"Oh, yeah!" said Yorky, leaping forward and taking the tickets from Becky. Laura watched as he gave her a super-enthusiastic smile. "Thanks. Thanks, Becky! Yeah, that's great. Just my . . . er . . . it's my, er, Snow Patrol tickets. Yeah!"

"It's your tickets for *We Will Rock You,* isn't it?" said Laura with an interested expression.

"Queen?" said Mr. Kenzo. "Ah, fabulous."

Yorky kicked her in the shin, and Laura took this as her cue to leave. "Thanks again, Mr. Kenzo. Bye, Becky."

"Er, bye, Laura," said Becky.

Laura pushed past Yorky into their flat, turned, and said again, "Sorry, Mr. Kenzo."

Mr. Kenzo's creased face smiled kindly at her. "Why you saying sorry? You are having bad day. Go in. And look after her," he said confidentially to Yorky.

"Thanks again," Yorky said to Becky. He swiveled from her to Laura, standing behind him in their hallway. "Er," he said.

Becky smiled at him expectantly. Laura cleared her throat.

"I'll—see you around, Becky," said Yorky. "I'd better go in. That's really kind of you. Great, thanks again."

As the door slammed behind him, Yorky turned to his flatmate with an exasperated expression. "You're awake. At last! I didn't know where you'd gone. You've been asleep all day, you know?"

"Yes," said Laura, walking toward her room. She stood in the doorway. "I'm going back to bed. I don't know when I'm coming out again. Go after Becky, Yorks. Ask her out. And when you get back, if anyone calls, tell them I'm not here."

"Laura—" Yorky was gazing at her with a plaintive expression.

"Sorry, Yorks," she said.

"But—"

"Leave me alone," said Laura, a sob rising in her throat, batting her hand at Yorky. "I'm so tired." She said it almost to herself. "I just want to sleep. Just leave me alone."

Laura went back to bed. She ate the food she could eat without leaving the bed. The wine she left—it wasn't a screw-top and she couldn't face getting the corkscrew from the kitchen. She ate a Crunchie bar in two mouthfuls. She was too tired to read the paper. She picked it up and scanned it, but the story about a school of orphans in Zimbabwe made her cry again, so she threw the paper on the floor and turned over, facing the wall, tears rolling across her face.

About an hour later, there was a knock at the door.

"Laura?" came a voice tentatively. Laura opened her eyes, but said nothing.

"It's me," said Yorky. "Look. Are you okay?"

Laura chewed her lip, praying he wouldn't come in, banking on a bloke's natural aversion to crying women. This was particularly strong in Yorky, sweet though he was in other ways.

"What's wrong, Laura? I'm . . . I'm worried about you!"

Laura pulled the duvet over her head as tears filled her eyes again.

"Look," he said, "I'm going out now. I don't want to bother you. I'm not going to come in. Will you just say 'Yes' to let me know you're alive and you haven't been attacked or anything?"

It was a good tactic. Laura patted the duvet away feebly with her hands, and said quietly, "Yes."

"Right," came Yorky's voice, sounding relieved. "Look, darling. I'm sorry about whatever's happened. Is it Dan?"

"Yes," Laura said. "Don't. Don't worry."

She didn't know why she said it, except she really didn't want Yorky thinking she was actually dying or something. It was her problem, not his, poor man.

Yorky said cheerily, "Oh. Well, you'll sort it out, I'm sure. I know you, Laura! You know what you want, don't you?"

Getting no answer, he said, "Well, bye, then," and seconds later Laura heard the front door slam. She lay there quietly for a moment, then put a pillow over her head and screamed, as hoarsely and loudly as she could, till the urge to shout had gone out of her and she was crying quietly again, until she fell asleep.

All through Sunday, Laura slept or lay in bed, feeling sorry for herself, not moving. She didn't have anything to do, and she had absolutely no one to answer to, and all she wanted to do was hate herself a little bit more, and the solution to that seemed to be to lie festering in a hot, sweaty bed, with greasy hair and greasy fingernails and skin, feeling achy and uncomfortable. She just wanted to be alone, to feel as totally rotten as it is possible to feel, to push herself far away from the hopeful, deluded girl who ran out to see

Dan every week with smooth, silky, tanned legs and clean, shiny hair.

She slept fitfully, and she kept dreaming. She dreamed she was running to tell Dan something, but she couldn't get to him; though her legs were long and she was running as fast as she could, she never seemed to make it any farther. She dreamed Dan was lying next to her, his arms wrapped around her, and that he was kissing her neck, her shoulders. She dreamed he had texted her to tell her it was all a mistake, but each time she woke up and checked her phone, there was nothing.

Early on Monday morning, she was awake, gazing around the room, looking at the detritus of her self-incarceration through the gray haze cast by the curtains. By this time Laura had been in her room for more than two days, and she was starting to freak herself out. But the thing about self-loathing is it stops you from taking the smallest of steps to make yourself feel better—even tying your hair back in a ponytail, or opening the window for some fresh air. She desperately wanted to get up, get out of bed, have a shower, but she couldn't. It was easier to lie here and not do anything. She couldn't go in and talk to Yorky. He'd told her all along she was stupid for carrying on with Dan! She couldn't tell her parents; the shock of the whole sorry mess would kill them. She couldn't call Jo, though she desperately wanted her wise, sanguine best friend's advice. Of course she couldn't call her—imagine what she'd say!

She thought about what she had to do now, and the enormity of it overwhelmed her. Fix things, fix things left, right, and center. And then, in the middle of it all, get over this man.

When she looked down the months to come, long Dan-less months of not sharing things with him, not telling him things, not being with him, her stomach clenched in sharp pain and her heart beat so loudly in her chest she felt it might burst. It was over. And so was that part of herself. When she thought about how she'd misjudged the situation, how she'd run ahead and fallen in love with him without stopping to look at whether he was the person she thought he was—well, she wanted to kick herself. Except this wasn't the first time, and she knew enough to recognize that she'd done it before. One thing was for sure, though: It was the last time.

Yes, the last time she'd fall like that. Absolutely the last time. A clean slate. A smooth, glowy feeling washed through Laura, stopping the cramps in her stomach. A clean slate, a project, someone to be, a new her. She looked past the gray-blue curtains at the crack that let the sunlight in. Yes, the good feeling persisted. She would be someone new. That was the only way to be. She was going to change.

The sun was growing brighter. Laura swallowed, tasting a bitter, moldy fur on her tongue. She sat up, her hands on her knees, and was considering what to do with this newfound zeal—whether to convert it into something by taking the first of a thousand small steps and jumping in the shower, or whether to lie back and think about it some more. What should she do? The energy of the question fazed her, and she probably would have lain back down and closed her eyes again when, thank God, fate intervened.

Laura didn't know which happened first, the sight of it or the sound, but as she was sliding back down under the duvet, there was a sickening *thump* and the window flew into a million pieces, hitting the curtains, and a pigeon hurtled in and landed on the bed at Laura's feet. Dead. Or dying.

It took a few seconds before Laura realized the person screaming loudly was her, her first spontaneous action of the last two days. She couldn't move. She sat staring and screaming at this twitching, bloodied pigeon, its feathers scraggly and ugly, its red-pink wormlike claws convulsing on her duvet, as Yorky burst into the room.

"Stop!" shouted Laura. "Don't come any farther! There's glass on the floor—STOP!!!"

Yorky slid to a halt, inches from a huge, dagger-shaped shard of glass. "Fuck! Fuck me!" he yelled. "What the fuck! Laura! What have you done!"

The pigeon twitched again. Laura suddenly heard her mother's voice saying, every time she wanted to feed the pigeons in Trafalgar Square or Piccadilly Circus, "They're flying rats, dear. Vermin. Crawling with fleas and God knows what else."

"Get away from me!" she said incoherently to the pigeon. "Fuck! Off!"

Yorky calmed down before she did. He looked from the broken window, where the curtains were fluttering plaintively in the summer breeze, across the path of devastation wrought by the flying glass in a shower across the floor, to the bed where the pigeon lay a couple of feet from Laura, who was surrounded by feathers, blood, and glass, as well as crisp packets, cans, chocolate wrappers, and bits of paper. He said slowly, "I think you should get out of there. Where are your slippers?"

"Don't know," said Laura helplessly. "I don't wear them in summer. They're too hot."

"Oh, good grief," said Yorky. "Flip-flops?"

"I don't know," said Laura. "Oh—there." She pointed at her chest of drawers below the window, which was covered in glass, and below it a collection of glass-strewn flip-flops.

"Wait there," said Yorky, and he trotted lightly down the corridor, returning with a pair of Wellington boots that he used for fishing trips (last year's Yorky craze).

"I'm going to throw them gingerly at you," he said.

Laura looked at him. "What does 'throw them gingerly at you' mean?" she said crossly. "Just throw them. Don't knock me out. And don't—urgh! Oh, Yorky—urgh. Don't throw them at the pigeon. Urgh!"

Yorky had prided himself on his spin bowling at school, and indeed was reckoned to be rather good at it. He tossed each wellie in the air, and miraculously each landed, in a slow, spinning arc, in Laura's outstretched hands. She pulled them on and climbed out of bed. Stepping around the glass and rubbish by her bed, she leaped across the mound of it at the bottom, and landed next to Yorky by the door.

"Er . . ." she said, not knowing how to ask. "Yorky . . . ?"

Yorky stepped forward and gently picked up the dead pigeon. He dropped it into Laura's wastepaper basket, and picked up the bin.

"Cup of tea?" he said.

"Yes," said Laura. She pulled her hair back and tied it into a ponytail. "Yes, yes please."

"Going to buy a new duvet and bin?" said Yorky as he pulled the bedroom door firmly shut behind them.

"Oh, you bet."

It was Yorky's last week of term, so he left for work a while later, by which time they had had several cups of tea, called a glazier (Laura), deposited the pigeon in some newspaper and a bag in the rubbish bins outside (Yorky), donned rubber gloves and begun the work of—once again gingerly—collecting each piece of glass that had managed to spray itself remarkably widely around Laura's room (Laura). By the time the glazier showed up after lunch, Laura had showered and dressed and had stripped the bed and washed her sheets. She threw away the duvet; she knew it was wrong and a waste of the world's resources, but it was almost fetid *and* covered in dead pigeon. There was no way she'd ever sleep under it again, she knew.

The glazier was a short, squat man who looked as if he had been born in blue dungarees. He was called Jan Kowolczyk.

"Well, well," he said, when Laura came to check on him after a little while. "Nearly finished here, young lady, then all will be good as new again."

Laura nodded. She agreed. It was all part of it, she knew, her feeling of having been evangelically cleansed. She had had her time in the wilderness, and A Sign had come to her to show her The Way. Sure, it was a disease-ridden pigeon, and it had almost given her a heart attack, but she had felt and interpreted its symbolism as keenly as if she were an A-level student reading Emily Brontë for the first time. And she knew what she was going to do next.

"Thank you," said Laura, smoothing down her long black linen skirt and then clasping her hands lightly in front of her. Her hair was clean and soft, tied up in a neat ponytail that brushed the back of her neck. The breeze through the window blew gently across her face and chest. She felt so in control now. She glanced around the room, her eye falling on the bookshelf piled high with her own books and videos, the self-indulgent ones she daren't have out in the sitting room. It was an unspoken agreement between her and Yorky. *The Godfather* and *This Is Spinal Tap* were out in the sitting room, along with various thrillers and classics and the usual clutter of shared possessions. But each flatmate kept his or her own personal tastes to the bedroom. So Yorky's room had all his weird sci-fi and fantasy novels, his *Buffy* and *Angel* boxed sets, while Laura kept all her Georgette Heyer novels and her romantic comedy videos in her room.

She looked at them affectionately, the rows of pink and purple plastic video box covers and the lines of paperback books, their spines cracked with repeated rereading. An idea came into her head, one so terrible she shrank from putting it into action; but she realized that to make a fresh start, she would have to. She gazed unseeingly at these architects of her doom. Really, she could blame them for a lot of what had happened. Putting ideas in her head. She needed a different role model now. Perhaps she didn't need them anymore. Perhaps—no, that was a bit too extreme, wasn't it?

Her eye fell upon an old hardback of *Rebecca* at the end of the shelf, and she picked it up, idly leafing through the pages. Maybe it was time to read it again. She needed cheering up. Laura adored *Rebecca;* it was one of her favorite books. She loved the poor, unnamed Mrs. de Winter with a passion, wanted to be her, and desperately loathed evil Rebecca, whom she saw in her mind's eye as looking very much like Amy. And Maxim . . . well, he was the embodiment of everything a romantic hero should be, in every way. Brooding, dark, passionate, brusque—just perfect. And she—

Laura brought herself up short. The breeze through the window picked up and she suddenly felt her blood run cold, as Mr. Kowolczyk whistled quietly in the corner.

That's it. You see? she said to herself. *This* is why you're in so much trouble. Get a grip! Mrs. de Winter was a complete idiot! She should have married some nice banker from Cheam and lived a nondescript life with him instead of falling head over heels in love with Max de Winter, driving around Monte Carlo, weeping hopelessly over people, and fleeing burning buildings. There, right there, was a symbol of what she was doing wrong. She, Laura Foster, would not behave like that anymore. She would emulate someone else instead. Mrs. Danvers, in fact. The good old reliable housekeeper.

At this idea, Laura felt her heart beat faster. Yes, Mrs. Danvers. Okay, she was a bit mad. In fact, you could call her a homicidal maniac with an obsession for a dead person, namely Rebecca, and an unpleasant penchant for appearing silently in doorways. And pyromania. But—but, Laura thought, as this idea took root, at least she wasn't a fool. She was neatly dressed, ran the house beautifully, moved silently, and was always in control of her emotions. It was so true, Laura couldn't believe she hadn't seen it before. Mrs. Danvers was the kind of person one would do best to follow. Mrs. Danvers knew keeping the house in order was best. Keeping yourself busy. Putting aside bad things. Having respect for one's friends and family. Okay, perhaps sometimes in a rather extreme way. But it was as good a place to start as any. As Laura ran through the list of broken fences she had to mend, she felt slightly sick, and then suddenly she realized what she had to do, whom she had to see. Not just because she ought to, but because she actually wanted to.

chapter ten

So, just before lunchtime, Laura rang the doorbell of Mary's flat.

"It's me," she said nervously, when the well-known, rather imperious voice of her grandmother said, "Yes?" over the intercom. "Your long-lost granddaughter, come to reintroduce herself to you."

"Goodness gracious," said Mary. "This is a surprise. Come up, darling, come up."

Laura had walked a lot of the way, enjoying being outside amongst the normal people and not in her head. But now she was tired, her early enthusiasm waning, and she felt naked and exposed, being out in the normal world again. She kind of wanted to go back to bed, but stiffened her sinews and climbed the stairs to the third floor. There in the doorway, a gin and tonic in her hand and a smile on her face, was her grandmother.

Mary Fielding was still as beautiful at eighty-four as she had been thirty years before. She carried her age with an elegance that owed nothing to expensive clothes or fine airs. She could tap-dance, she could sew, she adored Elvis and Clint Eastwood films, and she spoke five languages. She was the best grandmother, all in all, and as Laura saw her standing there, she knew she'd been right to come.

"It's been far too long," she said as Laura came toward her. "You're practically a stranger, darling." She saw Laura's face. "Good grief. What's happened?"

"Everything," mumbled Laura, wiping her nose inelegantly on her hand. "I'm sorry I've been so crap, Gran. I haven't seen you for ages."

"No," said Mary, "but you're here now. Let's get you a drink. Come inside and tell me all about it."

Laura sat on the gray velvet sofa, a drink in her hand, not knowing how to start or what to say next. She was feeling infinitely calmer now she was inside Mary's tidy, crowded flat, crammed with mementos of her old life with Xan. She looked around the room, thinking briefly how much it reminded her of all of her life, more in a way than her parents' house in Harrow, where she'd grown up. The photos on the wall; the drawings that each of them had done as children in a clip frame above Mary's writing desk; the tusks and knickknacks; Xan's pipe in the corner of the room—legacies of a life spent together, crammed into this flat for one person.

"I'm sorry I haven't been by for ages," she said awkwardly, breaking the silence.

"Me too," said Mary. "Well, you're here now, darling."

"Don't you want to know why I'm here?"

"Of course I do, if you want to tell me," Mary said, lowering herself into the chair next to the sofa. She looked across at her granddaughter.

Laura clutched the wide base of her tumbler, feeling the ice cool her hand. She looked out the window at the identical apartment building opposite, down toward where she had just been walking. Through the open window, the sun was shining and the purr of early-afternoon traffic sounded in the distance. From the balcony upstairs, she could hear the sound of laughter.

"Jasper and his boyfriend—they've just got back from Skye," Mary explained. Her upstairs neighbor, Jasper Davidson, was a painter.

"Right," said Laura, even then amused by the comings and goings of the inhabitants of Crecy Court. Mary took another sip of her drink, and looked expectantly at her granddaughter. Laura shifted in her chair.

"Okay. Shoot," said Mary, who had a fondness for the early oeuvre of Clint Eastwood.

"Well—I've messed everything up," Laura said calmly. "And I don't know what to do."

Mary leaned forward in her chair, her earrings glinting in the sunlight. "I'm sure it's not as bad as all that," she said. "Now, my love, suppose you tell me about it, and we'll see what we can do."

"It is bad," said Laura. "The worst."

"Well, you're still alive. I'm still alive. I got a postcard from Simon in some small village in Peru today, so clearly he is still alive, and when I spoke to your mother an hour ago, she and your father were still alive, so that's not true, is it, darling? Come on," she said, crossing her capri-pant-clad legs. "I'll just sit here, and you tell me in your own time, how about that?"

So Laura told her, absolutely everything, safe in the knowledge that her grandmother wouldn't judge her or frown or be shocked. As she finished, culminating in the dinner at the Newman Pie Room, the retreat to the bedroom, and the pigeon, there were tears running down her cheeks again.

"I'm sorry," Laura said, trying to breathe properly. "I just . . . God."

Mary smiled at her granddaughter. She put her smooth hand under Laura's chin and wiped away a tear with her thumb.

"My darling girl," she said. "Stop crying. Stop it. From what you tell me, I imagine you have had the luckiest of escapes. Now, dry your eyes, and sit still, and I'll get you another drink. It's over now, don't you see? Isn't that wonderful?"

"What?" said Laura, wondering what on earth she could mean. "It's not wonderful. I feel like a complete fool. I've lost my best friend, I've lost my job, I've behaved like an idiot."

"I think it is wonderful," said Mary, standing up. She went into the kitchen. "You fell in love, well, that's wonderful. All right, it was with completely the wrong man. But it's over now, and the best of it is, no more secrets. No more living your life in half shadow, which is what it seems to me you've been doing these last few months."

"Yes," said Laura, staring into the gloom of the kitchen. "I hadn't thought of it like that. But—I'm always doing it, always falling for the wrong person. I'm so stupid."

"No, you're not," said Mary. "You just haven't met the right one yet. And until then, at least you're not lying to everyone you know anymore."

"I know," Laura said. She squirmed a bit in her seat. "But . . . I know this sounds awful, but . . ."

"What?" said Mary.

"I quite liked all of that," Laura confessed. "The secrecy. The drama of it. If I'm completely honest, I think that was partly it. Isn't that awful? That's what makes me feel so bad about it all. What a nasty person I must be."

It was dreadful, when she thought about it with the tiniest bit of hindsight, to admit this was the case. That a small part of herself was such a masochist, so enjoyed putting herself through all of this. That she liked hearing sad songs on the radio and staring gloomily out the window late at night. The tears in her eyes as she walked home of an evening, thinking about how much she loved him and how great they were together. It was so adolescent.

"Laura, darling, every woman does it at some point in her life," said Mary. "You're not a nasty person. You're an honest person. You've absolutely shown how incompetent you are at cloak-and-dagger stuff, my love, and that's wonderful, too. It's not in your nature, Laura, it never has been. You've always been honest, since you were a tiny thing. It's best that way."

"It's boring that way," said Laura.

There was silence from the kitchen. Laura thought maybe her grandmother hadn't heard her.

"I mean, it's such a boring way to live your life," she said.

Mary appeared in the doorway, holding two more gin and tonics. She set them down on the raffia mat at the center of the coffee table. She put her hand on Laura's shoulder.

"Darling, never say that." She spoke quietly. "Never say that. Living an honest life is the best gift anyone can have, believe me."

She sat down heavily in the wicker chair.

"Really?" said Laura.

"Really," said Mary firmly. "Besides which, I think you may have had a lucky escape. No, listen"—because Laura's expression was mutinous—"honestly. This way, you'll come to realize you were better off without him. I promise, you will."

"Don't, Gran," said Laura. "I know. I know. It's just—really hard."

"It's true," Mary said. She drummed her fingernails on the chair arm. "You never got to the next stage, thank God. The stage when you're together with him, and both of you are walking down the street, and a girl walks past who looks exactly like—whatever the girlfriend's name is, what is it?"

"Amy," said Laura.

"Yes, exactly," said Mary, as if this was further evidence. "And instantly, the guilt starts up in your mind. The recriminations. Is he looking at her, is it awkward, does he still find her attractive? Does he think he made an awful mistake?"

"Well . . ." said Laura.

"It's a life half lived. That's what you would have had, believe me." Mary leaned forward to pick up her drink. "And that, my darling girl, is not your destiny."

"Well—"

"Trust me."

Laura didn't know what to say, but something about her grandmother's expression told her further questioning would be dangerous. After a few seconds, Mary sighed and smiled, and the twinkle reappeared in her eyes.

"You are a very great girl, Laura darling, you do know that?"

Laura didn't know what to say, it seemed such a completely untrue remark, apart from anything else. So she was silent.

Mary watched her, and she said, "I know you don't think so, but you are. I am so proud of you, of the way you are. Xan would be so proud to see how you've turned out, you and Simon."

"Hardly," said Laura. "He'd disown us. Well, me. If you can disown your stepgrandchildren, which I don't think you can."

"You're not listening," said Mary slightly sharply. "I am proud of you, Laura, and do you know why?"

"I am listening. Why?" said Laura, hastily swallowing some more of her drink.

"The quality you castigate yourself most about—your tendency to fall in love with the most inconvenient people—is what I love about you, darling."

"Oh, Gran," said Laura, trying not to sound impatient. "That's just not true. It's awful—I should get a grip, not—"

Mary banged her ringed hand on the arm of her chair, as if she were Elizabeth I inspecting the English fleet. "No, darling. You have a great capacity to love. Be careful. Use it wisely. But be proud of it. So much love in your heart. That's why I worry about you."

She coughed. Laura listened, relieved to be talking about it at last, but not really knowing what to say.

"I worry you will walk away from that. That this will close you up, make you forget how wonderful falling in love can be. Don't."

"Are you saying I should go out there and pick up the first man I see?" said Laura, trying to make light of it.

"No, no." Mary shook her head crossly. "Just—promise me, darling. Don't run away from it, not now." She closed her eyes briefly. "I worry that you will. That's all. Now, tell me," she said, lifting the glass to her mouth and holding it there. "If you have nowhere to go on holiday next week, might this mean that you might want to keep me company with your parents in Norfolk? And that you'll be there for my birthday lunch? Which, darling, I note you would have missed otherwise."

Laura's hand flew to her mouth. "Oh, shit," she said. "Sorry."

"What's that?" Mary said, alarmed.

"Holiday," Laura croaked, then stood up. "Holiday. With Dan. All booked. Have to cancel. No insurance." She sank back onto the sofa.

"Well," said Mary. "Ain't that a pretty pickle."

"No one in a western ever said that, Gran."

"The hell they didn't."

"What am I going to do?"

"I'll lend you the money," Mary said instantly.

"No," said Laura, shaking her head slowly. "No. I got myself into this mess. God. I'm going to get myself out of it. And then I'm never, ever looking at another man ever again."

"Really?" said Mary, smiling.

"Really," said Laura fervently.

chapter eleven

Slowly but surely, Laura's rehabilitation had begun. When she got back from Mary's in the early evening, slightly light-headed from the gin and wine her grandmother had pressed upon her, and full of good intentions, wanting to be like Mary, she cleaned the rest of her room from top to bottom, and then the rest of the flat, even vacuuming in Yorky's room. She went out and bought fresh flowers, bunches of sweet peas and cheap anemones, for she had long known that a broken heart takes a while to mend, but as Mary always said, flowers in vases to look at go some way to help. And she bought food. She made supper, spaghetti with clams, scrubbing them clean for ages, cooking them in white wine, garlic, and lemon juice.

She didn't feel suddenly light as a feather, or much better. She felt—numb. But a little hopeful. She was just glad she was out of bed, frankly. She told herself she would take everything as it came, not try to sort it out immediately, in the old impetuous Laura way.

When Yorky came back from work, they sat together and ate, chatting lightly over a bottle of wine, and Yorky asked, "What the hell happened to you?" and Laura repeated the story. Everything—Dan, the baby, the job, no money. Somehow, saying it all to someone her own age, who wasn't necessarily on her side, made it worse, because then it was out there, finally true, not just in her head. Yorky whistled through his teeth as Laura finished. She held her glass of wine by the stem, looked into her lap.

"I'm sorry, love," Yorky said. "I'm so sorry. I wish—"

"You wish you'd been wrong, and you wish I wasn't so stupid," Laura said lightly. "There's no need to say anything. I just wanted to say sorry, Yorks. I've been a crap flatmate. And an even crapper friend. Not anymore. Things have changed now, okay?"

"Oh, right," said Yorky uneasily. "How?"

Laura heard the tone in his voice, but carried on regardless. "How? How? Ha, well. New leaf, that's all. I've seen the light. No more romance. It's cold hard facts for me from now on, and that's that. I'm not going to go on about it," she said as Yorky coughed politely and settled back into his chair. "Seriously! I'm not. That's all I'm saying."

"Yeah, right," said Yorky. He smiled. "You don't have to change, Laura. We all love you just the way you are, you know."

"Thanks, Yorks," Laura said, "I mean it, seriously."

"Right," said Yorky, but she saw him hide a smile in his wineglass. Never mind, she thought. I'll just have to show them all.

"So," she said. "What about Becky? Any news?"

"Hah!" said Yorky. "She's got a bloody boyfriend!"

"No! Oh, damn. How do you know?"

"Because I effing saw him, didn't I?" Yorky said bitterly. "I was walking down the stairs today, *really* slowly, just in case she came out of the flat. Ha. She came out of the flat, all right."

"Yes? And?"

"With some bloke. Who she snogged for about five minutes outside. I walked past and they didn't even say *hello*," he finished sadly, as if it was the breach of manners that really upset him about the whole thing.

"Oh," said Laura. "Sorry, man."

"No sweat." Yorky raised his glass. "Onward and upward, yes?"

"Yes," said Laura, clinking his glass. "Onward and upward."

The next day, Laura got up at eight-thirty. She knew what she was going to do. She showered and got dressed, putting on jeans and a strappy tank top, and smoothed her thick, shiny hair back into a plait.

She opened her chest of drawers, and from it pulled a bundle of letters from Adam, her Romantic poets university boyfriend, a series of cards from Josh, and the tiny, pathetic scraps of memories she had from Dan. A photo of him. His expired work security pass. The bill from their weekend away in the Cotswolds (which she had had to pay for). A condom packet—God, how pathetic. Yet symbolic, she thought wryly as she chucked it in the bin. All the letters and papers went into the cardboard box she'd brought from the cupboard. Then, with a heavy heart, she turned to her video collection, stacked up on the bookcase.

Into the box went her beloved Doris Day collection. In went *My Fair Lady, The Way We Were, Pride and Prejudice* (TV boxed set), *Breakfast at Tiffany's, Gone with the Wind*, and *Brief Encounter*. She lingered over *When Harry Met Sally*—surely that was a comedy primarily, a fine piece of filmmaking, nominated for (she squinted at the case) an Academy Award for Best Original Screenplay—but she was firm, and it went into the box, to be followed by *Moonstruck, The Truth About Cats & Dogs, What Women Want*, and *Four Weddings and a Funeral*. Finally, with the heaviest of hearts, she picked up *The Sound of Music*, her personal favorite. Yes, the songs were great, but as far as Laura was concerned, it was all about the captain and Julie Andrews. The misunderstandings! The harsh words, the cross-purposes! The dance in the moonlight on the terrace! The— She stopped herself, and with her left hand pried the tape out of the frenzied grip of her right hand, and threw it almost viciously into the box. Gone.

She moved over to the bookshelf. Laura gulped. This was harder than she'd expected. She thought of Mrs. Danvers again, and hardened herself. Firm. Strong. Away with childish things. She put *Rebecca* on the bed, in case she needed to consult it. But into the box went all her Nancy Mitford books. In went all her Mills & Boon romances. She hesitated over her Jane Austen collection. Surely that was proper English literature, she shouldn't be throwing it away! But, no, the Mrs. Danvers in her spoke again. You have never read them for academic enjoyment, Laura Foster, she said. You read them because they make you swoon and sigh and have striding men wearing breeches in them. In they go.

Finally, she reached the top shelf of her bookcase. With shaking hands, she picked up her Georgette Heyer collection. She knew it had to be done, but, by God, it hurt. Tears came into her eyes. One by one, she dropped each book in the box, watched as they slammed onto each other, the pale colors of the old paperback covers gleaming up out of the box at her. It was torture.

But no. They were wrong, and they had to go. And the box was full. Slowly Laura taped it up, then carried it out into the hall, down the stairs. Outside in the sunshine, she squinted up at the sky as she staggered like a drunk person down the path to where the rubbish bins were kept. She balanced the box on top of one, and was debating whether to open the bin and throw everything in or to just give the box to Yorky for safekeeping when a voice said, "Hello, Laura! How you doing today?"

"Hello, Mr. Kenzo," Laura said. "I'm fine. Much better than the other day, you know."

"I'm glad, I'm glad," said Mr. Kenzo, who was carrying a balsa-wood box of fruit. He reached in, handed her something. "Have a peach, my dear."

"Thank you," said Laura, and bit into it. The rasp of the skin caught on the roof of her mouth, and she pressed her tongue up to the flesh and felt the sweet, musky juice flood down her throat. "Mmm," she said. "My goodness! That's delicious!"

"You look well today," said Mr. Kenzo, considering her. "Hair nice. New skirt? Much better than on Saturday. My dear, you looked—my Gahd. Like a dead, drowned cat. Old."

"Er," said Laura, taking another bite, not sure how to respond. "Thanks?"

"Let me help," said Mr. Kenzo, and before Laura could protest he had gripped the box firmly under his arm, lifted up the lid of the bin, and tipped the contents into its black mouth.

Laura gazed helplessly as videos, books, letters all tumbled out of the box one after the other, disappearing into the dark. "Oh," she said.

"Mistake?" said Mr. Kenzo. "Oh dear. That was rubbish, wasn't it? You did want to throw it away? Yes?"

"Yes," said Laura, finishing the peach and slinging the peach pit into the bin as well. She shut the bin lid. "Yes, I did. Thanks, Mr. Kenzo. See you later."

And she turned and walked up the path and up the stairs back to the flat. Another thing to check off the list. She was doing well. It was like having a New Year's resolution, she thought. I will get over Dan and I will sort out my life; also, I will go to the gym and have freshly squeezed fruit juice every morning. Well, little by little.

The phone was ringing as she came back into the flat, and though she'd been avoiding the phone, she instinctively picked it up.

"Hi, babe," Jo said.

"Er, hi," Laura said uncertainly.

"Look, I know it's none of my business. But Yorky just rang me. He told me what's happened." Her voice reverberated down the line.

"Oh," said Laura. "Right." She twisted the phone cord around her finger and sat down on the chair by the hall table. "Go on, then," she said, not really knowing what to say, not wanting to sound rude, but not wanting to get into it. She really couldn't cope with Jo if she was going to be sanctimonious and say "I told you so."

"Well . . ." Jo coughed. "I just wanted to say hi."

"Thanks," Laura said, fidgeting, feeling like a five-year-old.

There was a pause; then Jo said in a rush, "Look. It's none of my business. I'm not going to judge. You know what I think about it all. But I've been a really bad friend to you lately, and I'm sorry."

"You haven't been a bad friend!" Laura cried. "My God! I'm the one who's been bad! How can you say that?"

Jo's voice was a bit muffled, but she chuckled and said, "Well, it's over now, isn't it? Hey." She sniffed. "I really, really miss you, Laura. Can we—er, can we be friends again?"

"Of course!" said Laura. She hugged herself. "Oh, I'm so glad."

"Me too," said Jo, her voice quiet. "Look, I am really sorry. You poor thing. Are you okay?"

"Well . . ." Laura didn't want to sound pathetic. Then she said honestly, "Actually, no, not really. But I will be."

"Can I—can I pop round?"

Laura looked at her watch. It was only three o'clock. Jo should be at work. "Course," she said. "Where are you?"

There was a knock on the door, three feet away, and Laura jumped. "Argh!" she cried.

"It's me," came Jo's voice, down the phone and from outside. "Hello."

Laura opened the door. There was her best friend standing in the doorway, her tiny frame dwarfed by her enormous backpack. She was holding some chocolates and a bottle of wine. She raised a hand in greeting and her eyes met Laura's, and she smiled.

"Bunked off work," she said, rolling her eyes in the direction of her backpack crammed with papers. "I—I wanted to see you." And she came forward with her arms outstretched and gave Laura a hug. "Poor, poor baby," she said soothingly into Laura's hair, and both of them were crying, not just for Laura's predicament but because girls are a bit pathetic like that. "Poor baby."

"Yes," sniffed Laura, wholly in agreement. "Thanks," she added. "You must think I'm a complete idiot."

"No, I don't," said Jo firmly. "Just—no, I don't. *He's* the idiot, isn't he?"

"Yeah! But—well, I have been really stupid. And the worst of it is, you were right," she said in a rush. "All along. You're always saying it."

"Saying what?"

"You know," said Laura, looking at the floor.

Jo swung her backpack onto the ground and said nothing.

"Well," Laura said after a while, "just—it's not the first time. I should have learned my lesson by now. I have. Just so you know."

"Sure, sure," Jo crooned, putting her arm around her friend. "Yes, of course you have."

"No, I mean it," said Laura firmly. "You sound like Yorky. I have. Well, you'll just have to see. I'm a changed person. Anyway. Forget it." She eyed the bottle of wine. "Screw-top, yum. Come and get a glass."

"Great," said Jo. "So, tell me all about it. It happened on Friday, right?"

"Right," said Laura, retreating into the kitchen. "So . . ."

Laura suffered a setback on Wednesday. She knew she'd been doing so well, but it was hard being good and kind *and* Mrs. Danvers–like all at the same time. She woke up with a vicious hangover (Jo had stayed till eleven o'clock, and they'd got through a lot of wine together), and the dramatic avowals of friendship and cathartic chats of the previous night seemed a little empty the next day, when her tongue was furry again and she was tired and miserable and still jobless, penniless, Danless. She made herself a cup of tea and crawled back into bed, chewing her fingernails. What was she going to do with her life now? The practical side of her started to worry. How was she going to convince Rachel to give her another chance, trust her again? Future invented phantoms crowded into her mind; she couldn't stop thinking everything over, over and over, and she cried again, huge, self-pitying sobs.

She was still lying there when her phone rang. Laura reached out and patted the bedside table without looking at it, feeling blindly and knocking over her lamp and book. She picked it up and brought it under the duvet to see who it was.

Amy Mobile.

Laura pressed BUSY, her fingers fumbling. She turned the phone off and put it down the side of the bed by the wall, terrified, and curled up into a ball and hugged herself. It was more than an hour before she moved again and put her hand gingerly down to the floor, squeezing her knuckles through the tight fit between the bed frame and the wall, to pick up the phone. She turned it on. It seemed to take hours. The screen lit up, the welcome message trinkled at her, and then the voicemail rang. Laura pressed answer, her jaw set. Perhaps . . .

"Laura. You know who it is." She hadn't seen Amy for so long, hearing her voice came as a huge shock. Sickly sweet, slightly rasping, scary. It didn't sound violent, or overly emotional, or hormonal. It sounded in control. "Don't hang up on me, you *bitch*," she hissed. "You fat, spotty, spineless little *bitch*. Dan finally told me who he's been screwing, like I couldn't guess anyway. Okay? You're too fucking coward to talk to me after what you've done, are you? Fine. Let me spell it out for you. I know what you did. If you ever go near him again, I'll find you and I'll make your life misery. Even more miserable than it must be now. You fat, stupid *dog*. He told me how you chased after him, how you begged him, just like the ugly dog you are. Like you were at school, always begging. You're pathetic, Laura. You are *pathetic*.

"We're going on holiday next week, dog-girl. Just so you know. We're going to Florida. I would ask you along, but they don't allow dogs in the hotel. So why don't you just fuck off and think about what you've done. I hope it eats you alive. So long, dog-girl."

Laura couldn't feel her fingers, her hands, they were shaking so much, and the mobile fell onto the bed. She deleted the message and looked at the phone, terrified of its power all of a sudden, that something so nasty could come out of it. She turned it off again and slid it under her new duvet, feeling slightly sick. Would it always be like this? She could feel Amy's presence nearby, coming out of the phone, coming in through the windows. She was close, too close; so was Dan. Laura wished she were anywhere but here. She closed her eyes, but she didn't cry. She didn't know how to.

It was her mother who finally sorted her out. She swept into Laura's room on Thursday and drew back the curtains. Laura was watching a talk show on her TV, and her eyes bulged with amazement at her mother's nerve.

"How—how dare you! Get out!" she screamed, waving her finger at Angela rather like a French aristocrat to a peasant caught wandering in his garden.

"Hello, dear," said Angela, opening the window. "I spoke to your grandmother last night."

"Oh," said Laura, sinking down in the bed and chewing her little finger.

"She—well, she said she thought you've been having a hard time lately," said Angela, who wasn't half as insensible as her daughter thought she was. "Darling. Aren't you . . . needed at work at the moment?"

"No," said Laura, muffled.

Angela bit her lip. "And . . . are you still going on holiday next week?"

"No," said Laura, with the sheet over her head. "Go away."

Angela twisted her hands together and said, "Listen, dear. I have a suggestion. Why don't you come to Norfolk with your father and me instead? And Granny, of course. How about it?"

"Absolutely no way, ever ever ever," came the voice from under the duvet. "I'd rather eat . . . I'd rather eat—er—this duvet. No way!"

The next day—Friday—should have been Laura's last day in the office before her holiday. She should have been getting ready to go to Florida, packing her gorgeous new print hot pants, her halterneck bikini, her new digital camera, her cool cowboy hat.

As she was sorting through some clothes in her wardrobe, Laura found the cowboy hat. She took it down from the shelf and looked at it wonderingly, as if it were something from another planet. She stood there, running her fingers around the rim, letting her mind drift aimlessly over the past few days, weeks, months. Yes, in another life, the cab would have been coming to collect her in an hour. If it actually arrived now with Dan inside, calling up to her, telling her he loved her, that it was all a big mistake, what would she do? She put the hat back in the wardrobe and closed the door. She knew what she would do.

A few minutes later, Laura rang up her mother.

"Mum," she said. "I've . . . now that my plans have sort of changed, I was wondering . . . can I come to Norfolk with you?"

Angela knew her daughter far better than Laura realized. Laura could tell she was smiling into the phone as she said, "Yes, of course you can, darling. Oh, that's wonderful. How nice. I'll start on the packed lunch right now."

Laura put the phone down. Sitting there on the polished wooden floor, she leaned against the armchair and gazed around the sitting room. It was early Friday afternoon, too early for anyone to have left work. The air was still, and out on the street not a leaf stirred on the trees. It was very quiet. She brought her knees up under her chin and hugged her legs, and she stayed like that, thinking, for a long time.

part two

chapter twelve

The Foster family had been going to Seavale for their summer holidays since before Laura was born. About thirty years ago, when Xan and Mary started spending less time living as nomadic Bedouins or traveling through South America on diplomatic missions and more time in the UK, they had bought the bungalow overlooking the sea. The house had been built in the 1920s, a pretty, if small, Arts and Crafts villa, crammed with books and cushions and dancing light from the water. Beside the sitting room was a terrace, partly sheltered, and on the other side of the terrace was a single-room structure of glass and wood—Xan's studio, where he would spend the majority of the day in his smock, chewing his pipe and looking out to sea. It was now an extra bedroom, hung with his watercolors.

Mary's eighty-fifth birthday party was to fall on the following Saturday, when the clan would gather for one day only. Because it was a momentous occasion, Angela and George were to be joined that day by Aunt Annabel, Uncle Robert, and Lulu, Fran, and Fran's boyfriend, Ludo. Laura could only feel relief that she'd already said she had to be back in London that Saturday evening (some bollocks about a party somewhere, she'd told her mother), and would not be exposing herself to the Sandersons for longer than necessary. She could cope with the formidable Aunt Annabel, just about. Robert was a bore and a boor, but he was passable; he spent most of the time either drunk or asleep. It was Lulu and Fran whom Laura wanted to run in the opposite direction from. As with her mother's rather strained relationship with her stepsister, Laura wanted to like her cousins. She just couldn't bring herself to do it.

Lulu and Fran were famed throughout their teenage years for being creative, superintelligent, and well-behaved, always clearing up the tea trays, writing thank-you letters, and saying, "Oh! How lovely!" about things, rather than slouching grumpily around and grunting, thinking the world was against them, which was how Simon and Laura spent their teenage years. But Simon and Laura had *quite* liked them then, because they were naughty, too, and were up for things like the disco in the village next to Seavale, or having sneaky cigarettes in the sand dunes. But the years since had highlighted the gap between their respective families, and Laura now thought of them as snobbish, hyperartificial, and fake, and "creative" in the way that rich pointless people are, i.e., they become feature writers for *Posh Person's Monthly* or open their houses once a month to sell expensive jewelry they bought for next to nothing in Morocco. Lulu lived in Notting Hill and was skeletally thin and unbearable; Fran, actually, was slightly more bearable, but had gone native in Lulu's eyes. She lived in Putney with her boyfriend, Ludo, was a sports physiologist, had thick hair and thick ankles, and spent her life either running with Ludo or getting bladdered with him in an All Bar One–type pub on the river.

"Thank God they're not related to us," Simon and Laura would moan.

"I know," Angela once answered in a rare display of solidarity.

They were just different from the Fosters, and Laura didn't like the way she sensed the Sandersons looked down their collective noses at the Fosters, just because their house was a semidetached and they lived in Harrow, and only had one car. The Sandersons had two cars and lived in tony Holland Park; Lulu and Fran went to a super-exclusive school, and Annabel sat on several committees and cowrote cookbooks like *The Glorious Twelfth and Buffets for Debutantes,* or *Picnics for Countryside Alliance Marches,* which was ridiculous, since they lived practically in the heart of London and Annabel actually didn't like meat that much.

So, Laura had one week with her parents and her grandmother to get through, climaxing in the gathering of the extended family—with a guest appearance from Simon, who was supposedly returning from Peru on Friday and coming up on Saturday morning. Her brief was pretty simple, really: Be good, be nice, be kind. Put what's happened behind you and move on. A clean slate, a blank wall, a new dawn, *and* a new leaf.

But, of course, nothing ever turns out the way you expect it to.

Laura sat in her deck chair on the beach, her mouth knitted unconsciously into an expression of bitter disdain. She glared at her parents from under her sun hat, then realized she was actually *wearing* a sun hat, and threw it on the ground in a gesture of indignant irony—one that went totally unremarked-upon by her parents and grandmother, who were blithely unconcerned with her suffering.

She looked at the water. The sea was a rough, choppy gray. Clouds loomed overhead, menacing and bulbous, as if they might burst at any moment. The sand, which should have been glowing golden yellow, was a dirty cement color. And the huge beach was deserted, apart from a lone tatty-looking dog that was deliriously running around in circles in the distance, almost at the tide. An empty tar barrel rolled on its side, creaking. The sea grass rustled ominously in the wind. Why was she surprised the weather was bad? It was Britain. It was August. It was a typical summer holiday by the seaside.

George Foster hummed to himself as he carefully opened the National Trust Members' Guide on the blanket in front of him and fastidiously turned the pages till he got to "Norfolk's Stately Homes and Castles." Beside him on the blanket, Laura's mum was devouring her book club's selection, her mouth half open in absorption.

Mary was dozing. Her tanned hands rested lightly on her lap, one loosely clutching her book. She stirred slightly as Laura watched her, hitching an old shawl up around her shoulders again. Laura meanly thought about coughing sharply to wake her up, but she wasn't so far sunk beneath hope as to seriously consider giving her beloved grandmother a heart attack just so she could have someone to talk to. She picked up *Take a Break*, which she had thrown aside in disgust, and tried to concentrate on the story she'd been reading, about a woman whose husband was fooling around with their neighbor, but her attention wandered, or rather marched purposefully away, after only one sentence. She put the magazine down and gazed thoughtfully out to sea.

She'd been so good so far this holiday, but now she was in the grip of an irrational anger, and there was nothing she could do about it except hunker down and wait for it to pass. It was Tuesday, day four of the holiday, and acting like an angel with a blank slate, a new leaf, and all that was starting to wear her down because, much as she loved her parents and her grandmother, four days of constant exposure to them at a time when her reserves were low was not ideal. It put her in a kind of limbo—she didn't know whether she was a grown-up with a responsible place in society or a child, a total screwup with no job, no boyfriend, and no morals, who should just stop trying and give up. So she did a lot of gritting her teeth, till her jaw ached.

The first few days had passed, and despite the cold weather, Laura had tried to feel as if she were—well, not exactly *on holiday*, but still, away from it all. She helped her mother in the garden; Mary's hip was playing up. They all went to see a steam train display, and Mary made best friends with the driver and got to ride in his cab; George was jealous. They watched *Midsomer Murders* together, and Mary rolled her eyes and said things like, "It's the vicar, you total idiot!" while Angela gripped the sofa and screamed every time the incidental music played.

Laura made salad dressing, mixed drinks, and did not object to her parents' choice of television, newspaper, or plans for the week, one of which included the fulfillment of their long-held ambition to see the Seekers tribute band; as extraordinary luck—or ill luck, depending on your point of view—would have it, they were playing that week in the nearest resort's little theater. She'd managed to politely decline her parents' offer of a ticket. (They were actually called the Seekers Tribute Band, her mother had informed her that morning; Laura felt irrationally furious with them, that they couldn't have come up with a better moniker, Desperately Seeking the Seekers, or They Seek Them Here, or something like that. This did not contribute to a lightening of her mood.)

She had played Trivial Pursuit with her grandmother, who disputed the result every time the question was a modern one. ("*Britney Spears*? Well, how on earth am I supposed to know that? Ridiculous question. Give me another one. That's not Art and Culture, don't be stupid, Trivial Pursuit, you should be ashamed of yourself. Honestly.") She had tried to go for a long, moody walk by herself, but her mother and father had joined her and raved for a good two miles about the progress the National Trust was making with the coastline around the area, how the litter bins were so well placed, and how the cafés were much *nicer* than they used to be, until Laura tried walking slightly faster, ahead of them, but they merely caught up with her and carried on talking. So she had just smiled politely again, and gritted her teeth.

She had smiled agreeably at dinner each night as George briefly outlined the agricultural and economic history of Norfolk in the eighteenth century, and had asked a couple of pertinent questions, much to her father's obvious delight. She'd listened politely as her mother went through every family in their enclave in Harrow and delineated each member, what they were doing, what their children were doing, what their children's boyfriends or girlfriends were doing—people Laura hadn't seen for years, much less cared about. And she nodded wisely as Mary, for the umpteenth time, told Laura some marvelous story of derring-do about Xan and herself, this time in Jerusalem in the early sixties. Normally, Laura loved these stories. But this wasn't normal.

Laura shifted in her deck chair and pushed her hair out of her eyes. She looked around again, to see if Mary was awake. Nothing doing. She checked her phone, but there was nothing. Her mind wandered again. Scary Hilary had a party on Saturday night to celebrate being single again; Jo had promised to let her know what happened, and what the view was from the terraces, now that Dan and Amy were in the States and it was clear everything was out in the open. If Dan had told Amy, which he obviously had, who else knew? And would she have to pay penance for it? She wished she could ask him, but of course she couldn't, and she had heard nothing from him, nothing at all, after their last meeting. It seemed Amy was speaking for both of them now.

Thinking about Dan and Amy was all the reminder she

needed. It was her own fault that here she was, on the beach at Seavale, having the same stupid summer holiday she'd had since she was *five*. Only when she was five, she'd had Simon and Lulu and Fran and various other grubby holidaying children to play with. It was fine when she was five, Seavale was a nice place to go on summer holiday. The beach was vast, the tides were gentle, the sea was warm. There were ice creams and donkeys! And when she was thirteen and had kissed Robert Walden behind the beach huts and had her first cigarette with Lulu, or had gone to the disco in stonewashed jeans when she was fifteen, or had gone on a long last walk with Xan when she was twenty, over the dunes, into the fields, over the river and toward the next village, it was all fine—it was more than fine; it was her favorite place in the world. But not now. If only Simon were here now, she thought, moodily wrapping her scarf around her. But no. My brother *has a life*. He's *traveling*. And I'm *here*.

A seagull croaked viciously overhead, dangerously low, stirring Laura out of her torpor. She shook her head, ashamed to find tears were in her eyes. She pulled herself together and decided she'd be better off back at the house, rather than here making the others worry about her, because they already clearly thought she was mad. And it was freezing, apart from anything else. She turned to tell her mother this, and found her grandmother was watching her. Laura met her eyes, and saw that Mary was smiling with understanding.

"I'm going back up," Laura whispered. "See you in a bit." Mary nodded, gave her a quick smile, and picked up her book again.

Laura's dad murmured, "Mmm . . . mmm, see you, then," and Laura's mother looked up blankly and said, "You going back, darling?"

"Yep," said Laura briefly. "I'm cold. I'll put the kettle on, shall I?"

"Ooh, lovely," said Angela. "There's some of that fruitcake we bought from the craft fair in the tub, you could get that out."

"Right," said Laura, repressing the urge to scream, "I hate fruitcake! You know I do!" Instead, she said, "Okay, see you in a bit, then."

"Great," said Angela. "Dad and I are going to write our postcards later," she added inconsequentially, in the way that parents have when you are trying to leave them, a delaying tactic of some sort.

"Look, is that a crested grebe?" said Mary from behind her book, and Angela's head swiveled round. "Oh, no, my mistake." She carried on reading, the corners of her mouth twitching.

Laura flashed her grandmother a grin and, thankful for her escape, snapped her deck chair closed and propped it under her arm. Swaying slightly in the wind, she began the trudge across the cold sand up to the path back to their house.

Her bag made a vibrating sound as Laura reached the café by the lifeboat station. She stopped, fumbling eagerly in her bag, hoping against hope that it was Jo, or Yorky, that some kind of salvation from Parents World was on its way. She flipped open her phone eagerly.

Just reminding you to stay away from me, you stupid little bitch. And from Dan. Why don't you just fuck off? No one wants you, dog-girl. P.S. Miami is gorgeous, by the way. Wish you were here—not.

Stumbling blindly, her eyes stinging with tears, Laura ran back to the bungalow.

chapter thirteen

Back in her room, Laura threw the beach bag on the bed. She was trying not to crumble into little bits again, to go back to what she'd felt like before, but she couldn't help it. She cried. About five minutes later, footsteps sounded across the terrace, followed by tapping on the door.

"Darling, it's me," said her mother's voice anxiously. "Are you okay?"

"I'm fine!" Laura said unneccessarily loudly, and buried her head in the sodden pillow again. After a few seconds, the footsteps retreated. She howled silently for what seemed like several hours but was in fact about fifteen minutes, feeling deeply, deeply sorry for herself, the pitiable, unattractive, unlovable, friendless girl she was.

And then, all of a sudden, she stopped and sat up. She dried her eyes, wiped her nose on her hand, and looked thoughtful.

Laura had a pragmatic streak running through her, often not in tandem with the romantic streak, but following close behind. Listen to yourself, she said firmly. You have had your lowest moment, that was last week, in bed in your room. Remember the box of stupid romantic stuff now in the bin. Remember the pigeon. Your lowest moment was then; you're not allowed any more. You've been here four days now. Okay, it's pretty duff, but actually it's doing you a lot of good, and Mum and Dad and Granny are having a great time, don't ruin it for them. This is over, now.

She suddenly felt a hot bolt of anger shoot through her at Amy's text, at her message, at Dan's total weakness, the way he was willing to string both of them along and still end up the winner. This man, whom she'd thought was The One. He wasn't. Boy, he wasn't. Waiting for Mr. Right, The One, the great, great romance, was a waste of time—it had been a waste of time, and that's what she'd been getting so wrong all these years. It wasn't just Dan, it went back much further than that, but he was the one who'd totally, comprehensively stomped out her romantic strain. And perhaps she should thank him for it. She was going to be better off without it.

"Great," she said out loud. "Great." And she felt a little more cheerful.

Angela knocked on the door again. "Darling, we're having a sherry, do you want one?"

Laura was silent for a moment. Then she said, "Yes, please," and jumped off the bed. She pulled her tangled hair into a ponytail. "Just coming," she said, and opened the door.

That evening, as a storm raged around the bungalow and the leaded windows rattled and shook in their drafty wooden casements, the female Fosters and Mary sat around the table in the kitchen eating lasagna and not saying much, while George chatted merrily away about something. Conversation was slightly lagging, four days in, and Laura wasn't as much in the mood as she wanted to be. She knew her mother was staring at her, wanting to ask if she was okay, but she also knew Angela wouldn't. She knew her father was trying to jolly everyone along, but it wasn't really succeeding. And Mary, though Laura loved her, was always slightly hard to read, her mood hard to predict from day to day. She, Laura, had to make the effort.

She looked up as her mother said, "George, more broccoli, dear?"

"Yes, please," said George, breaking off his very interesting monologue about the great aristocratic families of the North Norfolk coast, and how they had fared during the Civil War back in the 1600s. Angela looked at him, her face softening with affection, and Laura's heart turned over. Her father took the bowl and smiled at his wife, the corners of his mouth crinkling, his ears wagging with pleasure, and Laura felt a rush of love for her parents. Yes, maybe Dad did often discuss heraldic symbolism at the dinner table for too long, and maybe he was just a normal bloke, not an orchestra conductor, or a deep-sea diver, or something. Deep down, Laura had always thought Mary found him a bit . . . *boring.* Laura knew why. Angela wanted a home, a family, roots. A back garden, a rose trellis. She didn't want the ex-pat life, the faded glory, the cocktail parties, stucco hotels, servants, bygone eras. She was normal, sensible. *Un*-romantic, if anything. Laura smiled at her mother, who was looking from her to her grandmother.

"Is there any more sauce, dear?" said Mary.

"Gosh, you two do look similar," said Angela fondly.

Laura stared at her grandmother. "Who?"

"You, dear, you and Granny."

Mary looked at Laura. "We do, don't we."

"It's odd sometimes," said Angela. "Just now, the two of you, next to each other. You looked rather fierce, Laura."

"Just like Granny, you mean?" Laura said, laughing, and Mary looked affronted.

"Angela dear, is there some more sauce?" Mary repeated. Angela shook her head. "Well, can you get up and check for me, dear? Thanks."

Angela stood up, looking from her daughter to her mother again, and went to the larder. Mary carried on eating quietly, and Laura gazed into space, her fork suspended in her hand. George was still talking as Angela returned with a small bowl of tomato sauce.

". . . fascinating that, actually, he *never visited the house* again! After she died. Heartbroken, they said. Of course, Sir John's additions were anathema to him, he loathed Palladian architecture, said it was a betrayal of the old English ways. . . . Still, fascinating to think that, wouldn't you say?"

There was silence. Neither grandmother, mother, nor daughter replied, partly because they couldn't think of anything to say, mainly because they hadn't been listening to a word.

"Well," said George, looking rather pink. "That's nice, isn't it. Was no one listening?"

"I wasn't," Mary said frankly. "I was thinking, Will Jasper remember to water my mint plant while I'm away?"

George scowled.

"I was, darling," said Angela. "I just had to get up to get the mustard, that's why I lost the train of what you were saying. Were you talking about the Devereaus?"

"No," George huffed. "Well, it doesn't matter. Let's talk about something else, shall we?"

Laura caught her grandmother's eye and smiled. Poor Dad.

"Pass the sauce, George," Mary said serenely, wiping her mouth elegantly with her napkin. "Now, I brought along the Elvis

'68 comeback special on DVD. Who fancies watching it with me after supper?"

"I'm going to mend the shed door," George said remotely.

"In this weather? Don't be ridiculous," said Mary briskly.

"The catch is very loose. Someone has to do it. I don't mind," said George with the air of one willing to martyr oneself for one's family over a loose catch on a shed. "I can talk to myself out there. At least the deck chairs don't answer back."

"I don't know," said Mary. "You carry on talking to them for long enough, they may well walk off to another shed."

"Mum," Angela said. "Don't be mean."

Mary smiled wickedly. Laura felt cross with her suddenly. It was irrational, she knew, but she wished Mary wouldn't do it. She looked at her dad. He pushed his chair back as if to stand up, in a rather defeated way. She took a deep breath.

"So, Dad," she said suddenly. "Where would you like to go tomorrow, then? If it's still raining? There's enough of those bor—er, I mean, big stately homes around here. Which one was first on your list? We could take a picnic, go for a walk, wander round the house. Make a day of it."

"Er," said George. He looked astounded.

"What?" said Angela, who was standing up, holding the salad servers in one hand and the bread in the other.

"Laura?" said Mary, moving forward in her chair. "Darling, are you okay?"

"Yes," said Laura, trying not to sound impatient. "I'm just asking, Dad, what do you want to do tomorrow?"

George's face turned pink again, but this time with pleasure. "Well, Laura, that's a very interesting question, love."

"Is it?" said Mary, sitting back again. "Is it really? Ask yourself, George, my dear man, is it?"

"Granny," said Laura warningly. She looked at her dad again. "Come on, where shall we go?"

"Well," said George Foster slowly. "If I had to pick one to kick things off with, I'd say . . . Chartley Hall."

"Lovely," said Angela. "Ooh, it's beautiful there. We haven't been there for ages, have we? Didn't they have a toy soldier festival a few years ago?"

Mary slapped her hands to her cheeks.

"Yes," said George. "And they used to have that lovely fete in the summer. Super. With the miniature train you could ride on? You and Simon used to love it. We went in '86. And '87. Do you remember?"

"Vaguely," said Laura. All their summers at Seavale blended into one for her these days, but her parents seemed to recall each and every one with the precision of an Exocet missile.

"Well, you'll see tomorrow," George said. "It's one of the great houses of England. Of anywhere. Beautiful. Inigo Jones. Finest collection of Hogarth's work in private hands. The library—all carved by Grinling Gibbons. And the most incredible books, a set of Austen first editions, of Henry James. The—was it the seventh Marquis of Ranelagh? A bibliophile, it consumed him." He cleared his throat. "Landscaped grounds . . . beautiful, just beautiful. In its heyday"—his eyes glazed over, and he reminded Laura almost of St. Teresa in her moment of ecstasy—"ah, it was the great house for miles around, its own kingdom, you know. The Needhams—there was no family like them in the area, no one at all."

"Why's that, then?" asked Angela, picking up the place mats.

"Well—more of everything than anyone else," George said simply. "They survived the Civil War, emerged with all their money intact, and they built themselves this great house to demonstrate it. They were a terrible lot to start off with. Brigands, extortionists. They made their money in the 1300s as debt collectors; then they married into money, then more money, then more, till they were the Needhams of Chartley Hall and everyone else had long forgotten they were thugs. Then Charles II's great mate, Thomas Needham, he was given the marquisdom. Mainly for letting Charlie have his mistress, I understand." George chuckled in an all-boys-together way, delighted at this behavior; then realized he was on his own and coughed. "So, yes. More money, more power, more of everything. The most glittering marriages—they married well, the Needhams. The greatest prizes—there was a Michelangelo plaster cast in the ballroom, till they sold it to pay off the—ooh, now, what was it? Which marquis? Nineteenth century, anyway. Terrible gambling debts, bad business."

"Hm," Mary said. "I remember the chap who was there when we went. Flew planes. He still alive? He was getting on a bit, wasn't he?"

"Yes, died two years ago. Terrible business, what happened to him. Broken man."

"Why?" asked Laura.

"Wife left him. Ran off with someone. Can't remember who, someone in the family. Big scandal, it was."

"His brother," said Mary. "His brother, Frederick."

"Really?" said Laura. "Blimey."

"She was the film star, Vivienne Lash," Mary continued. "You wouldn't remember her, Laura—she was big in the late fifties, sixties. Beautiful. It was this very high society match, the marquis and the actress. But, yes . . ." Mary pushed her glass backward and forward between her fingers, then looked around at them all. "Nice girl. I knew—I thought he couldn't have been much fun. Not a very nice chap, I hear. So she ran off with the brother, never saw her children again."

"Extraordinary," said Angela. "How could she do that to them?"

"Well, she was in love," said Mary, slightly sharply. "She would have done anything. And they weren't babies, they were grown-ups, I seem to remember. I met Vivienne and Frederick once, several years ago. They were—lovely."

Mary and Xan had met everyone. "Did you?" said Angela, refusing to be cowed. "Still—"

"Anyway, it's not him now," George interrupted his wife. "Died a couple of years ago. It's his son, Vivienne's son. Young chap. I saw her there once, you know. She was absolutely lovely. Stunning."

"Right," said Laura, wanting to say, "Get on with it, Dad!" but instead she said firmly, "Wow, sounds great, Dad. Tomorrow, then."

"Tomorrow," said George, looking round the cozy room. He rubbed his hands together. "And, Mary, we need to talk about the plans for Saturday, you know. What you want to do. Angela and I are going to buy the food on Friday. We need to prepare."

"Oh, yes we do," said Mary, her eyes twinkling at him. "Preparation is key, my dear boy."

"I've got to ice the—" Angela broke off suddenly, her hand flying to her mouth. "Oh. Nothing."

"Ooh," said Mary. "The dreadful suspense, my heart is in my mouth. What can you be talking about, darling?"

"Er," said her daughter. "Nothing. I'm icing—nothing."

"Great," said Mary. "How jolly. Just remember, I hate green food coloring with a passion. Thank you."

chapter fourteen

Laura woke up on Wednesday morning, forgetting where she was. She lay there in her light, airy bedroom, listening to the sound of the waves breaking as the gradual rush of memory slid into her waking brain. She got up and pulled up the blinds, to be confronted with a beautiful sunny day. The storm of the previous night had blown all the clouds away and the sun was dancing on the sea; there was a faint breeze, and the beach huts were already showing signs of life, colored doors open, windbreaks being erected. Laura's heart lifted.

Then, out on the terrace, she heard her parents having breakfast with Mary and discussing departure times for their expedition to Chartley Hall, and her heart sank again. Oh, Lord. It was one thing to cheer Dad up by encouraging him to reenact the National Trust guide at the dinner table; it was another to actually go with him to one of these places, just to keep the peace. Sure, she had liked them a lot when she was smaller. She especially liked the daydreaming you could do, pretending this beautiful silk-wallpapered room with its enormous bed was yours, pretending this marble staircase with the huge sculpture at the bottom was what you had to descend each night in a huge crinoline, skirts swaying from side to side as you greeted your guests, then were danced off onto the moonlit terrace by your husband, the terribly dashing Baron of . . . something. Or was that a scene from *Regency Buck*? She couldn't remember, and wouldn't, especially now that all her Georgette Heyers were probably languishing in an unecological landfill somewhere.

Anyway, it was nice to imagine, but quite another thing to have to pretend to enjoy now that she was twenty-eight, and actually basically thought stately homes perpetrated the myth of an outmoded class structure on British society and kept people like her dad firmly in his place, thinking they weren't good enough for other people, like the Sandersons. Apart from anything else, the idea of trailing round after her parents all day while they went "ooh" and "aah" over some boring carving in a library was dire, not to mention too depressingly embarrassing to imagine. She could stay at home with a good book; she had found an old Lord Peter Wimsey mystery on the bookshelf the night before and was looking forward to settling down with that for the day, perhaps outside if the weather held. No more romances for her.

She got dressed and went out to the terrace, and there was her dad, his head bobbing up and down enthusiastically as he passed his mother-in-law the milk.

"Aha, Laura! Morning! We thought we should set off in about an hour, what do you think, Laura?" he said, munching on toast and brushing imaginary crumbs absentmindedly off his rather bald head.

"Morning, love," said Angela. "Come and have some coffee,

I've just made it. Do you want toast?" She stood up. "I'll get you some, do you want some?"

"I'm fine," Laura growled. She cleared her throat. "I'm fine, Mum, I'll get it," she said, rather more lucidly.

"So, Laura," said her dad jovially. "Looking forward to our trip today, love?" He waved his guidebook at her.

"Yup," said Laura, reaching for a mug and pouring herself some coffee. "Look, Dad, the thing is . . . I was thinking. Do you mind if . . . if I don't come today?" She yawned in a deeply unconvincing way. "I'm really tii-iired. Aaah. I didn't sleep well. And I don't feel well."

Her parents looked at her.

"Also, I've got to do some work," she finished. "For the—the thing next week. My meeting. So, I really have to, actually. And—"

"Laura," Angela interrupted, holding her hand up as if to prevent her from speaking further. "Let me give you a piece of advice."

"Sure," said Laura meekly.

"If you're going to make an excuse, only make one excuse," said her mother sternly. "Don't make four. It makes it terribly obvious that you're trying to get out of something."

"I'm not!"

"Yes, you are," Angela said. "Never mind, dear. If you don't want to come, just say so. We're hardly going to be heartbroken, you know."

Laura looked at her dad. He didn't look heartbroken, of course. He did look quite sad, though. Laura shifted in her seat. She didn't want to go. She was twenty-eight! She didn't have to go if she didn't want to go and—she wasn't going to go, that was it. Silence fell upon the group.

After a moment, Mary said, "Such a nice postcard from Annabel, did I show it to you? She and Robert are really looking forward to Saturday, Angela. And she says Robert said to let George know he'll be able to give him a hand with the barbecue, too. Well, that's nice of him, isn't it. I suppose he's remembering George's slight mishap with the grill last year."

Whoa, thought Laura. Whoa, whoa. God, those Sandersons, they really were the pits.

"God," George muttered under his breath. Laura could have sworn she heard him say something else much ruder than that, but—no! not Dad, surely? She looked up at him in Foster solidarity, her chin in the air.

"Sure, I'll come," she said. "I just needed to wake up a bit. Great. Great."

"Great!" said George.

Mary smiled, and went back to her paper. "Have a lovely time."

Laura looked at her questioningly.

"I'm not coming, darling," she said serenely. "The garden needs doing and my hip's much better. You'll have a wonderful day without me, I'm sure."

"Hm," said Laura.

They left an hour later, and it was getting on for twelve by the time they turned off the road for Chartley Hall. Away from the coast it was a hot, still day; the trees along the quiet lanes around the house were heavy and green, the only sound a passing car or a lazily cooing wood pigeon high in the trees. They drove through Chartley, a small village crammed with B and Bs, shops selling tea towels of the house, and quaint old pubs, and a mile farther along came to the turn. A painted wooden sign, cracked and peeling, stood on a stake, partly obscured by cow parsley and trailing leaves. Laura had to peer to read it:

CHARTLEY HALL
Home of the Marquis of Ranelagh
Built 1650

Inigo Jones House · Hogarth's "Happy Marriage"
Grinling Gibbons in the Library
Picture Gallery · Tea Rooms · Gift Shop
Pony Rides · Castle Dungeons

A Fun Day Out For All!

"Here we are," said George, the excitement in his voice palpable. "On we go."

They turned into the drive and crawled slowly down the potholed clay surface, bumping along gently.

"Imagine what it must have been like in a *carriage*," said Angela, bouncing enthusiastically up and down in her seat.

Laura gazed out the window at the vast expanse of meadow framing the drive. No, she would *not* imagine what it must have been like in a carriage. That kind of behavior was over for her. Of course, the old her would have been busy thinking up fairy-tale stories. Thinking up some complicated scenario that involved her and her parents being asked to stay for supper, invited to a ball in the house that evening, the young marquis her dad was so excited about asking her to waltz. . . .

Well, there you go. Apart from anything else, she was wearing a faded old cotton skirt and a ribbon-strapped top from Marks and Spencer—that wasn't ballroom dancing gear. She'd seen *Strictly Come Dancing*. She couldn't waltz, she reminded herself. She gazed out the window at the view unfolding before her. Surely even her new unromantic self could enjoy a view, that was allowed.

The landscape fell gently away, and she could see trees, a stream, rising up to some kind of temple in the far, far distance at the top of a hill. She could smell freshly mown grass, and she could hear the wind rushing through the trees, even across the wide stretch of open land. The car slowed down as they approached a cattle grid, and drew up beside a tollbooth.

It appeared to be empty, but there was clearly some form of life inside. It was shaking, and muffled shrieks and growls were coming from within its narrow, dark interior.

"Morning!" said George jauntily, unperturbed. "Three, please!"

There was silence inside, then a muted coughing noise, and a remarkably pretty girl stood up suddenly. She was a few years older than Laura, with milk-white clear skin scattered with the darkest freckles, dark brown eyes that were almost black, and tousled auburn hair, which she flung out of her face as she smiled at them. She had on a strappy white top and a lot of jewelry, and she played with a thick gold costume necklace round her neck as she said, "Hi there."

Her voice was strangely mesmerizing, slightly transatlantic, slightly posh, slightly offhand. It was low and smoky. She smiled at George, biting her top lip. "How are you?"

"Er . . ." George looked round wildly, as if to ask his wife for the answer. "Er . . . I'm fine."

"Good, good," said the vision soothingly. "So . . . you want some tickets, yeah?"

Something in the bottom of the tollbooth made a shuffling, clunking sound, and the girl giggled huskily and stamped her feet. "Sorry . . . sorry about that." She glanced wickedly down. "Naughty. Right, then, tickets. Yeah?"

"Tickets . . ." said George again, seeming entranced by the girl.

Just as Laura was thinking she might have to get out of the car and slap her dad back into rational thought, her mother intervened.

"Three, please."

"Great," said the vision. "Great. How much is that?"

"Well," said Angela, much disconcerted by this question. "I don't . . . well, I don't know, do I?"

Suddenly the sentry booth spoke. "House and grounds, or just grounds," it said in a low Norfolk accent.

George and Angela jumped in their seats.

"What?" said George. "My goodness. What?"

Angela was suddenly alert. She peered toward the booth, her dark eyes flashing with interest. "Well, my goodness," she said. "Have you got someone down there?"

The vision chewed a lock of her hair. "Fuck," she said, apparently unbothered.

"She's got *what*?" said George.

"She's got someone down there. Whereabouts down there . . . I don't know," Angela said, showing a rare glimpse of camp humor. "Do let him get up and let us in, dear, then you can get back to what you were doing."

"Forty-five pounds for house and grounds, please," said the voice from within, even more quietly than before. Laura surreptitiously looked over to the tollbooth to see if she could see anything; suddenly its back door shot open and a lanky youth was seen bolting across the grass, behind the trees and out of sight.

His former companion sighed, and tossed her hair again. "Well, he said forty-five pounds, so I suppose he's right."

"Forty-five pounds!" said Laura in a stage whisper. 'That's bloody daylight robbery!'

As ever, the stage whisper was totally ineffectual, as it seemed to her everyone within fifty paces could have heard her. The girl shot her a look of pure dislike. "Have you got a problem with that?" she said.

"No, no, no," said George hastily, fumbling in his wallet. "There you go. It's cash, there you go."

"Great," came the reply. "Keep on driving."

"Any tickets with that?" said George desperately as the girl made to turn away. She was examining something under her fingernails.

"God, right. Uhm . . . yeah, here," she said, and carelessly flicked four tickets out from a roll on the counter. "Great. Have a . . . great day, then." She peered in at Laura, her stare of curiosity verging on the rude. "I'm sure you'll all really enjoy yourselves. Bye."

And she turned away and, tossing her hair, called someone on her phone. "Sean! Get back here and finish what you started. I'm so bored!"

As they drove on, George gazing about him wildly as if expecting other Titian-haired beauties to pop up in their path, Angela looking back and saying, "Well, *really!* Who was *she?*"

Laura gritted her teeth and scowled.

chapter fifteen

They drove on, through the near-silent park. The only sound was the faint rustling of the heavy leaves of the huge oak trees fanning out away from the drive. They were vast, sturdy things, standing in a line like sentries, and their branches hung low, casting a velvety green shadowy band across the landscape. The car crawled through them, out to the other side.

"Look!" said Angela. "There it is. Beautiful, isn't it."

There it was, and Laura turned her head to look. It was beautiful, it was true. The great house rose up out of the gently curving parkland, a crouching lion, noble and welcoming at the same time. The sun warmed the old stone, giving it a rich, golden glow. The windows glinted in the patchy midday sun, and the clouds that raced above the house were reflected in the glass. It was a huge, gracious thing; Laura could see additional wings and flanks stretching off it again and again, almost as if it were a small town. Though it had been built by hand, it was part of its own landscape;

and she found it very easy to imagine how it might have been three hundred years ago. Remove that family with the screaming toddler and the stroller at the front. Take out the sign saying CAFÉ THIS WAY, and the five old ladies in identical summer-print lawn frocks oohing over a guidebook, and the Range Rover peremptorily parked right outside—surely it shouldn't be there?—and replace all that instead with footmen in wigs, some Mozart in the background, and Laura herself, her hair piled up, one ringlet escaping and curling over her shoulder, dressed in a gown of beautiful red and gold, the door to her carriage being flung open as she was handed daintily down onto the gravel, waving a delicate fan made of ivory and silk. She allowed herself that one. It was a beautiful house. But as they parked in the car park, a field some distance from the house, and Laura got out of the car, a new rush of gloominess overtook her as the mundanity of the situation hit her again.

"Ha-ha!" said George, gripping his guidebook as tightly as if it were the key to a new Aston Martin. "Right, let's be off, then. Shall we start with the house first?"

"Great," said Angela, fluffing her hair out of her raincoat. "Then we can have the picnic, then look at the grounds. And the orangery. Oh, George! The orangery—"

"Yes, mustn't forget that," George said, winking at his wife.

"What?" Laura asked.

"There's an entire re-creation of the Battle of Waterloo in there," George said, pleased.

"Isn't the room a bit small for that?" asked Laura, deadpan.

George ignored her and strode on ahead. "No," said Angela beside him, as Laura brought up the rear, scuffing her flip-flops childishly along the dry gravel. "A *miniature* re-creation. Toy soldiers. Thousands of them. The eleventh marquis painted them all himself."

"Wow," said Laura as they rejoined the drive that led to the house. "That is quite simply incredible."

"The great hall was the first room to be fully completed, and it was here that guests would be welcomed as they arrived. This tapestry was designed especially for the north wall and woven in Mortlake, which was the preeminent location for tapestry weaving during the latter half. The seventeenth century. The chandeliers, moldings, and fixtures were designed as part of the overall décor for the hall by Jean-Bastide Rousseau, the preeminent artisan of his day in this area. This map of the county that you see above the great fireplace is very old. It dates back to 1485 and the final battle of the Wars of the Roses at Bosworth, in which the Danvers and Needham families both fought. On the winning side, of course. Lady Anne Danvers was betrothed to John Needham afterward, and the two great families were joined. This map was made to commemorate the union. Thus, it is central to the story of Chartley. And now we move through . . . into the ballroom. . . . Do follow me. Thank you. No flash photography. Thank you."

"Cynthia," said George keenly, annexing the fearsome woman who was their guide, "may I just ask about the significance of the map? It is interesting when one thinks that the Needhams . . ."

He danced alongside Cynthia, whose hair was set in tight curls of an iron and tin hue, and whose back was as straight as a wall. She frowned at him as they passed into the next room. Laura watched as her mother gazed around, Angela's birdlike eyes darting from one object to another, taking it all in, wondering what she should say and think about it all.

Their fellow day-trippers on this guided tour were as Laura had feared. Three clearly hysterical middle-aged women who were on some kind of day out, and who displayed such a degree of overexcitement about everything that Laura wanted to tell them never to go somewhere really *actually* exciting, like Las Vegas—the shock would kill them. Two separate dour-looking men, one very thin, one verging on obese, cameras round their necks. An overwrought family trying to pretend they were having a lovely day, whereas in fact the husband looked bored, the wife exhausted, and the children bewildered and tetchy by turns.

She seemed to have been there for about three days already. As the group returned to the great hall and ascended a majestic wooden staircase, she spotted her mum waving at her, pulled herself together, and trotted obediently over to join her, wearing what she hoped was a pleasant smile of enjoyment.

"And here is the library," said Cynthia, opening the door and flattening herself against it, sentrylike, to allow the group to file past her well-harnessed bosom into the final room on their tour. "Hm," she muttered, as the large camera-wielding man wedged himself between her and the doorframe, and eventually pushed himself out the other side, spluttering. Laura followed, trying not to laugh.

"The library is perhaps the most famous room in Chartley," Cynthia began. "It—"

"Excuse me, Cynthia?" one of the three ladies said, waving her hand in the air. "Hellooo."

Cynthia just looked at her as if she would like to have her executed for treason.

"It's so lovely to be here!"

The other ladies nodded enthusiastically.

"Can I ask you something?"

Cynthia inclined her head. "Of course," she said coldly. "Briefly."

"When was the last time you saw Lady Ranelagh?" said the first lady, as the other two looked on expectantly.

"Excuse me?" said Cynthia. "There is no Lady Ranelagh. His lordship is not married."

She turned to move on, but the second one stopped her. "Shh, Clare! Sorry. What my friend means is, the marquis's mother. Vivienne Lash. Has she never been back here? Did you ever see her?"

The rest of the group watched nervously as Cynthia looked at the three ladies in turn.

"Oh, Frances," the third one said crossly. "We shouldn't have asked."

"As I said before," said Cynthia, turning magnificently on her heel. "There *is* no Lady Ranelagh. I believe Mrs. Needham—as she is known now—lives in the south of France. *I* have never seen her."

There was silence. The three ladies looked crushed. Laura smiled sympathetically at them as Cynthia made her way down the room.

"Now," she went on. "The library."

It certainly was a stunning room, as George had said. It looked about as long as Laura's street at home. Shelves rose high on both sides, and light poured through the long, high windows on three sides—it took up the whole side of the house. It was like a big, glorious lantern, humming with interesting things, and although Laura desperately wanted to be interested, she was fast running out of steam. The old Laura would have cast herself as the bookish marquis's daughter, Lady Laura, creeping in here to study John Donne by candlelight while her brutish, unintelligent family slept on, but she simply couldn't work up the enthusiasm. She could almost block out the sight of George leaping up and down by a painting on the far wall.

"Yes, the famous Hogarth series," said Cynthia, marching the length of the gallery as the tour dribbled along behind her. "Harrem. The jewel of the Needham family's art collection. Long thought to have been unfinished by Hogarth. In fact, they were only discovered fifty years ago, by the present marquis's grandmother. Chartley Hall was used as a boarding school during the Second World War, and many of its most prized possessions were put into storage, in the attics above us here." She stopped in front of the painting. It was boldly executed, showing a man and a woman holding hands, emerging from a country church, with a plethora of characters—the grasping mother-in-law, the sozzled father, a beggar, and some children playing to the side—fanning out around the central bride and groom. "Some of his greatest work is shown in the eight different scenes that make up the series. All his life, Hogarth struggled to reconcile the twin demons of narrative subject matter and what he saw as great 'historical' painting in the grand manner. . . . With this sequence, which shows the happy courtship, wedding, and subsequent life together of a young aristocratic couple, he found it. Note the . . ."

Laura's attention wandered. What was Yorky doing at the moment? she wondered. Yorky, and Jo—and all of that—it seemed so far away, a lifetime away. It was good to be away from it all but—did she miss it? She didn't know, didn't want to think too closely about it all. She liked the fact that her life was on hold, as if she'd pressed the pause button on a video of her life and gone off for a while. On a tour of stately homes with her parents. Hm. She bit her lip and turned back to Cynthia, who was still talking, her clipped tones hurrying the information along.

". . . It was only when Amelia, the new marchioness, was taking these pieces out in 1947 that she stumbled upon a secret cupboard in the depths of the last room. There, rolled up and tied with twine, miraculously preserved—five of the eight paintings of this series. This is the only one of Hogarth's series that actually tells a happy story, I am pleased to say."

There was nodding of heads and pleased clucking from the group as Cynthia smiled benignly down at them.

"Where are the others?"

Cynthia looked around her. "I beg your pardon?"

Laura, to her astonishment, found herself saying again, "Where are the other paintings?"

Cynthia turned toward her, her smile a little more forced. "The other paintings?"

"In the series," Laura said. "You said they found five all rolled up. Why's there only one up, then?"

"Oh, dear girl," said Cynthia. "We couldn't hang the others. Too risky. Someone might cause them damage. They're very frail, you know. This one's the strongest."

"But—" said Laura. "What's—well . . ." She stopped, not wanting to sound rude.

"Go on, dear," said Cynthia, her eyes glinting.

Laura looked wildly around, regretting having started this conversation. Why? Why couldn't she just keep quiet? She felt the heat of someone's gaze on her and realized her mother was staring at her, eyes silently beseeching politeness. Laura plowed on.

"Sorry. But—well, what's the point of keeping them in storage? Why can't you put them on display so they can be together?"

"It's not as simple as that, dear," Cynthia said firmly. "And it's up to the trustees of the house. It's not really about putting every one out so the general public can enjoy it, is it?"

"Why?" said Laura, feeling heat rise within her, suddenly so impatient with this sad middle-England, middle-aged debate, setting, scene—everything. The new pragmatist in her rebelled. This wasn't fairy-tale, it was extortion! "You've charged us fifteen pounds each to get in, yet most of the rooms are roped off, the car park's miles from the house, everyone here is about eighty—no offense, Mum and Dad—no one seems particularly pleased to see us here, we're treated like cattle . . . I just wonder why you bother."

"Laura!" said Angela, horrified.

There was a short silence, broken only by the shuffling of feet on parquet floor as the majority of the group edged surreptitiously toward Cynthia and away from Laura, putting as much distance between themselves and this crazy, dangerous recidivist as they possibly could.

"*Well.* Really," said Cynthia slowly, puffing up like a tweedy balloon. "I mean, really. That's not nice, now, is it?"

"Sorry," said Laura. "My fault. I apologize."

Laura had been in a negotiation skills workshop a few months ago, where she learned how to deal with reluctant, lazy volunteers, undermined, exhausted teachers, parents who were sometimes demanding, sometimes hopelessly bewildered. The key, in most situations, was to apologize. Say sorry. People love it. It makes them feel much better, even if nothing gets done. The verbal action is greater than the mental commitment, in nine cases out of ten. It astonished Laura, depressed her, amused her sometimes, the power of an apology.

She looked around her, down the long hall at the sunshine that had suddenly broken through the great window at the end, the honey-colored books lining the shelves. She looked at the collection of flared-skirted, guidebook-clutching, middle-aged, middle-class tourists in front of her, and just wanted to be on her own. She should never have come in the first place. She should have stayed at home. What was she doing here, arguing with some tweedy woman about car parks and fees?

"I'm really sorry," she said again. "I'll wait outside. Mum—Dad—you take your time. I'll meet you back at the car, okay?"

Her parents nodded mutely. And so Laura turned and left, moving swiftly down the old wooden staircase that swept majestically down into the great hall. The sun was pouring through the great wide door and, with her flip-flops flapping on the black and white marble floor, she ran outside, away from it all.

chapter sixteen

Laura walked briskly away from the stable block, leaving the house behind her, the dry ferns and grass crunching satisfyingly under her flip-flops. Ahead of her was a grove of trees, cool and dark amid the yellow-gray meadow. Above her in a white sky, the hazy sun shone down. She could feel sweat pooling at the base of her spine.

Behind the trees was a huge field where, at one end, a mower worked methodically, making his way toward the heavy, nodding grass at the nearer end of the field. Laura could hear the humming sound of the blades, growing louder in the distance. In amongst the edge of the trees there was a little bench. She looked around anxiously, hoping against hope not to be accosted by yet another happy family or irritating fact-giving middle-aged people, such as those who had accompanied her here; but, happily, she was alone. She reached into her bag for her sunglasses. Her hand felt a square shape beneath the torn lining. It was a packet of cigarettes. She hadn't smoked for days; she only really had with Dan—in fact, she was pretty sure they were Dan's, from some snatched moment somewhere when she'd rammed them into her bag, in the rush to be somewhere, not late. How strange. They were a bit bashed around, but there was a lighter in the packet, too, so she leaned against a tree and lit a cigarette, closing her eyes and listening with blessed relief to the silence all around her, underpinned only by the sound of the engine growing louder as it came closer.

Something made her open her eyes. It was a deer, moving toward the copse at the edge of her line of vision. Its antlers were huge, fascinating to one who hadn't really seen a deer close up since she was six on a school trip to Richmond Park. Laura stared at it in wonder, mesmerized by its proud beauty, the contours of its body. The deer stared impassively back. I must take a photo of this, Laura thought, and rummaged in her bag again for her camera. Finally, something that might actually be a good photo, after four days of snapping remarkable road signs, or Mum, Dad, and Granny giving the thumbs-up sign whilst seated around a collapsible camping table.

Laura pinched out her cigarette and threw it on the ground. The noise from the mower was louder in her ears. She crouched amid the grass and tried to make a cooing noise, the better to lure the deer closer, but it stayed where it was, perfectly still, gazing dreamily at her in the sun. Suddenly, the noise behind her stopped, but Laura didn't care. She edged toward the deer, crouching and shuffling, camera in place.

The afternoon scent of mown grass and the tangy, sharp smell of a bonfire, crackling, filled her nostrils. In the distance, a bird cried harshly in a tree, and Laura remained as still as possible. Suddenly, the deer reared back and ran away, fleeing lightly back into the wood. Laura got to her feet, disappointed, as the smell of the bonfire grew stronger. Perhaps they were burning the fields now that harvesttime was here. Or something.

She turned around, and was appalled by the sight that met her eyes. The cigarette she had put out had obviously not been put out, and at her feet was a small, smoking black haze, with tiny flames that licked the brittle straw around it, that crept along the ground. It was alarmingly big, over a foot wide. Shit. Shit, shit. She was *so stupid*! Where was her cardigan? She knew you were supposed to put fires out with damp towels, perhaps it would do. . . . Damn! Her mum had it. Damn! She looked down at the fire, and for one mad second thought perhaps she should throw herself on it; then someone from behind grabbed her by the shoulders and pushed her out of the way.

"What the fuck do you think you're doing?" came a furious, low voice. It was a man, a tall man, and he was glaring at Laura as if she were a cockroach he'd found in his kitchen. He was wearing old jeans and a battered T-shirt, and a soft cotton shirt tied around his waist, which he pulled off, flung to the ground, and stamped on, his boots blacking out the center of the blaze.

"Stand back," he said briefly, not looking at her. "You'll burn your feet in those shoes."

"No, I won't—ouch!" Laura yelled, as she stepped on a small line of flames that had crept away from the main conflagration. She stumbled back and fell over.

He held out his hand and Laura took it, and he pulled her up to her feet with amazing ease. She realized he was furious.

"Are you okay?" he said, steadying her as she hopped backward to put her flip-flop back on. "Good. Do you realize how stupid that was, putting your cigarette out here? Apart from the fact you shouldn't be smoking in the first place, you idiot, we haven't had any rain for two weeks. This place could go up like a tinderbox."

"Right," said Laura, bending down again and picking up her bag and camera, to cover the embarrassment she felt at being told off. She caught sight of some keys in his hand and deduced that this cross, scruffily dressed, rude man must have been the person driving the mower. She looked up, a ready answer on her lips, but stopped as she caught sight of him.

Mr. Mower was obviously much angrier than she'd realized. He breathed as if he had been running. He was sweaty, and there was grass or hay in his messy black hair. His dark brown eyes were glaring at her with something akin to loathing. He was broad-shouldered, tall, powerful-looking; his face was tanned. Laura suddenly felt rather scared, as if he might pick her up by the scruff of her neck and fling her amongst the blades of the mower, to be shredded to small pieces.

She squinted up at Mr. Mower, annoyance written on her face. "Look, I'm sorry," she said, trying not to feel upset. He stared impassively back at her, his only expression one of enormous disdain. "But I'm not an idiot. It's a free country, you know, I can have a cigarette if I want. They should have signs up, if they're that against it, how was I supposed to know? I'd have picked it up afterward, and I certainly wouldn't have left it to catch on fire, not being blind or anything, you know," she finished with a note of triumph in her voice. "Sorry, okay?" She swung her bag over her shoulder and made to leave.

"Typical," said Mr. Mower behind her as she walked off. "Typical townie. It's not your fault, is it? It's always someone else's fault. I don't know why we bother sometimes." Laura carried on, pretending not to hear him. "Here," he said suddenly. "Hey. You forgot your camera case." He gripped Laura's arm lightly.

Laura turned around and smiled up at him, unable to be cross with him for long. He was nice, even if he was fairly rude, prone to throwing people around cornfields. "Thank you," she said. "I'm not doing very well, am I? Listen, thanks. I'd better get back. Good luck with the seed-sowing, or whatever it is."

"Crop rotational ecosystem, actually," Mr. Mower said. "Listen, you haven't got a cigarette I could nick, have you?"

Laura gaped at him. "Are you having a laugh?"

"No."

"Why on earth . . ." Laura said. "You don't deserve one, do you."

"No," the smoking farmer said. "I could go inside, but it's just such a hassle. Takes about fifteen minutes just to get to my room."

"Yes," said Laura, handing over the packet, her heart sinking. She really didn't want to be treated to some long monologue about the wonders of the estate, how great Lord So-and-So was, how friendly the people were. Fifteen minutes—she looked at her watch.

"Where do you live, then?" she said.

Mr. Mower lit his cigarette. "Over there." He pointed.

Laura followed his direction. "In . . . in the house?" she said.

"Yes, that's right," Mr. Mower said, laughing at her incredulous expression. "Someone has to, you know."

"Seriously?" Laura said, impressed despite herself. "You actually live . . . there?"

"Yep," said Mr. Mower. He ran his hand over the back of his neck self-consciously.

"So—how come?" Laura said. Her new inner self was saying, "No! Don't be impressed by this strange man just because he lives in a big house!" And her old inner self was saying, "Wow! Cor!" She shook her head, trying to drown out the voices, then realized she must look insane, so she smiled at him almost shyly.

Mr. Mower looked at her for a second. "How come—what? I live there?"

"Yes," said Laura. She couldn't help staring at him. He was . . .

well, pretty okay-looking. In a T-shirt, lean, kind of farmer way, she supposed. The old her would have gone for him like a shot, started batting her eyelids and wondering which room was his. The new Laura smiled pleasantly at him, wondering when she should get back to her parents.

Mr. Mower smiled back at her. He looked her up and down. "Well. I look after it, too. So I get to sleep there."

So that was what it was like, working for one of these places—you had to be able to make the frigging tea, sell people tea towels in the shop, *and* get out and mow the fields. What a life. She looked at him with something akin to pity, and he stared back at her with that glowering expression, his brows furrowed. He drew on his cigarette and said, "What about you? Where do you live?"

"In London," Laura said. "I'm on holiday here. With my . . . er." She stopped. "Er . . . with my boyfriend."

"And where is he?" asked Mr. Mower.

Slightly nettled by his nosiness, and unwilling to entrench herself too deeply in the lie she was already regretting, Laura said, "Er . . . looking at the soldiers. But I got bored, so I went for a walk."

An expression of annoyance strode across Mr. Mower's face. "So, you're on holiday together, then?"

"Yes," Laura said, putting the lighter back in her bag. "Look, I'd better go. Sorry again about . . . you know. Don't tell your—well, whatever you call him. Or perhaps you don't see him. Don't tell whoever your boss is."

"Hold on a minute," said Mr. Mower. "What's your name?"

"Laura. What's yours?"

"It's . . . Nick." He held out his hand. "It's nice to meet you, Laura. I'll let you get back to your boyfriend, then. Have a nice holiday. Thanks for the cigarette. Oh, shit. There's Charles. I need to speak to him."

Laura followed his gaze over to the house. There, under the spreading plane tree by the shop entrance, stood a tall, lean man about her age, stooping slightly as he stopped to talk to some visitors, who were drinking in the sight of him with obvious pleasure. One of them took a photo of him. He smiled, put his hands up in a semidefensive but still polite gesture, and the couple walked away, their heads together, twittering with excitement and looking at the photo on their camera.

"Who's Charles?" said Laura. "What does he do?"

"Er," said Nick, scratching his cheek. "Well—he kind of runs things. You know?"

Laura looked up at him. "Oh!" she said, realization dawning. "I'll let you get back to your boss, then."

"He's not really my boss," said her companion. Charles waved at them, and Nick waved back. Charles disappeared back into the house via a side door, and Nick turned to her and smiled wryly. "Well, he sort of is, I suppose. I'll catch him later. Couple of things he wanted to ask me about."

"Oh?" Laura said, happy to delay her return for a moment or two. She leaned against a tree and watched him. He looked at home there, standing almost arrogantly on the grass. She suddenly felt self-conscious in her pink top and skirt. A bit flimsy. Silly. "You are lucky to be self-employed." She thought of the decisions she hadn't made, the mess she'd left behind.

"What do you do, then?" he asked curiously.

"I'm a . . . I work with schools," said Laura uneasily. She could hear her own voice, knew it sounded like a lie, even though it was the truth. "For the council. I'm a coordinator. Sort of." She cleared her throat. "Well. It's kind of weird at the moment."

"What do you mean?" Nick said, looking at her rather strangely.

"Well . . . like I don't . . . I don't really know what I'm doing, even though I know it's what I want to do. Anyway." She shook her head, and Nick stared at her again. "That sounds stupid, forget it."

Nick was silent. After a moment he said, "No." His voice was matter of fact. "It doesn't. It doesn't at all. You love it, but you think you're rubbish at it. I'm the same."

"That's exactly it," Laura said. She stared at him. "It sounds so stupid when I think of it myself." She smiled at him gratefully. "Well, I'm going to be late. My parents want to spend a long time in the shop. A *long* time."

Nick laughed. "Doing what?"

"Well . . ." Laura scrunched her eyes up, trying to explain. "I don't know what your parents are like in a place like this, but mine like to finish off a long day somewhere like here by going to the shops, buying about fifty postcards of obscure portraits of the family who live there, and then having a really, *really* long, intricate discussion about the merits and demerits of every tea towel. 'Interesting Norman church fonts of Norfolk'? Or one in aid of the local RNLI lifeboat?" She ticked them off on her fingers, oblivious to Nick's quizzical expression. "Or 'Narrow Boats and Scenes from the Broads'? Or 'How to Make Cheese in Five Easy Steps,' printed on some cotton so you can dry the dishes with it."

"Right," said Nick, smiling.

"Right," said Laura. "So I have to meet them to get started with—" She stopped, suddenly remembering what she'd said before. "Them . . . and, and . . . my boyfriend, I mean."

Nick raised an eyebrow at her. He smiled sardonically, his eyes glittering with amusement. "So you don't have a boyfriend, then," he said, throwing his keys up in the air and catching them.

"Yes," Laura said hotly. "He likes tea towels, too. He's just not here. He's, er . . . oh, God. Never mind."

"Never mind," Nick agreed politely.

There was a pause.

"Boyfriends are for losers," Laura muttered after a while.

"Are they?" said Nick. "Really."

"Forget it." Laura said defensively. "It's not your problem."

"Not really, no," said Nick. "I have no boyfriend problems. Perhaps I should, though. Perhaps I should spend ages in my room reading magazines and writing about how horrible boys are in my pink diary with a padlock so flimsy and crap that a blind fingerless newt could break into it if they wanted."

Since this was how Laura had spent most of her teenage years, she didn't quite know what to say. She could feel herself blushing, and tried to cover her tracks by saying jovially, "Well! I've never done that, that's for sure! But—er, I do have some friends who did. How d'you know that?"

"I've got a sister," said Nick feelingly. "Well, two. But one of them spent about five years doing just that."

"Anyway," Laura said, feeling the conversation was veering wildly off the point, and reminding herself not to come across as a stupid person who *did* spend her teenage years scribbling "I love Mr. Wallace" in several different languages in a pink diary, "nice meeting you."

"I'll walk back to the house with you," Nick offered. "I'm going that way. Time for my tea. We can talk about your psychological disorder as we go."

"What psychological disorder?"

"The psychological disorder you have that means you need to invent imaginary boyfriends who like picking out tea towels with your parents."

Laura said, in what she hoped was a dignified manner, "No, thank you. I'll walk back this way, thanks. Good-bye."

She stomped off again. Nick followed. He strode easily, catching up with her. Laura ignored him.

"Can I ask you something?" he said.

"Go ahead," Laura breathed, increasing the length of her stride.

Nick stopped suddenly and stood in front of her so she almost fell onto him.

"*What?*" Laura said, steadying herself. "God, you're annoying, did anyone ever tell you that?"

"Lots of people," Nick said. He put his hand on her arm. "It was nice to meet you, Laura."

"You too," said Laura. "Thanks. And I'm—I'm sorry about the fire thing. Really stupid of me. I *am* really stupid."

Nick looked at her. "I'm sure you're not."

"Trust me," said Laura fervently. "I really am. Anyway, there are my parents, ho-hum. Better be off to meet them, get on with the rest of my lovely holiday."

"Well," said Nick. "I'm sure you'll have a whale of a time. Sounds like the perfect recipe for a really great holiday."

"Oh, yeah," said Laura. "If you like jigsaw puzzles and going through guidebooks looking for Roman roads. And going to craft fairs. And having to see the Seekers Tribute Band. Which is called the Seekers Tribute Band, by the way," she added bitterly.

"What a crap name," said Nick. "You'd think they could have come up with something better. They Seek Them Here, or something."

"*Exactly!*" Laura said, hitting him on the arm. "Sorry," she added, as Nick yelled with shock. "That's what *I* said, though! That was *my* suggestion! To myself, I mean," she said confidentially. "My other one was Desperately Seeking the Seekers—you see, I think that's much better."

"No, it's not," said Nick, rubbing his arm. "Who's heard of *Desperately Seeking Susan* if they're a Seekers fan? They wouldn't get the reference. No, mine's best."

"No way," said Laura. "But, hey. Let's agree to disagree. Well, agree, as well. I can't believe you said that, too. Hah." She was silent for a moment. "Anyway. I'm just glad I'm not going mad."

"Blimey," Nick said sympathetically. "Holiday not great, then."

"Like I say," said Laura. "Jigsaw puzzles, craft fairs, the Seekers. If you like that, well, great. Oh, and listening to endless monologues about some boring Marquis of Blah-Blah and his ancestors and their stupid house you have to pay millions of pounds to get into and then it's about as much fun as—as *botulism.*" She stopped, and her hand flew to her mouth. "God, Nick. I'm really sorry! Sorry. I know he's your—your boss and everything. And you work here. I didn't mean it. This is a lovely house. Really nice."

"What do you mean?" said Nick.

"Not my thing," Laura said. She tried to explain. "Just—well. You know how there's two sides to everyone? I used to like this kind of thing, going around pretending I was a countess or something."

"Really," said Nick.

"Yes," said Laura. "But not so much now. Anyway," she said, remembering Mrs. Danvers, "it's a long story."

"I'm sure," said Nick. "I barely know you, but I'm sure it is a long story."

"Shut up," said Laura. She liked him. She looked around again and said, "Look, I'd better go. And there's the lord and master himself, coming to find you."

Indeed, Charles had emerged from a door in the side of the vast edifice and was walking toward them.

"Fair enough," said Nick. He added, "Look, I know this is a bit . . . out of the blue, but how about a drink tonight, maybe some food?"

"Tonight?" said Laura. She felt awkward suddenly.

Nick said easily, "No big deal if you can't. I just thought you might want a bit of time out from your family. I always do." He looked up as Charles approached, then back at her. "So? What do you think?"

"Um," said Laura, not really sure. What did it mean?

Then she thought of the new her, and thought, Well, maybe, fuck it. Who cares if it is or not, it's a holiday, and it's an evening away from Mum and Dad and Granny. This is the new Laura, who dates casually and doesn't start replaying the plot of every slushy movie she's ever seen every time some new bloke crosses her path. She glanced at him, up and down, and smiled a small smile. And—well. Look at him.

"I don't know," she said.

"I'm not going to ravish you," said Nick, puncturing her pretensions. "It's just a drink, for God's sake. I know you appear to have taken some vow of asceticism, but you look like you might need a drink with someone under the age of forty."

"Yes," said Laura. "My God, yes."

"The George," said Nick, almost urgently, as Charles drew near. "Do you know the George?"

She did know the George; at least, she knew of it. It was the most popular gastropub in the area, booked up for months in advance, notoriously heaving with posh Londoners and those savvy enough to make their dinner reservations in January for July. She wanted to ask how on earth they'd get in there, but she didn't. She merely nodded, mutely.

"At eight?" Nick said. "I can get a table there. Yes? What do you think?"

There was silence.

"Okay, then," Laura said recklessly. "Okay."

She had no idea why she was agreeing to go out to supper with this total stranger, only that there was something about him she liked. She wanted to talk to him again. She was also curious to know how he was going to get a table there, but there was something about him that made it seem certain he would.

"Charles, this is Laura," said Nick.

Charles looked down at Laura and smiled. He was a tall man, a few years older than Laura. He looked sort of how you'd imagine a marquis to look. He was handsome in a rather gaunt way, with hollow cheeks and a hollow sternum. But he had a kind, wistful face and a courteous smile, and as Nick raised his hand in greeting, he bowed slightly as he bent over Laura's hand.

"Nice to meet you, Laura," he said. "Has this man here been a nuisance?"

"You could say that," said Laura, looking up at her companion, whose expression was impassive. "No, not really." She collected herself. She was talking to a marquis, after all. "This is an absolutely beautiful house," she said.

Charles nodded, obviously pleased. "It is, isn't it. We're very lucky."

He talked politely, asking about her holiday so far, as they crossed the grass back toward the house, Nick following a little way behind them, silent. As they reached the gate, Laura saw that the three middle-aged ladies from the house had gathered there and were watching their arrival. Charles lifted his head and smiled at them courteously, while Nick lingered in the background.

"Lovely house," said Lady #1, simpering and holding a bag from the gift shop.

"What a lovely day out, my Lord," said Lady #2, who had a wicker basket under her arm that was crammed to the gills with jams and marmalades with the Chartley logo on them.

Charles held up his hand in a gesture of thanks. "I'm so glad you've enjoyed yourselves," he said simply. "Do hope to see you back here sometime."

Nick nodded. "Thank you for coming," he said. "It's wonderful you came, isn't it, Charles?"

"Oh, thank you, Lord Ranelagh," said Lady #3 as Charles smiled politely at them, and they all dissolved into the near-hysterical yet deferential giggles that affect the British public only when confronted with the Royal Family or members of the aristocracy or people like Judi Dench or Joanna Lumley.

"Thanks again," said Nick, steering Charles gently but firmly away from them.

Charles pulled his cuffs down from his tweed jacket, and smiled at Laura. "Lovely to meet you," he said. "Enjoy the rest of your holiday."

"Thank you," said Laura as he drifted away. "I . . ."

"So," said Nick, turning back to her. "Will I see you tonight, then?"

He looked at her intently, and Laura felt herself losing her nerve. "Well—" she began.

"Look," he broke in, "shall we make an agreement? I'll be in the bar at eight. I normally am, in any case. So if you're there, you're there."

Laura didn't want to disappoint him, but she told herself it didn't seem as if he'd really mind that much either way. "Cool," she said. "I'm not sure what I'm doing for the rest of the day, anyway. So I'll see. Thanks."

"Well, Laura. I hope the rest of your day here is enjoyable. Thank you for coming. Apart from the low point of nearly burning down the house and its grounds, you've had a good time, I hope?"

He was already turning away, withdrawing. Laura said honestly, "Well, Nick—I know this isn't really your business, but since you ask—actually, I haven't had a very good time, to be honest. It's not much fun here, not for me, anyway."

Nick stopped and turned around. "What?" he said sharply.

Laura twisted the camera strap around in her hands. "It's just—well, it could have been better."

"Could have been *better*?" he said, incredulous.

"Yes," Laura said firmly. "It's a stately home, I know that. But it's a day out for most people. That's really important, you know? You can't just expect them to have to negotiate with two lunatics having sex in the ticket kiosk to get in, and then charge them a vast amount of money for the privilege of seeing some second-rate paintings in a few dusty rooms, and then round it all off with some rock-hard, stale scones in the café. On their precious holiday. I really don't mean to be rude, I'm sure Charles is lovely, he seems very nice and it's wonderful for you that you live here and everything. But since you ask, no, I haven't had a good time."

Nick flinched as she finished, as if someone had thrown cold water at him. "Well, thank you for that," he said after a while.

Laura bit her lip. "I'm sorry. But you did ask. Look—I've got to go now. Oh, hell, look, there's my mum. She can't meet you, she'd want to meet Charles, too, and that'd be like suicide. Bye, Mr. Nicholas Whatever-Your-Name-Is. Thanks, sorry about everything. I've been so rude, I can't believe it."

"Don't worry," Nick said. He took her hand. "By the way, Nick—it's short for Dominic, which I hate. You haven't been rude. You've been very interesting. Incredibly interesting, in fact. Enjoy the rest of your holiday, Laura. If I don't see you."

"Thanks, Nick-Short-for-Dominic," said Laura.

Nick touched his hand to his forehead and made a mock salute. He smiled at her politely, slightly formally. "Take care, anyway. Bye."

* * *

In the car on the way back, Laura was silent as Angela and George chatted enthusiastically about the things they'd seen, what they'd done, and the postcards and tea towels they'd purchased.

"What a beautiful house. I mean, one room after the other, so beautiful. You missed the picture gallery, Laura. It was—well, beautiful. All of it was! How do you live there, I wonder? It must be strange. Mustn't it?" Angela gabbled, like a six-year-old after eating too much candy.

"I agree," said George, taking a corner slowly. "A strange life, living there. I was talking to—harrumph—I was talking to Marjorie, that very nice lady in the shop. She was telling me the marquis is there full-time now. He hardly ever goes to London anymore. On that estate, day after day. He knows them all by name, ever such a nice chap these days, apparently."

"Of course," said Angela. "Yes, of course. He was the one who—"

"Yes," said George. "And his sister. One of them."

"Of course, there's three, isn't there."

"Yes, of course."

"Of course what?" Laura broke in, unable to contain herself anymore.

"We-ell," said Angela. "Yes—hrrm. Audrey—that's the very nice lady who was in the toy soldier display. Well, she said there was a time they were all very worried about him. The young marquis, I mean. Before his father died, the old marquis. Quite wild, apparently, when he was younger. Drink. Drugs. Women. You know, all sorts. And the sister, too. Rose. She had to go to a clinic, a rehab clinic, to sort herself out. This was after the mother left, you know. She went quite wild—and of course Audrey wouldn't have felt it appropriate to tell me, naturally."

"What do you mean, drink, drugs, women?" Laura said. "That doesn't really mean anything these days, you know. I mean, we've all—well. So he went clubbing a few times and got pissed. Big deal."

"Oh, no," said her mother, shaking her head sorrowfully, as if the Marquis of Ranelagh were the son of one of her friends from Harrow. "Really went off the rails. Few years after his parents split up. Well, poor boy, he was only eleven when it happened. It was awful. All over the papers. Well, some of the papers. Not the *Guardian*, naturally."

Laura couldn't work out if this was a veiled criticism of the *Guardian* for not having its reporting priorities right, or of her for reading a paper that did not concern itself minutely with the lives of the aristocratic, rich, and famous. So she said nothing, but a pang of sympathy for Charles shot through her. Poor Charles, poor thing. To have that everywhere, your family's misery, picked over by vultures and people who didn't know you, who made up their minds about you—it must have been bloody.

"Well, he seems okay now," she said in a neutral voice.

"Yes, lovely man, apparently," Angela said happily. "Audrey was telling us—he's Going Out with a very nice young girl. Cecilia Thorson. Her father is some Swedish millionaire. Very grand. Married to one of the Inghams, Lady Tania."

Laura rolled her eyes. She couldn't care less, she really couldn't. Even her old self, pre-purge, was completely uninterested in the lives of socialites and which posh person was shagging which other posh person. Maria the simple nun and Captain von Trapp—now, that was interesting. *Had* been interesting, rather.

"That's been in the papers, too, I remember now," said Angela. She swiveled round in her seat and lowered her voice, as if there might be a *Daily Mail* reporter hiding in the glove compartment. "I *hear* it's serious. They're all hoping she's—well, The One! You know!"

"Ooh, goody!" said Laura sarcastically, but it was wasted.

"Yes!" said Angela, nodding.

"So, when are the Sandersons arriving?" Laura asked, deftly steering the subject away.

Angela folded her hands in her lap. "Early Saturday, I think. Your grandmother was going to call them today to confirm who's staying and how long, that sort of thing."

"Are they *definitely* coming?" Laura said childishly.

"If you mean Lulu and Fran, yes, they definitely are," Angela said sternly. "And very nice it'll be, too. Yes. Annabel's bringing pudding, that's very kind of her."

"Is Robert coming?" George asked suddenly.

"Yes, of course he is!" Angela said.

"Oh," said George.

"Look, you two," said Angela as the car turned into Seavale and the wheels crunched slowly over the sandy stone path, "stop being childish. Yes, you, George," she said to her husband, who had opened his mouth to object. "It's Mum's day, and we'll all have a lovely time, and it'll be great. Besides, Cedric Forsythe's coming up, and he's bringing Jasper."

"Oh, great," said George, cheering up. Beneath her father's staid exterior, Laura had long suspected, there lurked the heart of a true romantic. He loved the old-British glamour of Mary's neighbors in the apartment block. Especially that of Cedric Forsythe, who had starred in George's favorite film, *When Victory Comes,* a stirring black-and-white epic about our boys in the Second World War. Cedric Forsythe was dapper, polished; at least, his onscreen persona was. The cinema Cedric smoked panatelas and wore silk dressing gowns; he raised his eyebrow as he talked—but he could still shoot a damned Boche at fifty paces and knew how to pull a plucky WAAF from a sinking boat, sling her over his shoulders, and swim four miles back to shore. In short, everything George Foster dreamed of being, but had long accepted was not his lot to be.

"I just hope it's what Mum wants," Angela said anxiously.

George flashed a smile at his daughter in the rearview mirror. Her frown lifted momentarily, and they shared a conspiratorial grin.

chapter seventeen

There was a message on Laura's phone when she got back to the house: "Hello, Laura. It's Jo. We—I miss you. Hope you're okay. Hope Norfolk's good—what you needed. Listen, give me a call. Wanted a chat. Just wondering if you're on for drinks on Sunday. Me and Hil. Hope so."

Laura had deliberately left the phone behind that day, afraid of the power it had since Amy's text message had disturbed the equilibrium of her day. The phone was her link with her life back in London, and she was still of two minds about it all. She missed it; she just wanted to be back in the pub with Yorky and Jo and Simon and all of that. And because she couldn't see the way to do it, while she was here in Norfolk being treated like a ten-year-old, she'd behave like one, renounce all responsibility for her other life. She texted Jo: *Drinks would be great. Looking forward to it. Hope yr OK. Love L.*

She brushed her hair, and thought about what had happened at

Chartley Hall. How embarrassing that was, to have nearly set fire to a whole estate. Stupid her. An involuntary smile crossed her face, though. It had been funny—the aftermath. Even though Nick had been, well, really quite odd, there was something she liked about him. She tried to analyze it. Basically, what she liked was that she could talk to him. And enjoy it. She felt, in a funny way, as if she could say what she liked to him and he wouldn't care. That was the great thing about strangers. Especially quite handsome strangers. She smiled at the memory. Ah, well. Nice of him to ask, but—she couldn't go. She wasn't here to go out drinking with strange but hunky farmhands. She was here to . . . get a life.

Outside on the terrace, George was fetching sherry for Angela and Mary as Laura joined them to watch the sun set.

"No, it was a lovely day," Angela was saying. "We had a wonderful time, didn't we— Ah, there's Laura. Didn't we, love?"

"Oh, yes," said Laura, handing the bowl of crisps to Mary and sitting down in one of the old wooden reclining chairs. "It was marvelous. There isn't a tea towel left in that gift shop, is there, Mum?" She stretched and yawned as her father handed her a sherry.

"No, there isn't. Wait till Saturday, you'll see," Angela said to her mother, nodding significantly. "Now, talking of your birthday—"

"My birthday present is a tea towel?" said Mary in rigid accents, sitting upright.

"What?" said Angela.

"It had better not be," said Mary. Laura stood up and wandered over to the edge of the terrace to look out at the sea.

"Of course not," said Angela impatiently. "I was joking, Mum. I'm not that bad, you know, that I'd buy my own mother a tea towel for her eighty-fifth birthday. Come off it," she finished rather bossily.

"No," said Laura mischievously. "Wait till you see the book of postcards they've got you. The first Marquis of Ranelagh, 1578. The seventh marquis, 1886."

"Not true," said George, but he was smiling in recognition. "Here, I did get a collection of postcards, though, you're right." He held out a small paper bag to Laura, who came over to collect it.

"Actually, you'll see," he said, taking out the postcards and showing them to her. "The seventh marquis was a great man, it's strange you should pick him. In 1880, he inherited the title from his father, you know."

"Right," said Laura, grinning. "I'll never make the same mistake again." She wanted to add, "I met the Marquis of Ranelagh today," but she knew it would prompt more questions than she wanted.

"I should hope not," said George, but then slightly ruined the moment of levity by clearing his throat and saying seriously, "Look at him, Laura. He was a very extraordinary man, the seventh marquis." He fumbled amongst the postcards as Laura stood over him, a sinking feeling washing over her. "Here we go. He was young, you know. And he did all these amazing things. This was all in the nineteenth century. He put proper drainage in the estate, overhauled the workers' cottages, all of that. He built the pub in the village, most of the cottages there, too. He added on the South Wing at Chartley. He's the one who collected first editions—he bought all the Jane Austens in the library. And he married his childhood sweetheart. But she died—it was terrible. Cholera. He never forgave himself. Dominic, seventh marquis. Amazing chap."

He handed Laura the postcard, and she took it, interested despite herself. There, in tight breeches, a viciously tailored jacket, and a top hat, standing rather stiffly against a country backdrop with Chartley in the distance, was the portrait of a young man, dark hair elegantly coiffed, dark eyes friendly and amused. He was smiling, holding a book in one hand, his expression relaxed and at odds with his formal stance. Laura stared at it. It was a very immediate portrait; the young man could be someone you'd walk past on the street today. He even looked vaguely familiar.

"Take it," said her father, and Laura put it between the pages of *The Nine Tailors,* which she'd brought with her to the terrace.

"We'll look at the rest later," said George. "All very interesting."

"Oh, yes," said Angela. "Ooh." She clapped her hands, and turned to Mary. "Now, then. I want to buy the meat for the barbecue tomorrow or Friday. What special requests do you have, Mum? It's your birthday."

"Chicken hearts," said Mary promptly.

"What?" said Angela.

"Chicken hearts. We used to have them when we were living in Brazil, you know. Xan loved them."

"Okay," said Angela, in a tone that said clearly, I will say yes now, but we ain't getting no chicken hearts. "But, some burgers? Chicken drumsticks, as well?"

"Don't mind, really," said Mary, slapping her hand down on the wooden arm of her chair. "Honestly, love, I really don't care. The main thing is having all my family there. It'll be so lovely. Annabel's making some amazing cake thing. It sounds fantastic."

"Great," said Annabel's stepsister, slightly icily.

"It will be lovely to see Lulu and Fran again, won't it?" Mary said. "And Simon will be back then, won't he?"

"He will," said Angela. "Well, I hope so." A frown crossed her face as George shifted in his seat and said, "Harrumph." Simon was not exactly renowned for his reliability, nor indeed for his communication skills when away. Although this time he had been quite good—they'd all had postcards, and the usual long e-mails detailing people and places that meant little or nothing to Laura, but seemed to give her parents and Mary no end of pleasure, since they kept rereading them out to each other.

Laura feared for her mother if he didn't make it back in time. She knew that in some small part of her mind, Angela had obviously, fervently, envisaged a scene where Simon strode in, tall and tanned and charming, with a lovely poncho-style present for his grandmother, greeted his family and aunt, and was a general hero for coming all the way back from Machu Picchu just for lunch, whilst skeletal Lulu and heavy-thighed Fran looked on and contributed nothing, and Annabel had to concede that, yes, for once, the Fosters had won this round.

Laura changed the subject. "What's for supper? Anything I can do?"

"No, it's all ready," said Angela. "Some salady things, I hope that's okay. Something simple so we could eat by eight." She turned to her mother and smiled brightly. "Mum, you must be tired after all that gardening today—you've really cleared it all out, haven't you? It looks marvelous, I must say."

"Thank you, darling," said Mary. "Good-o."

"Yes, yes," said George amiably, picking up the thread of his wife's conversation. "I'll give you a hand tomorrow." He paused, and rubbed his hands together. "Sooo. Tomorrow. Where shall we go, dear? I thought the windmill at Moxham might be nice. What do you think?"

"Well," said Angela excitedly, "we could try for the Seekers Tribute Band in the evening, couldn't we?"

"Yes, we must!" said George. "Tasks for tomorrow, Angela! Now, let's get the guidebook and decide what to do tomorrow, eh?" He loped over to the table and picked up the guidebook. "Hm."

He bent his head in concentration, as Angela looked happily

out to sea and Mary downed the rest of her drink. Laura glanced at her watch. It was seven-fifty. She looked up, out across the lawn. The sun was crowning the sea, casting long golden shadows across the water. It was very still. Suddenly she stood up.

"I'm going out," she said.

Her parents looked up at her, bewildered.

"What?" said Angela. "Where? Going out where?"

"Just out," said Laura. "Can I take the car?"

"Er—no!" said George. "You can't suddenly announce you're taking off just before supper. Where are you going?"

Laura bit back a sharp reply, and instead said, "Sorry. I just want a drive. Someone I used to work with—well, she lives up here. Naomi? Do you remember her?" Her parents' faces were blank. "She works for the Wetlands Trust now. Well, I got a text from her earlier. She's over at the George. I thought I might join her for a drink, but it's rude of me to leave without having supper"—she plowed on, aware she was laying it on a bit thick but hoping against hope it'd work—"so perhaps I shouldn't go, you're right. I just fancied a bit of a change, getting out, seeing some friends."

Laura's parents looked at each other, and Laura held her breath. She knew they were thinking, She's been through a bad time. Not sure how bad. But something's not right. Perhaps this is a good thing. Young people ought to get out and about on holiday. Shouldn't they?

They must have managed to convey these thoughts to each other by ESP, because they nodded at each other at the same time. George produced the car keys and dropped them reluctantly into his daughter's hand.

Laura pocketed them, grabbed her book, and turned to go. "Thanks, Dad," she said as she disappeared into the sitting room.

She grabbed a wrap and her handbag, dropping her book into it, and ran out onto the terrace again. "I'll take care of it, I promise."

"Don't be back too—" Angela began, then silenced herself as Mary shot her a warning look.

Laura ran across the gravel, and jumped into the car. The bushes on the path up to the house were already blacky green in the early dusk. She turned on the engine and drove away, leaving the house behind her. As she sped through the lanes in the evening air with the window open and her hair blowing in the breeze, she found herself feeling not like Mrs. Danvers for the first time in days, but more like Mrs. de Winter herself. With a bit more spine, hopefully.

When she arrived at the George, twenty-five minutes later, it was well after eight, and there was no sign of Nick. It was extremely crowded, as if the whole populace of Norfolk, indigenous and tourist, was having a drink there. Laura pushed through the throng, avoiding the glares of disapproval as she made her way to the lounge, where people were sitting with drinks, the doors flung open to the pub garden. She walked through them, looking left to right, but couldn't see him.

Standing there in the busy pub, she suddenly wondered if he'd meant it or not, this casual invitation he'd thrown at her. What would she and Nick the farmer, groundsman, estate manager person, *whatever* it was he did, talk about? They had nothing in common. Why had he asked her for a drink? And why had she come?

She breathed deeply. She couldn't go home just yet; it was too embarrassing. Apart from that, she realized that she would rather stay here and look like the loneliest person in the room than spend another evening with her parents. In fact, she quite liked it in a funny way, being here by herself, no ties, no responsibility, no dragging feeling of guilt about what she was doing. It was a drink with a nice stranger, no ties, nothing. She was a free agent, after all, she could do what she liked. Her new self rather liked that. She'd stay here, damn it, and enjoy herself, whether he showed up or not.

So Laura went up to the bar and got herself a glass of white wine, then went and sat outside at one of the tables by the French windows and opened *The Nine Tailors*; but she soon found she couldn't read. She fingered the postcard portrait of the seventh marquis and gazed into the distance for a while, thinking about lots of things. Imagining her parents' expressions if they could see her now, she allowed herself a small smile. Her sense of the ridiculous, which had lain dormant for a while, suddenly resurfaced, and she laid the book down on the table and grinned broadly. Here she was, basically having a date with herself, and it was the best evening she'd had in quite some time. It was tragic, really, when you thought about it, but she just didn't care.

So she sat there till it was nearly nine, reading her book and occasionally looking up to take in her surroundings. She felt perfectly content, enjoying her own company for the first time in a long while. But then suddenly, a deep voice behind her said, "Excuse me, are you waiting for anyone?"

At last. Laura looked up, a quick retort ready on her lips. But standing in front of her was a tall, large man with a rather fleshy face whom she'd never seen before, tucking his shirt into the back of his waistband and looking impatient.

"Sorry?" she said, taking a moment to recover.

"Are you expecting some friends?" the man said again.

"Er," said Laura warily. She really wasn't in the mood to be chatted up. Good grief, men were incredible. Just because she was on her own and reading a book! Six months ago, perhaps she would have smiled and said, "No! Sit down!" and then developed an inappropriate crush on him, but now . . . "Well—" she said, trying to let him down gently, and grimaced. "You know . . ." She shrugged.

The man looked at her as if she were a half-wit, and Laura felt even more uncomfortable. He definitely worked in the City, a banker or something, Laura thought, nodding to herself.

She glared at him rather crossly, but he said, unheeding, "Look, it's just there aren't any other tables, and we're having food. There's five of us."

"Eh?" said Laura.

"Is there any way you'd mind moving"—he pointed at one of the sofas, where there was a small square of squashy leather free—"over there, so we can sit here?"

Highly embarrassed, Laura shot up out of her seat. "Ha-ha! No! I mean, yes, of course you can! Ho!" she practically yelled, and then felt like an idiot.

"Thanks a lot, seriously," said the large man, heaving himself onto the bench. "I should buy you a drink." He slapped his wallet and drink down on the table, and as he did, the beer slurped up out of the glass and over Laura's skirt.

"Oh, shit," said Laura, wanting to be irrationally cross and shout at him, all of a sudden.

"God, I'm sorry," he said. "Are you okay? Can I buy you another drink?"

"No, don't worry," said Laura, in a tone meant to convey that she was not okay and he should buy her another drink; moreover, he should get a towel.

"Really sorry," he said. He patted ineffectually at the table with large, meaty hands, and looked at her skirt as if he should do the same there. "Erhm. I'm such an idiot. So sorry."

"It's fine, honestly," said Laura, turning to smile magnanimously, and found herself humiliatingly talking to thin air, as the man had turned back to his friends, who were huddled together, waiting for her to leave.

"Great," said Laura out loud, feeling suddenly exposed, rather like someone whose skirt has been ripped off.

She threw an evil look at the tall man as she turned to go, her good mood evaporating as she pushed her way back through the throng, which seemed to have grown in the intervening hour. The queue for a table was just as long, would-be diners lounging in a bored fashion, waiting for the bills of the previous occupants to be paid. She pushed politely past them, and stumbled as she stepped out into the car park. She headed for the car and fished for her keys. Definitely time to go home.

"And where do you think you're going?" came a voice from behind her.

Laura froze, her key poised above the lock of the car. She turned slowly, and there was Nick, striding easily toward her across the floodlit gravel. He looked smarter; he'd changed out of the T-shirt and jeans and was wearing a worn but clean, freshly ironed shirt and khaki trousers. He was tall, she remembered now, taking in his close-cropped hair, the almost harsh contours of his face, the strong cheekbones, the dark eyes. She almost didn't recognize him. He looked . . . different, somehow. Like a different person.

"Where have you been?" he said as he came closer. "I assumed you'd stood me up."

"Me!" Laura squeaked uncoolly. Her voice was unrecognizable to her own ears. "I waited for you for"—she looked at her watch; it was after nine—"for at least forty-five minutes! How dare you!"

"So you got here around eight-thirty. Hm," said Nick easily. "And you're surprised that, having said I'd be there at eight, by eight-thirty I'd assumed you weren't coming and went upstairs to say hi to someone in the office."

"You said you'd be here *from eight,*" said Laura accusingly. "I didn't—I wasn't going to come—anyway, well . . ."

She turned back to the car and stabbed ineffectually at the lock with her keys.

"Oh, calm down," said Nick. "Look, you're here now. Why don't we have supper? Come on, you might as well, and I haven't eaten yet—I'm hungry."

"Ooof," said Laura, staring helplessly up at him. "I—God. I'm tired."

"Me too," said Nick. "Look, Laura—I'm apologizing. Come and have some food and then go home. You can't not eat, for God's sake. The food is amazing, I promise you. What were you going to have with your—with your boyfriend back at home instead?" He smiled mockingly at her.

"Oh, shut up," said Laura, but she smiled back into his face, and put her keys into her bag. "Thank you, that'd be lovely. I'd love to have supper with you." She looked him up and down. "You look smart."

"There was a reception at the house," he said easily. He looked down at her. "Let's go inside. They won't keep the table forever."

"Great," said Laura. She stared at him.

"Get a move on," said Nick unemotionally. "There's a bloke over there I don't want to spot me. We'll be here for hours if he does."

"Where?" said Laura. Nick pointed at the table-nicking, pint-spilling large man, who was guffawing loudly with his friends in the corner of the garden at Laura's table.

"Ha," said Laura. "I know him."

"You do?" said Nick, slightly surprised. "City chap—can't remember his name. Works for a bank? Sorry. I didn't realize he was a friend of yours."

"God, no," said Laura, slightly hysterically, in case Nick

thought she was consorting with strange, annoying men while waiting for him. "He split a pint over me. Spilt, I mean, he spilt a pint, and I was all—"

"Look," said Nick, "mind if you tell me this story upstairs? He's looking over."

"Right," said Laura. "Sorry."

"No problem. Looking forward to it. It sounds great."

He held the door open for her, and they stepped through into the pub together.

chapter eighteen

They threaded through the crowded pub together in silence. Safely out of view of the table-stealer in the corner, Laura watched as Nick shook hands with various people and had his back slapped. She hung back a little, not wanting to announce herself to a roomful of strangers who obviously all knew this man well. It was his local, after all, and who was she? Some girl he'd met that afternoon whom he'd asked for a drink. But why?

Stop it. *Stop it,* she told herself. This is why you're always getting into trouble! Your imagination runs away with you. She looked at Nick, who was shaking off some old fellow-farmer bloke. He looked rather uncomfortable, and he pushed her gently ahead of him through the rabble, almost as if he were in a hurry to leave them all behind. Laura liked the feel of his warm, firm hand on the small of her back, then brought herself up short. Remember, Laura, she said to herself, he is *not* Prince Charming. He is a nice, good-looking man and you are going to have a drink with him. Just because he made an amusing joke about the Seekers, *don't* go casting him in the role of romantic hero. You don't know him. He is a virtual stranger, he's not Rhett Butler. Reality. Reality.

She pinched herself on the arm, hard, to remind herself as Nick got waylaid again, then looked up to find him staring at her as he listened to the old wizened farmer who was droning on about something to do with his family. His eyes met hers, and he jerked his head toward the stairs. "Come on, Laura," he said. "Sorry, Mr. Withers. I'd better get on," and he took Laura's arm and steered her lightly upstairs.

Mr. Withers glanced happily at Laura, looking super-pleased for her, muttered something about how grateful he was, and crept backward, almost bowing, toward the door.

"Nice old chap," said Nick, holding the door open as they reached the upper floor.

"He seemed very keen on you," said Laura, impressed.

"He said he was glad I was having supper with such a pretty girl," said Nick. He nodded as Laura looked at him skeptically. "It's true," he said lightly.

"Aah," said Laura, self-conscious. "That's nice."

"It is nice," said Nick. "Very—er—nice. Right, let's get some drinks. And the menu. I'm hungry, aren't you?"

"God, yes," said Laura. "I'm completely starving."

She was glad she'd given herself a stern talking-to just now, and thought with relief how relaxing it was to *not* be thinking of this as a mega-serious date, worrying about whether it was seemly to be quite so eager to wolf down some food. She was hungry. She wanted to eat. That was it.

Nick smiled at her. "Steak okay? They do a great one here. Fantastic béarnaise sauce. With chips."

"Thin chips?" asked Laura.

"Absolutely," said Nick. "I wouldn't come here if they weren't. Fat chips are wrong, I think."

"Me too," said Laura. "Like half a potato each. They're impossible to eat. And they're always cold in the middle."

"Yet again we agree," said Nick. "Never trust someone who says they prefer fat chips to thin chips. That's my motto."

"I concur," said Laura. "Strongly concur."

"Great," he said.

Nick ordered a bottle of wine, and soon the food arrived. The steaks were, as he had predicted, delicious: tender, melting, juicy, drizzled with garlic and parsley butter.

"God, I love garlic butter," said Laura. She rubbed her hands together. "I could drink it."

"Please don't," said Nick. "And I sincerely hope you're not going out on the pull later if you're planning to scarf garlic all evening."

"Why?" said Laura. "Where does one go on the pull around here?"

"Well," said Nick, "there's a nightclub about thirty miles away from here. Champagne's, it's called. There's usually a fight there about eleven-thirty every Saturday night. If you eat quickly, you can get there in time to pull *and* watch a fight."

"There was a club like that in Harrow, where I grew up," said Laura. "Called Ballyhoo. I used to love it there. Till it got shut down."

"No, really?" said Nick. "Why?"

"The loos got blocked one night and it flooded and the electrics fused. Permanently." Nick raised his eyebrows. "I'm sorry. We're eating."

"Well, if you want a trip down memory lane, I'd be more than happy to drive you to Champagne's and leave you outside, so you can revisit your misspent youth," said Nick politely. "Sound nice?"

"I'm okay, I think," said Laura, laughing. "I'm going to scarf away instead."

"Good," said Nick. "Right decision."

Laura *was* starving, and she ate happily away, genuinely enjoying herself for the first time in ages. Nick was good company—compared to the company she'd been keeping all week, most people would have been to her by then, but she couldn't help thinking he really was. He was his own man; he wasn't in Charles's pocket. They found common ground almost immediately, as any two strangers can if the basic ingredients are right. They discovered that they both loved *The Sopranos*, that they had both stayed in the same hotel in Edinburgh, a day apart, and that both their birthdays were in May.

"So, Laura Foster," said Nick, several glasses of rich, velvety red wine later. "Why did you come tonight? I'm curious." He wrapped his long fingers around the stem of his glass and smiled at her. "I must say, I didn't think you would."

"Why not?" said Laura curiously.

"Just thought you'd think it was weird."

"I know," Laura agreed. She opened her hands to him in a gesture of disclosure. "But I just thought, well, why the hell not. It's got to be better than another evening at home with the parents."

"Well, thank you."

"You know what I mean."

"Actually," he said, "I don't, really, no."

"Well. Have you ever been on holiday with your parents?" Laura said. "After the age of sixteen, it's a pretty terrible idea."

"So—why are you on holiday with yours, then?" Nick said, taking a sip of wine. "If it's such a bad idea."

"Long story," said Laura. "I—ah." She looked down, not really knowing how to go on.

Nick poured her another glass of wine. "Doesn't matter, though, does it?" he said, his voice light. "Right. Do you want some pudding?"

Laura looked up gratefully. "Oh, I'd love to. But I shouldn't, really."

He laughed, and said, "Go on. Have one if you want to. No one's going to stop you."

"No, I know," said Laura. "But I won't, honestly."

"You sound like my sisters," said Nick. "Women! You go mad if someone tries to say you're all the same, but that's the exact same response my sisters always give if anyone asks them if they want pudding. And they couldn't be more different. You'd barely know they were related."

"You've got two sisters, haven't you?" asked Laura.

"Yes. One of them lives in London. She—ha." A cloud passed over Nick's face. "She used to be rather wild. Quite good fun, always turning up off her head on something, with someone. She—yes. Anyway, now she's married to a very uptight businessman. She's gone all grown-up and boring. Wears suits, sits on committees, that kind of thing. She's a real snob these days. Whereas Lavinia— God."

"Why, what's wrong with her?"

"Oh, she's a liability," said Nick. "She moved back here a few months ago, and she's shagging this bloke on the estate. Does the tickets. Sean. She basically stalked him into submission. He has no choice in the matter. Not that he seems to care that much, he's—God, he's almost as thick as her."

Laura thought of the red-haired beauty they'd encountered on their way in to the Hall earlier that day. "Do you know, I think I met her today," she said.

Nick groaned. "Oh, God. Where?"

"In the ticket box. With Sean. They—"

"Don't tell me," said Nick, holding up his hands. "Oh, God, they're the lunatics having sex in the kiosk you were complaining about earlier. Aren't they?"

"No," said Laura, blushing. "I was just being rude."

"Don't spare my feelings, Laura." He looked resigned. "She's a nightmare, and I've got to do something about it now she's living back at the Hall. At some point."

"It's very nice of Charles to let her stay there," said Laura.

"What? Oh, yes," said Nick. "He's always been fond of Lavinia. Think he has a crush on her, actually."

"He seems lovely," said Laura. "Really nice. It must be a weird life for him, I suppose."

"Why do you say that?" There was a note of defensiveness in Nick's voice.

"Well," she said carefully, "I just mean it's a big responsibility, that house, all those people. And it's not like he's married with loads of kids and a wife, or he has someone to share it all with. It must be weird."

"It is," said Nick.

"Would you want to be him?" said Laura. Nick looked blank for a second. "I mean," she went on, trying to explain, "would you want to swap places, be the marquis? Do you ever think about that?"

"No," said Nick slowly. "You know, I sometimes think I wouldn't be him, not for all the money and estates in the world."

"Well, he's lucky to have you as his friend," said Laura.

Nick was silent. Then he cleared his throat and said, "I'm not so sure about that. More wine? Here, have the rest." He poured the last of the wine into her glass, and his hand touched hers momentarily as he set the bottle down again. Their eyes met, and they smiled at each other. Laura sat back in her chair, relaxing a little more. There was something so comfortable about him, about his company. Her mind flew back to the mess of tangled friendships and relationships she had left behind in London, and she thought suddenly that it was funny, but here in this pub, with this nice, strange man, she felt calmer, like she was breathing properly, like she could see the vista of her life stretching out over the next few months more clearly than she had for—she didn't know how long. That for the first time she was looking forward to it.

"So, when do you go back to London?" said Nick.

"Saturday," said Laura. "Yeah." She gazed reflectively into her glass. "Got a big birthday lunch for my grandmother on Saturday. All the relatives coming up."

"Oh, God," he said, looking at her with amused sympathy. "If they're anything like mine . . ." He trailed off.

"They're a bit grim, to be honest," said Laura. She finished her glass of wine. "They mean well, I'm sure."

"What does that mean?"

"Well—take my aunt Annabel. I'm sure she's not *evil*, but if you were stranded on a desert island and she rescued you after six months, she'd criticize you for not tidying up the grains of sand. And she'd say the jungle was out of control and you should have pruned it back."

Nick looked at her, trying not to laugh. "Right," he said. "That's some aunt."

"She's not really my aunt, really," said Laura. "Actually, she's like my stepaunt. You know."

"Er," said Nick politely, after a pause in which Laura thought, Oh, no, I'm gabbling. She opened her mouth to ask about his family, but he said suddenly, "So. Do you have brothers and sisters?"

"A brother," said Laura. "Just me and him. He's called Simon."

"Are you close?"

"Yes, we are," said Laura. "I miss him. He's been away, in"—she scrunched up her face, trying to remember the location of the last postcard—"some mountain village in Peru, anyway. I haven't seen him since March. But he's coming back for Granny's lunch on Saturday. Hurrah!"

He smiled at her enthusiasm. "Hurrah, indeed. You sound like a close family."

"Well," said Laura. She looked at him. "We are, but—you know."

"What?"

"Well, families. It's all complicated, isn't it? We are close, but we're all quite weird at the same time."

"How so?"

"My aunt, and her brood. That's why I . . ."—she fiddled with her napkin—"I'm not looking forward to it much. We're all quite different." She was silent then, and twirled the stem of her glass between her fingers. "Sorry," she said, meeting his gaze. His eyes were warm, understanding. "I don't mean to gabble on."

"You're not," said Nick. "Really, you're not. That's families for you. It is, as you say, complicated."

"How about yours?" said Laura. "Same thing?"

"Yes," he said, standing up. "All very complicated, and it's not on the surface, is it? Give me a moment, I'll settle the bill, and then I'll walk you to your car."

He left her, and Laura watched him go. She felt as if he were holding her at arm's length, and she didn't know why. She looked around the pub, frowning. Then she told herself not to be so silly, not to jump ahead again. She'd only just met him. And it was strange, how she felt she could tell him anything and it wouldn't matter. For the first time in ages, no judging, no agenda, nothing. Just a friendly stranger on a warm summer's night, a glass of wine, and a proper conversation.

chapter nineteen

They walked outside, onto the moonlit gravel path, out of the floodlighting. As Laura approached the car, she had the sensation of two sides of her brain, the subconscious and the conscious, rushing together for the first time that evening. The subconscious had been hiding something from her, and it suddenly hit her, with the full force of an oncoming train.

"Shit!" she said suddenly.

The violence in her voice made Nick stop in his tracks. "What?" he said. "Laura?"

"Shit, shit," said Laura, turning around and banging her fist on top of the nearest car. Luckily, it was her car. She turned back to face him. "I can't drive!"

"You can't drive?" Nick said, perplexed.

"No, not that! I completely forgot. I've had . . ." She quickly added up how many glasses of wine she'd had, and gave up in despair at three. "I've had far too much to drink. At least three glasses. Argh." She banged her forehead gently on the roof of the car and let out a muffled groan.

How could she have been so *stupid*? How could she have forgotten she had the car outside? She'd relaxed, let herself enjoy the evening—and this was what happened.

"It's okay," said Nick calmly. "Don't worry. You can stay with me."

"No!" said Laura, so loudly both of them took a step back. "Sorry," she continued in a quieter voice. "Oh, stupid! Stupid me! How could I have forgotten I drove here?"

"Do you make a habit of this kind of thing?" asked Nick. "Drinking nearly a bottle of wine and forgetting you drove to the pub?"

"No, never," said Laura. She was cold all of a sudden in the night air. "I don't, in London. I don't have a car. So I always drink when I go to the pub."

"Well, there you are, then," said Nick. "It's different up here, you know."

"I know," said Laura miserably. "I was—enjoying myself, that's all."

Nick watched her for a moment. "Don't look so tragic about it, Laura. It's not a crime to enjoy yourself, you know."

"Yes, it is," muttered Laura, feeling as if she were in some biblical parable, the one where the Lord wreaks vengeance on the stupid girl who is a foolish wanton by removing the last shred of common sense in her brain.

"No," said Nick firmly, "it's not. But it will be if you drive. Look, Laura, come back to the Hall with me. It's five minutes away. You can either stay the night or call a cab. But at this time of night, a cab's going to take over an hour to get here." Laura shifted from one foot to the other, unsure of what to say. "Which is why you might as well stay the night."

"Oh," she said eventually. "But—look, Nick—"

"This isn't a come-on," said Nick in amusement. "Seriously, this isn't my dastardly way of taking advantage of you."

He laughed at her, his voice soft in the velvety darkness. Laura stepped away from him, feeling embarrassed. She didn't want him to think—she couldn't bear the idea he thought she might be angling for something, that this was some ploy of hers. Especially not when they'd had, well, the perfect evening, she thought. She didn't want to spoil it, the memory of it, and now she had.

"I know—of course. Really—"

She couldn't see his face, but his voice said in a kindly tone, "Look. I'm your only friend in Norfolk, aren't I?"

"You are actually my best friend in Norfolk," said Laura.

"Well, there you go," said Nick. "Come back, and we'll get you a cab or find you a room."

"It won't be a problem?"

"I shouldn't think so," said Nick gravely. "There's about thirty-five bedrooms, Laura, I'm sure we can find somewhere for you to sleep."

She gave a snort of laughter, then clapped her hand to her mouth. "I didn't mean that! I meant, you won't get into trouble, will you? It's okay for you to—to ask some—some random gir—person back and give them a room for the night?"

"Yes," he said. "I promise you, it won't be a problem."

She shivered. Nick put her wrap around her shoulders and said, "Come on, then, new best friend. Come back to mine. You're getting cold and I'm not standing here all night. You can pick up the car in the morning."

Laura was mightily amused. " 'Come back to mine,' eh? You make it sound like you live in a flat next to the post office. And how do I explain what happened to my parents? And how do I explain I'm staying the night, without them getting totally the wrong end of the stick?"

Nick started walking ahead of her. He said shortly, "Well, you make something up. What did you tell them tonight?"

"It's really only a five-minute walk?" said Laura, following him. "I don't believe you. The bloody driveway alone took ten minutes."

"We're round the back; this is the edge of the estate to the north," said Nick, leading the way. "The fields over there are corn—the combines are arriving soon, in a couple of weeks, you know."

He strode ahead in silence, Laura following. What a curious mixture he was, she thought, admiring his rear view dispassionately. Face to face, he was diffident, closed-off, flippant. In repose, or when he thought he wasn't being watched, he was a different person, almost two sides. One, the polite, almost remote man who could make you laugh and was endlessly flippant, never serious. The other, the broad-shouldered, outdoorsy country boy who talked enthusiastically about animal husbandry, whose face and attitude were more relaxed, more human, almost. It was hard to believe they were the same person, and it was strange that she felt so comfortable with him.

"Thanks," she said suddenly. "I'm sorry. About this."

"My pleasure, Laura."

"If we bump into Charles—" she said abruptly.

"I'll make something up," said Nick. "Don't worry. I'm not a slave there. I'm allowed to bring people back, you know. But you're right. Best if no one sees. People will only gossip."

They had reached the gate beyond the pub's garden. He unpadlocked the bolt and drew back the tall, solid wooden door.

"Okay?" he asked.

"Okay," said Laura, but as he said, "Mind the—" she stumbled into a tiny ditch, a hollow on the other side of the door. Nick caught her hand.

"Sorry," he said, putting her on her feet again and releasing her. "Must get that sorted out, you know. I keep meaning to talk to the guys about it. You okay?"

"Absolutely," said Laura.

Their feet made scraping sounds along the dry earth of the pathway. An owl hooted in the woods to their right. Ahead of them the path swung round by the trees, and as they walked past them Laura drew her breath in.

"The house. Look. It's . . ."

There in the moonlight, the side view of Chartley Hall appeared in front of them, like a proud lady in profile. The stone gleamed in the moon's light, but the windows were dark. Ahead of them lay a formal garden, knotted with rows of black yew. It looked old, forbidding, magnificent—and nothing like someone's home.

"Nearly there," said Nick. "I love this view."

"It's beautiful," Laura said simply. "Beautiful. You must—" She stopped.

"What?" said Nick.

"Well, it must be quite lonely sometimes."

"It is," said Nick. "Yes, it is." He was silent, standing still. "Right," he said after a moment. "Here we are." And they walked down the gentle slope past the woods to the monolith in front of them, toward a side door in the center of two wings. It was as if the house were swallowing them up, taking them in its jaws, Laura thought, and she craned her neck, looking up to the roof, as Nick unlocked the door and held it open for her. They stepped into a small hallway with a staircase, wood-paneled and painted green, ghostly in the nighttime light. It was tiny, incongruously small, given the vast shell that lay beyond it.

"God, this is weird," said Laura.

"What do you mean?"

"Well, when I stagger back from the pub late at night, the walk home is slightly different," said Laura. "More rubbish bins in my way. Lot more empty fast-food wrappers. A few people lying on the curb, you're not sure if they're alive or dead. That kind of thing."

"Well, this is weird for me, too," said Nick, leading the way up the stairs. "When I stagger back from the pub, I don't usually have some pyromaniac girl with me who keeps hitting me and can't drive because she's drunk too much and she's forgotten the car right outside the pub that she drove there."

"Oh . . ." Laura cast around for the appropriate response. "Shut up."

"Well done," said Nick. "Excellent comeback."

They reached the top of the stairs. Ahead of them was a prim, neat, very long corridor. Laura looked around, almost disappointed not to be confronted with some magnificent vista, a sweeping staircase, a vast airy ballroom, or some such. Nick could obviously sense this, because he said, "Sorry. I should have given you the guided-tour version, shouldn't I, rather than just rushing you up the back stairs. This is my front door, you see."

"Oh, no," said Laura. "Please, don't worry. I had the guided tour today."

"And you hated it. I remember," Nick murmured, then put his fingers to his lips. "I hear something. Come this way."

They walked down the long corridor, and the unmistakable sound of someone coming up the stairs behind them could be heard, echoing toward them. Someone down below, a rather tentative voice, said, "My lord? Is that you?"

Laura looked at him in alarm, and without warning, Nick opened a door and virtually pushed Laura inside.

"This is my room," he said apologetically. "Charles is just down there, they must think it's him. Sorry about that, don't want anyone to see us, don't want you to have the third degree and all that."

"Goodness, no," said Laura.

"Okay," said Nick. He glanced around, ran his hands through his hair. The room was big, high ceilings, painted white, virtually without any decoration or personal touch whatsoever. There was a clock radio, a portable radio, a mahogany chest of drawers, and a door leading to a bathroom. A dressing gown hung on the back of the bathroom door. It was, in short, a very typical boy's room.

"Look," he said. "I think what's best is if you sleep here, and I'll kip somewhere else. I don't want to plonk you in another room only to find someone trying to hoover you up tomorrow morning. They're pretty fascist around here about hoovering. But they don't ever bother me in my room. Is that okay? Can you sleep here? Sheets are clean on today, which is great."

"Yes, of course," said Laura, giving herself up totally to the adventure of it all. "No problem." She was suddenly very tired. She reached up to take her wrap off, but Nick leaned forward and unwound it from her shoulders. It slid off and he handed it to her, and then he kissed her on the cheek. It was a strange moment; it felt like a strange gesture, intimate yet not intimate, and there was a silence as both of them stood there, rather embarrassed. Laura looked up to find his eyes on her.

"Okay, best friend in Norfolk," she said after a while. "Thank you, thanks a lot. I'm sorry about this."

"No problem at all," said Nick. He walked over to the dresser and took out a big old T-shirt, which he handed to her. "Here. You can borrow this."

"Thanks."

"I'm sorry this is all a bit cloak and dagger. I just don't want you to have any hassle. I'll knock on the door after eight sometime, is that okay?"

"Great," said Laura.

He raised his hand in a gesture of farewell. "All right," he said. "Sleep well. Don't rifle through my personal possessions, and if you do, ignore the hard-core porn."

"Sure, sure," said Laura. "No judging. Night."

"Night," he said, and smiled at her as he shut the door behind him.

The wine, the walk, the unexpectedness of the day—Laura barely managed to text her parents and take off her shoes and skirt, before falling into bed and into a sleep so deep she didn't think till afterward how strange it was that she was here, and how strange it was that it didn't feel strange.

When she woke, funnily enough, Laura knew exactly where she was. She opened her eyes and looked around the room, taking in its appearance in the daylight that shone through the thin curtains at the far end, opposite her bed. She sat up and rubbed her eyes, feeling deliciously relaxed, looked down at the baggy blue T-shirt Nick had given her. It said THORSON TECHNOLOGIES in huge red letters—trying to read it made the letters dance in front of her eyes. Out of the window she could see pine trees in the distance, a mass of greenish black to the north of the house. A wood pigeon was cooing somewhere nearby. Other than that, it was completely quiet. She snuggled down again and pulled the duvet over her. The bed was huge, the sheets smooth and clean. Laura stretched her arms and legs wide, and still couldn't feel the edge of the bed. She made a star shape with her limbs, like a windscreen wiper under the sheets, and she was laughing to herself at the sheer randomness of it all when there was a knock on the door.

"Laura?"

"Yes," cried Laura in a strangulated tone, getting tangled in the sheets.

"Er—are you decent?"

"Yes, yes! Come in!" Laura said chirpily.

The door opened about half a foot, and Nick's head appeared around the door, his short, thick hair sticking up in tufts. He looked in, obviously rather afraid of what he might find. "Ah," he said with relief, as he saw Laura was sitting up in bed, her arms crossed, under the duvet. He came in and shut the door behind him. She suddenly had a pang of fear—after all, it was a weird situation to be in. Perhaps this was all really embarrassing; perhaps she had in fact made a total fool of herself last night? Was there something she wasn't remembering, some repressed memory where she'd licked him, or broken a Sevres vase?

"Hello there." Nick smiled at her in a friendly way. He looked younger in the morning light. "You sleep well?"

"God, yes," said Laura gratefully. She looked at her watch. "Blimey. It's nine-thirty! I didn't realize it was so late."

She hadn't slept for nine straight hours since . . . he couldn't remember when. Over a year ago. She stretched again, smiling at him. "Thanks so much, Nick. I'm so sorry about last night—how completely emba—"

Nick raised his hand to cut her off. "Really, Laura, don't apologize. It's as much my fault as yours. I should be apologizing."

"I threw you out of your room, though," said Laura.

"No, I did. I'm a big boy. And it's a big house, you know. I found a study farther down where I could lay my weary head. Two chairs pushed together will do me fine."

Laura's hand flew to her mouth. "Oh, no! Really?"

"No, not really," said Nick in withering tones. "The guest bedroom next door but one, actually."

"Oh," Laura said. "Ha-ha."

There was a pause. Laura was suddenly aware of what a peculiar situation it was. She slapped her hands on the duvet and said, "Well. Thanks again. I'd better be going."

"I've asked for some coffee to be sent up," said Nick. "Thought you might like some before you go."

"Oh, great," said Laura. "Thanks a lot."

"No problem."

"I'm going to get dressed," said Laura.

"Oh," said Nick. "I'll avert my gaze, then."

"Well, it'll only take a minute or so," said Laura, as he turned around politely. She hopped out of bed and slipped the T-shirt off, put on her bra and skirt and cardigan, slid on her flip-flops, and pulled her tangled dark-blond hair into a messy ponytail.

"Are you decent?" Nick said after a while.

"Yup," said Laura.

Nick turned round, amused. "That's your daily toilette, is it?" he said. "Very extensive."

"Absolutely," Laura said. "It just saves time. Wear the same panties for a week and they double up as pajamas. It's very handy. You get so much more done."

"I bet," said Nick. "Wow, you must be popular."

She raised her eyebrows at him. There was a knock at the door and the sound of something on the floor outside. "Coffee, sir."

"Ah," said Nick. He waited a second for the sound of footsteps walking away before going to the door; Laura was amused to see that, while everything was utterly relaxed between the two of them, he was not quite so relaxed about anyone else knowing he had had a strange girl in his room last night. What would Charles say? she wondered, as Nick put the tray on the bed. She thought he was probably more austere about these things than his friend. Might not like it, even though it couldn't be more innocent.

Nick handed her a cup of coffee. "Pastry?" he said, indicating a plate of delicious-looking croissants.

"It's like a hotel here," said Laura. "Wow!"

Her host was pouring some more coffee. "Yes," he said. "Slightly different, though. You can check out anytime you want, but you can't leave. Like the song." He looked up and smiled, that disarming smile.

Laura didn't quite know what to say. She looked out the window. "What's that?" she said suddenly, standing up and going over to the window.

Nick followed her pointing finger. "What?" he said.

"*There.* Jesus, what *is* that?'

"Oh," said Nick. He came and stood behind her. "Fuck." He gazed out the window. "That's a helipad. And that—*that*—is a helicopter. Help, I'd forgotten. Rose is coming for the weekend."

"Rose?"

Nick ran his hands through his hair. "Yes. Er—the sister. Charles's sister. With her awful husband. Bloody Malcolm. There's a thing on Saturday evening, a dinner for . . . Shit. I should go and . . ." He groaned, and looked out gloomily. "Damn. She *has* brought Malcolm. Help."

There was a light tap on the door. They froze, as if caught in the act. Nick was first to relax. He smiled ruefully. "God, this is ridiculous. Yes? Who is it?"

"It's Charles," came the calm voice from outside. "Man, Rose is here. I was wondering where Mrs. Hillyard is, I can't find her. Can I tell her—"

Nick leaped up, went to the door, opened it, and had a muffled conversation with Charles in the hallway, leaving Laura realizing suddenly that she really should go, she was getting in the way. She looked out the window, from high up on the top floor of the house. How strange it must be to wake up here, even if you'd known it all your life. The countryside sloped gently away from the grounds, the woods of the estate to the north merging into pinewoods, which stopped abruptly, and there beyond them was the sea. There was a fresh breeze, and Laura breathed in, catching the scent of pine and seawater. She felt calm, awake.

"It's a lovely day," she said, as Nick came back into the room.

"It is," he said. He was looking at her, his hand on his forehead.

Laura inhaled again, closing her eyes. It was gorgeous, air you could taste. She sighed, and shivered suddenly.

Nick watched her. "Goose walk over your grave?" he said.

Laura nodded. "Something like that. Right, I'd better go, I think." She allowed herself one last glimpse out the window, and said dreamily, "The beach looks so lovely from here, doesn't it? You must want to spend all day there when it's like this."

"I suppose so," said Nick. "I—where? Oh, it's there. I've never really been."

"What?" Laura gaped at him. "You've never been to the *beach*?"

"Not really," he said, looking out the window again.

"Nick, sorry, sorry," said Laura, holding up her hands. "You live overlooking that beach, the beautiful sea, and you've never been there?"

"Yes, of course I have," he said impatiently. "I used to go, but when I was small. I mean, I haven't been—you know, since . . ." He waved his arm vaguely. "It's always too crowded. With people. You know. And I don't really have time to go. Since I came back."

"How long ago was that?" said Laura

"Two years ago." Nick backed away, walked across the room. He chewed a nail. "I moved back two years ago."

"Oh," said Laura. "Why did you come back?"

Nick scratched his head. "I had to, when my father died. Before that, I didn't come here much. I was . . . being stupid, mainly. Pissing my life away in London. That's why I hate London. And I love it here. It saved me, basically. Charles did, too. And—I'll do anything—well." He stopped suddenly, and sat on the edge of the bed. "That's all."

"Well, you should go to the beach," Laura said, following the thread of the conversation, not really knowing what else to say. She slung her bag over her shoulder. "Right. Well, I'd better be off."

"I should, I know," said Nick unexpectedly. Then he stood up and said casually, "Listen. What are you doing later?"

"What, later today?" said Laura. "God, no idea. Going to a windmill. Or a buttery or something, I expect."

"I meant tonight," he said.

"Oh," said Laura. "Oh." She wanted to see him again, she knew it, but—

"Not that that doesn't sound lovely," he said. "Well—give me a call if you need rescuing or you fancy a drink or whatever." As Laura involuntarily opened her mouth, he said, "Relax, old chum. I feel it's my duty, since I'm your best friend here, to make sure your holiday goes well."

"Well, thanks to you," said Laura, "it's actually much better than I thought it was going to be."

"Cool," said Nick.

"Cool," said Laura.

They said good-bye by the back door, the one through which they'd entered last night, a few minutes later. It was nearly eleven, and the sun was climbing higher in the sky. Nick had offered to walk her to the car, but Laura said no, she'd be absolutely fine. He'd given her his number, too. They stood in silence for a moment, suddenly awkward, and then Laura saw Charles approaching them, skirting the formal garden at the back. Laura pushed her sunglasses on her head, held out her hand, and said, "Thanks. I'll—I'd better go."

He took her hand in his, and shook it firmly. He smiled down at her, a smile that was so familiar to her now, so strange.

"Remember what I said about tonight," he said casually.

"Yes," said Laura. "Thank you."

"Fine," said Nick. They grinned at each other. "Are you going to tell your parents where you were?"

"Nope," said Laura. "They'd just get overexcited. I told them when I texted last night. You're Naomi. You're a friend from my first job, and you work for the Wetlands Trust."

"I do, do I?" said Nick in amusement, as Charles reached them.

"Hello there, again. It's . . . Laura, isn't it?"

"Good morning," said Laura, resolved not to be embarrassed or obsequious. She smiled at him, then turned back to Nick and said, "Maybe I'll see you later, Naomi." She reached up and kissed him on the cheek. "Thanks for a lovely . . . er . . . thanks for a lovely evening."

As she walked away, her heart was beating strangely fast. She looked back, but Nick had already turned and was heading toward the front lawn, his tall, rangy frame solitary against the vast expanse of grass, toward where a voice was bellowing forth.

"Nick! You're there. Hello. Where's that useless sister of yours? Lavinia not up yet? The roses have got ash-rot, you've been overwatering them, you must tell Fletcher . . ." came a voice from behind him, heels on the terraces. Lady Rose Balmore's strident tones rose above the garden and floated over to them. Nick answered, his voice inaudible, and the sounds of greeting, familiar exchanges, gradually faded away as he slipped back into his life, and Laura continued on her way across the lawn, up to the path she'd taken on that strange night before. She was in no hurry. She'd slept so well, the tired feeling behind her eyes had gone, and she could feel the sun on her arms, on her hair, as she walked away from that strange world, back to hers. She turned and looked at the house as she reached the gate. It looked so different in the morning sunshine, gold and glittering, with green all around it. Windows were open all over its façade, and she could hear the hum of a tractor in the distance, and the coos of the fat pigeons in the dark trees to the north.

chapter twenty

As Laura walked round the side of Seavale over an hour later, dodging the deck chairs, she could hear her parents and Mary making polite conversation over what was clearly an early lunch.

"Pass the ratatouille, would you, Angela dear?"

"Yes, Mum. Would you like some more water?"

"No, thanks. Is there any wine left in the bottle?"

"George?" said Angela. "George, is there any wine left?"

"No," said George. "Oh, well."

"Hm," said Mary.

Silence fell as George and Angela Foster carried on eating. Laura watched them through the window, mesmerized by her own family and the contrast to the scene she'd left behind.

"How about opening another bottle?" said Mary. "I think I'd like another glass."

George looked up, aghast, as Angela frowned. "Really, Mum? Do you think . . . ?"

She trailed off as Mary gave her a stern look. George and Angela were not great drinkers, but Simon and Laura took after their grandmother. The idea that three people could get through more than a bottle at lunch clearly appalled George, whereas the idea in reverse appalled Mary. But George was a good son-in-law, and so, as Laura watched him fondly, he dabbed at his mouth with a napkin, stood up, and said, "Of course. I'll just see if there's any . . ."

"In the wine rack, the Hamilton Russell," Mary said firmly. George crossed the sunny dining room and disappeared into the tiny kitchen through the corridor.

"Lovely." Mary looked pleased. "You know, after lunch I think I shall sit outside and do the crossword for a little while. It's such a beautiful day."

"Yes," said Angela, though it was clear she was actually thinking, No, you should have a nap and a glass of water. "I wonder where Laura is," she said out loud. "Her text message did say she'd be back from Naomi's by lunchtime, didn't it?"

"Naomi. Yes," said Mary musingly. "Funny. I've never heard her mention Naomi before. Have you?"

Laura hurried across the lawn and through the French windows. "Hello," she called, putting her bag on the floor as her father appeared with the wine.

"Laura!" said Angela, her face alight with pleasure. "Here you are, and there's still some lunch left. Ratatouille, you like that, don't you? Would you like some ham? Here, have this sandwich."

They looked at Laura expectantly, as one.

"Did you have a nice evening, darling?" Angela said. "How was Naomi?"

"Er." Laura cleared her throat and stared at them.

"Bread?" said George, proffering the bread basket.

"Wine?" said Mary, pushing a spare wineglass toward Laura.

Laura cleared her throat again and ran her hands through her unruly hair. She was starving again—why was she so hungry all of a sudden?—but felt like a savage come amongst civilization and did not trust herself to form a full sentence.

"Thanks," she said, and sank into the chair her grandmother pulled out for her.

"So," said Angela. "We were surprised to get your text message. But how nice. Did you and Naomi get to chatting, then? Reminiscing about old times?"

"Yes," said Laura. "Yes, we did."

In answer to her mother's curious stare, she tried to expand.

"Because it was nice to see her."

"Great," said George, talking to his ham. "Well, you missed the windmill this morning, Laura, but we've got some great news!"

"What?"

"Great! Laura, we've managed to get tickets to see the Seekers Tribute Band! The box office just rang to confirm they're holding them."

"For me?" said Laura in a slightly strangulated voice. "Oh—well, I—"

"They thought they might be able to get you one, too, Laura. Come on, love," said George. "It'll be terrific fun. Oh, I know, they're not that popular with you lot"—he waved his hand in the direction of Laura and Mary, leaving Laura unsure whether he meant not popular with young people, old people, or merely people with ears—"but I promise you'll have a good time." He stood up. Laura swallowed a remark in her throat.

"Mary, are you sure you don't want to come? We can get Laura one if she wants, there's one for you, too, I'm sure. Tickets are still available, you know."

"What are the odds?" said Mary to her plate of ham. "Amazing."

"Yes," agreed George happily.

"No, thanks," said Mary. "Just fantastic you can go, of course, and Laura, I'm so jealous. But at my age—whew. I think the excitement might be a bit too much for me, you know. I think I'd better stay in and get an early night." She smiled serenely at her daughter.

"Excuse me a moment," said Laura, pushing her chair back and getting up. "I'll be right back."

She went outside, plucking her phone out of her bag, and texted: *You were right. Going to Seekers Tribute Band tonight. Help.*

Mary was standing up when she got back. "I'm going to sit in the sun for a while," she said. "Enjoy the calm before the storm tomorrow."

"Why?" said Angela, who was collecting the plates. "What's tomorrow?"

Mary gave her a look. "My birthday, Angela dear. Don't be silly."

"It's on Saturday, Mum," said Angela.

"Oh." Mary smoothed her gray hair. "Oh. Of course it is. It's—it's Thursday today, isn't it. Yes." She looked rather uncomfortable, her hand clutching the back of the chair. "Silly of me."

"Let me give you a hand," said Laura, coming forward. Her phone rang in her bag. "Oh."

"You get that, darling."

"No," said Laura, thinking it could be Amy. "Let's go outside. If they leave a message, I'll hear."

"So, you had a nice time yesterday," said Mary, walking slowly, her grip on Laura's arm tight as they went outside. She relaxed a little in the sunshine, pushed her sun hat on as she sat down again.

"Yes," said Laura uncertainly.

"Did you hear all about the wetlands yesterday?" asked Mary.

"They're not that special, are they? Personally, I've always thought they were rather dull." She fixed a beady eye on her granddaughter.

Laura breathed in as she met her grandmother's gaze. She could have just told the truth. There was nothing to be ashamed of; she was a grown-up, she could do what she liked with whom she liked. And it was hardly as if she'd actually *done* anything, anyway. She could just say, "I met this nice bloke yesterday, he lives at Chartley Hall, and I stayed in his room but nothing happened." But something stopped her. She breathed out again.

"It's funny," said Mary. "Xan and I, when we used to come here, do you know what we'd do?"

"No," said Laura. She sat down next to her grandmother. "What?"

"We'd read. And go for long walks. And watch films. Eat lots. Listen to the radio, do the crossword."

"Nice," said Laura, because it was, and she loved hearing Mary talk about Xan.

"He loved fish," said Mary, her eyes closed. "Grilled fish. That barbecue"—she waved in the direction of the barbecue at the edge of the garden—"we'd use it every night. Just the two of us, some wine, some classical music on the radio, sitting out here watching the sunset."

She was silent.

"Your parents don't go in for that sort of thing, though. They like being told things. Seeing things. Cramming in as much as possible. Your grandfather and I—well, we liked doing our own thing."

"Your way's the best way, I think," said Laura. Because it was still Xan and Mary she looked up to more than anyone else in the world, not her parents, and it was Mary's approval she craved all the time, rather than her mother's.

Mary looked up sharply. "There's no right or wrong way, Laura," she said, sticking her neck forward and tilting her hat up so she was looking at her granddaughter. "That's not what I meant. I mean, each to their own. What's sauce for the goose, and all that."

"What?" said Laura, confused.

Her grandmother lay back in the chair again. She said quietly, "You're twenty-eight. Aren't you?" Laura nodded. "My memory's so terrible these days. Darling, all I'm saying is—you're not your parents' age. Yet. Or mine. You should enjoy yourself while the going's good."

"Right," said Laura. She stared out across the sea, wanting to ask more; but when she turned to her grandmother to say, "Do you know where I was last night, then?" Mary was asleep.

She picked up the sandwich her mother had given her and munched it happily; then she dozed for a bit in the sunshine, her mind stretching lazily back across the previous twenty-four hours, sifting through everything that had happened. It was refreshing, really, she decided. For so long her life had been so narrow, so confined to what one man was doing, when he could see her, at the expense of everything else, that to be here, to have met Nick—and Charles, of course, and seen the house—it was all really interesting. Yes, that was it, nothing more than that.

Yes, it was true that Nick was attractive. In fact, he was gorgeous. It was also true that he lived in a huge house, one of the greatest houses in the country. And there was also the other stuff—how easy it was to talk to him, how funny he was, how she felt she could tell him everything even though they had nothing in common. She thought of the previous night, sitting high up in the soft glow of the dining room overlooking the darkening woodland, each of them leaning into the candlelight, their elbows on the table, drinking wine and talking, talking and laughing. It was a great Brief Encounter, that was all, and Laura told herself that it was a really good sign that she could get out there and meet someone as nice as him. It boded well for the future, even if she wasn't going to see him ever again. She wasn't. It was just too weird. Leave it at that, a perfect evening, a nice experience, an amusing story to tell Jo and Yorky when she got back, to show them she was over Dan, that everything was okay and all of that—yes—

Her phone rang again and, without thinking, she picked it up out of her bag. *Nick Mobile.* Well—just to be polite.

"Hello," she said softly, not wanting to wake Mary. She got up and walked to the low wall on the other side of the garden.

"Hi," said Nick. "Get home okay?"

"Yes, thanks," said Laura. "Thanks again."

"It was . . . a good evening, wasn't it?" said Nick.

"Really good," Laura agreed, wanting to say more but not wanting to go too far.

"I mean it. I really enjoyed myself, Laura."

"Well, I did, too," she said. "I mean it, too." She smiled into the phone. There was silence, and she knew he was doing the same thing.

"You know," said Nick, "it's a real shame about tonight."

"The Seekers?"

"Yes," he said. "I'm sorry."

"I am, too," said Laura. "You have no idea."

"Do you have to go?"

"What?"

"Can you get out of it?" he said.

"No," said Laura. "They've got me a ticket and everything."

At that moment, her father appeared at the French windows and called, "Laura?"

Mary shifted in her chair, and lowered her hat even farther.

"Laura, we're going for a walk," her father said, bending down to brush something off his Gore-Tex sandals. "Come with us? We're going to look at the marsh, about two miles away. Marvelous birds."

"Oh," said Laura.

"Wait a minute, George," her mother called, disappearing back into the house to fetch something. "My binoculars."

"Oh, God," Laura whispered into the phone. "Help." Then she realized Nick was still there, and said, "Sorry."

"Don't be," he said, and she could hear laughter in his voice. "So, you're going to the marsh, and then to the Seekers Tribute Band concert, and you're not going to let me take you out for a drink?"

"No," said Laura sadly. "I've said I'll go. I can't get out of it."

"Right."

"Right."

"Of course," he said, "I'm not the kind of man who'd ask you to lie to your parents and get out of an evening with them so I can see you again."

"No," said Laura. "You're not."

"And you're not the kind of girl who'd agree to lie to get out of the evening in the first place."

"No, Nick," said Laura again. "I'm not."

"So," he said, "I'll meet you at six-thirty, then?"

"Where?"

"The north gate?"

"See you there," said Laura, smiling into the phone again as her mother emerged from the house.

"Ready?" her dad said.

"Oh, dear," said Laura, putting down the phone. "Mum, that

was Naomi again. Her boyfriend. He's just dumped her. She was really upset."

As she walked across the lawn to her parents, Laura distinctly heard Mary chuckle softly beneath her hat, but she ignored it, knowing she would pay for it on Judgment Day, but also knowing that, as lies went, this one was almost excusable.

chapter twenty-one

...That's why you don't seriously like them. Name one single player."

"Cole."

"Exactly," said Nick. "You don't even know his first name."

"Yes, I do," said Laura. "Joe. No! Ashley! Ashley! And the French bloke. Thierry Henry. There."

"Right, right," said Nick, pushing aside a protruding branch and waiting for Laura to pass by. They were walking through the wood to the south of the house, having met at the north entrance. "Yes, of course, so you can name two members of one of the most famous football clubs in the world, so that makes you a really big fan of theirs."

"I like them," said Laura obstinately.

"I'm sure you do. I'm just saying, you like them because you live in North London and you're deeply middle-class and think you have to support Arsenal as a result."

"That's not true, and don't be rude to your guests," said Laura. The evening sunshine was filtering through the branches, creating a kaleidoscopic effect of hundreds of tiny flecks of light shimmering over them in the slight breeze. "Where now?"

"I thought we'd walk over toward the pond, then out to the village. There's a nice pub there, too, we can have a drink."

"Great," said Laura, following her host along the path. Even after a summer of sunshine, it was dark and damp, and the way was cool after the heat of the day. It was deliciously green, the air mossy and moist, in contrast to the already parched, yellowing land of the fields nearby, dry and brittle now that summer was so far advanced.

"So," said Laura, breathing deeply, enjoying the cool on her arms, "what did you do today?"

"Today?"

"Yes."

"Why?" said Nick, fiddling in his pocket for something.

"Well," said Laura, slightly taken aback. "I wasn't being nosy. I just wanted to know. I have no idea what someone like you does all day."

"God, no, sorry," said Nick. "I was . . . thinking of something I forgot at the house. Sorry. Of course. Right." He took his hand out of his pocket, picking a switch off a tree as they passed. "Today—well. I spent the morning in the kitchen garden with Fletcher—he's the head gardener—talking about what our yield will be this year. What we're likely to get, where we'll put it, and so on. How much we can use. I want the estate to be as self-sufficient as possible, you see."

"Right," said Laura. "Is that possible?"

"Not really, no," said Nick, laughing. "Although we do make all our own jam and scones for the tea shop, which I'm very proud of. All Chartley products, which is good, isn't it?"

"That's great."

He picked a flower growing out of the mossy bank nearby. "Here. Have a white campion." He handed it to her, and she took it, startled. "Especially when you realize how many damn cream teas we sell on a day like today."

"Must be hundreds," Laura said, tucking the flower behind her ear.

"Hm? Oh, yes, it is. Hundreds and hundreds. We have nearly a hundred thousand visitors a year, did you know that?"

"Oh, my God," said Laura. "Seriously?"

"Absolutely." Nick tapped a tree with his branch. "All of them wanting a slice of heritage. They come, they have their cream teas, they see the tapestry and the Hogarths and the staircase, and they wander round and hopefully buy a tea towel, and then they go home."

"It's bizarre," said Laura.

"No," said Nick. His voice was determined. "It's not. It's great that they want to come, and it's our job to make sure they have a good time. I feel . . . we need to make it somewhere people feel genuinely welcomed."

"And do you think it is?" said Laura, remembering how she'd criticized it yesterday. He read her thoughts.

"Well . . . yes and no. I've been thinking about what you said, you know."

Laura looked down at her feet as she followed the path. "I'm sorry. I was really rude."

"No, you were honest. Which, believe me, people usually aren't."

"Honesty's not always the best policy," said Laura ruefully.

"It is," said Nick. "Really it is." He stopped. "Anyway, I—it was helpful."

"Are you going to talk to Charles about it?" said Laura.

"Charles? Oh—yes. Yes, I suppose I am."

"That's nice of you!" said Laura, laughing.

"Ha," he said. "Yes. You're right, though. I—we should do something about it."

"Get the sign repainted," said Laura.

"The what?" His face was blank. "What sign?"

"When you arrive, on the drive," said Laura. "The sign looks awful. It's the entrance to the house, and it's cracked and peeling, and it just looks like the place is falling apart. And your sister and that bloke in the ticket booth," she continued, getting into her stride. "Sorry, but I don't think that's what Charles would want people's first impression of the house to be. Especially when they're paying fifteen quid for the privilege. You need some friendly, nice, welcoming person who says they're just completely delighted you're there and gives you a guidebook and is sensible."

"That flower suits you, in your hair," Nick said. "You're pretty when you rant, did you know that?"

Laura felt herself going red. "Am I?" she said, rather stupidly.

"Yes," he said solemnly. "You are. Well, don't get distracted. I take your point. You're saying an encounter with a randy young woman and some confused, exploited, sex-mad youth isn't the right way to say 'Welcome to Chartley'? Well, I can't think why. Look, here we are. Here's the pond."

They had come to the edge of the wood, and he stopped, Laura next to him. In front of them was a wide expanse of water surrounded by thick gray reeds waving gently in the breeze. Over on the other side was a tiny bridge of golden stone, and a stream flowed under it, cutting through the grass. They were high up, Laura realized—she looked over in wonderment and there, as the land sloped away, was Chartley Hall below them, a hundred yards or so in the distance. They were looking at the north side and the back view, with the formal gardens stretching out behind the house. The dark green of the tiny formal hedges looked like perfectly drawn letters of the alphabet, a secret message to someone. The stream ran away through the landscape, following the contours of the hill until it reached the formal gardens, where it became part of the layout, flowing into the fountains at the foot of the terraces, sparkling in the setting sun. The stone of the house glowed; on the terraces there were people, tiny as ants, taking pictures, sitting in the sun. Around them was the green of the landscaped park, the dull gray-yellow of the shorn fields, rolls of hay puckering the view, and in the distance to the north, the thin blue band of the sea, behind the wood at the north of the park. The people looked so small, incongruous, compared to the breathtaking size and grandeur of the house and its surroundings. Laura turned to her companion to say this to him, and found him watching her, a strange expression on his face. He leaned toward her, and then very slightly stepped back.

"You like it?" he said.

Laura laughed. "It's okay." She looked out again, not wanting to move. "You are lucky, living here, you know."

"I know," Nick said. "I'm very lucky." He checked his watch suddenly. "Right. Shall we get a drink? It's not that long to Chartley village. Have you got time?"

"Oh, yes," said Laura. It was nearly eight. "I told my parents I didn't know when I'd be back."

"Don't you feel horrible?" said Nick gravely. "Lying to them, making them think some imaginary friend of yours is in trouble."

"She's not imaginary," said Laura. "I used to work with her."

"Naomi. Excellent. Poor Naomi."

"She doesn't even know I'm here," said Laura. "I shouldn't think she's losing sleep over it; she wasn't even that nice. She . . ."

"What?"

"Nothing."

Laura felt a bit embarrassed. In fact, Naomi had stopped speaking to Laura when she'd finished with Josh—they'd all worked together. She'd told Laura she was a bitch, and that Josh deserved much better than her. Naomi had then got really drunk at Rachel's birthday do a couple of months later—God, they were fun, those evenings, especially Rachel's birthdays—and thrown herself at him. Josh had politely said no, and then no again and again, as she virtually started to stalk him. People at work had said that was why he'd moved to Australia—to get away from her—and Naomi had moved to Norfolk to try to live down her stalker shame. So it was hardly likely she'd be overjoyed to hear from Laura, really.

"Go on," said Nick, putting his finger on his chin. "I'm all curious now."

So Laura told him about Naomi. He was highly amused, and let out a yelp of laughter. "She sounds lovely."

"She was pretty awful. I feel sorry for the wetlands, you know, being looked after by her."

"Well, I love her," said Nick firmly, as they turned their backs on the view and walked south toward the gate.

"Don't."

"I owe her a lot. Thanks to her, I'm your best Norfolk friend. Right," he said, walking swiftly on.

They walked across the high, wide downs at the top of the park, then through a gate that led them out of the grounds onto the road, Nick chewing bits of grass and telling Laura the names of the various flowers along the banks. Laura picked a bouquet of flowers in the hedgerows, some hedge parsley, vetch, goosegrass, and pale pink dog roses, already in bloom. They chatted, not really saying much, walking easily, soaking up the sun as they approached Chartley, skirted the edge of the village, and came to the Needham Arms at the top end of the High Street.

The interior of the pub was small and dark, and though it was nearly empty, Laura noted, impressed and amused at the same time, that Nick was greeted like a young prince, rather than the bloke from the estate.

"What do you want?" he asked Laura, looking down at her as they stood by the bar.

"I'll have a pint, please," said Laura firmly.

"You don't want any—"

"No, thanks," said Laura. He nudged her. "Oh, all right, then," she said, giving in.

Nick turned to the barman. "Sorry. A Pimm's, please. No, make that two."

"Good choice," said Laura, and they nodded at each other, smiling, as the barman watched them curiously.

They were ushered to a quiet parlor at the back, and Laura was touched to be given a wet napkin by the barman in which to wrap her flowers.

"Does Charles ever come in here?" Laura asked, once they were settled. She was more and more curious about the elusive, shy marquis and how he coped with his role. He seemed too, well, *old-fashioned* to actually be able to keep up to speed with the needs of the estate, more like someone who'd be happier in the library deciphering obscure Latin texts.

"No," said Nick. "Not really his scene."

"It must be difficult for him."

"How?" said Nick.

"Well," said Laura. "Because he's . . ." She trailed off.

"Tall? Got pustulating boils on his face? Two noses?" said Nick. "What?"

"Well, because of who he is. The *marquis.*" Laura spoke in a whisper.

"Why should it make any difference?" said Nick. He sounded impatient. "Why shouldn't he come in here?"

"All right, all right, don't get shirty with me," said Laura, trying to make a joke out of it.

"Well, he's a person," said Nick, his voice still sharp. "He's not an alien, you know. It says NO DOGS outside. It doesn't say DON'T COME IN, YOU'RE TOO POSH, does it?"

"You're impossible," said Laura.

He relaxed and smiled at her. "You're right. One more drink?" he said.

"One more. I'll go," Laura said, standing up. "I'll watch out for any aristocratic-looking people trying to get in and eject them. Don't worry."

"Thanks," said Nick. "That's a weight off my mind."

She came back bearing the drinks and sat down. Nick took a sip from his and said suddenly, "So, Laura. Can I ask you something?"

"Anything," said Laura recklessly.

Nick paused. "Well . . ." He looked carefully at her, and put his glass down on the table. "What's your favorite film?"

"Ha," said Laura. Her heart, which had been beating loudly, slowed down again. "That's a hard one, you know. What's yours?"

"*Raiders of the Lost Ark*," said Nick. "Seriously," he added, as Laura looked surprised.

"I agree," said Laura. "I'm just surprised you think so."

"Why?"

"Well . . ." She paused. "I'd have thought you were more of a . . . *Godfather*, *Citizen Kane* kind of guy. You know—films with themes."

Nick obviously found this amusing. "I like that. You think of me as this serious, grown-up man who relaxes by reading biographies of Hitler, don't you?"

"Er, a bit," said Laura. "And I don't know why, when—" She broke off, not wanting to sound rude. When your life on the estate is quite easygoing, even if it is hard work, and Charles is obviously a good boss, and you seem to have quite a nice life, so why are you so closed-off and prickly about so many things? Why don't I know your surname?

"When what?" said Nick.

"Nothing," she said, smiling at him. "Nothing." She put her hand on his arm impulsively. "It's my favorite film, too."

"Really?"

"Yes," said Laura. "Didn't used to be. It used to be, er—*The Sound of Music* or *Four Weddings and a Funeral.* When I was into all of that."

"All of what?" said Nick. "It's not crack cocaine, they're just films."

She shook her head, trying to explain without explaining, not wanting to give herself away—and then realized she was doing exactly the same thing as he was, closing herself off, and it was weird but okay. "Ah . . ." she said. "When I was younger. And more stupid. Than I am now." She looked down.

"Okay," said Nick, nodding as if he understood. He stroked her arm gently, just once. "I'm going to ask you something else, then."

"Yes?" said Laura, staring at the table.

"So . . . why are you here?"

"What do you mean?" Laura looked at him over her Pimm's.

"I mean, here on holiday. I still don't quite understand it. Yesterday you said something about how your job was weird at the moment. And you keep darkly mentioning how you've apparently fallen out with various people, which I don't get either—you don't seem like someone who's constantly making enemies."

"I . . ." Laura began, but she didn't know what to say.

Nick said lightly, "So—what happened?"

"Ah." Laura looked at him, not sure how to answer. She said tentatively, "Well . . . it's complicated."

"Complicated. I see," said Nick. He paused. "Don't tell me if you don't want to. I don't mean to stick my nose in."

"No, no," said Laura, relieved that his curiosity was only that, nothing more. "Well—it was . . . well, it was just this bloke—this bloke I was seeing. That's all."

"Right," said Nick. He drained his drink. "It is none of my business, don't worry."

There was silence.

"He had a girlfriend," Laura said in a rush, unable to bear it. "We had an affair, he was—Dan—he was still with his girlfriend. I got it wrong, I got a bit—er, ah—I fucked it up, basically. Big-time. Kind of got everything out of proportion." She cleared her throat and said in a small voice, "I thought he loved me. It's stupid. Anyway, that's it. It's over."

"And where's Dan now?" said Nick in a neutral tone.

Laura chewed a fingernail, looked up, and said, "With his girlfriend. Pregnant girlfriend. On holiday in Miami. We were . . . supposed to go away together. But I found out about her . . . being pregnant."

"When?"

"Two weeks ago," Laura said, smiling ruefully. "Lost the money on the holiday. Been suspended from my job, too. Oh, yes," she said, meeting his eye, almost enjoying the surprise on his face, "I've really screwed it up. For the moment, anyway."

"So you came here to get away from it all," Nick said.

"And so I came here." She looked up and said definitely, "It's over. That's it, end of story. I'm getting over him."

She smiled at him over her glass. And suddenly, something clicked inside her. She *was* getting over Dan. She wasn't there yet, but it didn't really hurt so much—the whole thing didn't, suddenly. She hadn't thought about it, couldn't bear to, and now that she said it, she realized she was. It seemed . . . a million years away.

"Good for you," said Nick, and he smiled at her, the hard lines of his face softening as he patted her arm. "Sounds pretty rough."

"It was—a bit." Laura looked at him gratefully, surprised at how much the gesture meant; he knew she didn't want sympathy, just a bit of human understanding. "But you're right. I'm here to get over it. This is the turn-over-a-new-leaf approach, this week. So far, not too bad. Well, now I've met you, that is. So, thanks."

"Well," Nick said, raising his glass, "thank you, too. Here's to the new-leaf approach. Or the Norfolk Outreach Program for Mental People. After you leave, I'm going to start hanging around the station waiting for the London train, to pal up with the next unstable person on holiday and in need of a friend."

"Well, that's really kind of you," said Laura.

They were silent; both took sips of their drinks. Laura looked at her companion under her eyelashes until his eyes flicked up toward her, and she looked elsewhere, at the old photos, the dried flowers in baskets on the windowsill, the clock on the wall. It was getting on for nine-thirty. But she could still see his face in her mind's eye, like she had taken a snapshot. The close-cropped, curling black hair; the bony face with its rather harsh expression, tanned by the summer sun. The expression in the eyes that gave away so little, and occasionally so much. It was strangely familiar, that face, and he reminded her of something, someone; but for the life of her, she couldn't remember what.

"When do you go?" he said suddenly.

"What?" said Laura, still lost in a dream. "Oh."

"When do you go?"

"Saturday evening," she said. "But I have the birthday lunch all day on Saturday, so—"

"So . . . what are you doing tomorrow?" he said, shifting in his seat on the wooden bench.

"Evening?"

He nodded, his expression inscrutable.

"Nothing," said Laura. "Well . . ." She felt a bit guilty suddenly. Shouldn't she be spending more time with her parents? With Mary? But she saw them all the time, a voice inside her said. And there was the lunch on Saturday, after all—she'd see them then. Surely that was—

Laura jumped and glanced down. Nick had put his hand on hers. He said quietly, "I know you have to go. But tomorrow—do you fancy a picnic at the beach? Since it's your last night?"

Suddenly Laura didn't know what to say, which was weird because, up till now, she'd felt she could say almost anything to him. She looked anxiously up at him, into his eyes. They were narrowed, watching her almost fiercely, the old expression of kindness, humor, arrogance, and sarcasm mixed with . . . something else, something undefinable. His grip tightened slightly; then he released her hand and sat back.

Laura said slowly, "Yes, of course."

He nodded, and they looked at each other again, rather blankly, until he said, "Meet me there at seven. I'll bring the picnic."

"Really?" said Laura. "No, I'll bring something, too."

"No, it's my pleasure. Someone in the kitchens owes me a favor."

"Right," said Laura.

"How are you getting home tonight?" said Nick as he took another sip of his drink, watching her over the glass.

"I'm getting the bus." She laughed at his bemused expression. "Seriously. There's a timetable at home. I checked it before I left. The bus goes from just outside here, every half hour. So I won't have to force you out of your bedroom again. I've planned ahead."

"Great," said Nick. "Well—that's great."

There was silence between them, and this time it was awkward. Something had shifted imperceptibly. Nick said nothing. He looked down at the table. Laura wanted to say something, but she couldn't.

In the end, she said, "So, I'd better go soon. . . ."

"You don't have to," he said abruptly. "You could—"

"No," said Laura softly. She drummed her fingers on the table. "I . . ."

They were alone in their tiny alcove; the murmur of the other drinkers in the pub was faint. Nick slid his thumb under her hand and wrapped his fingers around hers, stopping the tattoo she was beating on the table. They stayed like that for a few seconds, her hand in his. Laura looked up at him, her heart beating so loudly she was sure he could hear it. He was watching her with that strange, familiar expression. His face was pale under his tan. She noticed how plump his bottom lip was, how biteable it was, compared to the sharp lines of the rest of his face. And then he put his other hand behind her neck and gently pulled her toward him, and kissed her.

His lips were soft, his arm was wrapped around her, and she could taste fine, salty sweat on his skin as she kissed him back. They pulled apart. She looked at him, drinking in the sight of him, and they said nothing again, but smiled at each other in understanding. Nick was still holding her hand; he squeezed it, and then put his other hand up to her mouth. He touched her lips gently with his fingers, and his hand dropped to his side again.

"Well," he said, his tone noncommittal, but he was smiling at her.

Laura smiled. A feeling of happiness was washing through her, like sunshine after a cloudy day. She looked into his eyes. "Well," she said, and tightened her grasp on his hand, as they stared at one another.

"What's your surname?" she said suddenly.

He laughed, and stroked her cheek with his index finger. "How very Victorian of you, Laura. I didn't know you were so old-fashioned."

She blushed. "I just meant . . ."

"It's Needham," said Nick. He paused, his eyes on hers. "Better now? Any more questions?"

"No," said Laura dreamily. "Not at the moment."

So he kissed her again.

"I'll see you tomorrow, then," said Nick, as they walked along Chartley High Street. It was a warm evening, the sky a deep royal blue, not quite night yet. "Are you sure you—"

"I'm sure," said Laura firmly. Mrs. Danvers had told her in no uncertain terms she had to get on that bus, much as she wanted to stay in the Needham Arms and carry on making out with Nick for the rest of the night. She looked at her watch. It was nearly ten. She was suddenly tired, and moreover, she'd promised her mother she'd help with the shopping bright and early the next morning (it was one of Angela's great obsessions, going to the supermarket at the crack of dawn, to avoid any possible danger of having to queue). And she couldn't hang around two nights in a row and invade this poor man's house, which wasn't even his. No, with regret, she knew she ought to leave him, and whatever this unexpected, lovely thing was between them.

"So." Nick took her hands in his so she was facing him, still clutching her rather bedraggled posy of flowers. The air was still, the horse chestnuts lining the road heavy and scented, stirring faintly.

She took a deep breath. "Thanks," she said. "A lot."

"No," said Nick. "Thank you. You have no idea." He held her hands tightly, but his face was in shadow under the tree and she couldn't see his expression.

"You neither," she said.

"Well, let's just agree we're both total screwups, and we won't fight about it," he said.

"What are you a screwup about?" Laura said, curiosity getting the better of her.

"Trust me, Laura, we don't have time for that now," said Nick. "I won't bore you with the many ways in which I've screwed up. You wouldn't want to see me again."

He didn't sound self-pitying, merely detached, amused. It was impossible to gauge his real meaning, so Laura said cautiously, "Nick, about what I said earlier."

"About what?"

"About that guy—the one I—"

He kissed her. "Forget about it." His hands tightened on hers again; there was hardly any gap between them as they stood facing each other, her hips pressing into his. "That was then. This is now." He stopped. "This *is* what this is, isn't it?" He threw the question out snappily, as if it didn't really mean anything.

Laura said hesitantly, "Nick—"

"I know," he said, his voice full of laughter. "Let's worry about that tomorrow. Or whenever."

"Absolutely," said Laura, as the sound of a heavy engine grew louder, coming toward them. She turned her head—there was the bus, its incongruous primary colors out of place in that lovely old street, this perfect, perfect evening.

"See you tomorrow."

"Seven o'clock," said Laura. "Tell Charles thanks for letting you out another evening."

"I'll tell him," he said. "The Marquis of Ranelagh says thank you."

"I'm honored," said Laura, as the doors shuddered open.

He leaned down and kissed her, hard and swift, again. "Bye, gorgeous," he said casually, stepping back onto the pavement.

The bus driver gave him a salute, doffing an imaginary hat. Laura sat down by the window and smiled at this piece of faux courtesy. She waved at Nick as the bus rolled gently down the road, out of the village, toward home.

She put her head against the glass and found she was smiling insanely, grinning ear to ear. She pulled her book out of her bag and tried to read, but couldn't concentrate. Nick. Nick! Nick. She couldn't stop smiling, and she told herself she had to calm down, that Mrs. Danvers would not be pleased at her schoolgirlish behavior. She pinched herself on the arm. Good grief, she was almost having a relapse. No. No more old Laura. She carried on looking out the window, thinking how sudden, how strange the whole thing was. She *mustn't* start being her old self again, the person who had taken up running to impress a boy at university and sprained her ankle. The person who had convinced herself that the man who'd painted the office, Julian, was her future husband, because they both had grandmothers called Mary.

The book fell from her lap as the bus swung around the corner. Laura put her hand over her mouth and yawned. She ran her hand down over her lips, her neck, to her breastbone, wanting to remember how it felt to kiss him, touch him. She bent down to pick up the book, and saw that the postcard her dad had given her had fallen out and skidded across the scuffed lino floor. Smiling with recognition, glad Nick hadn't seen it, she picked it up, and turned it over, and her mouth fell open with shock.

The seventh marquis smiled up at her from the card, his dark, intelligent eyes boring into hers. She gasped.

It was Nick. It was the spitting image of him. How could she not have seen it before? The hair, his eyes, the bony, rather arrogant face. Just a hundred fifty years earlier. She turned it over again, as if to check that she hadn't picked up another postcard that happened to be lying on the floor of the Coastal Hopper. She read the caption on the back: "Dominic, Seventh Marquis of Ranelagh, Earl of Albany Cross, 1867–1928. In 1895, the *Illustrated London News* called him 'England's Most Eligible Bachelor.' "

Dominic. Nick.

chapter twenty-two

"Is it okay if I stay with Naomi tonight?" Laura asked casually the next day, as she was pushing the trolley around the supermarket with her mother.

Angela was humming with nerves, rapidly repeating ingredients under her breath. She turned her attention momentarily away from the bag of onions she was holding, and squeaked slightly as someone pushed past them. It was lunchtime, it was Friday—the supermarket was packed full of locals and holidaymakers alike, stocking up for what promised to be a boiling-hot weekend—perfect barbecuing weather. Laura waited behind her. She was tired and hadn't slept well. Her head ached.

"Lulu doesn't eat meat, does she?" Angela said, not listening.

"Lulu doesn't eat anything, Mum," said Laura, prying the onions from her mother's frenzied grip and picking up a smaller bag. "Here, Mum, you wanted red onions. I asked you a question, do you know what it was?"

"Er . . ." Angela had wandered down the aisle and was looking at crisps. "Annabel's always so snooty about these," she said, brandishing a huge packet of semi-posh crisps. "Says they're full of additives. But I rather like them, what do you think?"

"I think they're great, and Gran likes them, too, remember? She asked you to get that exact flavor," said Laura patiently.

"Oh, my goodness," said Angela. "My memory."

"Mum!" said Laura. "It doesn't matter what Annabel thinks. Or what she wants. Gran's *your* mum, isn't she? And this is *her* birthday! Isn't it!"

"Yes!" said Angela, slamming her fist down into the crisps section. There was a loud crunching sound as several packets burst. "Oh, dear," she said, looking amazed at her own strength. "Good grief."

"She winds you up," said Laura. "Don't worry about her. Simon's coming back tomorrow, it's Granny's birthday, the sun's shining, and everything's fine." She pushed the trolley on, blocking her mother's way. "Now, is it okay if I stay with Naomi tonight? I'll be back early tomorrow to help you before the others come, I promise."

"Yes!" said Angela. "Bless you, darling. You're quite right. Yes!"

"Yes to Naomi?" said Laura, hopping from foot to foot with frustration.

"Naomi?" said her mother, as if hearing the name for the first, not the third, time. "Oh. Again, dear?"

"Yes, I know," said Laura. Her head was throbbing. "I'm sorry, but tonight is my last night, and it's been so lovely to meet up with her again."

"You've really enjoyed it, haven't you?" said Angela, stopping to look at her daughter.

"Yes," said Laura. "Yes, I have."

"Do you think you'll stay in touch?"

Laura gazed into the distance. "Not sure," she said. "We need to talk about that tonight. About a lot of stuff." She came back into the present with a jolt. "I—er, I mean, Naomi needs to sort all that out. With her ex. She's got a lot of things to sort out."

"Ah," murmured Angela sympathetically. She picked up a bag of salad. "What about this? Looks nice."

"It's washed in tons of chlorine, and it's really ecologically unsound," said Laura, throwing the offending bag of salad back. "Oh, Mum," she said in a rush of confidence, "I don't know what she's doing, to be honest."

"Why?" said Angela, her head on one side. "Oh, dear. Why, what's the problem with her boyfriend?"

Laura was silent for a moment. Then she said slowly, "She's only just met him. But she thought—she thought he was great. That they were really good together. But he's kind of lied to her." Her eyes filled with tears; she turned toward the bags of salad again. "Oh, look," she mumbled in a muffled voice. "Watercress."

Angela wasn't really paying attention, having drifted toward the vegetables. "Oh, dear. That's a shame," she said vaguely, covering her tracks, her eyes scanning the shelves like an SAS operative. "Carrots, ooh, yes," she said. "Leeks."

Laura leaned against one of the shelves and put her hand to her forehead. She felt hot and rather tired. A night of sleepless tossing and turning, of reaching out to grab her phone, wanting to text him and say, "I know who you are," of wrestling with the knowledge she had now acquired, had brought no more answers. She liked him; he liked her—wasn't that enough? It didn't matter, did it? she told herself, through the long night, as the sky filled with light and the morning came. Surely this didn't really change things?

Then, following simultaneously on, would come the doubts,

the questions. Was it really true that he was this person? Someone she felt she knew, and now just didn't know at all? She couldn't reconcile the two: Nick, who loved thin chips, made her laugh, and kissed her as if it was just right; and the Marquis of Ranelagh, this symbol of ancestry and wealth, of formality and duty—this person about whom she had heard so much, as if he were a thing, rather than a living, breathing man. She had turned over and over in bed till the sheets were loose and crumpled, trying to make sense of it, desperate for some calm. That house—the treasures inside it—the history—the family, Lady Rose, Lady Lavinia . . . the mother who'd left him, the scandal. The publicness of a life like that. Then she knew why he hadn't told her, and she felt a cold feeling start inside her, that this was stupid, doomed, that she shouldn't take it any further.

After all, she'd only just met him. Perhaps even worrying about it was stupid. Perhaps thinking about it was the last thing to do. She wasn't angry with him, or even with herself, for once. She just wanted to see him again, to be with him, and perhaps then she would know what should happen next. Because at the moment, she wasn't sure.

"Naomi's boyfriend lied to her, did he?" Angela said vaguely, putting some leeks into the trolley. "Oh, dear.'

Laura shook herself out of her reverie, and followed with the trolley. "Well," she continued, not really minding whether her mother was listening or not, "yes. She knows he's lied. But he doesn't realize she knows."

"What did he lie about?" said Angela, looking curiously at her.

Laura said sadly, "About who he is."

"What, is he a convict?"

"Kind of. The opposite. Sort of."

Angela looked at her daughter as if she were mad, and Laura said hurriedly, "Well, she doesn't know what she should do about it now. And that's not even the biggest issue," she continued, warming to her theme, as Angela made sympathetic noises and moved around the corner to the condiments, where she bent over slightly, humming and putting her finger to her lip, to run her gaze over a row of mustards. "The biggest issue is, now that she knows he's what he is, that makes *everything* different."

"What would your grandmother say?" asked Angela. "Dijon? Or whole-grain?"

"Dijon," said Laura, plucking a jar viciously off the shelf and throwing it into the trolley, where it clattered loudly.

Angela frowned, obviously rewinding the sounds in her head so she could respond to her daughter's last sentence. "How is everything different?" she said with astonishing clarity. "Does him having not told the truth about who he is really make that much of a difference, if she feels that strongly about him? Doesn't matter if he's a convict. Unless it's for something *really* awful, of course," she said, lowering her voice. "But it doesn't, does it?"

Laura stopped still in the aisle. "Don't know," she said, chewing her lip. "I'll have to see. See her and see."

"It is Dijon she likes, isn't it?" said Angela, moving on. "Ask your grandmother when we get home, just to make sure."

"I'll ask her," said Laura. "Good idea."

Before lunch, as Angela stood in the kitchen chopping, dicing, preparing marinades, getting things ready for the next day, and George crouched down by the barbecue, oiling it, speaking tenderly to it as if it were a temperamental dressage horse, Laura wandered out onto the terrace, carrying a huge bowl and a massive bag of broad beans to shell under her arm. Mary was crouched over a flower bed, deadheading a pink scented rambling rose that clung to the side of the house. She was wearing sunglasses and had tied an old printed scarf over her hair.

"Ah," she said, standing up with a groan as Laura approached. "Come and talk to me."

"I will," said Laura, pulling a chair up to the table and sitting down.

Mary brushed the dead leaves off her gardening gloves, and winced as she bent down again. "Got everything you needed this morning?"

"Absolutely," said Laura. "You like Dijon, not whole-grain, mustard, don't you?"

"Oh, yes," said Mary. "Loathe whole-grain. Those little bits. In fact, I was thinking we should have some mayonnaise, too. Xan used to make garlic mayonnaise, you know. Delicious, it really was. When we were in Morocco, he—"

Wanting to steer her thoughts in a different direction, Laura said, "Sorry, Gran." Mary looked up, rather crossly. "Can I ask you something?"

"Of course," her grandmother said. She leaned against the slatted wood of the house and undid the scarf covering her hair, shaking it out. "What's on your mind, darling?"

"You—you said you'd met the marquis's mother," said Laura hesitantly. "Vivienne something. Didn't you?"

"Golly," said Mary. She patted her cheeks. "Vivienne Lash. Yes, ages ago. Xan and I met her and Freddy both, when we were living in the south of France for the summer. Saw quite a bit of them, actually."

"Have you met her son?"

"The new marquis?" said Mary. "Oh, no. She was the outcast, you know, darling. She left his father when he was—ooh, barely a teenager, I think."

"Right," said Laura, not really knowing what to ask next, or what she was hoping to get out of this conversation. "So—did she talk about her children?"

"Vivienne?" Mary sat down next to Laura and lifted up her sunglasses. "Not much. Think it was too painful for her. We knew all about it, of course. Everyone did."

"How come?"

"Well, it was a huge scandal. Massive. Kept the tabloids busy for weeks."

"Really?" said Laura. "Why on earth? People run off with people all the time."

Mary smiled at her. "Oh, darling. You are naïve about things like this. Just because it doesn't interest you, just because you'd rather read about it in the pages of a novel, doesn't mean it's not endlessly fascinating to the rest of the public. Or the newspapers, at least. No, it was all rather juicy to them. For a variety of reasons."

"What?"

"She was terribly famous in her day, you know, Vivienne. Real A-list British star. When she married the Marquis of Ranelagh, it was like a real-life fairy tale. Beautiful actress marries richest peer in the land, that sort of thing."

"And they are . . . that rich, are they?" Laura said in a small voice.

Mary flexed her right hand, squeezing the secateurs tightly together. "The Needhams? I should say so. Laura, they're *the* great aristocratic family, you know. Vast wealth. That house is only the tip of the iceberg. There's the place in Grosvenor Square, that castle in Scotland—and they own half of Belgravia, too."

Something caught in Laura's throat; she breathed in the wrong way and started choking, coughing violently. "God," she rasped, as her breathing returned to normal.

A seagull flew overhead, croaking loudly. Mary looked up, and her gaze followed it as it flew out to sea. She said distantly, "Yes. You know, though, it wasn't enough for her. She shouldn't have married him. I think she loved him, but it was Freddy she really loved."

"Freddy?" Laura said, breathing deeply.

"The brother. I think William—was that it? William? Xan would remember, he—oh, well," said Mary, her face clouding. "Anyway. Yes, it was the scandal for a while. Because she was so well known. And the Needhams were so rich. And she was running off with his *brother*, you know, that's really not on in some people's eyes. And then there were the children. There were three of them. Yes, that was it. Rose was the eldest. Then there was Lavinia, yes, that was it, gosh, I'd forgotten. And then the boy. The heir. She did worry about him. He was only—what? Nearly twelve when it happened? Still quite small."

The seagull squawked in the distance. Laura stayed very still, her arms around the bowl, not wanting to disrupt anything. She gave a tiny nod, willing her grandmother to tell her more.

Mary sighed, and stretched out her arms. She cleared her throat. "Yes," she said. "I loved her. But she did suffer about leaving that boy behind. Dominic. Nick, she called him. The heir to the whole damn thing. What a life. Can you imagine?"

"No," said Laura. "Absolutely not."

"Can't imagine it. Losing your mother like that."

"Well, but she didn't die," said Laura.

"No, but they weren't allowed to see her. Or she them. She missed them dreadfully, you know. I sometimes wonder . . ." She stopped, and looked out across the lawn, over the wall, down to the sea.

"What, Gran?" said Laura.

"Was it worth it? But they were so in love. And she was so miserable with her first husband, you know. Still."

"Still . . ." Laura said encouragingly.

"I think she hated herself for it, for doing such damage. Still does, probably. I haven't seen her for years, you know. She was lovely." Mary sighed. "But she was punished for it. She didn't deserve it, I think. She was only human. We all are, you know." She put her hands lightly on the arms of her chair.

"Yes," said Laura. "We are." She patted her grandmother's hand, and nodded at the bag of beans. "I'll get on with these, then."

The rest of the day passed as if she were sleepwalking, counting down the hours till she saw him again. Against the backdrop of preparation for the next day, as the sun shone down and the Fosters put up bunting, cleaned and cleared everything, tidied the house, put the newspapers outside, Laura worked almost silently, still tossing it all over in her mind like the mounds of salad she washed in the spinner, still thinking so hard her head hurt, without ever reaching a conclusion about what to do. She only knew that she liked him, more than she could say, that it felt so right.

But that was exactly what was terrifying her. Because she'd been there before, and had been proved utterly wrong; and if she'd thought Dan was someone who hadn't come clean about his life, Nick could win an Olympic gold medal in the same event. She had to see him, to talk to him, to try to work out why, yet again, this had happened to her. And why it mattered so much.

chapter twenty-three

He was waiting for her when she arrived at the beach. The last of the day's holidaymakers were leaving in dribs and drabs, brightly colored nylon sun umbrellas rolled up under their arms, clutching towels, goggles, rubbish—the paraphernalia of family holidays. Laura passed one such family as she made her way down to the beach past the rustling sea grasses and beach huts. There was something real and comforting about them, about the way the father held his son's hand, the little boy quiet and dirty after the day's exertions, about the way the other son, who looked about five, trailed behind his parents, his face tearstained, his mouth lolly-stained, the excitement of the day obviously too much for him. That was real life, she thought. This, the encounter she was walking toward in a red sundress, the silver bangles on her wrists jingling, this wasn't real, was it? But here, now, with the sun setting and the calm of evening falling on the sea, she just didn't know. All she knew was that she couldn't wait to see him again.

Nick turned at the sound of her step. He frowned slightly as he recognized her, his eyes squinting against the evening sun. There was something intensely familiar about him, Laura realized. Not because he looked like some postcard of his ancestor. Not as if it had only been three days. She watched, like a neutral observer, as he straightened up from the post he was leaning against, his tall, muscular frame moving easily under his shirt, his tanned, dark face, so distant and arrogant in repose, now smiling quickly at her as she drew near. How comfortable he looked here, in this landscape. Laura knew she looked like what she was—a tourist. Utterly different.

"Hello," he said, taking the bottle she'd brought and clasping her hand. "My name's Naomi, great to see you again." He shook her hand, grinning at her. "Can I show you some interesting bog weeds?"

"Hello," she replied, her hair blowing behind her in the breeze. She looked up at him, suddenly shy. She'd forgotten how attractive he was, how *nice* to look at he was. Marquis or no marquis. He was still holding her hand, and he pulled her toward him and kissed her. She remembered with a jolt how much she enjoyed being with him, how kissing him was something she wanted to do all evening. She broke apart from him, and stood back.

"How are you?" she said abruptly.

"Fine, I'm fine," Nick said, scanning her face. She could see a note of uncertainty in his eyes. He was still holding her hand, his face inches away from hers. "I'm glad you could come."

"Me too," said Laura. Their eyes met briefly, and suddenly she wanted to put her head on his chest, stay like this forever. But she shook her head, withdrew her hand, and stood back a little.

"Shall we go this way?" said Nick, jerking his head to his right.

"Great," said Laura. This was strange; it wasn't working out the way she'd expected. He was still the same. She'd expected to notice the difference in him, now that she knew, but there was none. The same distant, detached amusement at the world, the same politeness, kindness. That same feeling that she could totally be herself with him—it was still there. She did not move as he set off, and he turned back to find her watching him, the knuckles of her hands pressed against her cheeks.

"Everything okay?" Nick said easily.

"Well," said Laura, suddenly feeling a bit sick, "not sure, really. Nick. Why didn't you tell me who you really are?"

A tiny muscle ticked in Nick's cheek. He was silent for a moment, then gave a harsh, short laugh. "I see," he said, putting the cooler box down. "I assume you're referring to the title I happen to have, rather than to my unbeaten record as Chartley District Junior Darts Champion in 1985."

"Don't joke, Nick," said Laura. "I'm serious. You—you lied to me."

He looked as if he were about to protest, but then said quietly, "Yes. Yes, I did."

"Nick—"

"I lied about a couple of little details, Laura. That's all they are, I promise you. They're unimportant to me."

"But they're not to me!" said Laura. "You're—you're a freaking *marquis*, for God's sake! How could you not tell me? Do you do this to people all the time?"

"No," he said, holding out a hand to stop her. His voice was low, his expression serious. "Laura, listen to me. Listen. This is important. It is not a big deal, I promise you. The person you met—that's me. You know my name, you know what I do all day—that *is* what I do all day, mostly. You—you—I didn't want to tell you the truth, because you'd got the wrong end of the stick, and then I found, well . . ." He smiled at her. "I found I wanted you to like me for myself, more and more. So I didn't tell you."

"You should have."

"Yes," he agreed. "I should have. But"—he stepped forward and grabbed her fingers, enclosing them in his strong hands—"Laura, I swear to you this doesn't make a difference to us. Whatever this is between us, it mustn't make a difference." His hands tightened. "It already does, too much. It's not going to change this."

The pressure of his hands suddenly hurt. She winced. He released them, and said, "I'm sorry. It's just—my life is odd. Extraordinary. And when I'm with you—it's seemed more normal. And, believe me, that's quite rare." He shook his head, and made as if to turn away. "Look, I'm sorry."

Laura suddenly saw how comic the situation was. "Don't apologize for being a multimillionaire aristocrat," she said. "I should be impressed, I suppose, not having a go at you." She smiled at him to let him know it was okay, not wanting to tell him what she was really thinking.

"Shall we go and eat?" said Nick. "And we'll pretend it's yesterday, and you still think I'm your local friendly farmer, or whatever it was you assumed I was when you started shouting at me and trying to set my estate on fire."

"I thought you were unbelievably rude and a big bully, and I still do," said Laura.

"Great," said Nick. "Glad to see you're still the same charming girl I took a chance on and asked out. Nothing's really changed, has it." She smiled at him. "Has it?" he asked more seriously, looking at her for the answer, and Laura shook her head. He picked up the cooler box and handed a couple of bottles to her, and they walked down toward the beach together in silence, casting long shadows in the setting sun.

"Potato salad, some biscuits—ah, there's some cheese in here, too. Crisps. Some ham. And mustard. Great."

"You didn't make this, did you?" said Laura, leaning forward on the sand to peer inside the box.

Nick paused as he lifted out a bottle of wine. He said, "Er, no."

"So, who did?" Laura said mischievously, genuinely curious. She stretched her legs out on the blanket, feeling more relaxed.

Nick lay on his back, looking slightly embarrassed. "Um . . . the housekeeper." He scratched his face.

"Who is called . . . ?"

"Mrs. Hillyard."

"And does she have a scrubbed red face and wipe her hands on her apron all the time and say things like, 'Ooh, I say, Mr. Hudson'?"

"No," said Nick, trying not to smile. "She's a very elegant lady from a very expensive agency, and I'm terrified of her." He handed her a glass of wine. "Charles persuaded me."

"To ask her to do a picnic?" said Laura incredulously.

"Yes," said Nick. "I know. Pathetic."

"A bit," said Laura. She laughed. "I don't get it."

"What?" said Nick.

"Your relationship with him, I really don't. If I was him, I'd have cleared out long ago."

"Relationships are funny things," said Nick. "Now, have some wine."

He clinked her glass.

"Talking of relationships . . ." said Laura carefully.

Nick looked up. "What?" he said.

"It's stupid of me to ask," said Laura, hating herself for remembering in the first place. "My mum mentioned it—when we were coming back from Chartley, after I'd just met you."

"Yes?" said Nick. He put his hand on her ankle, which was the bit of her nearest to him.

"She read it in the paper," said Laura. "Believe me, I don't read that kind of thing. She loves it. It's none of my business anyway."

"What on earth are you talking about?" said Nick, rolling over so he was facing her.

"You've got a girlfriend, haven't you?" Laura said.

"Laura," said Nick. "Don't."

"It was Cecilia something, wasn't it? Oh, God. I shouldn't have mentioned it."

Nick shook his head. "Cecilia Thorson. It's not true." He drank some wine.

Laura said uncertainly, "But Mum said she saw a picture of Cecilia Whatsis and the Marquis of Ranelagh in the paper, and it said they were going to get engaged."

"That's what she thinks," said Nick roughly. "Let's not talk about it, please, Laura?"

She was silent, a worm of fear crawling through her, turning the wine in her stomach into vinegar. This was how it was going to be, wasn't it? Did she really not matter at all to him? Was she just a holiday fling while his posh girlfriend was away? Already things were different, were altered, because of who he was. It was unfair—and it wasn't right, most of all.

"No, Nick," she said suddenly. "Tell me. I can't help knowing it, can I? You owe me that much, after all. Come on. I know it's hard for you—but it's hard for me, too, having just found out. And really"—she flung up her hands in a fleeting gesture—"it's not as if we're married. We've only just met."

His face softened. "You're right," he said. "It's ridiculous, I'm sorry. I shouldn't be even bothering you with all that stuff." He put his hand on her ankle again, and she put her hand on top of his and moved closer.

"Cecilia—she thinks she's seeing me. But she's not."

"Right," said Laura, confused. "What the hell does that mean?"

Nick sat up. "It doesn't mean anything. I'm single. I swear to you. But she—we were set up, by my sister Rose. Her husband, Malcolm—he works in the City. He knows Cecilia's parents, the Thorsons. When Dad died two years ago, he was very helpful when I had to move to Chartley, take over the house."

"How?" said Laura.

"Dad—well, he hadn't been the same since my mother left. You know. Things were starting to slide, and he'd left some significant debts. Malcolm was very helpful; so was Lars Thorson. They gave me advice, helped make some investments, so I could get things on an even keel again, or begin to."

Laura felt a rush of admiration for him, again. "It's only been two years?"

"Yes," Nick said. He waved it aside. "Anyway. Cecilia. They set us up, and we went out on a few dates, to a few parties in town, that sort of thing. Charity dos, you know. But that's it."

Charity dos. Parties in town. It sounded hilariously unlike Laura's life; the gap was so wide, she could have laughed—perhaps that would have got rid of the sick feeling she had. "So you haven't slept together or anything," she said, trying to be calm.

Nick looked uncertain. "Well," he said. "Yes, we slept together, of course."

Boys, Laura thought. I love the way their idea of not going out with people is completely different from girls'. "Right," she said.

"But she's—um. I finished it with her, last month. Not that there was anything to finish, but I didn't want her getting the wrong idea."

"The wrong idea?"

"We're not compatible," Nick said. "She's obsessed with the

house, all that. Having a title. And I can't stand that kind of stuff. It's tacky."

"Oh, I don't know," Laura said, feeling some sympathy for Cecilia. "The old me—wow, I'd have loved that."

"Who's the old me?" said Nick. He topped up her glass. "Is this something else you haven't told me? Do you have two personalities?"

"No," said Laura, trying to think how best to explain herself. "No, it's stupid. Just—the old me, well . . ." She ran her hand through her hair. "Nothing."

"Go on," said Nick. "I won't laugh, I promise."

"Well, I was a bit . . . head in the clouds," Laura said. "Fairy tales and all that. I wanted to meet Prince Charming. It got me into a lot of trouble."

"Really."

"Yes, it did. Well, not anymore. I threw away all my videos. There," she said fervently. "I haven't told anyone that."

"What videos?" said Nick, bewildered.

Laura reddened. "Forget it. Just . . . stupid films and stuff. And books and things. I only read improving books now. And I watch interesting foreign-language films."

"You do?" said Nick. "What interesting foreign-language films have you seen recently?"

"Er. I haven't yet. But I'm going to when I get back to town. You know what it's like. Well, you don't," she said, wondering if Nick ever went to the cinema. Perhaps he had his own private cinema. No, he didn't seem the type, really. Suddenly a mental image of him dressed like the postcard of his ancestor, all medals and morning dress, striding into the King's Lynn multiplex popped into her head, and she laughed. The wine in her glass slopped over onto the blanket and her arm. "Sorry," she said, and knelt up to reach for a napkin.

"Here," Nick said. He leaned over her, caught her arm, and wiped it with a tea towel, rubbing the bare skin gently. They looked at each other, saying nothing, and Laura sat back down again.

"So," he said. "We're okay, then? The Cecilia thing? I'm not avoiding it, it's just that it's nothing."

"No, I know," said Laura. "It's just a bit weird. I don't want you to think I'm making a big deal about it either. It's just, there's lots I don't know about."

"I know," he said after a moment's pause. "And I'm sorry. For being uncommunicative. I don't like talking about myself much. As you may have noticed."

"Just a bit," said Laura.

"Even to you," he said.

"But—" Laura was taken aback. "I hardly know you."

"Yes and no," said Nick. "Does that make sense?"

"It makes a lot of sense," said Laura. "When I think that a week ago I'd never met you—that's weird."

"It is," he said. "It's almost unbelievable."

They looked at each other, and fell silent.

Nick produced a bottle of whisky as it grew colder, and poured some into Laura's glass.

"Here, have this, it's getting chilly," he said, and threw her his sweater.

Laura took it gratefully and put it on. She didn't want to move or dispel the magic charm of the evening, knowing that when they left more things would be said, things would change; wanting to leave it like this, perfect, suspended in a bubble. She wrapped her hands round the glass, gazing contemplatively across the sand.

"It's getting late," said Nick after a while.

"Yes," said Laura, looking out at the dark petrol gray of the sea in the night.

"You're not driving, are you?" he said, laughter in his voice.

"I brought the car, yes," said Laura. She rolled over on the blanket, so she was facing him.

"So . . ." Nick said. He put his hand on her shoulder. His skin felt warm against hers.

She said, "But I don't think I can drive it home."

"Ah," said Nick softly, and she could feel his breath in her ear, on her neck. "I was kind of hoping you'd say that."

"So . . ."

He sat up and leaned over Laura in one fluid motion, his hands on either side of her arms. She said nothing, just lay there and looked up at him, watching him and, behind him, the stars in the black sky.

"Laura—" he said. "God."

"Yes?" she said softly.

"You are coming back with me, aren't you?"

"Yes," she said, reaching up and putting her arms around him. He lowered himself gently onto her and kissed her once. Then he groaned and sat back.

"Let's go home," he said. "Let's not waste any more time, Laura. Let's get back." He stood up and held out his hand, pulling her up. "It's definitely your last night, isn't it?"

"Yes," said Laura. "Nick—don't let's—"

"I know." He nodded. "No big deal. You can't stay for one more night, can you? It's just—"

"No," she said firmly. "I can't." They were still for a moment, and Laura felt incredibly sad, and she didn't know why.

"Here," he said, suddenly practical. "Take this blanket. And, oh, I'd better warn you. Just—watch out for my sister."

"Lavinia?" said Laura.

"I'm not worried about Lavinia so much. No, Rose. We don't want to bump into her. Disaster if she saw us."

"Right," said Laura, feeling like a sluttish scullery maid being seduced by the master in *Upstairs Downstairs.* "I'll be careful," she said, brushing the sand off her dress.

chapter twenty-four

They walked back, talking quietly, until they reached the edge of the house again, as they had done two nights earlier. Laura felt as if she were in *Groundhog Day*, or *Groundhog Day* meets *Gosford Park*. She said so to Nick, who laughed. He reached over to kiss her, but broke away, looked up, and said under his breath, "Damn."

"What?"

"Rose is still up—look, there's her light."

"I don't mind—" Laura began, but Nick took her hand.

"It'll be a real pain if she sees us."

"Yes, of course," Laura said automatically, wondering if she should offer to fold herself up and climb into the cooler box.

"I know," said Nick suddenly. "I've got an idea. Come with me."

He led her down the path and through the trees, so that they skirted the house, which was almost entirely in darkness. This was his *home,* Laura thought as she followed him, shaking her head in disbelief at what she was doing.

Finally they came to the front of the house, their feet crunching quietly on the gravel.

"We'll go in through the front door," said Nick. "Rose is at the back, she won't hear, and the people who live on this side won't notice. They'll just think it's Sam, one of the footmen, doing his rounds."

"Er . . . through the front door? Right," said Laura, bemused by the mention of footmen.

They walked up to the center of the great façade and up the stairs, which Laura had climbed only two days before, dragging her heels behind her mother's exclamations of pleasure and her father's comments about Doric columns. On the small, balustraded terrace before the black-paneled door, almost twice the size of Laura's whole sitting room, Nick paused and rummaged in his jacket.

"Keys. Ah, here they are."

He slid a huge brass key into the lock, turned it smoothly, and pushed the door open. He smiled sardonically, as if he were aware of the strangeness of the situation, and inclined his head.

"After you, madam."

Through the ghostly, dark house they walked, as quietly as possible. Through the great hall, where Laura looked at the huge map of the county and smiled; past the ballroom, where George had got his digital camera stuck on pause, precipitating a mini-crisis; up the great staircase, where their feet slapped on the cold, hard marble, and under the immense chandelier that hung over them dead and still, its crystal pendants dull.

They reached the library in silence, and Nick stopped, put his hand on her arm. "Nearly there," he whispered in her ear. "I'm sorry about this, this is ridiculous, but we'll have to go through the house. Quietly—I don't want James to hear. He's Sam's nighttime partner in crime. Or not."

"It's fine," hissed Laura in a stage whisper that made both of them jump apart a little. "It's fine," she repeated.

Nick gave her a strange look. "You okay?" he said. "Not having second thoughts?"

Laura wasn't having second thoughts; she rarely did once she'd got to this stage with someone. She was, however, trying not to freak out about everything else to do with the situation. Normally, when she was climbing the stairs of someone's house in silence, it was to avoid a sleeping flatmate, or a drunk friend passed out on the sofa.

"No, no," Laura whispered again. "I'm not very good at whispering, that's all. Sorry."

"That's okay," said Nick. "I'm not surprised, knowing you as well as I do. You're a bit too much of a ranter to be able to whisper particularly well." He smiled and took her hand. "Hold my hand. I've just got to check they've locked up."

He walked toward the library door, Laura following. She watched as he grasped the old brass handle and looked in. His gaze ran down the long room, where moonlight was starting to creep onto the carpet through the slivers left by the blinds.

"*The Happy Marriage,*" she said out loud, looking toward the lonely painting at the end of the great room.

"Yes," said Nick, almost to himself. "It was my mother's favorite."

"Really?" said Laura.

"Yes. She loved it. She used to dance along the room with me when I was little, doing a jig. And then my sisters used to make me reenact it with them when we were small. I had to be the bridesmaid."

Laura laughed quietly.

He smiled. "And now we're advised that we can't afford the insurance to have the whole series out on display during the summer. Pathetic, isn't it."

"It's beautiful," said Laura inadequately, feeling foolish.

"Beautiful," Nick said slowly, looking around him, leading her into the library. "Do you think so? Yes. Of course it is."

She caught the fleeting expression on his face, and it disturbed her. It was dark, ugly, his mouth curling in an unhappy smile.

"It's all yours," said Laura impulsively, saying something to break the silence. "Isn't that weird?"

"It's very weird, especially when you find yourself getting used to it," said Nick quietly. "You start to think this is what a normal life's like. It's not. I have to keep reminding myself of that; otherwise I'd go insane."

Laura didn't know what to say. She agreed with him.

"I'm sorry I lied," he said frankly, almost to himself. "It's just you get in here, and *this* becomes the big deal." His gesture encompassed the room, the fields outside. "Not the important stuff, and I don't want you to think—"

"Stop worrying," said Laura. "I mean it. I'm not here because of all of this. I'm here because of you."

She looked around the big, beautiful room. It was completely still, not a sound within or outside. As if it were just the two of them, nothing more in the world, in this room alone. Nick took her hand and held it. She watched him; the skin on her palm was creamy white in the moonlight streaming through the great windows. He raised her hand to his lips, and kissed the tips of her fingers gently.

"I just keep thinking perhaps you're made-up," he said softly.

"Me too," said Laura. "Me too."

They stayed like that in complete silence, staring at each other, in the center of the long, silvery room.

"Are we still friends, then?" he said, his voice light.

Laura looked up at him. "Oh, Nick, I don't think we're friends anymore, do you?"

No one disturbed them as they continued on their way through the corridors, and it was almost a relief to reach the strangely familiar surroundings of his room, a comparative haven of normality tucked inside this great shell of a home.

Nick dumped the cooler box and the blanket on the floor, then took off his jacket, his back to her, while Laura took off her shoes. She felt suddenly ill at ease, and the white noise of questions she had about all this and him, how strange it was, how something was bothering her about it but she didn't know what, started to rise within her. But then he turned around, and she wondered how she could have thought he was anyone else but him, how she could have thought she didn't know him, because she did.

He walked toward her. "I've wanted to do this since the moment I laid eyes on you, you know that?" he said, and he calmly put his hands on her hips and kissed her again. As his lips met hers, Laura felt as if she were melting into him. He kissed her slowly, wrapping his arms around her, so that he held her tightly. As she returned his kiss more urgently, his tongue inside her mouth, pushing, sliding slowly into her, she could feel the strength of his body against hers, as if they were breathing together, as if they were in their own world. She stopped thinking, for the first time in days, weeks. She simply felt, in her heart and head, and soon she barely knew where she was.

Nick's eyes were black. He gave her that old, sweetly familiar smile, half mocking, half comforting. She knelt on the edge of the bed and wrapped her arms around his neck, and he buried his face in her skin.

"Don't go tomorrow," he said, his voice husky. "Laura—don't go. . . ."

Laura put her finger to his lips, and he pushed her back. They fell on the bed together, and Laura remembered fleetingly how big it had felt when she had got into it alone, two nights ago. How strange that seemed now. Nick was on top of her; she could feel that he was hard already, and her last thought before she gave herself up to it, to him, was how strange it was, too, that it should feel so right, as if she had known him for years. Her very own romantic hero—yet it turned out that who he was couldn't matter less to her; all she wanted was to feel him, to be joined to him, to stay like that forever.

chapter twenty-five

Laura dreamed that she was back at home in her flat with Yorky. He was walking toward her, smiling, pleased to see her, and behind him were Jo and Chris, Simon plonking his backpack down on the ground, Hilary and Hamish. Rachel was there with a picnic hamper, looking overjoyed, and they all had a picnic, until Dan appeared with Amy and three small children; and suddenly all their friends dispersed like pale, insubstantial ghosts, leaving her alone in the sitting room as Amy advanced toward her, holding a child in each arm, screaming at her, while Laura called out for help, but no one came, and Dan stood in the background, wringing his hands. . . .

She woke with a start, for the second time, in Nick's sparse, bright bachelor bedroom. She sat up, realizing where she was, and her heart lifted at the view of sunlight out the window. Nick wasn't there. She lay back again, remembering the previous evening, the night, Nick's hands on her body, all over her, the two of them together, and she stretched again, smiling. Funny to be alone in the bed, when the two of them together . . . Almost the perfect date, she thought, and she put her hand to her breast to calm her heart, which was fluttering most alarmingly.

She sat up again and bit her lip, turning her thoughts to more pragmatic matters, to the day ahead. She was in charge of meeting and greeting when the relatives arrived for Mary's lunch, handing out drinks and crisps, almost like a maitre d'. She looked at her watch. It was ten, she realized with horror. At this very moment, the Sandersons were on their way, getting closer and closer. As was Simon—she was going to see Simon, hurrah. She had to go, she had to help Mum. Right, she told herself. Get dressed, find Nick, and say good-bye.

Say good-bye. At the thought of doing just that, her heart turned over and sank. Good-bye. She couldn't. She wished he were here, so she could ask him—so she could convince herself it was the same with him, that she wasn't this convenient fling. That this whole sleeping-with-a-marquis thing wasn't a really bad idea. It didn't seem like it, here in the relatively comforting surroundings of his room. It hadn't seemed like it the previous night, as they lay together, tightly entwined, his hands stroking her hair, Nick whispering softly to her as she fell asleep. But today . . .

There was no point in reliving it, not just yet, she told herself. She got dressed, pulling on her sundress and gathering her things together. She opened the window, straightened the duvet cover. She was pragmatic, organized. It was what Mrs. Danvers would do. Then she sat on the edge of the bed to wait for him to come back, feeling rather marooned, not knowing why she wanted to cry, why suddenly this all seemed much sharper, more real, with more potential to hurt, to give her pain.

She was just admiring her post-bed hair, which looked like a tousled bird's nest, in the mirror when there was a knock at the door. Laura grimaced. What should she do? Pretend there was no one there? She was silent, hoping the person would go away.

The knock came again, and there was a pause. She could hear a light cough. "Nick?" came a low, tentative male voice.

The door opened slowly. Laura froze on the other side of the room, not sure where to go or what to do, feeling insanely English all of a sudden.

It was Charles. He caught sight of her and stopped on the threshold, looking horrified. "Ah. Oh, my goodness. Laura? I'm so dreadfully sorry. I had no idea."

"Hello," said Laura, feeling very unsure of herself. Had Charles known she was here? Did he know anything about the situation? Argh! It was embarrassing, she thought, then collected herself. Was it against the law? No, of course not.

Charles advanced a little way in and leaned against the thin edge of the door in an attempt to look natural and casual. It didn't really work. He was nervous, she noticed.

"I was—I was just going," said Laura, picking up her things.

"No, no," said Charles, looking alarmed. "Please, don't go on my account. I was looking for—for Nick. Do you know where he is?"

"No," said Laura, shoving her knickers into her bag and standing up straight. "I don't, I'm sorry. I woke up—er, he was gone. I was wondering where he was, too. Shall I give him . . . give him a message?"

She leaned nonchalantly against the side of the bed, misjudged its height, and nearly fell over. "Ah," said Charles, somewhat discomposed, as she flailed around trying to right herself. "Well, it's a couple of things, really, that's why I thought I'd better . . ." He looked at her, his pale blue eyes smiling shyly at her. "His sister's looking for him. Lady Rose, you know, she's staying here."

"Right," said Laura. "I don't really want to—" She looked up at him rather helplessly.

"Stay there," said Charles decisively. "He is useless, abandoning his—er, guests. I'll go and find him. You must want to—be on your way. Er." He coughed, mortified. "Not that I mean you're not welcome—ah."

Laura laughed. "Please don't worry, Charles. I do need to be off, though, I should find him."

"Of course," said Charles. "You know what he's like, starts talking to someone about something and he has to listen to all their problems for hours. That's Nick, though. You know how passionate he is about it all. The estate." He waved his arms vaguely.

"Yes," said Laura, not feeling she could tell the truth, which was, No, I don't, actually.

"It's the big dinner tonight," Charles confided, relaxing slightly. He folded his arms and leaned against the wall. "Phew. That's why Lady Rose is down. Hordes of Needhams gathering from all round the country."

"Oh," said Laura. "Why? What's the occasion?"

"Well," Charles said with enthusiasm, "Sir Guillibert Danvers, in—gosh, thirteen-something—anyway, some ancestor of Nick's, a knight in service to Eleanor of Aquitaine. Old boy got stabbed in some plot to oust the king. They got the pope to make him a saint by way of thanks. It's his feast day today. The whole family always gathers for it. It's a great evening."

Laura suddenly felt as if she were having a conversation with her father, so she said politely, "How interesting."

"Yes," said Charles. "Yes, yes. And it's rather a big do. Lady Rose does like everything just so. You know how these family gatherings can be—it's the same the world over."

Since there was no way Laura could reply "It bloody well is not the same, I'm telling you," she smiled instead. "Well," she said, "I bet they couldn't do it without you."

Charles looked shocked. "Oh, yes, they could," he said. "Absolutely. It's Nick, you know. He takes it all very seriously, the tradition of the thing. He's been up since the crack of dawn, discussing it with Mrs. Hillyard, sorting out everything."

"Oh," said Laura.

Charles coughed delicately. "Are you—er, are you coming tonight?"

"God, no!" said Laura. She looked around her wildly. "I mean—you know. This is—just a casual thing, you know. We've only just met, I don't think he'd invite me tonight, seriously."

"He asked for another place setting at his table," said Charles doubtfully. "That was yesterday. Perhaps—"

Perhaps Cecilia Thorson's suddenly available, Laura thought miserably, assailed by doubt and fear and hating it. This had to stop, it was ridiculous. She looked up at Charles. "Well, if you're off to look for him, then . . ."

"Yes," said Charles, collecting himself. "Sorry to have kept you. Laura, it's so nice to see you again." He walked to the door. "I'll send Nick up to you. Ah—see you soon, I'm sure."

"Thanks," said Laura.

Outside, a wood pigeon cooed softly. She walked to the window and looked out, taking in the view, thinking how beautiful, how unreal it all was, and she was actually here, it wasn't some film. Which was why it was so awful that it was all starting to feel so wrong. She closed the window, slung her bag over her shoulder, and left the room.

She walked quietly down the stairs, trying to remember in this huge labyrinthine maze of doors and corridors how best to find her way out without bumping into a tour party, a relative, or the man himself. She didn't want to go without saying good-bye, but what else could she do? It was the coward's way out—but then, she was a coward, not up to living this life. She reached the bottom of the stairs and opened the door that she was sure led out to the rose garden at the side, when suddenly a voice called from above her, "Laura!"

It was Nick, coming down the stairs toward her, breathing hard as though he had been running. "Where are you going?"

"I'm—I have to go," said Laura, standing in the doorway.

"You were going to leave without saying bye?" he said, his tone light but his eyes dark in his tanned face. He stepped outside, motioning her to come with him, and shut the door. "You know, it's polite to thank the host for the lovely evening."

"I know," said Laura, blushing in the sudden sunlight and feeling horrible. "I know, thank you, thank you so much." She allowed her eyes meet his. "I didn't know where to find you—and I didn't want to come barging in—then Charles said you were busy—I thought I'd . . ." She trailed off, knowing it sounded pathetic.

"Laura," Nick said. He took her hands in his, folding them into his clasp. "I'm so sorry. You were asleep. I tried to wake you, but you turned over and ignored me. Then you hit the pillow and said something, and I thought I'd better clear out in case you tried to attack me in your sleep. I had a few things to do, boring things to sort out for tonight. So I came downstairs. I checked on you, but you were still out—I should have come back earlier, I'm sorry. Do you have to go right now?"

"Yes," said Laura. "I really do, I'm afraid. The relatives are descending any moment now—and from what Charles tells me, the same's true of you."

"Yes," he said. "Look—"

"Thanks," said Laura. "Thanks again, Nick, it was a wonderful night. All of it." She stood on tiptoe and kissed his cheek. "Look, I hope—it'd be nice to . . ."

He didn't say anything, just stood there staring at her. A muscle ticked in his cheek. Her heart sank, though she didn't really know what would be best.

At that moment, a sturdy blonde with rigid hair appeared from around a corner, talking to Charles. "Nick must know I wanted to discuss the apples with him—good God! Hello?" She glared at Laura as if Laura were wearing a stripy top and an eye mask and carrying a bag labeled SWAG.

"Nick!" she said, still staring at Laura. "There you are. I've been looking absolutely bloody everywhere for you."

"Rose," said Charles, collecting himself. "Rose, this is Laura. She's a friend of Nick's. She's just—are you going?"

Rose's eyes bulged, and she smoothed her rather strained, correct shift dress over her hips. "And how do you do?" she said, nodding at Laura.

Not having been addressed like that by anyone since she had met Father Christmas on a Brownies trip in 1983, Laura let out an involuntary snort of laughter, which she tried to disguise as a sneeze. Nick was staring at her in bemusement, and she realized how strong the family resemblance was as she turned from brother to sister and said, "I'm so sorry—lovely to meet you. I must go, I'm afraid."

"Laura," said Nick. "I'll—"

"Nick, the roses really *are* a frightful mess," said Rose, turning to her brother and almost blocking Laura out. "Sam says he's started on them, but how, I want to know. And about the apples, I have a good jelly recipe from someone. And Great-aunt Teresa's arriving by train, can someone please be sent to pick her up? I particularly asked, but no one seems to know anything about it."

Laura was waiting for him to say something else to her, but he didn't. He stared distractedly at her, and then at his sister, and said, "Oh, God, Rose. I don't know. I—"

"Bye, then," said Laura. "Thanks again, Nick. Bye, Charles. Bye—er, Rose," she added uncertainly, not sure how you addressed someone like Lady Rose Balmore; and that, if anything, was surely reason enough that she shouldn't stick around much longer. She raised her hand in a gesture of farewell and walked briskly around the back of the house, up toward the woods and her car, and she didn't look back once.

chapter twenty-six

By the time Laura pulled up in front of Seavale, it was after eleven, and there were two new cars in the drive. She sat in the car for a moment, pulled the mirror over, and looked at herself. She didn't look any different. Tired, maybe, with dark smudges under her eyes. Not older or wiser, which wasn't surprising, since she still hadn't learned anything, it would seem. She rested her head on the steering wheel briefly, her mind racing back over the past eighteen hours or so.

Was she *so* stupid that she still hadn't learned a thing, despite everything she'd been through? The dreadful thought that Nick was just another one to add to the list, the most spectacular cock-up of all Laura's failed romantic endeavors, was almost too much to handle. It looked like it could be, she had to admit. Meet some guy, fail to spot he's the ideal romantic hero to beat them all, spend your holiday with him, fall for him, sleep with him, and never mind that a) he's one of the richest people in the country; b) he owns more land than is covered by the distance from Mum and Dad's house to your titchy flat in North London; c) you have nothing in common—he's a marquis, for God's sake, and you're a reading coordinator for a local council; and d) he has a girlfriend. Well, he claims he doesn't, but really—Laura banged her head against the steering wheel softly—it's clear that's what *she* thinks she is.

No, she thought. Best that it ends like this, a lovely memory, a beautiful summer interlude, like something out of a book. Leave it there, recognize it for what it is. And now, go inside, smile brightly, and help your mother with the Foster family's equivalent to Nick and his Sir Elephant Something-or-Other evening. At the thought of how hilariously disparate those two gatherings were, she smiled, realizing she was right to be putting it behind her, and pulled the keys out of the ignition. Her heart ached, a stab of something, but she said briskly out loud, "Indigestion," and got out of the car.

"Mum, Mum! It's me, I'm back!"

Angela appeared from the lawn, rubbing her hands on a tea towel. She smiled thinly. "Oh, Laura. There you are. At last!"

"Sorry, Mum," Laura called, as she walked across the gravel. "It was all a bit complicated. I'm really sorry. Here, now, what do you want me to do?"

"Well, set the table, maybe," said Angela, still rather frosty.

"Are they here?" asked Laura in a whisper. "Simon? Is he here?"

"They're outside, having drinks. Robert and your dad are doing the barbecue," said Angela, unbending somewhat at her daughter's apology. "Fran's brought Ludo, that's nice, isn't it."

"Right," said Laura, rolling her eyes. She threw her bag into the corner of the room. "What can I do?"

"Get Annabel another drink, I think," said Angela demurely. "She had a somewhat . . . *fraught* journey up here, I think. Cedric and Jasper were rather . . . boisterous, I understand."

Since the last time Laura—who was too young to recognize Cedric Forsythe as the demigod he was to George and a generation of impressionable young British schoolboys—had seen him, Cedric had taken her and Mary to see *Anything Goes* and had alarmed everyone by breaking wind violently and deliberately throughout, Laura was not surprised. And since she knew that he and Jasper were incredibly naughty when they were together, she was even less surprised when a voice came booming from the lawn, "Is that Laura? Is that gorgeous Laura? Ha-ha, hahahaha. Come here, beautiful."

Laura found herself being swept into Jasper Davidson's navy-besmocked chest. He kissed her on the head. "You're too thin, gorgeous. Far too thin. Ah, Cedric, look who's here."

"Dear girl," said Cedric Forsythe mellifluously, advancing toward her with a happy smile on his face. "I am truly glad to see you here." He handed her his glass of champagne. "Come and find your grandmother. God, your cousins are awf—ah, Annabel! Dear lady, how are you?"

Aunt Annabel, obviously hearing the commotion, had arrived in the doorway and was regarding Laura with minimal warmth. Laura went over and kissed her, feeling rather like she was in some kind of random 1930s farce. Annabel was wearing a strangely formal all-in-one buttoned-through housecoat in striped khaki with fake cuffs, adorned with several pieces of carefully understated—but nonetheless ever-so-slightly ostentatious—gold jewelry. She was about fifty-five, but she was suspended in time. She could have been seventy, or thirty—one never really knew. She was so correct, seldom betraying any emotion, that Laura couldn't remember her aging or acting any other way. Where Annabel's stepsister waved her arms, worried, dropped wooden spoons covered in batter on the floor, and generally despaired of herself, her husband, her children, Annabel had, Laura thought, probably never suffered a moment's self-doubt in all her life. And she kind of wished she were Annabel, for one brief moment.

"Ah, Laura, you're here," she said. "Goodness. You have been ages, haven't you? With your friend from the wetlands place, dear me. Angela"—she redirected her steely gaze toward her stepsister—"your mother's getting rather hungry. How long till we eat, do you think?"

"Grrmshowalla," muttered Angela as she turned toward Annabel. "Not long, Annabel. Shall we all go outside and finish our drinks?"

Angela made a sweeping motion that included everyone, and Cedric and Jasper turned away from the drinks cabinet and shuffled toward the door.

"Yes, but—" Aunt Annabel said, looking over toward the kitchen.

"I suppose it depends on how long it really takes for Robert to get the barbecue going," Angela said serenely, and sailed outside.

Round one to Mum, thought Laura, settling back into her normal life, and she raised her glass to George as she stepped out onto the terrace. It was hot, almost too hot, and George was slaving over the barbecue, sweat forming perilously on his jaw, while Robert lounged next to him chatting negligibly about something, a bored expression on his large face. Laura's father glared at her as she appeared; then his expression softened, and he rolled his eyes and flipped a burger in a fluid motion that impressed his daughter deeply.

"Where's Simon?" she said again.

Annabel made a *moue*. "Oh, dear."

"Not here yet," said Angela tightly. "I'm sure he'll call, though. He knows it's today."

Laura knew from long experience that the phrase "he knows it's today" absolutely meant the person concerned did *not* know it was today, or was *not* going to turn up.

"Oh, man!" she muttered as she followed her mother into the kitchen, unreasonably cross with her absent brother, although deep down she had never seriously thought he might turn up on time. She was cross because she missed him, and the thought of having a normal person here had been sustaining her these seven days. "Shall I call him?"

"I've tried," said Angela. "His phone's switched off."

"It's always switched off," said Laura. "I don't know why he took it there. I'll try him again anyway. Perhaps it's just because he's in a tunnel on his way to King's Lynn. Don't worry, Mum, it'll—"

"Lawww-rah!" came a booming voice behind her, and Laura turned around, to be snaffled in a headlock by Fran and patted painfully on the back by Fran's indecently hefty boyfriend, Ludo.

"Lululu! Laura's back. Hi, Laura! Wow, how are you?" Fran stepped back, bouncing on her huge sneakers, her stubby ponytail wagging behind her head like a pug's tail. "Wow!" she said again. "You're here! We thought you'd just decided not to bother! Lululu thought you'd pulled, but I said, 'God, no *way*, Laura never pulls, can you imagine!' Hey, Ludo, get Laura a drink!"

"Hey, Laura," said Ludo, who was a huge man-mountain. His bulk momentarily blocked out the sun as he stood facing Laura, his hands on his hips. "Hi. *Really* great to see you. What do you want? Some poo? We bought a couple of bottles."

"Argh," said Laura, disentangling herself from her cousin's grasp. "Can you just . . . give me a moment? I just want to dump my stuff."

"LULULU!" screamed Fran, even louder than usual. "Come and say hiiiiiiiiii to Laura!"

"I'm not going anywhere," said Laura desperately. "I'll be back in two seconds, I promise—oh, hi, Lulu."

"Hiiiiiiiiiiii, Laura," said Lulu, as thin and sepulchrally pale as ever. "So," she continued as Ludo handed Laura a glass of champagne, "where have you been? Really great to see you." She said this with the enthusiasm of one who has just been given the present of a dead rat.

"Mum said she thought you weren't going to show up, just like Simon!" squeaked Fran behind her. "Wow, Laura, we've got loads to fill you in on. Ludo and I are buying a flat! In Battersea, well, it's kind of Battersea, toward Clapham. It's *really* lovely. You're still sharing, aren't you?"

Laura cast an anguished look about the patio. She didn't know what to do, how to react. Her father was still slaving over the barbecue; Mum was talking animatedly to Annabel, who was looking bored; Jasper and Cedric were throwing olive pits over the wall into the sand dunes, trying to hit day-trippers. Suddenly she caught sight of the person she'd been looking for.

"Sorry, give me a minute," she said briskly. "I just want to say hi to Granny."

Leaving her cousins gaping behind her, Laura strode over to where Mary was sitting in her wicker chair, watching the progress of the olive-throwing and nursing a gin and tonic.

"Hi, Granny," she said, and bent down to give her grandmother a kiss. Mary's cheek felt cold and papery, beautifully soft to the touch. She patted her shoulder. "I'm so sorry I'm late. Happy birthday. Are you having a good time?"

"Oh, yes, darling," said Mary, opening her blue eyes very wide. "You're here, then. Thank goodness; I'd given you up."

"God, Granny," said Laura. "I didn't mean to. I overslept. I'm so sorry."

Mary bent her index finger, motioning for Laura to come closer. "It's fine," she said. "You're here now."

"I know, I know. I feel—I feel terrible. Anyway, we're all here, and it's such a lovely day," said Laura manically, feeling like a children's entertainer. All she needed was a stripy jacket and some huge clown's shoes.

"Go and see if your mother wants any help," said Mary. "I'm afraid your aunt rather puts her on her mettle." Laura nodded obediently and turned to go. "And—Laura?"

Laura turned back to face her. "Yes, Gran?"

"Will you tell me who he is one day?"

"Who who is?" Laura said stupidly, blinking in the sunlight.

"Whoever he is you've been spending all your time with." Laura gaped at her. "I know you, darling. Now, go."

"Er," said Laura, feeling that since she'd arrived home, all she'd done was speak in a series of grunts. "Ur. Argh. Well—it's complicated."

"I'm sure it is." Mary smiled. "It always is."

"It's nothing," said Laura, standing firm. "Nothing at all. Part of my new rule."

"We shall see," said Mary. "Darling, be a dear and get me another gin and tonic." She held out her glass.

"You don't want any champagne?"

"Loathe the stuff," said Mary cheerfully, glaring balefully at Ludo, who was flexing his muscles and showing them to Fran and Lulu, amidst screams of delight. "Some ice and a—"

"—thick slice," Laura finished. "Sure, be right back."

They were everywhere, these Sandersons, blocking her way to the kitchen, making loud noises, cheerfully insulting her father—"No, old man, that burger's charcoal on the outside, but you've left it raw inside, look"—and subtly digging at her mother: "Angela, your salad was rather small, so I've taken it out of the fridge and added some spinach." Laura leaned against the wall of the kitchen and breathed deeply. The events of this morning seemed an age away already. She would have time to digest them all when she caught the train home that night and said good-bye to all this. Tonight she would be back home, back in the flat with Yorky watching TV, flicking pistachio shells into the bin, having a beer, telling Jo on the phone all about her holiday. If Laura wanted to tell—she thought she probably didn't. She checked her phone. There was a text message from Yorky:

Need your help asap. Please advise return time. Having romantic crisis with Becky downstairs. She is single. Think we're going on date tonight. Not sure. Need you to be laughing flatmate who thinks am great. V important. Love to yr gran. Yx

The phone in the hall rang, and she ran to answer it. "Hello?" she said uncertainly.

"Laura?" came a distant voice, accompanied by what sounded like someone waving sheets of metal in the background. "It's—mon."

"Simon!" Laura yelled. "You're here! Where are you? Ely? Cambridge?"

"Callao," came the distant voice.

"Where?"

"It's near Lima."

"Simon—" said Laura. "Oh, God. Why aren't you here?"

"I—chew—amazing!" Simon's voice said happily. "Can I speak to—?"

"Who?"

"Um!"

"Mum? Hold on." Angela appeared in the corridor, a squeezed

lemon in her hand. "So you're not coming back?" Laura yelled unnecessarily.

"Isst my—!" Loud metal sheet waving in the background. "Ing to see the—gasts!"

"Oh, good grief," Laura said, turning to her mother.

"Give me the phone," Angela said crossly. "Silly boy. What happened?"

"Tell Gran I—her!" Simon said in Laura's ear.

"What?"

"Yes!"

"Simon! Are you—" Laura began, but the line went dead. She banged the phone hard on the cradle in annoyance.

"He's gone?" Angela said.

"Yes," said Laura.

"Where is he?"

"Somewhere called Callao. It's near Lima. That's all I could get out of him," said Laura. "Sorry, Mum. He sounded okay, though."

"Hm," said Angela. "It's just as well I didn't speak to him. I'd have said something unforgivable."

Laura reflected with some amusement that the safety and well-being of her son came a very distant second to Angela's desire for him to fulfill his family commitments. She looked at her phone again; another text message had just arrived;

Pls reply re return time. Y. PS Just had call from Simon. Not coming back till next month. In Callao. Is near Lima apparently. Sounds nice.

"Argh!" Laura growled, surprised only that she was still surprised at the crapness of blokes. From the garden, George said loudly, "Lunch is ready," and Laura followed her mother outside, with a heart as heavy as Aunt Annabel's mashed potatoes.

They sat down to eat a few minutes later, and as the others tucked into their food, Laura sat there staring at her plate, half expecting it to talk to her. She felt suddenly very weary. As her father munched happily away on his burger, equilibrium briefly restored as Sandersons on both sides ignored him, she gazed around the table, unsure of what to say or do.

She speared a leaf of salad, looked at it, then put it back on the plate. She wasn't hungry.

"You all right, dear?" said Cedric Forsythe.

"Ye-yes," said Laura. "Just tired, that's all." She pulled herself together. No, not again. She'd be home this evening, ready to advise Yorky on Becky from downstairs. That sounded promising. And there was the hearing at work on Wednesday, she reminded herself. She had to get through that. That was what she'd focus on. That, and the shape of the lettuce leaf she was eating. Focus, focus. Don't let this become a thing, like all the other times. Just don't think about it, she told herself; and second by second, minute by minute, the lunch went on its way, as Mary relaxed, the sun shone, and this odd assortment of quasi-relatives concentrated on trying to have a good time, unconscious of their nearest neighbors' most fundamental hopes and dreams. It was ever so.

chapter twenty-seven

The clock ticked on, nearer the time she'd be able to get away, go back home, while Laura nodded and smiled and said things like "Yes, I love rugby" to Ludo and "Yes, I love sushi" to Lulu. Annabel held court at one end of the table, ignoring George and batting her lashes at Cedric in an alarming way. Cedric, in turn, was making overt eyes at Mary, who was frankly not repelling them as she might, while Robert was locked deep in conversation with Jasper, expounding upon the art market and its relative value in recent months. Jasper's eyes were drooping, and he stifled a yawn. Ludo and Fran joined in—they knew someone, a guy who'd been traveling, who'd taken some really wonderful wildlife photos in Africa, he should contact Jasper, shouldn't he? Wasn't Jasper's gallery looking for young new photographers, too?

When the conversation moved on to Lulu's latest career path—in this case, her burning desire to be a singer-songwriter—Laura tried not to let her incipient hysteria overwhelm her.

"So, what kind of thing . . ." Angela asked politely, piling up the bowls.

"Lululu's had a lot of interest already, haven't you, Lulu?" said Annabel, a fond smile cracking across her wintry expression. "She made a demo tape—that's a demonstration of her songs, Mary. At her friend Barrett's house. Some record producers are *very* interested, apparently. She'll have to pick and choose who she goes with."

"It's like—it's kind of my own stuff, my own message?" said Lulu, coming alive a little. "Like—like Dido, but she's so kind of . . . you know, *commercial.* Really hackneyed. It's sad, really. I don't want to be a sellout, you know. I just wanna do my own stuff, really say something with it. Stuff . . . that's happened to me. Really personal stuff, you know. Just for me, not for anyone else."

"So—you don't want to sell any copies," said Laura acidly, as Angela disappeared into the kitchen, followed by Jasper and Cedric.

"Yeah, of course I do. Obviously, if people like me . . ." She smiled coyly. "But"—Lulu's eyes glazed over, and she ran her finger around the rim of her glass so it made a chalky, whining sound—"I don't want to be on *Top of the Pops* or any of that shit. I don't want to be on magazine covers. I really don't want that stuff. I just want to write, songs and stuff?"

"Right," said Laura. The sound of Lulu's long fingers on the glass was excruciating. "So, who's asked you to be on the cover of a magazine, then?"

"No one," said Lulu, staring at her as if she were talking to a moron. "I just won't do it when they do ask."

"Right," said Laura, getting up. She said in a friendly tone, "I really hope no one's interested, then. Good luck, fingers crossed for you."

"How's the job, Laura?" Annabel called from the other end of the table. "I've hardly said two words to you so far. How is everything? Mum says she hasn't seen much of you lately."

"I didn't say that," said Mary patiently. "I said it was lovely to have her here and spend all this time with her."

"Yes," crooned Annabel, as if she were talking to an imbecile. "I know. *Lovely.*" She swept on. "That reminds me," she said inconsequentially, "I did a talk to a lovely group in Bexleyheath the other day, on preserves and the larder. And guess who was there?"

"Who?" said Mary, as Laura picked up the plates.

"Lady Rose Balmore," said Annabel.

"Who?" said Mary again, as Laura put the plates sharply down on the table.

"You know. The Marquis of Ranelagh's sister. *Lovely* woman. Chartley Hall."

Cedric was standing by the French windows, watching the group with a detached air. He said, "Vivienne Lash's daughter."

"Who?" said Annabel sharply, turning round to see who had interrupted her so rudely. "Oh, Cedric! Hello! Er—well, we obviously didn't talk about *that*, of course."

"I did a few films with her," said Cedric reminiscently. "Stunning creature. Flighty, though. Pretty mad. Still, gorgeous. Beautiful breasts."

"Belle, old girl, you remember," said Robert, harrumphing a cough into his big fist. "Actress. Nice looker. In all those fifties comedies. Ran off with the brother. 'Member?"

"Yes, of course I remember," said Annabel. "Anyway, Lady Rose Balmore. I had the chance to meet her, most interesting woman. We discussed Chartley, you know—"

"Yes," said George, coming alive abruptly. "We went there on Wednesday, had a great day, didn't we, Laura?"

"Ah," said Annabel, not particularly interested. "Well, we talked about Chartley. I asked her—I hope she didn't mind!—how her brother was getting on. He's younger than she, you know. Dominic. And she said very well, and then I told her the apples at Chartley were perfect for jelly, and she must be sure to make some this year. She said she would pass it on. Well!"

With a lightning flash of certainty, Laura knew, as sure as the tide was coming in, that this was what Lady Rose had been coming to find Nick about less than two hours ago, and the cosmic irony of this made her want to laugh out loud, but of course she didn't. She sat down again, rather weakly, and poured herself another glass of wine. There was some dead dry skin on her feet, and she bent down to pull it off in a small act of bad manners directed at her aunt.

"Anyway, I mentioned—only in passing—that my stepmother had a house on the coast nearby, and she was most kind about it, very nice. She even asked—"

"There's a car just pulled up in the drive," said Jasper, wandering out onto the terrace, drying a glass with a tea towel. "I wonder who . . ."

On the stone stairs by the side of the terrace, the sound of footsteps rang out, and a deep voice called tentatively, "I am—I'm sorry to disturb you. I just wanted a quick word with—is this where Laura's staying? Is she here?"

Laura sat up sharply, or rather tried to, and banged her head hard on the table. "Shit," she muttered, and turned around.

There, walking toward the table, walking toward her, was Nick. Right there. A real-life marquis, the most eligible man in the country, and he was looking for her.

Opposite her, Aunt Annabel's jaw dropped, so low that a bone clicked loudly in the silence.

chapter twenty-eight

"Can I help . . ." Robert began, half rising, but the words died on his lips.

"Oh, my God," said Lulu. "I know who you are! You were in *Harpers* last month! You're—"

"It's you," breathed George.

Aunt Annabel tried to pull herself together. "Good Lord," she said. "You—you're—"

"Ah," said Mary. "Of course! It's you."

"Hello," said Nick. "I'm Nick."

"Oh, my God!" said Angela, appearing on the terrace with a summer pudding in her hands. "You're . . ." She regained her composure remarkably fast, and said, "Pudding?"

Dominic Edward Danvers Needham, twelfth Marquis of Ranelagh, Earl of Albany Cross, returned the gazes of those grouped around the table. Lulu giggled and turned her stringy frame toward him, her huge eyes even more enormous than usual.

"Er, no, thanks," Nick said. "I'm so sorry to interrupt your lunch. I just wanted a quick word with Laura here . . ." He stared at her intently across the table. "Laura?"

Laura, meeting his gaze, stood up instantly. "I'll be back in a minute," she said to the others. "Er—start pudding without me."

"Fine," said Cedric, hugely enjoying the street theater going on in front of him. He took out his pipe.

Annabel glanced at it disapprovingly. "We're having pudding now," she said firmly, her eyes following Laura. "You can do that later."

Laura escorted him away from the goggling family group, down the stone steps that led to the beach.

"Sorry about that," said Nick as Laura shut the gate. "I hoped you might have finished." She turned to face him. "Hello," he said.

"Hi," she said uneasily. "I—"

"Look," said Nick, scratching his cheek, "I won't disturb you for long. I just wanted to see you again. You were so strange this morning. I wanted to make sure you were okay."

"Yes, of course," said Laura, impulsively reaching out and putting her hand on his chest. "I'm sorry, really sorry. I know you've got loads on today—I knew I was in the way."

He held her hand, pressing it against his rib cage. "That doesn't matter, Laura. Seriously. You're not—I was worried you might have regretted it. Last night."

"God, no," said Laura, rather too frankly. She clapped her hand to her mouth, as he smiled. "I mean . . . no, of course not. It was—" She met his eyes, and smiled back. "It was great. You know it was."

"It was," he agreed. He was still holding her hand. "I'm glad. I thought you might have had second thoughts. About it all."

"No," she said. "No, I haven't."

Nick looked up at the sky. He was suddenly serious. "It's getting late," he said, switching gears. "I can't stay long, either. I wanted to ask you to come tonight."

"Tonight?" said Laura, not understanding. "But you've got the . . ."

"Yes," said Nick. "It's the family dinner thing. It's good fun. Charles'll be there. And Lavinia." He grinned quickly. "You've met her, remember?"

"Yes," said Laura. Her head was spinning. "Yes, but—Nick—me? Come tonight? Why?"

"I want you to," he said simply. "I want to have you there. Please."

"Nick, it's a family thing," said Laura uncomfortably. "I wouldn't want to—"

"It's lots of people," said Nick. "Laura, I keep thinking I've shortchanged you this week. Not telling you who I was." He shook his head. "I thought perhaps you might like an evening at Chartley, just one more night, Laura. I don't want you to think I didn't tell you because of . . . some stupid reason."

"Go there—with you?" said Laura.

"Yes, absolutely," said Nick. "And I won't leave you on your own. I promise."

Laura felt slightly sick, like before a big meeting at work. How could she say no? How could she say she didn't want him like that, that she *didn't* want to be his date, the one everyone was staring at, like Prince William's new girlfriend or something? That she just wanted him, by himself, them together, nothing else . . . ? Oh, this was ridiculous, it was getting out of control. "Er—" she said, not knowing how to say that she couldn't, she didn't want to, that they weren't meant to be together at things like that.

But then she was saved. Her phone, which was in her pocket, rang.

She whipped it out of her pocket and jammed it up to her ear, turning away from Nick, who stared at her, obviously rather taken aback. "Hello?"

"Laura?" came a jagged voice, crackling over the sound of the sea and the wind.

"Yorky!" Laura said. "I've missed you! How are you? I didn't reply, did I? I've . . ."

"*Why* didn't you reply?" Yorky's voice was aggrieved. "Laura, I'm freaking out, man. Becky's coming up here! She's coming up here at eight."

"I can't believe you finally asked her out," said Laura. "Well done, man. What happened to the boyfriend?"

"I didn't ask her out!" Yorky practically shouted. "She asked me! And before I could screw it up, I said yes, without thinking! What am I going to do? She says she thinks I'm a lovely guy!"

Nick walked away, toward the sea. Laura watched him, the cast of his dark head, his wiry frame, the way he walked, his slightly stiff bearing.

"No!" she said, not paying attention. "She never said that, seriously?"

"Thanks," said Yorky. "Thanks for your support."

"Sorry." Laura tore her gaze away from Nick and swiveled round toward the dunes.

"So, when are you back tonight?" Yorky said. "You need to be here, to have the nuts in bowls ready, and all of that. While I'm cooking."

The last time Yorky had cooked for a girl on a date, he'd made salmon and cucumber mousse, which he'd whipped up in the food processor so much that it looked like gray foam. He'd served it with some carrots, and that was it.

"Why are you cooking?" said Laura. "Don't cook. Take her out! And why do I need to be there?"

"To talk me up!" said Yorky, his voice rising. "You have to say things like 'Hey, Yorks! Did you mend that cupboard while I was away? How did you reach it?' And I'll say, 'Well. Because I'm a big strong—' "

She was standing on the edge, the edge of the precipice, and she couldn't stop herself, didn't want to . . . "Yorky," Laura interrupted. "I'm not coming back tonight."

Nick heard. He turned around.

"Laura! No!" said the voice on the phone crossly.

"I'll be back first thing tomorrow. Promise. We can have a debrief then. I've got lots to tell you."

"Really?" Yorky sounded dubious. "So, sorry to be a bad flatmate. How are you? How's it all been?"

"Great, actually," said Laura, as Nick walked toward her. He raised his eyebrows. She put her finger to her lips, smiling gently at him, trying to breathe normally, pushing aside the voice that told her she was in too deep, she was vulnerable. He was there, in front of her, looking at her with those eyes; nothing else mattered—for the moment.

"So," Yorky said, recalling her to herself. "What are you doing tonight? Something mega-exciting, eh? Night at the pub with Ange and George?"

"No, a ball at a stately home with a marquis," said Laura, and Nick wrapped her in his arms and kissed her neck.

"Absolutely," said Yorky on the other end of the phone. "Me too. After I take Becky for a drink at the Cavendish, we're going on to dinner at Buckingham Palace."

"Well, there you go, then," said Laura. "Ow."

"You sound muffled, is something in the way?"

"No, just bad reception," said Laura. "I'd better go. See you tomorrow."

"Bye," said Yorky, as Laura dropped the phone on the ground, and Nick kissed her again.

"Who was that?" he asked after a minute or two.

"My flatmate. He's having a romantic crisis," said Laura, twining her arms around his neck. Trying not to sound anxious, she added, "Nick—tonight. Am I mad? It is going to be okay, isn't it?"

"I promise," said Nick. "You'll have a great time. Don't worry about any of the other crap." She scanned his face, and his hold on her tightened. "Honestly, Laura. I'll be there, won't I? We'll be there together."

She looked at him and smiled, and at that moment Fran, leaning over the wall up at the house, yelled down at her top decibel level that they were cutting the cake, and was Laura coming back up again or not?

Aunt Annabel appeared next to her, and boomed graciously, "Your lordship, you are, of course, *more* than welcome to—to eat the cake with us."

Laura's toes curled up in their flip-flops. She and Nick looked at each other, and she saw his lip curl, too. "Sorry," she said instantly.

"Don't be," said Nick. "Thank you," he called, his voice carrying up to Annabel. "I must go—thank you again, though."

He turned to Laura. "You'll stay the night, Laura?" He pulled her toward him. "So, can you get to mine for eight?"

"Absolutely," said Laura, ignoring that his invitation to make her way to his thirty-five-bedroom, five-thousand-acre, Grade One–listed estate by eight o'clock was phrased as "Can you get to mine for eight?" She smiled to herself, something she thought she might be doing a lot of before the evening was over and she got to be alone with him again. "I'll drive, then."

"That okay? I can send someone, if you want."

"No," said Laura, smiling. "You are funny."

"God. I really have to go," he said, looking at his watch. "Why am I funny?"

"No reason," said Laura. "I'll see you later."

"It's going to be great," said Nick. "I'm so glad you're coming."

chapter twenty-nine

She should have listened to herself, when she was getting ready that evening, thanking the God of Odd Packing she'd brought along a simple little black dress. She had wondered why on earth she'd seen fit to pack it, but thank God she had. It was nothing special, but she could just about get away with it tonight. What did you wear to something like this, anyway?

As she showered, as she brushed her hair, there was a voice in her head telling her to be careful, to watch out, not to go too far, too fast. To make sure she could get out of this thing, this falling feeling that she had, without hurting herself again. Mrs. Danvers kept telling her to be careful, as Laura looked at herself in the mirror and put on her makeup. She kept telling her she should go back to London, that she shouldn't go to Chartley.

You'll be going there as his girlfriend. You'll roll up that driveway in your car and get out, and you'll see yourself running up the stairs, the Mrs. Danvers voice in her head said. *You'll imagine what it'd be like to live there. All that good work you've done, not daydreaming, not believing in that stuff—gone.*

Laura said impatiently to her reflection, "I know. I know. But it's too late now, isn't it?"

No, it's not, said the voice. *Look at you. You're doing exactly what you always do. Yorky needed you tonight, and you were too busy snogging some bloke on a beach to go home and be there for him.*

"But this is different," Laura told herself. "It is different, isn't it?"

No, it's not, the voice said again. *This is like Dan all over again, Laura.*

Dan. Dan Floyd. Dan. Laura said his name out loud, as if it were a foreign word on her tongue, amazed at how neutral it sounded. "Dan." When was that? When had it been? It seemed to have happened months ago. The last three days, four days—they, in turn, seemed like years.

She put her hand in her sponge bag, looking for mascara. There at the bottom were two diamanté scallop-shaped clips, pretty things. Jo had bought them for her for Christmas. She'd never got the chance to wear them, much as she loved them. She slid one onto each strap of the dress, feeling rather glamorous suddenly, excited.

Oh, Laura, said the voice in her head as she looked at herself in the mirror, her hand on her breastbone, trying not to get too nervous, trying to tell herself not to care as much as she did. Suddenly, she felt utterly defenseless, like the baby bird she and Xan had rescued from the street of their house in Oxford when she was small. The egg had fallen from a tree and shattered. The baby was ugly, tiny, totally exposed, and though they gave it water, though Xan stayed up to look after it, it died. Being out in the open, too soon out of its shell with no protection, was just too much for it. It had upset her so much, the ten-year-old Laura. She remembered how distressed she had felt, watching herself now.

She shook her head, her eyes dark, her pupils huge, her reflection in the mirror strange to her, like someone she didn't know. "Oh. Just be careful."

She should have listened to the voice, she thought as she drove along the winding lanes, her palms sticky on the steering wheel in the sticky summer's evening. And as she turned into the drive, and crawled along in solitary, splendid isolation, she suddenly felt self-conscious in her parents' Rover. What did posh people drive? Not Rovers, probably.

As she reached the house, she could see a figure waiting for her on the steps. She looked up expecting to see Nick's face, and found it was Charles, in black tie, hands behind his back, hair combed back. The machine was in operation.

"Leave the car there," he called as she wound down the window to say hello. "Someone'll take it around the back for you."

"Oh," said Laura. "Cor." She coughed. "Thank you so much," she added. She wondered if she should mention her overnight bag, lying so neatly packed on the backseat, and then decided that would complicate things far too much, so she left it where it was, got out of the car, and climbed the steps to meet Charles, who gave her a kiss on the cheek. "Jolly nice to see you again, Laura," he said. "So pleased you're here."

"Oh, well," said Laura. "It's great to be here." She looked down at her strappy silver evening shoes; they were worrying her. She normally wore them with jeans. They were high but not too high, in fact strangely comfortable, considering their silver-high-heeled-evening-shoe pedigree. But the heels were scratched, the silver covering torn, and she wished with all her heart that she were in something glamorous, nice. She clicked her heels together. Perhaps they would magically transform into gorgeous new shoes. But no.

"Jolly nice diamond clips, those," Charles said as she looked up. "Very pretty."

"Oh, thanks very much," said Laura, fingering one of them. She smiled at him. "Jolly glad. Don't want to let the side down," she added, then stopped, alarmed by the role she was giving herself, which was, she realized, Virginia McKenna in *Carve Her Name with Pride.* She'd cried over that film one long Saturday afternoon a few weeks ago during a particularly low moment with Dan, but really, there was no need to start talking like her.

"Hey," said Charles, patting her arm. "Shall we go in? Everyone's here, pretty much."

"Really?" said Laura, taken aback. "I'm not late, am I?"

"No, no," said Charles. "They've been having drinks for a while. In the great hall. Most of them arrived in the afternoon, you see. Staying the weekend, and all that."

"Ah," said Laura. She looked past him, past the balustrade into the great hall. "Er . . . right. Where's—er, where's Nick?"

"He's in there," Charles said. "Shall we go and find him?"

It would be pathetic to say "Can you get him to come out here while I wait, I'm scared, I don't want to go in?" It was, wasn't it? Laura pulled herself together. "Yes," she said. She slid her arm through Charles's. "Let's go in."

"So," said Nick's great-aunt Teresa, five minutes later, "Laura. Where are your people from, then?"

"Oh," said Laura. She took a nervous sip from her heavy champagne glass. The alcohol tasted chalky; the bubbles rasped in her throat. Over on the other side of the room, Nick was talking to Sam and Penelope, two cousins from Somerset. Laura had said hello to them both briefly, and Nick had squeezed her arm and whispered, "I'll come and find you in a minute, okay?"

The room was crowded; fifty or more relatives of varying ages, but tending toward forty-plus, were talking loudly, laughing, greeting each other. Ripples of amusement, of shared jokes or reminiscences, floated to Laura's ears as she stood there, trying not to feel too much like an outcast: "Well, hello there! Terrific to see you again, old thing." "Minty's in Cornwall." "John? Wife died a few months ago. No, he's up at Balmoral." "Damn nag fell at the first fence. I know.' In front of her stood one such specimen, Nick's great-aunt, well over ninety, clad in upholstered purple velvet and wearing a small diamond brooch, with beady eyes that bored into Laura in a most disconcerting fashion.

"Sorry?" said Laura, who felt as if all she could hear was a loud buzzing noise.

"Hello? I said, your people. Parents. Where are they from, dear?"

Laura dragged her gaze away from the back of Nick's head to Great-aunt Teresa, who was regarding her intently. "Oh," she repeated. "Sorry. My parents? They're from Harrow."

"How lovely," said Great-aunt Teresa, politely but vaguely. She grimaced, sucking her lips into her mouth. "I don't know it very well, I must say. Although my brother was there. Beautiful."

"Oh, Harrow boys," said Lady Lavinia. She was standing next to Charles, who was gazing at her as if she were an exotic princess. "Gosh. Lucky you, living so near them." She smiled, her little pink tongue darting out between her tiny white teeth, and tossed her auburn hair over her shoulder.

Charles scowled, and rubbed his face; Laura had never seen him so discomfited.

"Not really," said Laura. "I mean, the school—it's not that near where I love—I live, I mean."

"Right," said Lavinia. She smiled at Charles from under her eyelashes. He blushed rosily, and Lavinia lapsed into a vacant silence that seemed to say "I've done my bit."

Great-aunt Teresa picked up the gauntlet. She peered at Laura's dress. "Those clips," she said. "Very pretty."

"Oh, thank you," said Laura. "My friend Jo—"

"The diamonds are lovely. What is the setting? Platinum, or silver?" Great-aunt Teresa peered at one of them, her beaky nose almost jabbing Laura's arm.

"Oh, no," said Laura, laughing. "They're not real. They're fake. But they're pretty, aren't they?"

"Fake?" said Great-aunt Teresa loudly. "Oh. I see."

"My friend Jo," Laura said again weakly. "She gave them to me."

Nick left the cousins and was moving across the room. Her heart leaped, then sank again as she watched him shake hands with someone else, a dark-haired, bearded man.

"So, Laura, you're off back to London tomorrow," said Charles, turning to her.

"London?" said Great-aunt Teresa. "Whereabouts do you live, then?"

"North," said Laura noncommittally.

"Regent's Park?" said Great-aunt Teresa. "Near there?"

"Er—yes," said Laura, reasoning that in relation to, say, Newcastle, her flat *was* near Regent's Park. "Lovely, isn't it?" She added politely, "Where do you live?" She felt with unease that she should know how to address Great-aunt Teresa, whom she was sure was a lady or something and moreover not *her* great-aunt; but, as with Lady Rose earlier in the day, she wasn't sure enough to ask.

"Where do *I* live?" said Great-aunt Teresa in tones of astonishment. "At Dearden."

"Dearden Hall," Charles murmured in her ear.

This meant nothing to Laura, not even with Charles's kind clarification; it only made her feel even more gauche, were that possible. "Right," she said politely, hoping that was contribution enough to the conversation, knowing that it wasn't.

Great-aunt Teresa, of Dearden Hall, and Lady Lavinia moved off in different directions, to be greeted with shrieks of joy by their respective new companions, and Laura was left standing next to Charles, trying not to feel like a shorter, fatter Audrey Hepburn in *My Fair Lady*, that she was failing some subtle, silly test. This was the twenty-first century, what the hell did it matter who was who and where they lived and all that? It didn't make them important. It didn't matter that she was from Harrow and lived in Tufnell Park. She was here because of Nick, because of how she felt about him. The rest of it wasn't a big deal.

Why did it *feel* like a big deal, though? Why couldn't she shake the idea that she was about as welcome tonight as a cockroach infestation? She glanced at Charles gratefully. He was watching her, and smiled as she looked around the room again for Nick, who was talking politely to the same man as before and a couple of other people about her parents' age. One of them said something, and Nick nodded seriously. He was so handsome, she thought. The white of his shirt gleamed against his dark hair, black tie, and black dinner jacket, and stood out in the cavernous gloom of the great hall. He looked grown-up. Remote. Different. Very different from the Nick she knew.

Of course, he was, though, Laura thought, and her hand flew to her cheek, because thinking that upset her, though she knew it was stupid. He was a marquis. He was an important person, not just because he was so rich, so posh, so well connected, but also because he was the employer of hundreds of people, the person who ran the estate, who had investments, who sat in City boardrooms while people presented plans to him. She didn't know that Nick at all; and it was all very well for him to say it didn't matter, that only the two of them mattered, but she couldn't help feeling the rest of it mattered more than he could see or she had realized.

Then she thought, You stupid girl. You think he's wonderful, don't you? You've fallen for him, for this handsome marquis in his huge stately home. You've convinced yourself you know him, that he knows you. You've had three wonderful nights together, and you've bloody fallen for him. And then she heard Mrs. Danvers loud and clear, and this time, Laura listened.

It's been three days. You met him three days ago, Laura. How could you let yourself do this again? Haven't you learned anything?

But, Laura said to herself, staring into her empty glass, it's Nick. He's not like that.

Laura, Laura. Come on. Three days. How can you possibly know? Of course, he's nice. He's lovely. He's kind, he makes you laugh, you get each other really well. But isn't that just because of circumstances? Isn't it something to do with the fact that he was the first person you'd had a normal conversation with in days, when you met him? Because he's tall, and so handsome, and looks at you with those big dark eyes like he's falling in love with you? Oh, Laura. It doesn't mean he is. . . .

Her throat hurt, she didn't know why. She wanted to be alone, but she knew she was just being silly. She smiled and pulled herself together, taking a deep breath. She turned to Charles, still standing there politely, carefully, nicely.

"What about you, Charles?" she said, trying to get onto something approximating common ground.

"What about me?" said Charles, smiling at her.

"Well," said Laura, waving her hands vaguely and trying not to sound like the queen asking someone questions in a lineup, "what do you do? Er, in your spare time, I mean?"

"When I'm not running after Nick, or sorting out the house, or his crazy family, you mean?" Laura nodded. "Ha. Well, that leaves about five minutes in the day."

"Really?"

"Oh," said Charles. "No, not at all. I'm very lucky. Don't really want any spare time, to be honest."

Laura didn't believe him. That didn't sound like luck; it sounded like about as much fun as botulism. She pressed him again, genuinely curious. "No," she said. "I mean, if you had a night off, could do anything? What would you do?"

"Well, I'd potter around the garden, I suppose," said Charles. "I've got my own bit, out the back, by the kitchen garden."

Oh, good grief. This was awful. Laura nodded politely. "Still," she said gently. "Like a night out. If you could do anything at all."

"American sitcoms," said Charles unexpectedly. "I'd watch them all day if I could."

"Really?" Laura said incredulously.

"Yup," said Charles. "Love 'em. I've got a digital box in my room. *Seinfeld. Larry Sanders. Curb Your Enthusiasm. Arrested Development.*"

"Seriously?" said Laura, feeling as if she were on a weird trip. "Wow. I love *Arrested Development.*"

Charles's face lit up. "Isn't it amazing?" he said. "So clever. So hilarious! Did you know, Ron Howard's the person who narrates it?"

"No!" said Laura. "Really? I always thought he sounded familiar. That's so cool! I must tell Yorky that."

"Yorky?" said Charles.

"My flatmate," Laura explained. "He . . ." She trailed off, suddenly remembering that at this moment, Yorky would be having a drink in the sitting room, on A Date with Downstairs Becky. How she wished she could be there. . . . She looked around the room, thinking again that this was odd. This was effectively Nick's sitting room. She cleared her throat. "Anyway. Ron Howard's the executive producer, isn't he?"

"Yes," said Charles seriously, and Laura realized she was the only one finding it at all incongruous, out of place, this conversation. In fact, this whole situation. Perhaps because it was just her who was out of place. Incongruous.

chapter thirty

Five minutes later, the gong sounded for supper, and Laura felt unease creep over her again. She could talk about telly for hours, and she enjoyed talking to Charles, who was so lovely and whom she genuinely liked, with his pink and white face and sweetly intelligent, shy manner. But she knew he was looking after her, and that he probably had things to do or people he wanted to talk to. She knew he'd rather be talking to Lavinia than to her, or discussing the harvest or something, rather than having to be her bodyguard.

Charles said, "We should go through, ah, just here," as a swarm of unknown relatives bustled past them, seemingly unconcerned with Laura and Charles, though a couple looked back at her as they passed and gave her rather appraising stares, as if to say "You stand out. What are you doing here?" Charles put his hand gently on her back and steered her toward the ballroom.

Suddenly she felt another arm steal around her waist, and Nick kissed her lightly on the neck and murmured, "I am so sorry, Laura. Here you are. You look beautiful. Thanks, Charles."

He took her hand and they walked in to dinner together, and Laura's heart sang at the feel of his fingers entwined with hers, the reassuring press of his heavy dinner jacket against her bare arm. The crowd parted as if they were Cleopatra and Mark Antony, and people stared and whispered, heads bent together, as the combined Needham family suddenly realized who that bland, uninteresting, unglamorous girl talking to Charles was. She was Nick's date. From the look of openmouthed shock on some people's faces, she could tell this news wasn't exactly welcome.

They entered the ballroom, and Laura glanced around, thinking how strange it was that the last time she'd been in there, her father had been asking Cynthia about dynastic successions, and her mother had been saying, "Do you think they have a lampshade similar to that in the shop? I should ask, shouldn't I," and Laura had never even met Nick; and here she was now, standing next to him, his hand squeezing hers. It all felt slightly unreal, as if she were watching a film about someone else.

The room was a mass of dinner jackets and brightly colored taffeta. Scanning the long table, set in the middle of the room and laden with glittering crystal and flowers, silver cutlery, snowy white tablecloths, Laura looked at the row of Needham relatives ranged opposite her, and saw there was a family resemblance; a faint one, but there nonetheless. It was something in the cheekbones; the high, rather narrow faces; the dark hair. It was extraordinary, she thought—centuries of interbreeding, all in one room; and she looked down at her hand, tangled with his. He squeezed it again reassuringly, and then held out her chair for her to sit down.

"Thank you," said Laura formally. He touched the bare skin of her shoulder lightly, and sat down next to her.

"So," he said. "Bearing up okay?"

"Yes," said Laura, smiling at him. "Just about."

"I kept meaning to come over and introduce you to people, but every time I made a move, someone would annex me," Nick said. He turned toward her and smiled, the Nick she knew, even in a dinner jacket. "And then you looked like you were having such a good time with Great-aunt Teresa and Lavinia—I'm glad."

"Yes," said Laura. She stared at her lap, feeling rather helpless. Strange though it was to think it, when he'd lied to her for most of the time she'd known him, she hated lying to him about this now. It felt . . . like everything was wrong. But she had to, so she did. "Yes," she said again, as he stole his hand onto her lap and squeezed her thigh gently. "It's been just great, Nick, thank you."

A waiter unfolded a napkin and waved it gracefully onto Laura's lap. Nick moved his hand, and they were both silent until he'd moved on.

"Well," he said, "I don't know about that. I don't really like these things, you know. But I have to do them, and we all actually quite enjoy seeing each other." He scratched his head, and a shadow crossed his face briefly. "The one thing to watch out for is . . ."

"What?" said Laura.

"Well, someone's bound to bring up my mother. They always do, after a few glasses, and then . . ." He shook his head. "Forget it. That's an even longer story. Do you—" He looked unsure, then angry. "I hate this. It's so stupid, asking someone you—if they know about how your mother ran off with your uncle. Because it was in the paper every day for about a year."

"I know," said Laura. "My grandmother told me yesterday. She met them."

Nick looked amazed. "My mother?" he said rather loudly, and next to him his cousins Clare and Oliver stopped talking and looked appalled, as if Nick had just made a Nazi salute or punched a waiter or something.

"Yes," said Laura. She added softly, thinking she sounded like *her* mother, "Shall we talk about it later?"

"Yes, let's. You're right," said Nick. His fingers gripped his napkin, screwing it into a ball, and he looked up and down the room impatiently, his gaze traveling the length of the table until it came to rest on her. "Oh, Laura. I'm sorry. This—perhaps this was a bad idea."

"What?" said Laura, feeling sick again.

"Asking you tonight," said Nick. "Thank you. White, please," he said to the waiter. "I don't mean—you know. I just mean, perhaps it's a bit rich, expecting you to get all of this so soon."

Feeling slightly like a disease-ridden barefoot chimney sweep, Laura tried to smile reassuringly at him, but his attention was claimed by an old lady across the table and he turned away from her. The last of the guests were being seated. Across the table, Charles sat down opposite her. And next to her, a chair was drawn back, and a voice said, "Good evening. It's nice to see you back at Chartley so soon."

It was Lady Rose, corseted in pale brown lace and silk, looking exactly like Queen Mary, a cool smile on her face. She caught sight of her place card next to Laura's; Laura saw the look on her face. Laura looked back at the table and concentrated on the huge bowl of flowers in front of her, trying not to eavesdrop.

"Nick," Rose said softly to her brother. "I wasn't supposed to be sitting here."

Nick smiled. "Hello, Rose. Well, you are now," he said. "I moved things around a little, hope that's okay. Malcolm's next to Lavinia, he's fine. You're next to Laura."

"But—" said Rose. Her voice grew louder. "I always sit next to you."

"Rose," said Nick firmly. "Sit down, please."

Laura, unable to avoid listening to this exchange, was torn between wanting to stand up and offer Rose her seat back and wanting to slide gently under the table and crawl out of the room.

There was a pause; the tension was palpable. And then Rose sat down next to her, and smiled graciously.

The doors closed behind them, and Nick stood up, and waited for the babble to subside. Down the long room, the noise fell, and fifty or so faces turned to look at him expectantly. The only movement was the glint of diamonds in the light of the chandeliers.

"Just a minute, please. Thank you. Hey!" Laura jumped as Nick banged his hand on the table. He called down the room to two old men who were still talking, "Alec! Geoffrey! This won't take long. I just want to welcome you all. All of you."

He paused infinitessimally. His voice was softer, and she did not dare look up at him, but she felt as if he was talking to her.

"We're all family, aren't we? And it's rare that we are all together. So perhaps we should drink to that. To this evening. I'm so glad you're all here tonight. To the Needham family."

There was a shuffling of chairs as the assembled company stood up. "The Needham family," they chorused.

Laura looked around the room. If my friends could see me now, she thought. Imagine if I called Jo and told her where I was. Or Yorky. They'd never believe it. She looked at the offending Geoffrey and Alec, stout and bespectacled; at Great-aunt Teresa, leaning heavily on a stick, staring beadily into space; at Charles,

Lavinia, and Malcolm Balmore, who was short and squat and looked very disgruntled about something. At the massed ranks of Needhams, scanning along the row until her eye rested on Rose, stately and gracious, nodding at someone opposite her; and then she turned to Nick, her Nick, so tall and grave in his dinner jacket, and felt overwhelmed. She didn't know what she was doing there at all.

chapter thirty-one

Dinner was not a nine-course gourmet affair; it was a huge roast dinner for all, with the toast to Sir Guillibert Danvers scheduled to happen halfway through the evening, followed by more wine and pudding. Laura smiled inanely at no one as the roast beef was served, as if she were having a simply fantastic time. Around her the Clan Needham talked amongst itself, and Rose inclined her head graciously toward her from time to time. And, of course, Nick was next to her, chatting politely to some ancient aunt and uncle opposite him, occasionally turning to her to see if she was okay, and looking so pleased when she would smile and simply say, "Yes, I'm having a great time, thank you."

As seconds were being served, Rose swiveled her attention around to Laura. She leaned forward and reached for her glass. "So, Laura. I hope you're enjoying yourself tonight?" she asked in polite tones.

"Oh, yes, thank you," said Laura. "I'm very glad to be here."

Rose said nothing, but inclined her head graciously.

"It's beautiful here," said Laura, knowing this was a pathetic thing to say, but not sure how else to break the silence.

"Yes. Yes, it is," said Rose. "Tell me something, Laura." Laura nodded. "How did you meet my brother? I'm so curious."

"Er, well," said Laura. She toyed with the idea of saying "At the Sandy Lane Resort in Barbados" or "St. Tropez last year." What did it matter how she'd met him? Why was it important?

"I was here on Wednesday with my parents, for the day," she said. "I bumped into him then—we got talking, and we ended up going out for a drink in the evening."

Rose's expression was undefinable. "Your parents?"

"Yes," Laura said carefully. "We're here on holiday. We were going round the house." She took a deep breath.

"How nice," Rose said eventually.

"Yes," Laura said. "I go back to London tomorrow, so Nick was kind enough to ask me tonight."

Rose nodded. "I see." And then she was silent.

Laura found herself gabbling. "Which is rather weird, because I know it's a family night, and I'm a complete stranger! But I'm incredibly touched to be asked." She knew she sounded like a fourteen-year-old, that she wasn't saying the right thing, but with no idea of what that might be, she thought she'd better keep talking.

Rose raised her glass. "Well, so here you are, then." She paused, then smiled brightly. "Forgive me. It's rather a surprise, that's all. My little brother is rather useless, isn't he?"

"Yes," said Laura, blindly agreeing. "Well," she amended hurriedly, "no, I don't think—"

"You see," Rose said, unheeding, "I rather thought he had a girlfriend. That's why I'm surprised. He *was* seeing a girl called Cecilia."

"Yes, he told me," said Laura, refusing to be ruffled.

"Oh, you know? Of course," said Rose. 'She's terribly nice. I don't know if you know her. Her father's a very good friend of Sir Malcolm's. We've known the family for ages. The Thorsons."

"Right," said Laura.

"They were terribly kind when . . . my father died." Rose cleared her throat. "You see, there were debts, when Nick inherited two years ago. And the Thorsons have been so helpful, advising him, all of that. So kind. We thought he and Cecilia would get on. It was going rather well, I'd heard."

"They're not seeing each other anymore," said Laura. "We talked about it."

She sounded rather gauche, schoolgirlish, she realized. Rose looked pleased, like a cat.

"Oh you did, did you? Well," she said, and her tongue darted out of her mouth; she looked like her sister, Lavinia, for a fleeting second. "I'm sure if that's what he told you . . ."

"Yes, it is," said Laura. She felt she ought to distance herself a little from this. She didn't want to sound like a stalker. "But, of course, I have only known him for a very short time, so . . ."

"Yes," said Rose, almost purring. "You're quite right. So." She smiled and waved at someone farther down the table. "Ah, there's Emily. Dear thing. I must say hello to her afterward." She cleared her throat, as if drawing the line under the conversation, now her point was made. "Well, I'm glad you're enjoying your time here."

"Thank you," Laura said.

"We're all family here tonight," Rose said. She ran a short, plump finger around the rim of her glass. "Except you, of course."

"I'm very lucky."

"Yes," said Rose. "I'd say you were."

And with that, she turned back to her neighbor, leaving Laura staring down at her plate, not knowing what to say.

It's almost impossible to have a relaxed conversation with

someone when you know everyone else is looking at you, appraising you, judging you. And, in Rose's case, wishing you weren't there. After this, Laura felt even more exposed, and when Nick turned to ask her how it was all going, she found herself making small talk with him, as if he were one of Mum and Dad's neighbors at a barbecue in Harrow. She didn't know what to say to him, all of a sudden, how to talk to him. She wanted to be alone with him on the beach, or in his room. As if it were last night, or the night before, or before that. Before real life got in the way—and what a reality it was.

Because it was different now, all different. Among Laura's opening salvos to Nick were:

"Do you have job-share schemes on the estate?"

"Is the soil good for growing potatoes, then?"

"Who handles the insurance for the paintings?"

"That's an interesting chandelier, how old is it?"

What she didn't say was:

"Can I punch both your sisters?"

"How do you cope with this, all the time?"

"Why can't it be the two of us, like it was before?"

And,

"Do you realize I've fallen for you?"

Eventually, the plates were cleared away after the first course, and Charles stood up to announce, in his polite, soft voice, that there would be a break and then the toasts to Sir Guillibert Danvers would begin. Nick turned to her, and put his napkin on the table.

"Why don't we go for a walk?" he said, smiling at her, just her. "Outside, for a couple of minutes. I don't really feel like I've been a very good host to you tonight."

"I'd love that," she said, gazing up at him, thinking how perfect he was to her in that moment, with his long, bony face, tanned skin, kind, clever eyes. How much she wished they could just leave this evening behind, forget it. Perhaps they could—perhaps the feeling that was growing inside her, this feeling of doom, perhaps she was wrong about it. Perhaps it would be okay.

He touched her hand lightly. "Right. Let's go. I'll—"

"Nick! M'boy! Damn good to see you."

"Leo, hello," said Nick, turning around and standing up. Laura turned to see a large, purple-faced man whose dinner jacket strained alarmingly at the buttons. "Leo, this is Laura," Nick said, holding Laura's elbow and urging her forward.

Laura shook Leo's hand. "Nice to meet you," she said.

"And you," said Leo, looking at her breasts and not at her face. "And you, m'dear. Good that you're here," he said to the breasts again, before coming to with a start. "Before I forget, Nick. Need a small word with you in private. Now?"

"Now?" said Nick. "I just—"

"Can't stay afterward, m'boy. It's about Pickleton. The cottages. Now Ned's dead. Really think we should discuss it." Leo looked rather anxious. "Not sure what to do, if the truth be known."

"Of course, of course," Nick said, patting his shoulder. "Laura, do you mind? Why don't you wait here? I'll only be a minute."

"I'll go outside and wait," said Laura, who didn't particularly want to be left alone. "I'd love some fresh air. See you on the steps."

He raised his hand and smiled briefly, turned away, and walked out. She could see his retreating back and Leo's as they disappeared through the great hall into a room off to the side.

Laura sat down, and drained her drink. She looked for Charles, but couldn't see him. Across the way from her, various old ladies chattered happily amongst themselves; she thought how like her grandmother they were, and how Mary would get on beautifully in this situation, would take to it like a duck to water, in fact. She stood up, trying to look inconspicuous, and headed out to the great hall. She didn't feel inconspicuous, though. She'd never felt more out of place in her life.

She went outside and waited on the steps. The landscaped grounds were in near darkness now, with only the glow from the floodlit house illuminating the gravel, the drive, a little of the way beyond down to the fountain in the distance. A few people from the dinner—she didn't know their names—walked past her or came out and saw her, but they didn't bother her. The stone was warm from the heat of the day.

So she sat and waited, and thought about the last four days, and how she had come to be there. She thought about Mary's birthday, about how stressful family affairs were, but how it was worth it to see her grandmother surrounded by her family and friends, to realize how lucky she was to have her parents as her parents. How funny this afternoon had been; she suddenly saw Lulu and Aunt Annabel's incredulous faces as Laura said good-bye to the assembled group and drove off in her black dress to Chartley Hall. She thought about Yorky on his date, how it was going, and felt a sharp pang as she found herself wishing she were there waiting for him to come back, so they could sit up and chat about it over a late-night drink. About popping round to Jo's; sitting at her and Chris's kitchen table reading the Sunday papers, laughing and drinking coffee, being normal. Tomorrow was Sunday; when she got home, she knew there would be a letter waiting from Rachel confirming her meeting about coming back to work. A job. A life again, on an even keel, now that the madness of the previous few months was over. She thought about Dan, and shook her head, her hand pressed to her heart when she remembered how blindly she had loved him, wanted to love him, to be with him, and how utterly different the reality was, the cold hard facts of daily life.

She looked behind her, to the house. It was funny, wasn't it.

This was reality now, right this minute. The last few days with Nick, just being with him, just the two of them, walking, talking, kissing, making love—they hadn't been real, because they weren't the truth. This was real, sitting on the steps now, waiting for her romantic hero to come out the door to meet her; and the irony was it was like something out of one of the novels she'd wanted so much to live in.

As she sat thinking, sifting all these thoughts through and through, gradually Laura realized what she had to do; and the idea of it was awful, she didn't know how she would get through it, but she knew it had to be done. She looked down at her dress, her feet in their strappy sandals, shimmering silver against the dark stone. She wanted to remember it, remember being here, preserve it, so she would always know what it felt like to know he was here, on his way out to find her, that he wanted her.

It seemed as if hours had gone by, but it was only a few minutes later that she heard his footsteps behind her, and he came and sat down next to her.

"Hello," he said, and he slid his arm around her waist. "Sorry to keep you waiting." He kissed her. "Leo does go on rather a lot. He's a great chap—he was my dad's cousin, you know. He runs the estates in Lincolnshire, does a fantastic job. But he's rather . . . wordy, you know. I'm sorry."

"Don't worry," said Laura. "Honestly."

There was silence between them.

"We should go back in in a minute," said Nick. "I have to propose the toast, and wear this ridiculous hat. I'm sorry. And there's a rhyme thing. God, it's ridiculous, but it keeps them happy for another year, and . . ." He trailed off as Laura stood up.

"I'm going, Nick," she said, trying to keep her voice neutral.

"What?" said Nick blankly. He looked up at her. "Inside?"

"No," said Laura. "I'm going. Going home."

"But it's—" He stood up. "What are you talking about?"

She knew she had to play a part. "I'm not staying here," said Laura in the tone of an offended, stroppy girlfriend. She stood and started to walk down the steps, clutching her bag. "I'll get the car myself. Thanks for a lovely evening."

"Laura!" Nick caught her by the arms. He was almost laughing, but there was panic in his eyes. "What are you talking about? You can't leave, it's—we haven't had pudding yet." He shook his head, as if aware of how silly that sounded. "You know what I mean. We haven't spent any time together. I want—I thought you were staying with me. Tonight, I mean."

She shook free from his grasp, looked away, took a deep breath, and then faced him.

"Stay here? And be treated like this? You must be joking." Her voice was shriller than usual. She let the muscles in her face form an ugly expression, and she smiled at him spitefully. "Who are you kidding, Nick? I've had a crap evening, and you've treated me like dirt. You've barely spoken a word to me! You let your sisters be rude to me!" Her voice rose. "I'm not used to it, okay? I'm used to being treated politely by my date. Like a lady." She thought, feeling sick, that might be going a bit too far; she didn't want to sound like Sybil Fawlty. But he had to believe her. She put her evening bag over her shoulder. "I'm really sorry, Nick," she said. "We had a laugh, didn't we? But I'm going to go now."

Nick was staring at her, shaking his head. "No—no," he said. He moved closer to her. "Laura? Why are you being like this? I don't—aren't you glad to be here? I thought you wanted to—I thought you didn't mind all this . . ." He trailed off, his eyes beseeching her.

"What, you think I'm going to be on my knees with gratitude because the big lord's invited little old me to his stately home? Eh? Like a fucking geisha, is that what you think? Thanks so much, sir,

I'm nothing and I'm so grateful." Laura was trembling, shouting as she said it. It was horrible. She hadn't imagined it could hurt this much. "Well, I'm not. So perhaps you'd better look around for someone else who's more up your street. Okay?" She ran down the last two steps.

"Is this about Cecilia?" said Nick, coming after her. "Rose just cornered me and asked me lots of stupid questions about her, about why we broke up. I'm *not* seeing her, Laura. Rose is just trying to bully me into marrying some fucking millionaire's daughter just so she and Malcolm can have the proprieties observed. Is that it? What did she say to you?"

Laura saw her chance and took it. "How am I supposed to believe you?" she said, making sure she kept her voice shrill. "Your sister didn't know you'd broken up with her—how am I to know if you're still seeing her or not? You lied to me about being a marquis, Nick, you could lie to me again."

He was staring at her, his expression totally bewildered. "I don't understand you, Laura. I thought we—I thought you . . ."

Laura turned and walked away so she didn't have to look at him anymore, because she was on the verge of losing her resolve, and she was nearly there, it was nearly done, and she couldn't believe how much it was hurting her.

"Just leave me alone, Nick," she said, her voice breaking.

He followed her, around the house, toward the stables at the back, and grabbed her hand. She snatched it away as he swung her round to face him. They were standing on the gravel in the shadow of the huge, dark stables. The trees behind them sighed in the nighttime breeze.

"This isn't you," he said quietly. "Laura, why are you doing this?"

She looked at him, and her shoulders heaved. A sob welled up in her throat. "I can't do this," she said softly, her voice breaking.

He drew her to him, holding her tightly. His buttons pressed into the thin fabric of her dress, digging into her ribs. He kissed her hair and murmured, "Laura, oh, Laura. What's wrong?"

She drew back from him slowly, wiping a tear from her cheek. "Nick," she said. "Please. Don't try to stop me. Just let me go. I'm not pissed off, I'm not pretending anymore."

"Good," he said with a glimmer of humor. "I didn't know who you'd turned into back there. I thought—"

"Nick, I mean it. This is never going to work."

Two lines of annoyance appeared between his dark brows. "Come on, Laura. We've talked about this. It can work."

"No," Laura said, her voice rising. "We *haven't* talked about this, Nick. And it can't work. Look at us. Look at tonight."

"Why?" he said. "Come on, I know they're a bit hard to take, but—"

"You don't get it, do you?" said Laura, trying not to shout at him, to cry, to hit him. "Can't you see? You're them. They're you. You're part of this." She waved her arms around her. "The whole thing, the house, the history, all of your family. All of it. It's massive. And you're trying to pretend it doesn't matter, but it *does,* Nick. You talk about it as if it's something abstract, or as if it's a condition, like being allergic to apples, or having a fear of spiders, as if it's just a vague inconvenience. And it's not, it's the whole damn thing with you."

"It's not," he said, taking her hands, folding them in his like he always did. He shook his head blindly. "Laura. If I can't have a normal life outside it, I'm doomed. Of course all this is important to me, it has been since Dad died and I had to come back here and start looking after things. It's been the most important thing. But there are other things, too," he said, and he leaned forward and kissed her.

His lips were on hers, insistent, hot against her cool skin, and her heart physically ached; she hadn't realized it could. She would never forget how it felt when he kissed her, what it was like. How it felt to hold him, to feel him on top of her, inside her, his hands on hers. Perhaps that was all that mattered. But then she remembered the expressions on the faces of his relatives as they walked in. She remembered the portrait of the seventh marquis, proud and handsome. Cynthia, the tour guide, telling her rapt audience that the Needhams had fought in the Wars of the Roses. Nick and his sisters, reenacting their own personal Hogarth paintings as children. The gardeners, the servants, the houses, the lands . . . it all whirled around in her mind, Rose's voice telling her how lucky she was when Laura knew she wasn't, she'd probably just got it wrong. Again. And she had to get out, before she hurt Nick more than she'd already hurt herself.

She pulled away from him, and saw George's trusty, beloved Rover lined up in the darkness next to the battered old Range Rovers and a Rolls-Royce.

Nick stepped back, his arms falling heavily by his sides, and looked at her in disbelief. "You're actually going to throw this all away, because you're an inverted snob," he said angrily.

"If you like," said Laura, keeping her emotions in check with one last herculean effort.

"You're a coward," he said, his voice harsh, his fists clenched. He shook his head. "Coward."

She turned and walked toward the car; she took the keys out and, trembling, tried to unlock it. Her hands were shaking. He watched her as she opened the door.

"You know, I actually thought I might be falling in love with you," he said quietly. He stepped away, turned around, and walked toward the house, and didn't turn back once.

Laura drove out of the stables onto the long, wide driveway, not daring to look in the mirror in case she caught sight of Chartley behind her, or the figure climbing the steps at the front to disappear inside. Tears rolled down her cheeks; she gripped the steering wheel, and put her foot on the accelerator.

"The trouble is, I've already fallen in love with you," she said softly to herself as she reached the end of the long, long drive, and turned onto the main road, back toward home.

part three

chapter thirty-two

"So, what's she like?"

"What are they like together?"

"I heard she stayed the night, did she? God. So has she seen him being himself yet?"

"Yes, you know. Really Yorkyish. Awkward and yet bizarrely self-confident," said Hilary, stubbing her cigarette out in the ashtray, her long, elegant fingers squashing the butt like a helpless insect. She wiped her fingers and looked up expectantly. Next to her, Jo nodded patiently.

"I don't know!" said Laura, laughing and holding her hands up in protest. "I haven't seen them together yet."

Jo moved the crisps into the center of the table. "But you have *seen* her, though, right?"

"Becky? Of course!"

"So, she's not . . . imaginary?"

"No!" said Laura. "Poor Yorky. Of course she's not imaginary."

The three of them were sitting in Jo and Chris's newly designed garden, enjoying the warm evening and Jo and Chris's John Lewis garden table and chair set, a wedding present of which Jo was inordinately proud. The French windows were flung open, music was playing softly in the kitchen, and, way back in the sitting room at the front of the house, Chris and his brother, Jason, were watching telly. It was Sunday evening, and Laura had arrived back from Norfolk early that morning.

She had crept out of the house, waking only her mother, saying she had a lunch to go to that she couldn't miss. She had left a note for Mary, and had already embraced her inner guilt about not saying a proper good-bye. But she couldn't stay there any longer. She had to come back to London, or else go mad with thinking about what she was leaving behind.

Here, in Jo's tiny, welcoming back garden, sitting with Jo and Hilary and a bottle of sauvignon blanc, she could imagine it had all been a dream. She knew she would think about it later, that it would hurt, that she would think about him, but here, right now, on a warm July evening, she asked nothing more than to sit with two friends and chew the fat over a few glasses of wine.

"So," said Laura. "What's happened while I've been away?"

Jo and Hilary looked at each other. "Nothing, really," said Jo. "Yorky having a date with someone is the most exciting thing that's happened to me for a long time." She paused. "Ooh, though. Me and Chris are going to Australia next month! I forgot that bit. And we bought some lovely eggshell paint for the bathroom."

Hilary looked disgusted and rolled her eyes at Laura, but Laura said, "Right—eggshell, that's great, but—Jo! You're going to Australia, wow!"

"Yes," said Jo, clapping her hands. "I am so excited, I can barely speak. It's like a delayed honeymoon, and we weren't going to go, but we had three weeks booked off anyway, and we got these flights, and . . . so we're going!"

"You lucky things," said Laura. "I'm going to miss you! Three weeks, my goodness."

Jo took her friendship responsibilities very seriously. "I know," she said, patting Laura's hand. "Perhaps I . . . well, obviously I'm not going to *not go*, but we should talk. If you need me. You know."

Laura laughed. "I'm not that hopeless, you know."

"Yes, you are," said Hilary. "Look at the mess you got yourself into when you and Jo weren't speaking back in the spring."

"Thanks," said Laura. "Charming."

"Sorry. But you know what I mean," said Hilary, as Jo held Laura's hand. "Talking of which, I hear all is not well in paradise. Or Miami, to be more precise."

"Eh?" said Laura, pouring Jo and herself another glass of wine. She looked up to see Jo making cut-throat gestures at Hilary. "What do you mean?"

"Miami?" said Hilary. "Who's there at the moment, do you remember?" Laura looked blank, and then recognition dawned on her face. "There you are. I bumped into that ghastly friend of Amy's yesterday. Camilla? The fitness instructor?"

"She *is* ghastly," said Jo loyally.

"Anyway, she let slip that Dan and Amy were on their way back. Early. They've had a massive row."

"Really?" said Jo. She looked at Laura anxiously. "Oh, Laura . . ."

Laura smiled at her. "It's fine, really."

"Oh, Laura," Jo said again, staring at her. "He'd better not . . . ooh, if he tries to get in touch with you, I'm going to tell Chris to Have a Word."

"Have a fag," said Hilary unemotionally. She gave Laura a quick smile. "Thought you'd want to know, anyway."

"Thanks, Hil," said Laura. "No thanks. Look . . ." She shook her head. "I can't explain why, but it really is okay. Good luck to them. I hope they work it out, seriously." She rummaged in her bag as diversionary activity, looking for her lip salve. As she was holding her phone, it beeped, a text message. It was from Nick. She didn't open it, see what it said; she just stared at her phone, almost in disbelief. No, no. This was her real life now, that was a dream.

"Who's it from?" said Jo, mildly intrigued by Laura's sudden silence.

"Er—" said Laura. "No one."

Jo looked at her. "Why didn't you see Becky last night?" she asked.

"What?" Laura took some more crisps.

"Becky. You came back last night, didn't you?"

"No," said Laura. "This morning." She was still looking down at the phone; she felt Jo's eyes on her. She put it away, shoved her bag under her chair. "I stayed up in Norfolk an extra night."

"Why?" said Jo doggedly.

"I . . ." Laura faltered. "I wanted to. Granny's birthday, you know. We—er, I . . . in the evening, I . . ."

Hilary was watching Jo with something like impatience. "Great," she said. "Back to the main event though, Jo." She grabbed Jo's arm and jerked her head in the direction of the house. "Tell me. Is Jason still single?"

Jo was still watching Laura. Laura looked back at her uneasily, until with horror she saw something like realization dawn on her friend's face. "You met someone in Norfolk, didn't you?' she said slowly, aghast. She shook her head. "My God. You did."

"What?" said Hilary. She swiveled her head around. "You've met someone? Already? Laura!"

"She has, hasn't she," said Jo, nodding at Hilary. "Who's the text from?"

"I haven't read it. No one," said Laura, only half truthfully.

"Good grief, Laura . . ."

"It's nothing, I promise," said Laura.

Laura didn't feel surprised, or annoyed, or patronized, or cross, or any of that. No. She ran her finger up and down the stem of her glass and she felt glad, glad that she could justify her behavior of the previous night to herself. It meant that she knew she had made the right decision last night, to leave him, leave it all behind, even if at the moment she still felt raw. Even if, at the moment, it seemed—had it really only been last night that she was there? With him?

"Who is he this time?" said Jo, shaking her head.

She tried to imagine Jo and Hilary's reactions if she told them the truth, if she blurted out, "You're right. I did meet someone. He's a marquis. He owns a huge stately home. He's a millionaire. He's really handsome. Oh, and I actually think I love him, I'm not just falling for him because I'm me and this is what I always do. You don't believe me? *Really*? Why on *earth* not?"

No, she wouldn't say anything. Even if Jo was looking at her with her big brown eyes, and even if more than anything she wanted to tell her about it, talk to her about what had happened, try to make sense of it all. She'd flirted with the boy who cried wolf too many times.

Taking a sip of her wine, she shook her head again. "I swear, honestly," she said. "Nothing happened in Norfolk. Very boring. We saw some really interesting windmills, though."

Hilary cracked a smile, then Jo, and Laura tried to persuade herself that she'd got away with it, even though there was something in her best friend's expression that told her this was not over.

Jo blinked rapidly, and stood up with the bowl of crisps. "Let's have something to eat. How's Simon?" she asked, clutching the bowl—varnished beechwood, part of a set of three, also from the wedding list—to her chest.

"Who knows?" said Laura. "He didn't make it back in time for the party," she explained to Hilary.

"Typical," said Hilary.

"I know," said Laura, but she added dutifully, "I'm sure there's a good reason."

"Some Brazilian pole dancer called Evita," Hilary said. "One night only."

Jo nodded in agreement.

"I know," said Laura. "Well, we'll see."

"When's your thingy at work?" asked Jo.

"What thingy?" said Hilary.

"I have to go in and kind of, er . . . reinterview for my job," Laura explained.

"Oh," said Hilary, looking embarrassed, as one does when confronted unexpectedly with someone else's problems. "Course. Sorry. When is it?"

"Wednesday," said Laura. She stood up as well. "I have to do my homework before, though. That reminds me," she said, putting her bag over her shoulder. "I think I'm going to head off."

"But I was going to make some food," said Jo, astonished.

"Yeah, Laura, stay," said Hilary.

"Thanks, thanks," said Laura. "I'm just really tired." She kissed Hilary. "Thank you, Jo, so much for tonight."

"But—" said Jo. "I want to talk to you!"

Laura ran her hand over her forehead. "Please, Jo," she said.

"I'm sorry, I—I need an early night. I'll call you tomorrow. Can we go over what they might ask me on Wednesday, maybe?"

"Course," said Jo. Laura kissed Jo good-bye, and Jo walked her through the kitchen to the hall.

"Bye, Chris!" Laura shouted, but there was no response.

"He's useless. Honestly," Jo said, but she smiled.

Laura looked at her. "Thanks again for tonight," she said. "It's been great."

"I'm glad you had a good time in Norfolk," said Jo. She shifted from foot to foot. "Are you sure there isn't something you're not telling me?"

"Absolutely," said Laura, trying to keep the tremor she felt in her voice from coming out too much.

"Don't want you making the same mistakes as before, that's all," said Jo. "I'm allowed to say that, I'm your best friend and I love you," she added, patting Laura's cheek as if she were her mother.

As Laura walked down the path, she heard Chris shout to Jo from inside the house, "What's up with Laura? She gone?"

"Yep," she heard Jo call back.

"She okay?" Chris said.

"I don't know," Laura heard her best friend say. "Not sure."

Laura walked down the road toward home, the flat, down the dusty, quiet Sunday streets. She pulled her phone out of her bag.

Laura, still think last night was a bad joke. All of it. Reply to this. Tell me I'm right. N

The image of Jo's face, leaning over her lovely wooden garden table, asking in tones of dread, "Who is he this time?"

Hilary's sympathetic expression—which in itself was rarity enough.

Her mother's worried stare that morning as she knocked on her door and told her she was leaving, there was a cab waiting outside, she was sorry.

Yorky's blissful smile when she'd got back to the flat at lunchtime, having just waved good-bye to Becky from downstairs, eighteen hours after their date originally commenced.

There were dry leaves on the dry street; they crunched under Laura's feet as she walked home, dog-tired, as she thought about it; and gradually it became clear to her: The only way this would work was if she did precisely what she'd never done before—just blocked it out. Blocked him out, tried to forget the whole thing as soon as possible.

Usually, when Laura broke up with someone, she almost enjoyed the post-split wallowing. She embraced the playing-sad-songs, getting-rid-of-shared-possessions, crying-to-friends-over-wine portion of the whole experience. The post-dumping analysis of subsequent texts and e-mails. The his-friends-think-he's-mad conversations—all of that could be immensely soothing to a hopeless romantic like her, someone who needed to believe that the person she'd just split up with was actually The One, and thus worthy of weeks more lolling around and sighing.

She knew this about herself, post-Dan, and this was where it had to stop. She looked down at Nick's message, and thought again about how she'd explain to Jo that she'd fallen in love with someone, and how she'd explain who he was. Of course, it was ridiculous. Of course, she had to get over it, as quickly and painlessly as possible, because they couldn't be together, and that was that.

Ahead of her loomed the apartment block. She pressed DELETE, and slowly put the phone back in her bag, rummaging for her keys and trying not to think about him, about him typing that text message. The thought of Nick standing there in the stables, his expression bleak and angry, tall and dark yet so oddly comfortable and easy to be with, made the breath catch in her throat. She couldn't bear to think of him in pain, couldn't bear to think she had upset him. She wanted, more than anything else, for him to be happy and well, and to be able to get on with doing what he had to do.

She climbed the front steps and let herself in. *That*, she reasoned, as she leaned against the door for a moment, was why it was better this way. He was better off without her, without a doubt.

Yorky had left her a note:

Your mum called! I'm EXHAUSTED! What a weekend! See you tomorrow!

chapter thirty-three

"So, Gareth, do you have any questions at this point?" asked Rachel, turning toward her colleague politely.

"Hhrm . . . yes," said Gareth, crossing his arms and leaning forward on the table, a pen in one hand. "Laura. I accept that you were going through a difficult time personally, which led to your work suffering as a result. What I have yet to be convinced of is that the same thing won't happen again in the future. What I mean is, I suppose, without prying too far—can you assure us this was a one-off?"

Laura sat opposite them, ankles crossed neatly, hands clasped lightly in her lap. She looked from Rachel to Gareth, and gave a tiny smile that didn't quite reach her eyes.

"I assure you it was," she said. "There's no reason for you to believe me, I quite appreciate that. All I can say is that I look back on my behavior over the last year or so, my conduct and my attitude to work, and I'm horrified. I don't recognize myself, and I'm appalled that I let it go that far." She cleared her throat and said calmly, "I understand I've let you down. I let myself down too, massively. I'm incredibly sorry."

Rachel nodded at her, looking mollified, but Gareth said rather sternly, "That's great, Laura. But we can't just let it lie there. Can you be more specific?"

Laura didn't get rattled. She just said, "How so?"

"Well . . ." Gareth looked around Rachel's tidy, bright office as if seeking inspiration. "If you were to get your job back—if—can you tell me what areas of your job you'd need to focus on, if there are any projects you'd like to implement, stones being left unturned, and so forth."

"Gareth, I don't think it's quite fair to ask her—" Rachel began, but Gareth shot her a warning look.

"Well," Laura said. She breathed in, collecting her thoughts, remembering what she and Jo had talked about on the phone the night before. Don't get rattled, don't.

"Our fund-raising scheme isn't working," she said calmly. "I know I haven't been paying enough attention to it. But it's more than that. We need a special initiative. Something new." Rachel was nodding furiously. Laura took heart, and went on, "And I had been thinking we don't do enough to involve local businesses with schools. That we should be acting more as an introduction agency, if you like. Our catchment area of businesses is incredibly diverse. It's big City firms, and small local businesses, shops, and so on. And lots of them want to be more involved with the school nearest to them. We get these lawyers or people from the banks or some café going to read with children in these schools, yet we don't do anything else with that link. It's often just four people in a company of a hundred. We should empower that company a bit more. Get them more involved in the school. And we could get them to donate to that school, specifically."

"Right," said Gareth. He nodded expectantly. "Give me an example."

"Well," said Laura, leaning forward a little. "We should appoint a special coordinator in each company. Assign them each a school. So it's not just reading they're doing with them. They could have the students into the office, show the children what a working environment's like. Do sponsored events, half marathons and so on, to raise money, if they liked. Give them talks about different things. Show-and-tell, as it were."

"Great, great," said Gareth, smiling at her enthusiasm. "What do they get out of it, though? The person working at the local bank branch or the person in the law firm. Why would they want to do it?"

"The call of altruism is a powerful thing," said Laura wryly. She sat up in her chair. "If you're some big lawyer, and you go and read with some six-year-old kid, show a class round your company, and then you get to go to their carol service or their school concert, and these children are coming up to you going, 'Hello, Gareth,' or whoever, you know it makes them feel good. Like people who wear those plastic wristbands. All in a good cause."

"You're right," said Gareth with emphasis. "Most of those people—pathetic. They're rich, they have no idea what it's like. Big nobs. How the other half lives. Gah, it makes me so angry."

Laura swallowed a smile. Gareth Lunn was the original conservative phony who still liked to think of himself as Old Labour through and through.

Gareth stared ruminatively into the distance, and Rachel caught Laura's eye. Laura met her gaze nervously, still unsure of how Rachel felt about her, and was immensely relieved when Rachel gave her a sweet smile and winked confidently.

"Right," said Gareth, snapping out of his reverie. "Time, time. I have to go. Meeting on the other side of town. With . . ." He tapped the side of his nose. "Laura, wait outside for a moment, will you? This shouldn't take long."

Laura stepped out into the main office, wondering what that meant. She felt it had gone well, but who knew? She looked round and leaned against the wall, taking in the scene. Nasrin was reading a magazine, per usual; Shana was on the phone, arranging something; and Tim had just come back from a training session, it was clear, because he was loading the videos back onto their shelves. He caught sight of Laura, and smiled shyly at her.

It was very strange, being back in this place she knew so well she didn't even have to think to look for the light switches or find something in the filing cabinet by her desk. It didn't feel like it was barely three weeks since she'd run out of there. She felt as if she'd been away for months, in a different world.

"Laura?" came a voice from Rachel's office, and Laura stepped back inside.

Rachel and Gareth were looking serious. "Sit down," said Gareth.

Laura sat down obediently, and found to her annoyance that her legs were shaking. Please, please, don't let this be it, she prayed.

"Look, Laura," said Gareth. "I'm going to level with you. Okay? I was all for letting you go, to be honest."

"Right," said Laura, nodding earnestly, feeling she should agree with him, anything to keep him on her side.

"But Rachel persuaded me, and I'm really glad I came today. I think you're good, Laura. I think you've got potential. The education authority needs people like you."

"Thank you," said Laura, but too soon—Gareth raised his hand in a gesture of impatience.

"But I have to say, you're lucky to have a job. We're giving you the job back, but on a three-month probation period, subject to review at the end of that time."

"Thank you. Thank you so much—" she began again.

Gareth said, "But you have to be aware, Laura, you have done some damage, and you're going to have to sort it out. Pull something big out of the bag. Rachel tells me you haven't heard about Linley Munroe."

"What about them?" Laura said sharply.

"You remember Marcus Sussman?" said Rachel. "The one Mrs. McGregor complained about? The banker?"

"Oh, yes," said Laura, searching through the fog of her Dan-skewed memory of this year. "Goodness, yes."

"She had a real go at him. He's gone mad. Furious. Says it's a two-bit operation. Turns out he's quite important there. Anyway, he's told the coordinator to pull the plug on the whole project. It's a real shame, Laura. They're a big firm, they wanted to play a part. They were looking to sponsor a school—perhaps plow some serious money into the local community. And now it's not going to happen."

"God," said Laura. "That's awful. Right." She scrunched her face up, trying to work out what had happened, how much of a part she had played in this. They were watching her expectantly, waiting to hear her response; and Laura looked at each of them in turn, trying not to panic. And then she stopped herself. Took a deep breath.

"Leave it with me," she said, looking from Rachel to Gareth. "I'll get them back." She smiled at them, nervously but candidly. "I'll get them on board. And the whole company'll be at their carol service at Christmas in a few months' time, you mark my words."

Even Gareth grinned a little at this. He stood up, as did Laura and Rachel. He held out his hand. "Well done, Laura. Good luck. Great to have you back."

Laura shook his hand. She found herself saying, as if she were on *L.A. Law,* "It's great to be back, sir."

Rachel took her hand in both of hers and leaned over the desk. She kissed Laura, and whispered, "If you fuck this up again, I'll kill you."

Laura laughed, and shook her head.

"See you tomorrow," said Rachel. "Bright and early, remember?"

Laura nodded emphatically, slung her bag over her shoulder, and walked out behind them. A small part of her wanted to shake her head in annoyance, to ask Rachel: Couldn't she tell, couldn't they all tell, how different she was from that Laura person of before, who was late and careless and self-obsessed and useless, that reminding her to be on time was totally pointless? Could she really not see? She was new, different. That Laura had gone, gone forever.

chapter thirty-four

Outside the office, Laura stopped and got her phone out of her bag. There were text messages from Jo and Yorky, both asking her how it had gone, saying to call them, good luck, as well as a voice message from her mother: "Hello darling! Just wondering how everything . . . er . . . went today!' as if Laura had been at the circus, not interviewing to be reinstated at work.

She dialed Jo's number, and turned away from Kingsway into the Victorian redbrick back streets of Holborn.

"Yes. . . . I know! I know. Can't believe it. All good now. . . . Well, I don't know about that. . . . Yes, they have. . . . Tomorrow! I know. . . . Oh, thanks, love, thanks for your help, seriously. . . ."

The battery on her phone was low, so Laura turned it off and threw it back in her bag. She threaded her way through the tiny warren of roads behind the Law Courts tucked behind the roar of central London, past the gown-makers for the judges, the minute little pubs, the rambling small bookshops tucked into courtyards.

Eventually she came upon the wide, leafy space of Lincoln's Inn Fields, and she headed to the north side of the square, looking for a diminutive figure outside the Soane Museum. She was there.

The Soane Museum was Laura's favorite in London. Mary used to take her and Simon there as children, and they would walk down to Simpsons in the Strand afterward and have tea. It was the holiday treat of their childhood. Laura loved the higgledy-piggledy nature of the house, the way it had been meticulously assembled by its creator for an atmosphere of chaos, sensation. It was the kind of place you could look around for hours and still find something new to surprise you.

"Granny!" Laura called as she approached.

"Hello, darling," her grandmother said, lowering her huge sunglasses and pushing her headscarf back a little. She looked like a daintier version of the later Gracie Fields, the Capri Years. "You're here. How did it go?"

"I got my job back," said Laura, nodding and smiling with pleasure.

Mary clasped her hands together and brought them above her head. "Oh, that is marvelous," she said. "Just marvelous. Oh, my dear, I am so relieved. You must be, too, hm?" She put her head on one side.

"You could say so," said Laura grimly. "Thank God. Seriously."

"Never mind," said Mary. "All that's over now, yes?"

"Yes," said Laura, slightly apprehensively, and then she added, "And now I have to find a way of persuading some company that hates us to donate thousands of pounds to their local primary school."

Mary rolled her eyes. "Golly."

"Yep," said Laura. "But, you know, I'm going to do it."

"Well, the main thing is the job's yours again," said Mary. "It's just wonderful. Tell me exactly what they said. Tell me what you have to do. Let's go inside." She indicated the steps up to the Soane Museum.

"Right," said Laura, hesitating.

"I want to see the Hogarths," said Mary. "They've been rehung in the picture gallery. Last time I was here—oof, in some cramped little back room. My favorites, don't you know. Shall we go?"

"Gran," said Laura. She stroked her grandmother's arm. "Do you mind if we don't? It's such a lovely day, after all. Can we go up to Lamb's Conduit Street, get a coffee, sit down instead?"

"You don't want to see the Hogarths?" Mary said. "I thought you liked them. Didn't you do that sweet project on them in school about *Marriage à la Mode*—do you remember, darling? You had to make a costume, and Xan found you that wonderful piece of material for a dress. Where did he find it?"

Laura pretended to hunt in her bag for something, not trusting herself to speak.

"In the attic, wasn't it? Wasn't it from a ball gown of mine, something I had in Cairo?" Mary smiled at the memory. "Yes, I'm sure it was. You were a countess, weren't you? Anyway. Are you sure you don't want to look at them?"

"No, not really," said Laura, her face still in her bag.

Mary looked at her, and suddenly said, "How stupid of me. Hogarths. Oh, darling, how stupid of me. Let's go and get a drink. Let's talk about it all."

"I don't—"

Her grandmother put her arm firmly through hers and said, "Shh. We're going to have a little chat."

They found a pretty little pub in Lamb's Conduit Street, and chose a table outside on the cobbles. When Laura appeared back from the bar with two gin and tonics and sat down, Mary said, "Darling. Cheers. Congratulations. Well deserved."

"Well, hardly," said Laura, taking a sip. "I wouldn't have had to go through all this if it wasn't my fault in the first place."

"Maybe not," said Mary, putting her glass down gently on the slatted wooden table. "But still, you obviously proved to them just why you're the great girl you are. Well done, darling. Have you rung your mother?"

"Not yet," said Laura. "My mobile's dead."

"Eh? Oh, I see. Well," said Mary, patting a ring of condensation on the table, "do call her later. She's worried about you."

Laura said nothing.

"We all were, a bit." Mary looked at her from under her eyelashes.

"It's fine now," said Laura after a while. "The job's okay, and all that stuff with Dan—it's over, honestly."

"I don't mean that," said Mary. "I mean that handsome young man who appeared so dramatically at lunch and was clearly so terribly, terribly keen on you."

Laura sometimes wanted to tell her grandmother to lay off sounding like someone at a film dialogue school run by Noël Coward, and never more so than now. She peered into her glass. "Don't worry," she said, sticking her plastic swizzle stick into her slice of lemon. "It's nothing."

"Really?" Mary said. "Hm. It didn't seem like nothing."

"Holiday fling," said Laura. She felt that if she said as few words as possible, she might be able to convince her grandmother, she might not have to stop and take a deep breath.

"Well. It doesn't seem like nothing when you come back at ten o'clock at night, go straight to your room, and lock the door," Mary said frankly, knocking back her drink. "And when your mother knocks on the door, you tell her you've gone to bed and are very tired. And it doesn't seem like nothing when you leave the next morning at the crack of dawn, without saying good-bye to anyone."

"I'm sorry, Gran," she said honestly. "I really am."

"Don't apologize, darling," said Mary. "You missed your aunt's face at breakfast, and that was something quite special."

Laura loved it when Mary was rude about her stepdaughter; it was all too rare, considering how rude Annabel was 98 percent of the time. She grinned. "Really?"

"Absolutely," said Mary. "Your mother did her best, you know. She told Annabel you had severe hayfever and had to go home early before the pollen count rose during the day, and that you had to get back for a very important birthday lunch in town."

Laura thought of her mother, chiding her gently for using too many excuses to get out of going to Chartley, and laughed. "Seriously?"

"Yes, I quite admired her for it. But I fear your aunt will have told everyone she knows that her niece is going to be a marchioness anyway."

Laura looked down at her drink again.

Mary pushed her large sunglasses into her hair. "So, Laura. Tell me, darling. Why did you leave so early?"

"I had to," Laura said quietly, viciously jabbing the lemon slice.

"Why?" Mary asked.

"You wouldn't understand."

"I would," said Mary. "More than I think you know."

"You always find these things easy," said Laura in a rush. "You know the right thing to say, Gran, you get it right. I just—screw it up. I wish . . . Oh, never mind."

"What are you talking about?" said Mary with asperity. "What exactly happened? What did he do?"

"I can't explain it," said Laura. She knew it sounded weak. To set out exactly why she had to leave that night would take too long; it was too complicated, too bound up in everything to do with the past and the person she had been. She shook her head. "Gran, it was never going to work, that's all. Trust me."

Mary didn't say anything for a moment. She pulled her glasses back over her eyes. "Was it the title? Did all of that rather scare you off?"

"Yes," said Laura fervently. She wished she could tell her grandmother about it, about all of it. "We're too different. I—oh, let's not talk about it."

"But," said Mary, "those days before, when you were supposedly dancing off to see that girl in the marshes. You were with him then, weren't you?" Laura nodded. "Just the two of you?" She nodded again. "And, well, it was jolly good then, wasn't it?"

"Yes." Laura smiled despite herself. "It was . . . perfect. When it was just us. Oh, Gran . . ." she said, and she felt sunshine flood over her again at the memory of it, until she clenched her fist and said, "It was perfect. He was perfect. But we realized it was never going to work in the real world. It's just too hard. He's too different. I'm not what he needs. And he's—" She couldn't finish the sentence.

"That's what you think, is it?" said Mary.

"Yes," said Laura, looking at her grandmother, hoping for her approval, praying she would understand.

"What rubbish," said Mary.

Laura stared at her in shock. "What?"

"What total rubbish, Laura. I didn't think you'd ever be like this. Not you," Mary said, waving her glass at her. "Darling, you fall in love all the time. You can't run away just because it doesn't quite fit into your exact romantic dreamworld, you know."

"I'm not," said Laura, so surprised she didn't know what to say. "Gran, don't say that. Please."

"I mean it," said Mary. "Honestly, I'm surprised at you. If you love him, it's worth it. And from the way you were acting about him, it seems to me it is worth it." She laughed. "Good grief. It's not as if he's a warder on a convict ship bound for Australia, or a vivisectionist, or anything. He's a marquis, for God's sake! I know it's a little different from what you're used to, but, goodness! He's a multimillionaire, he's got a beautiful house, and—well, even an idiot like your uncle Robert could see he was mad about you, darling. So what if you're a bit different?" she said, impersonating Laura. "So what if his family was stuck-up? Who cares? If you loved him enough, it wouldn't matter."

Laura put her hand to her throat and sucked air into her lungs, slowly, calmly. "Well," she said. She looked sadly at her grandmother. "You may think I fall in love all the time. I obviously didn't this time, did I? Because I'm always screwing this kind of thing up, and it *does* matter, and that's why it's over."

"Let me say something," said Mary. "Just one more thing, and then I shall stop, and we'll finish our drinks and go into Persephone Books and buy something nice to read."

"Yes," said Laura.

"I nearly didn't have your grandfather. Xan, I mean. When we met, it was all . . . rather complicated. During the war, and all of that." She coughed. "I'll tell you, one day. Not now. But you know, don't you, darling, that he was the great love of my life."

Laura nodded.

There was silence for a moment, nothing to be heard but a bird calling in a young tree behind the pub. Mary said softly, "If I imagine how life would have been without him, Laura—what would have happened to me, carrying on living for all these years, not knowing what it feels like to be with the one person you love. . . ." She leaned forward and put her sunglasses on the table. Her beautiful eyes were bright with tears; Laura thought, with shock, how old she looked all of a sudden. Mary clutched Laura's hand. "I've never said this to you before. Now I say it to you. Don't run away from it, just because it's difficult. Don't."

Ever since she was little, she had been getting it wrong, Laura knew, because all she'd ever wanted was the perfect romantic hero, the man who would rescue her from everything. She couldn't tell her grandmother why it wasn't that it was difficult, or too hard, or that Nick wasn't right for her. It was that, on that evening not even a week ago, as she had watched him with his relatives in that vast ballroom, she had realized that they couldn't be together. She didn't want to make a romantic drama out of it; she didn't want to sigh and mope or scream hysterically to impress others with how awful it all was, even though she felt as if something fundamental, deep within her, had been taken from her. She was simply trying to cope, to get on with her own normal life. Which, she knew, was something he could not be part of.

So she smiled, and squeezed her grandmother's hand. "Thanks, Gran," she said. "I promise you, I'm not running away. Not this time. It's not this one."

Mary gave her a look as if she didn't understand her, and swallowed the rest of her drink. "I need a present for your aunt," she said eventually. "It's her birthday next week. Shall we go?"

"Yes," said Laura. She felt she should try to qualify the conversation a bit. "It's good it happened, you know," she said. "I needed to get it out of my system."

"Get what out of your system?" said Mary, sounding rather imperious.

"My Mr. Darcy/Prince Charming complex," said Laura. "And now I have." She faced down her grandmother, who was pushing her bag onto her arm. But her grandmother didn't look at her.

"If you think so, darling," she said.

* * *

Later, after she had deposited her grandmother back at Crecy Court and walked on to Baker Street, Laura stopped and looked around her. It was early evening, and there was a freshness in the air that belied the summer heat. She didn't want to get into a cramped, airless Tube carriage, not on this, her last day of freedom. She crossed busy, hectic Marylebone Road, walking briskly, and headed into Regent's Park. She would walk home.

Half an hour later, when she reached the row of shops near her flat, Laura went into the mini-market and bought some lemons and a fat, frothing bunch of coriander. She was making supper. She climbed the steps to her flat, tired but happy, swinging her string bag beside her.

When she opened the door, the stereo was on, and she could hear the sound of low conversation. Yorky said, "Is that you?" and appeared in the hallway, breathless, his feet bare, a strange expression on his face.

"You okay, loverboy?" said Laura, putting her keys on the table. "Did you get my message? I turned my phone off. I got the job back! Hey. Did Becky call you?"

"I got your message, yes, yes," said Yorky, looking agitated. "I tried calling you—Laura—I thought you wouldn't be back till later—"

"Laura?"

A voice came from the sitting room, so familiar to her, yet so alien, but Laura knew exactly who it was. Her hand flew to her mouth and she dropped the string bag. The lemons rolled out and trundled across the floor.

Dan appeared in the doorway. "Hello, Laura," he said, and he smiled that same old smile. "I'm back."

chapter thirty-five

The only noise for a few seconds was the sound of one breakaway lemon coasting across the floorboards. Yorky bent and picked it up.

"Laura, mate," he said, as if Dan weren't there, "I'm really sorry. He turned up about an hour ago, I couldn't get him to go. He wouldn't leave."

"Right, right," said Laura in a detached tone. She looked at Dan, drinking in the sight of him again. It wasn't possible that it was less than three weeks since she'd seen him. It seemed like a lifetime. Here he was in front of her, this onetime figure of myth, this fantasy, this "ideal man," every detail of him familiar to her, as obsessed over by her as anyone could ever have been, and she felt nothing, just curiosity. How fickle she was. If anything was proof of that, this was.

"Er—hi. Why are you here?" she said, in what she hoped was a polite voice.

Dan flicked a glance up and down at her. "You look amazing. Have you been away?"

Laura was suddenly overtaken by the urge to laugh. She nodded, and said again, "Dan—why are you here?"

Yorky was hovering in the doorway to the kitchen. He said, "I'll get a beer . . ." and disappeared.

"Come and sit down," said Dan.

"I will," said Laura. She couldn't help feeling slightly annoyed that she was being made to feel like a guest in her own home.

She sat down on the sofa, Dan next to her, and she stared at him as if he were an alien. He was tanned, but there were dark circles under his eyes. He cleared his throat, rather awkwardly, and sat up. "Listen. Laura. This isn't a big deal, and I tried to call you, but your phone was off."

"Okay," she said, looking at him, trying to remind herself of how she'd felt about him. Nothing.

"I felt shitty that I haven't spoken to you. Since—you know. I came because I just think I should pay you back. For the holiday."

"What?" said Laura.

"The holiday. You must have had to lose the booking, me dropping out like that." He said it as if he'd been prevented from going because of the flu, rather than because of the termination of the relationship and the appearance on the scene/ultrasound screen of his firstborn by another woman.

She said, "Oh, well—you know. There's no need."

"There is," said Dan. "Seriously, Laura, I won't take no for an answer."

Since Laura had had, the day before, a fairly unpleasant conversation with her credit card company, she had to admit this was welcome news. "That's really kind of you," she said practically. "It'd be—helpful, let's say."

"Of course. I mean it," said Dan. "The whole thing. I'll pay."

"No, no," said Laura. "Honestly. Just your half, that'd be great."

"I want to." He pulled his checkbook out of the back pocket of his jeans. "Look, I've been a complete dick."

"You have," said Laura, handing him a pen from the table.

Dan laughed. He took the pen and started scribbling. "I'll make it blank, so you can work out what it cost. The whole thing. Please, Laura. Let me pay for it all. It was my fault, totally my fault."

Laura said slowly, "No, it wasn't. It wasn't all your fault, you know." She patted his hand. "Just half. That's all. You need the money for the baby, for God's sake. It was me, too. I should have—been a bit wiser." She stared out the window. "I've learned my lesson."

Things are different now, she wanted to say. It'll be a cold day in hell before I lose my heart to you again or get hurt by you again. Or someone like you. And, by the way, your girlfriend's a complete psycho.

He signed the check with a flourish, tore it off, and gave it to her. "Here," he said. "And let's—let's be friends, shall we?"

"Right," said Laura, taking the check. "So . . . how's Amy doing? How's she feeling?" she asked politely, wanting to sound as if they were fellow parents outside the school gates, not people who a month ago were in the throes of a torrid affair.

Dan shifted on the sofa. He said blankly, "She's fine, thanks. Fine. Yes—Miami was, er, great, thanks. We had—a great time."

"Really?"

"Yeah," said Dan. "We—I don't know if you heard? We had to come home a few days early. Amy not feeling so good, you know."

"Oh, I'm sure," said Laura.

Dan said in a rush, "It's an amazing place, South Beach. The Art Deco hotels, wow. They're wonderful." Laura nodded politely.

"The weather was great, too—we were lucky, apparently. And the food's incredible." His voice rose a little. "And loads and loads of designer shops and boutiques. So Amy was delirious, as you can imagine. God, I'm dreading the next credit card bill. I kept saying to her, 'What's the fucking point when you won't be able to *wear* any of this stuff for the next six months?' But apparently, that's the wrong thing to say. You know how touchy she is."

"Yes," said Laura. Several responses to this rose to her lips: Yes, I know how touchy she is, you were always going on about it, and anyway, she's pregnant, give her a break. . . . Yes, I know she's an acquisitive little cow, but you're the one who wouldn't leave her, mate. . . . Do you actually think it's appropriate to blithely be having this conversation with me?

But she said nothing. Getting up, she took his arm gently and steered him toward the door. "Thanks so much for coming round, Dan. And thanks for this." She waved the check. She looked at him and smiled gently. "You really didn't have to. I—"

"No sweat," said Dan. "It's the least I can do." He bent and kissed her on the cheek, and she felt nothing, it was strange. Or strange that it wasn't stranger.

"So—I'll see you soon," he said.

"Well," said Laura, "probably not, I expect."

"You're right," said Dan, nodding vigorously. "Yep. Uhm . . . where are we, then?"

"What?" said Laura. "You and me? We're nowhere, Dan."

"I know," said Dan. "I just—well. I'm sorry, that's all." She inclined her head; he looked at her curiously. "You okay?" he asked.

"I'm fine," said Laura. "Quite tired, I've had a long day."

"You—you're different," said Dan. "You seem different." He was standing in the doorway, leaning against it with that old air of confidence she used to love so much.

"Am I?" she said. "I don't think so."

"More . . . grown-up," said Dan, nodding. He looked at her soulfully. "Oh, Laura."

"More over you," said Laura. "That's it. I promise." She patted him on the shoulder. "Bye, Dan."

Dan looked slightly startled, and then he smiled. "Yeah. Right. Bye, Laura. Good—good luck with everything."

Amazing, thought Laura, as she closed the door quietly behind him and leaned against it, her hands flat against the cool painted wood. She was touched by the gesture. It was more than she'd expected of him. But that was Dan, she thought. It didn't occur to him that it was at all weird for him to be chatting merrily away, signing checks for holidays, pressing himself just *slightly* too long against her as he said good-bye. That he couldn't see that he hadn't been in love with Laura at all; he just didn't love his own girlfriend, and was looking for some way out, or some penance to pay for not wanting to be with her. Laura knew clearly now that it wasn't that he should have been with her, Laura. No, he should just not be with Amy, and that was all there was to it. She didn't feel relieved, or justified, or sorry for either of them. She didn't know what she felt, other than a curious blankness about it all.

There was a strange, acidic smell coming down the hallway. In the kitchen, Yorky was hopping around in an agitated fashion, cutting up the coriander. He'd chopped it with such nervous energy that it was in tiny, tiny slivers, only millimeters long.

"Ah," he said as he saw Laura watching him from the doorway. "Hello, old girl. Are you—are you okay? I started on the supper."

"I'm fine," said Laura. "Absolutely fine. He was sweet, actually." She smiled.

"Oh, God," said Yorky to himself.

"No, no," Laura hastened to reassure him. "Nothing like that, I promise. He wanted to pay for his half of the money I lost, canceling our holiday."

Even saying "our," like there ever had been an "our" as in her and Dan, sounded weird. She opened a bottle of wine and collected the glasses. It was still light outside. As Yorky cooked some chicken, sloshing in a little wine, and sliced some crusty bread on the side, Laura set the table. She went to the window and threw it open, breathing in the evening air. Across the treetops, streets, houses, more houses, cars, big roads, shops. She looked north, to the horizon.

Somewhere, in a huge house a hundred miles away, was Nick. Sitting there eating supper by himself, in an empty room, a great rattling house stuffed with treasures and relics of the past. But nothing that was actually *his*, his own personal stuff, until he climbed those long winding stairs to his room at the top of the house, a room with a radio, his own clothes, some paperbacks, that bed—and another, very different view out the window over the treetops. Was he on his own? Was anyone with him? Did he have someone to talk to, like Charles? She stared out the window, willing herself to see more, if only for a second, before the picture left her mind.

"Ready?" came Yorky's voice behind her. Laura spun around.

"Yep," she said.

Yorky looked at her. "Sit down, and pour that wine," he said. "You've had a lucky escape." She looked confused, so he said, "Dan."

"Oh," said Laura. "God, yes. You know, it's fine."

They clinked glasses.

"Tell me what's happening with Becky," said Laura, switching tack. "So, she hasn't replied to any of your texts yet?"

"Right," said Yorky.

"Have you seen her on the stairs or anything?" Laura asked.

"Nooo," said Yorky. "Not since she left my place early on Sunday morning. Oohoo."

"You said she fell asleep on the sofa and nothing happened," Laura reminded him.

"Er," said Yorky, deflated. "Er, yeah."

"So," said Laura encouragingly, "what have you done about it?'

"I've taken action," said Yorky, looking pleased. "I thought, okay, perhaps she didn't get any of the texts. So I'm on my way back from school today, and I think, I'll go round to where she works. You know that little gift shop in West Hampstead?"

"Oh, God," said Laura.

"Yes, absolutely," said Yorky, unheeding. "I get there, it's about six-ish. I can see her clearing up and stuff. And when she comes out, I say, 'Hi, Becky, how are you, okay?' And—God, I don't understand girls, I really don't."

"Why?" said Laura.

"She pretends she hasn't seen me, and runs back into the shop! And I follow her and say, 'Hey, look, I only wanted to make sure you got my text messages. And, by the way, do you want to go out next week?' And she said she was really busy, but she'd think about it and let me know. I feel confident, though. Strangely confident."

"How come?" Laura asked, trying not to grin.

"Er . . ." said Yorky. "Not sure, really."

"So . . ." Laura said after a pause. "When are you seeing her again, then?"

They both cracked up, and then Yorky said, "Seriously, Laura. I'm really proud of you. Norfolk did you a power of good. You're so much better off without him, you know. I'm not just saying that. It's the truth. And . . ." He looked slightly embarrassed. "I don't want to sound pervy, but you look amazing at the moment."

"Really?" said Laura.

"Whatever it is, you look—er, very nice. Really well. And you know, you're better now. Time for a fresh start, eh?"

"Yep," said Laura. "Fresh start."

"Got your eye on anyone, then?" Yorky said, helping himself to the chicken and avoiding her gaze.

It was as if someone had asked her if she were an ironing board, or if she liked drinking raw meth—a completely outlandish, freakish question. "God, no," Laura said. "Me?"

"Yes, you!" Yorky said, chuckling. "Don't look so amazed! You've always got someone you're mad about, haven't you? Come on, Lara. Who is it?"

Can't you see? she wanted to say to Yorky, just as she had with Rachel earlier that day. Can't you see I've changed, that everything's different?

"No one, honestly," she said after a bit. She pulled the bottle toward her.

Yorky waved his wineglass at her and nodded, in an ancient-sage sort of way. "You should get back out there, Laura. Get over him, get under someone else, you know. You're the best, Loz, so don't leave it too long before you fall in love again, okay?"

She said nothing, but smiled. Yorky raised his glass. "All better now. To fresh starts, eh?"

"Fresh starts," Laura echoed, knowing he was right.

Yorky was right, it *was* a fresh start. And she wasn't going to screw it up again. She was at work an hour early the next day.

"It's lovely to see you again," said Rachel, who was waiting for her as she walked through the door. She handed her a bunch of tulips.

"Oh, my goodness," said Laura. "That's so sweet of you." She kissed her. "Thank you, Rachel." She bent down, put her bag on the floor, and switched on the computer.

Shana waved at her across the large table they shared. She was eating a doughnut, and after a minute she said, "You okay?"

"Fine, you?"

"Yeah. Good to see you again, Laura."

"Thanks."

The phone rang, and Shana grinned at her and picked it up.

"Come into my office when you've sorted yourself out," said Rachel. "We'll talk about what you're going to be working on next. This major fund-raising drive's about to take off, and I want you to work on it."

"Thanks," said Laura. She tapped Rachel's arm as she turned to leave. "I mean it. Thanks."

"Don't let me down," said Rachel quietly. "That's all I ask, Laura love. Show me you've turned over a new leaf."

"Trust me," Laura said. "I mean it—I have."

And she had. For the next month, work became her obsession. She loved throwing herself into it, proving to Rachel that she'd changed. And she started walking everywhere. There were fresh flowers in the flat each week, and Laura's room was always tidy, her clothes sorted and hanging neatly, freshly ironed. She remembered birthdays; she cooked a meal for Yorky and Becky (which he could pass off as his own); she organized a picnic for Hilary to celebrate her promotion at the museum where she worked, and helped Jo paint her bathroom while Chris was away. She couldn't undo the way she'd behaved in the past, she knew that; but there was a grain of comfort from realizing, as she looked around at her friends, that she was back in her old life, in some small way.

For the short rest of the summer, Laura felt the zeal of someone on New Year's Day, trying to suppress their deep depression about it being cold and dark and having to go back to work by distracting themselves with a new keep-fit regimen, some bulbs in a window box, learning to cook, taking tap lessons—anything rather than give in to it. This was her life; she knew it and recognized it for what it was. At last she felt she was being a proactive, organized, serene person. The feeling of emotional isolation, of being able to look back at her life, her mistakes, and feel nothing, or virtually nothing, continued. And if she occasionally had to bite her lip when an involuntary memory of those brief few days flew back to her—walking down a leafy country lane, sitting on the beach at nighttime, creeping through the great hall, lying quietly holding hands with him in bed looking at him, or his face when she said she was leaving—well, she simply told herself to add it to the box, the box of memories of the past.

chapter thirty-six

Early in September came the return of the prodigal son. Simon Foster arrived home from Peru, where he had acclimatized to the altitude, learned to speak Quechuan, grown an impressive beard, and bought or made a selection of brightly colored, simply woven garments that hung, Guevara-like, about his person. What does someone having acquired all these skills and possessions do with such a trove? Move back in with his parents in Harrow, of course. He arrived back on a damp Saturday afternoon, and Angela phoned, delirious with excitement, to ask Laura—and Yorky, too, of course—round for Sunday lunch.

Though she couldn't wait to see her brother again, Laura had to admit she was kind of reluctant to go to her parents'. She hadn't seen them since she got back from Norfolk. It wasn't that she was avoiding them; it was more that she . . . she'd been busy. She knew they wondered what had happened with her and Nick. Her mother called fairly often, wanting to "chat," and Laura always managed to steer her off the subject. She felt awful, since she knew her mum must be bursting with curiosity, if nothing else; but she just couldn't talk about it, and she knew Angela would never ask directly. Angela wasn't the only one Laura was trying to avoid, little though she liked to admit it.

There was Mary. She felt guilty about her, too—she hadn't seen her for weeks, either. But Laura pushed that to the back of her mind, along with everything else. The trouble was, she was working very hard these days, and not that she was in a lovelorn frame of mind, she told herself. It was all very well, going round to Mary's and listening while her grandmother told her about the time she and Xan stayed in a palazzo in Venice and met Nancy Mitford, or how they had visited a maharajah in Jaipur and been woken by the sound of fighting tigers; yes, that was all very interesting, romantic, fascinating, when you were younger and not concerned with other things. Now, she just didn't have the time. A voice in her head was telling her that was rubbish, that she could talk to Mary about anything, always had done. No. But Laura consoled herself with the thought she'd call her. Soon.

The third member of the trilogy Laura was holding at arm's length was Jo, and Jo had gone on her trip of a lifetime with Chris to Australia (Yorky and Laura referred to it as Their Trip Before They Get Pregnant). It was a fortnight since they'd left. Laura felt guilty about Jo, too, but a slight sense of relief that she was out of the country for a while, because Jo knew something was up, and Laura knew Jo knew something was up, and this gave her some breathing space. Laura wasn't worried—it wasn't a secret, after all. She just wanted control, she wanted to keep a lid on it all. Maybe that way it would just go away. Jo, Mary, her mother—she loved them all, but while they were capable of concern, she wanted to keep them at bay. Just for a while.

* * *

"I know what it'll be like," said Laura gloomily as she and Yorky walked up Heathcote Road toward her parents' house. "Me sitting there like a spare part, or tidying away, being a good daughter, while Mum has kittens because Simon's back and you're there, too."

"Well, so she should," said Yorky reasonably, though slightly smugly. He was secure in his knowledge of Mrs. Foster's deep and lasting affection for her children's oldest friend. "He's been away for nearly four months now, Laura. Remember those two weeks when you didn't hear from him? She thought he was dead."

"He wasn't dead!" Laura exclaimed impatiently.

"Well, obviously," said Yorky.

"You know what I mean! He just couldn't be frigging bothered to drop his own parents an e-mail saying, 'Hello, I'm still alive'! He's a lazy bastard!"

"You don't know that," said Yorky. "Your poor mum." He coughed self-consciously and increased his stride, looking bashfully down at the bunch of tulips he was clutching.

"You are such a suck," said Laura, reverting to the behavior of her teenage years. She'd been so grown-up lately. Simon brought out the childish side in her, she knew.

"Laura! Hello, dear!" cried her mother, flinging open the door. "And James! So wonderful that you could come, we're all so pleased. Darling," she said, hugging her daughter. "How *are you*?" She emphasized the question delicately.

"Great, thanks," said Laura, thrusting a bottle of wine at her mother. She gave her a kiss. "Where is he, then?"

Simon appeared in the doorway to the kitchen, and Laura had to stop herself from running toward him. She smiled. "All right?"

"Yeah," said Simon, leaning against the cellar door. "You all right, sis?"

"Yeah," said Laura, coming forward and giving him a big hug. " 'S nice to see you."

"You too." Simon squeezed her tight, and punched her on the arm.

Laura kissed him. "Where's Dad? I'll go and say hi. Back in a min."

Simon was hugging Yorky, patting him on the back. "Out the back. Hey, man."

Laura wandered into the kitchen, which was, as always, immaculate. The white surfaces spotless, the plants in little tiled bowls on the windowsill, the childish nursery drawings by her and Simon in clip frames. The National Trust calendar by the fridge, annotated neatly by both George and Angela. She looked at it. September had a picture of a beautiful garden at a stately home in Shropshire. She grimaced.

"SIMON BACK!" it said on the Friday, covered with stars and underlined. Then, the following weekend: "*The Real Inspector Hound,* Harrow Am Dram Soc, 7:30 p.m." "Dentist, 1 p.m."

From the door out to the little conservatory at the back, George Foster emerged, wearing his gardening gloves. He looked up and saw his daughter, and smiled. "Oh, hello, love," he said. "How are you?"

"Fine, Dad," said Laura, watching him. He took his gloves off gingerly, hung them carefully on the pot by the conservatory door, then neatly wiped his weekend loafers on the doormat and shook out his dark blue corduroy trousers.

"All okay with you, love?" he asked.

Laura wondered what her poor dad must have made of her over the past couple of months, lurching from one crisis to another. She nodded emphatically. "Yeah. Really good. Thanks, Dad."

"Good, good, ha-ha, good," said George, visibly relieved he didn't have to say anything more. He rubbed his hands together.

"Well, hello, James." He advanced into the room and shook Yorky's hand. "I'll get the drinks," he said, smiling with pleasure as he went over to the fridge. "Nice to have everyone here, isn't it."

Laura nodded happily, and sat on the seat watching her dad take a new lemon from the bowl.

"Slice this for me, love, will you?" he said.

In the corridor, Simon was saying earnestly to Yorky, "I *am* well, mate. Peru—it changed my life. I can't wait to tell you all about it, you know."

"Lunch in five minutes, darling," her mother said, bustling into the kitchen as George picked up the drinks tray and headed for the sitting room. "How's work, Laura?"

"Fine, Mum. Great, actually."

"Oh . . ." said Angela, pleased. "That's wonderful. I'm so glad. And you—you're . . . About that chap, you know. The marquis—I haven't liked to ask, but . . ."

"Oh, it's absolutely fine," said Laura. "Good grief, I've totally forgotten about it, Mum, really."

"Your granny said that—" Angela began.

"Gran likes to gossip," said Laura furiously. Her mother looked hurt. "Sorry, Mum, but I promise you, I'm fine."

Angela didn't say anything. She just looked rather quashed. "Oh, love. I know you like talking to Granny about it, but you know I'm here if you ever want—" she began timidly.

"Yes, of course," said Laura, feeling guilty, and guilt making her even angrier. "Come on, Mum, let's go." She grabbed her drink and went into the sitting room, Angela following slowly. As they entered, her brother looked up.

"Now she's here. Hurrah. My favorite sister. And my darling mum. I just want to make a toast. To being back home again, with all of you." Simon raised his glass in one hand, and took his mother's hand in the other. "I've felt very far away from here the last few months, you know. But this is where I come from. It's home. And it's just great to be here. Cheers. Thanks, Mum and Dad. Cheers."

"My boy and girl, under one roof," Angela said, with a catch in her throat. "Oh, it's so nice." She caught sight of Yorky, looking rather left out. "Oh, James. And you, too."

"Chocolate, James? Go on," said Angela. She waved a plate under Yorky's chin, so it loomed in his face and his eyes squinted to focus.

"Oh, thank you, Angela," said Yorky. It always sounded awkward, Laura thought, when he called her mother by her first name.

Angela spun brightly round. "Well," she said, rubbing her hands. "Everyone having a good time? You all right, Simon dear?"

"Yes, Mum," said Simon patiently, for the fourth time. "I'm fine. Sit down."

Looking at him, Laura realized Simon was indeed transformed. He didn't look like her younger brother. He looked huge, tall, imposing. It was as if Aragorn had suddenly turned up in the lounge in Harrow and was drinking a glass of Waitrose best pinot noir on the sofa next to Angela and George after a nice lunch of roast chicken. The conversation over lunch had been chitchat, Simon telling them a few stories here and there but never really going into detail; but Laura could feel he was gearing up for it, for something.

"So!" said George.

"We want to hear *all* about it!" said Angela.

"Yes," said Yorky, more noncommittally.

"So," Laura said weakly. "Tell us all about it then. . . ." She loved her brother, and she really did want to know how he'd got on, but Laura was generally bored rigid by tales of other people's holidays, especially of the four-month traveling variety.

"Try to contain your indifference a bit more successfully, sis," Simon said, leaning back in the sofa and sighing a deep sigh of pleasure. "Well, it was great. But it's really nice to be back now, I must say. I really wanted to see you all. I've got a lot to tell you."

"Oh, great," Laura said. "Highlights?"

Yorky nudged her. Simon smiled. "Highlights. Okay. Being attacked by a wolf. Nearly getting shot during a drug raid. Um—the mountains early in the morning. And dancing round a campfire with the girl of my dreams."

"Oh!" said Angela. "How lovely!"

"Eh?" said Yorky. "Who's that, mate?" He looked curious.

"Jorgia," Simon said, an expression of great serenity creeping across his tanned face. He turned to his parents and opened his arms wide. "I'm in love, Mum and Dad. She's the most wonderful girl, and I can't wait to bring her home to meet you."

"Are you being serious?" said Angela, whipping her head round. "Who is she, Simon darling?"

"Oh, Mum," said Simon, taking his mother's hand again. "She's just amazing. She's from a tiny village, high up in the mountains near Machu Picchu. She—she—well, I want you to meet her."

"Right!" said Angela, smiling slightly mechanically. "My goodness. Ha! She sounds wonderful." She winked significantly at her husband. "Doesn't she, George?"

"Er . . ." said George, twirling his wineglass in his hand. "Great. Really great. So, what does she do?"

"She lives with her parents at the moment," Simon said, smiling broadly at them. "Her father's a doctor, in the village! Simeon Questodora. Jorgia is his only daughter, he has two sons. He's a good man, a wise man. He has welcomed me into their family." Simon nodded, half bowing, as if Dr. Questodora might be watching him via a secret camera hidden in the vase of dried flowers on the mantelpiece. "Anyway," he went on, "I'm going back there, Mum and Dad. I want to live there." He coughed as his parents gawped at him. "I want to marry her. Not now—I know it's all very sudden. I want to see if we can have a future together, the two of us, and how we can make it work."

"Eh?" said Yorky.

"It may not work," said Simon. "I'm fully aware of that." He cleared his throat again and said quietly, "But I've never been happier. You know me. I didn't used to believe in fairy tales. Well, now I do."

Sitting on the sofa, Laura could barely believe her ears. Yes, of course, this was happy news; but Simon was the man who had shagged identical twins at university (Yorky had told her this), who had had an affair with his boss for a year and managed not to get fired, but promoted. Simon was kind, he was charming, always honest—but he had never wanted a serious relationship. This was incredible!

Besides which, setting aside Simon's historic aversion to falling in love, she thought, surely if you claim you're about to marry some random Peruvian villager you've known for three minutes, you must have gone mad. You shouldn't be talking about it in a mature, balanced way. She could see that this was affecting their parents deeply, and that instead of saying, "My God, have you gone completely mad," they were instead likely to—yes, there it was—

"Congratulations, son," said George, striding across the room, clutching Simon's hand. "That sounds—er, wonderful."

"Oh, Simon," said Angela, tears in her eyes. "You're sure? Well, that's just, just lovely."

"I am sure," said Simon, standing up and putting his arm round his mother, as Laura watched in amazement, scowling at both of them. "I'm sure she's the one for me. I love her. But we have to think about what to do next. Jorgia—she . . ." He looked down and blushed, then smiled shyly at them. Laura felt slightly nauseated. "She wants to come over to meet you all, as soon as possible, but she is very proud. She won't let me pay. She is saving up herself for the flight."

"How long will that take?" said Laura waspishly. Yorky gave her a sharp look.

"A few months at least. She is very proud, like her father, like her family. So—until then"—he ground to a halt, rather uncertainly—"I'll be here, if that's okay. You see, you see—I've handed in my notice at the charity."

"Oh," said Angela and George together. Angela reached out and clutched the enamel box that stood on the mantelpiece for support. "That's great, dear," she said faintly, and looked at her husband.

"They wanted me to go to India next month, and I can't, if she's coming here. I had to say no, and when I did, well . . ." He held up his hands, rather helplessly. "I know it's a bit reckless—but it just seemed like the only thing to do. I couldn't let her get away, you know."

Reckless? Laura wanted to shout. I should say so! Jeez Louise, the world has gone mad!

Her father said, "Well. You had worked there for five years, it was probably time for a change, eh?"

"I'm pleased for you," said Yorky, nodding wildly.

"Yes," said Angela. "Well! Travel really does broaden the mind, doesn't it!"

"So, Laura, what do you think?" Simon said, sitting down next to her and putting his hand on her shoulder.

Good grief, thought Laura. The world has gone mad. Here am I being a sensible person, and what reward do I get? Whereas Simon has clearly got some brain disease, causing him to lose all grip on reality. No job! No home! A girlfriend halfway up a mountain on the other side of the world! And this is good news?

Simon was looking at her expectantly, and she found it hard to breathe all of a sudden, though she couldn't have said why. And she felt a bit sick. Well, she reasoned, it was a lot to take in, for anyone. She gripped his wrist with her hand, and said, "It's fantastic, Simon. Great. I just hope—you know, it's a big step."

"For fuck's sake!" Laura ranted to Yorky, when they were safely on the Tube heading back. "He's gone completely *mad*, and I'm the one they think's the bad guy! Jesus!"

Yorky said nothing. He looked up at the Tube map.

"Seriously!" said Laura, warming to her theme. "The hypocrisy! Bloody Simon! He misses Gran's birthday, he's lost his job, he waltzes in after months away and announces he's shacked up with some Peruvian gypsy from the mountains, and Mum and Dad! God! They just smile and say, 'Wow, that's great!' "

"But it *is* great, isn't it?" said Yorky.

"No!" cried Laura. "Well, yes," she said, amending herself hurriedly. "Of course, it's fine, whatever. But really, has he lost his *mind*? He can't be in love with her, can he?"

Yorky looked at her, then turned away slowly. "Oh, just shut up, will you?"

Laura gaped at him. "What?"

"Yes!" Yorky said, and there was real disdain in his voice, disdain mixed with anger. "Just shut up! What's happened to you, Laura! I know you're on this No Romance kick, ever since Dan, and I know you hate men, and I know all of a sudden your job's the most important thing to you since—since sliced bread, but, God! Sometimes . . ." He trailed off.

Laura was completely bewildered. "Sometimes what?" she said, trying to make sense of what Yorky was talking about. She'd never seen him quite this cross.

"You're—you're just so—so weird about everything these

days!" Yorky said. "God, you've been like this ever since you came back from Norfolk."

"What do you mean?" said Laura, her heart hammering in her chest.

"Well!" Yorky threw his hands in the air. "I thought it did you good, but you've changed, Laura, you're just . . ." He shook his head, bewildered. "You sit there in front of the TV and you don't concentrate, you're in a world of your own. You work all the time. You don't go out anymore. You're really negative about everything, you don't want to do anything. You won't look at another bloke—every time me or Jo mentions some guy you might like, you look as if we've just thrown up over you." Yorky twitched his nose and scratched it. "Look, mate. I know Dan hurt you, but what did he do to make you this fucked up about everything?" he said sadly. "Here's your brother, okay, yeah, sure, he's gone a bit mad, and he thinks he's in love with some girl he met traveling. But you're his sister! Just support him, okay? Don't be snide, don't think you know it all. You don't."

"I know I don't," Laura whispered. "I know."

Yorky looked horrified. "Listen, I didn't mean—"

Laura said, "It's fine. You're completely right, I'm sure."

chapter thirty-seven

The Simon situation rankled Laura, though she didn't understand why. Over the next week, she kept thinking about what Yorky had said on the way back from Harrow. Sometimes she thought he was mad, totally out of order, and she would feel a calm within herself that she-was-right-he-was-wrong, and no action was required on her part. And sometimes, the peeling away of that layer beneath which lay all her insecurity made her numb with fear.

Perhaps Yorky had a point about not going out enough, though. She had been a bit of a hermit since she'd got back. And she should be trying to meet someone else, she knew. But where was she supposed to meet someone, even if she wanted to, which she didn't? Laura started thinking, How did I used to do it? Fall in love like that at the drop of a hat? How did I used to meet men so easily, so happily, be so relaxed about it all? It seemed completely alien to her now.

Still, she hated not having things right with Yorky, just hated it. The following Saturday evening, she was in on her own when her flatmate returned from an afternoon out with Becky, walking along the canal by Regent's Park. He was mysteriously silent on the subject, which Laura assumed meant nothing had happened; instead he suggested a "casual" dinner the following Saturday to welcome Simon back. Laura knew this was in reality a chance for Yorky to drop round and ask Becky if she wanted to swing by for supper (nothing special, just a few friends coming over, no pressure). She was glad, because it meant things were okay again, so she sounded enthusiastic about it, and waited for Yorky to talk about Becky for the next ten minutes. But he didn't. Again, this was strange.

"I'll cook," said Laura as she opened a bottle of wine.

"No, *I'll* cook," said Yorky firmly. "You call Simon, get him to come. And Jo and Chris are back next week, can you text her on her mobile, get them along?"

"Fine," said Laura, conceding defeat happily. "That'll be great. Have some wine."

"Love some," said Yorky. "You in tonight, then?"

"Yep," said Laura firmly. "Just a quiet one."

"Great," said Yorky. "Me too. Let's drink lots and tell each other sad stories of the sea."

"Er . . . okay," said Laura. "How's it going with the girl downstairs, then?"

"Great," said Yorky, nodding. "It's early days, you know. But—she's just fantastic. That's all there is to it." He shrugged, and simply smiled at her.

Laura felt panic shoot through her, and she didn't know why.

"Come on, Yorks," she said, struggling to find the joke in it. "Haven't you got some funny story about it to tell me?"

"Not really," said Yorky. He yawned, stretched his lanky body, and reached up to get two glasses out of the cupboard. "We had a good chat yesterday, you know. We're going to take it slowly. But—it's just going really well. That's all."

Laura watched him, amazed. "That's . . . great," she said, hating herself for not thinking it was great. "Wow. I'm really pleased."

At eight-thirty the next morning, Laura was—like most right-minded people at eight-thirty on a Sunday—fast asleep. But gradually she stirred, for something was ringing in her ear; it kept on ringing. It would stop, and then start again. It took a good few minutes before she realized that the sound was the phone in the hallway, ringing, then stopping when the answering machine kicked in, then ringing again.

"Shut up!" Yorky croaked from his room down the corridor.

Knowing that Yorky would happily ignore the phone while it rang for a good few hours yet, Laura fell out of bed, cursing, and shuffled down the corridor.

"Hallagh," she growled into the receiver.

"Laura? Hello, dear. It's Annabel," came a voice down the phone, disconcertingly close by. "How are you, dear?"

"Er . . ." Laura coughed. "I'm fine. Are you—is everything okay?"

"Yes, of course," said Aunt Annabel, sounding astonished. "I rang to say hello. So—how are you, dear?"

Waking up more and more by the second, Laura shook her head and ran her free hand through her hair. "Yes, well, like I said. I'm fine. It's—it's a bit early for me, though. How are you?"

"Well, I'm fine, too," said Aunt Annabel. "Really very fine."

There was a rather tense silence for a few seconds. Laura waited for her aunt to speak, because she wasn't really sure what to say next.

"So, Laura. Have you seen the paper today?" said Aunt Annabel.

Laura wanted to yell, "It's eight-thirty in the morning, of course I haven't seen the paper today. Go away!" but instead she said, "No, why?"

"I think you should," said Aunt Annabel. "I was really ringing to say hello, of course. But I did just want to check you'd got a copy!" She cleared her throat, and said almost reverentially, "To see *him* in it. Number three, no less! My goodness."

"In what?" Laura asked, her mind beginning to whir.

"Britain's Most Eligible Bachelors," said Aunt Annabel. "You know who, dear!"

Annabel had never called her "dear" before, nor rung her at home before, nor indeed ever expressed much interest in any aspect of Laura's life before, and it was this that struck Laura first, before the mist cleared and she realized what her aunt was talking about. "Oh," she whispered, clutching the receiver with both hands. She leaned against the wall. "What is it?" she said, trying to keep her voice normal. "Nick?"

"Well, I think you should read it for yourself!" her aunt said gaily. "But we knew you'd want to see it, so we thought we'd better let you know."

"Right," said Laura, wondering who "we" was.

"I'm sure everyone else will be calling to say they've seen it, too, but it's quite something to say you're an item with the Marquis of Ranelagh, especially after this!" Annabel said in tones of delight. "And you were so *mysterious* about him in Norfolk, I didn't even say good-bye to you. Lulu and Fran were *so* sorry to have missed you, you know. So sorry!"

"Me too," said Laura, crossing her fingers. "How are they?"

"Good, fine, wonderful. Fran and Ludo are in Singapore at the moment! Having a wonderful time, back in a few days' time. And Lulu's in the south of France. It's just little old me and your uncle Robert, you know. On our own! Very lonely! So when your uncle saw the article this morning, he said, 'Annabel, you must call Laura.' And I thought, Gosh, yes, I must."

Since Uncle Robert was notorious for saying nothing and contributing nothing, Laura found quite a lot wrong with this assertion. But she merely replied, "Thanks, Aunt Annabel. Look, I'd better—"

"Yes, yes," said Annabel. "I'll let you go—you know, it's marvelous. That's all. And, Laura—do hope to see you soon. Both of you, maybe?" she said coyly.

"Both?"

"Well," said Annabel, "you . . . and the marquis, of course."

"Aunt Annabel," said Laura. "Really, there's nothing going on with me and Nick."

"Oh, really?"

"Really," Laura said firmly. She forced herself to sound blithely unconcerned. "In fact, I'm sure he's forgotten all about me. It was just a fling, seriously. I'm afraid if you're thinking we're an item . . ."

"Oh, no!" said Annabel, backtracking hastily. "Actually, it says, you know. In the article. It says he's got a girlfriend."

Laura's knees turned to water; she swayed against the doorframe. "Oh," she said. "Right, then."

"I just thought that was probably rubbish, you know these newspapers," said Annabel, blissfully unconscious of any irony. "And he did seem awfully—*keen* on you, you know. . . ."

"Annabel!" came a voice gruffly in the background. "Any more tea?"

"Oh, there's Robert," Annabel called gaily. "Must go. Lovely to chat, Laura!"

"What?" said Laura, then hastily: "Of course, thanks, Aunt Annabel, sorry I'm not really awake. . . ."

"Please, don't worry! Good-bye!" Annabel said, and the line went dead suddenly.

Laura shook her head, confused, and then she went into her room and pulled on some clothes. Was she going to buy the newspaper? Of course she was.

Ten minutes later, Laura smoothed open the Sunday paper on the kitchen table. BRITAIN'S MOST ELIGIBLE BACHELORS, ran the headline. She tore her eyes away from the photo of Nick standing in front of Chartley, pulled the cuffs of her sweater over her fingers, and read rapidly:

> Number Three: Dominic Edward Danvers Needham, 12th Marquis of Ranelagh, Earl of Albany Cross. Okay, so the Princes have to be at Nos. 1 & 2, but many are more intrigued by the deb's delight, Dominic Needham (above). Thirty-five, single, handsome, worth roughly around £300m, the Marquis of Ranelagh is the matrimonial jackpot for almost every ambitious mother with a socialite daughter to marry off—and the heart-throb of a generation of boarding-school girls. And, of course, there's also the house.
>
> Chartley Hall is regarded by many as the finest stately home in England. Built by Inigo Jones, nestling next to the wild North Norfolk coast, it is full of the most fabulous treasures (the Hogarths, the greatest collection of Renaissance drawings in the country, the Grinling Gibbons woodwork throughout, the magnificent library, and the notorious soldier collection begun by his father). Visitors flock there year-round. But does the notoriously private marquis have anyone to share all this with?

"Oh, God," she whispered to herself. "This is dire."

Happily, girls, the answer is—for the moment—no. For beneath the glittering surface, all is not well in the House of Needham. Rarely has there been a great aristocratic family so rocked by scandal in recent years. First came the notorious affair between the present marquis's mother, the beautiful British actress Vivienne Lash, then 11th Marchioness of Ranelagh, and her husband's brother, notorious gambler and playboy Lord Frederick Needham. They ran off together when the present marquis was just eleven, and now live in the south of France. The 11th Marquis forbade all contact between his ex-wife and her children, and to this day Nick and his two sisters, Lady Rose Balmore and Lady Lavinia Needham, have made no effort to keep in touch with their mother, who now, in her late seventies, is said to be in ill health.

Her children have fared little better. Her eldest daughter, Lady Rose, seemed set to follow in her mother's footsteps when, in 1978 at the age of eighteen, she eloped with Gareth Ringwood, a drummer with the heavy-metal band Roxattax. It was a tempestuous marriage that ended in divorce in 1980, and coincided with her heroin addiction reaching its height. After an overdose that nearly killed her in 1982, she entered rehab, and six years later married the multimillionaire industrialist Sir Malcolm Balmore. They have two young children, Samuel and Elizabeth, and Lady Rose is active on many committees, tireless in her work for various charities.

"My *God!*" said Laura, unable to stop herself from grinning. "Fantastic. Who'd have thought it?"

Lady Lavinia has not taken the same path as her elder sister. She might be called rootless, in fact. She spent several years in India in various ashrams, and ran a stall in London's Portobello

Road market, selling leather goods she had sourced herself. She spends six months of the year in Thailand, where she has a house—paid for by her family, it is presumed, for she has never worked a day in her life. Ethereally beautiful, she is as famous for her love life as anything, having dated several rock stars and actors. She is currently living with her brother in Chartley Hall, where sources close to the family say she is having an affair with the marquis's oldest friend and estate manager, Charles Potter.

He wishes, Laura thought. God, this is a load of rubbish.

She read on.

So, what of our handsome romantic hero, Dominic (known to all as Nick)? Until recently, friends said, he was increasingly remote, shunning the London society that was once his lifeblood. A regular on the smart London social scene, where young rich aristocrats regularly pay £1,000 for a bottle of champagne in the nightclubs of Mayfair and Chelsea, he withdrew almost entirely from public life after his father died in 2003, when Nick went up to Norfolk to take over the estate. His father was much loved in the county for his management of Chartley and its lands and properties. His son, who has made a few attempts to alter the running of the estate without any great success, is often regarded as standoffish and arrogant by those who don't know him. Friends say loyally that he is merely shy, growing used to the role he must play as one of the highest peers in the realm.

In recent weeks, however, his behavior has changed, and the gossip on the circuit is that he has finally fallen in love. Since June, he has been seen several times in town with Cecilia Thorson, trust-fund daughter of millionaire financier Lars Thorson and his wife, notorious socialite and seventies beauty Lady Tania Ingham. The Thorsons are well known in fashionable circles, seen as the A+ of the A list, and Nick could look no higher for a future wife. Friends say he is very much in love, spending more and more time in London and increasingly absent from his post at the estate, where he still has much to learn.

Is this true love? Is this an apprenticeship? Or is the marquis too wrapped up in himself to find the solution to his problems—a wife who will provide an heir for one of our greatest national treasures? Many would like to know—and many girls would love to be that solution.

"Who was that?" came Yorky's voice blearily from his room. "The phone?"

"Nothing important," Laura called back. "Coffee?"

"Yes, please."

Laura stood up, arching her back and stretching. The kettle was boiling. She got the coffee out of a cupboard. She screwed up her eyes as if trying to stare into the distance. They stung with tears. Stupid to have any kind of proprietorial feelings about him, she told herself. You haven't heard from him in a month, and that was your decision; you know it's too hard, that you can't be together, you haven't let yourself think about him, so that's why it's so weird to read about him now. Just recognize that, you'll be fine. He's not for you, this life is not yours, the whole thing is ridiculous.

She knew all that rubbish about Cristal-drinking toffs was idiotic, but at the same time, she also knew that there was no smoke without fire. He *was* different, she knew it. And apart from anything else, he was obviously going out with that girl, the millionairess Cecilia. Laura tried to feel noble. It was obviously the right thing for him—a blue-blooded, blond millionaire's daughter, that was absolutely what he needed.

It couldn't be further away from what she was, an ordinary girl making coffee in a slightly scuzzy kitchen in North London on a Sunday morning. So what if it still hurt—that was the way it was. She looked down at the article again. Best thing would be if she were to chuck it, straight away. She poured the coffee, biting her lip as she read it all through again.

chapter thirty-eight

I'd love to, Laura. But I'm not sure. Really. Don't have a go at me."

"Simon! But it'll be great! Jo and Chris will just have got back from Oz, they really want to see you. And Yorky's invited the famous Becky, you'll meet her, too."

Simon said apologetically, "I'll try, Laura, but I'm just not sure. I have to speak to Jorgia on Saturday, too—we've got a lot to sort out. And it's so far . . ."

Laura said, "Whatever, Simon. Fine." She crouched over her desk at work and started tapping on her keyboard loudly, to try to let him know that she was a Very Busy Person. It was a waste of time speaking to Simon these days, she thought crossly. Of course he should be coming over on Saturday, to catch up with everyone, but was he? No. He wanted to stay in with Mum and Dad knitting tea cozies and coo down the phone to his girlfriend. Pah. It was ridiculous—even Yorky was starting to think it was ridiculous, a grown man living at home in Harrow with his mum and dad, helping them out, going to the supermarket, taking care of all their recycling.

"It's just . . . it's such a nightmare coming all the way in from Mum and Dad's, you know."

"If you weren't living with Mum and Dad, it wouldn't be a problem," said Laura pointedly. But Simon didn't take the bait.

"Come on Saturday, Simon, go on." Laura tapped her fingers on the receiver. "Come on, bro. I miss you! You can even kip on the sofa if you want."

"Okay," said Simon, relenting. "Okay, of course. I'd love to. Er. Are you cooking?"

"Yorky's cooking. Well, perhaps we're getting a takeaway. Listen, I have to go, I'll be late."

She said good-bye, put down the phone, pulled her hair back into a ponytail, and picked up her bag.

Her latest project, which she was just starting, was Operation Bring Linley Munroe Back into the Fold. She had had a meeting there last week with Clare Swynford, the coordinator for the company, and had prepared a pack of stuff about the programs they did, the investment opportunities (tax-free), and lots of pictures of smiley children, which had won Clare over most convincingly. Today was a different matter, though. She was going back this afternoon to meet Marcus Sussman, the man at the root of all the problems, the one who'd insulted Mrs. McGregor and then been outraged at his treatment. He was head of the banking division at Linley Munroe; and since he'd been the first to volunteer and the first to pull out, Laura was being made very clearly to understand—by Rachel, by Gareth, and by Linley Munroe as well—that he was the cause, but also the solution. He was an important man, and Laura couldn't help feeling he wasn't the kind of person to go gooey-eyed over a cute photo of three children drawing with some crayons.

She wasn't, truth be told, looking forward to it much. She knew what Marcus Sussman would be like. Pleased with himself, too rich, arrogant. But it had to be done, so Laura slung her bag over her shoulder, picked up her phone and the folder she'd made for Marcus Sussman, and headed out of the office. On her way, she passed Rachel.

"Where you off to, then?" said Rachel.

"Linley Munroe," said Laura briefly. "Can't stop, I don't want to be late. The rehabilitation begins."

"Great!" said Rachel. "Good luck. Let me know how it goes."

It was a little more than ten minutes' walk to Linley Munroe; Laura prepared her lines in her head. It wasn't a big deal—they had some great new companies who were interested in investing money, she told herself. Linley Munroe wasn't the be-all and end-all. She knew she'd caused the breach in the first place, indirectly. There was funding missing, vital funding, because of her, and getting Linley Munroe to give money, plug the financial hole they were in, represented the last of the mistakes she had to rectify.

The first signs were not promising. Laura was shown into an office that was a bizarre hybrid of formal leather-bound boardroom chic mixed with glass futuristic Canary Wharf–style modernism; the company clearly wanted the best of both worlds. The air conditioning was turned on full blast, and Laura shivered. It was warm outside and she was in a thin top. She wished she'd brought a sturdy cable-knit sweater to pop on. She gazed around the office, taking in the black office furniture, the neatness of everything. There was one piece of paper in the in-tray; everything else was filed away. There were no personal effects anywhere, unless an invitation pinned up on the board to an Autumn Black-Tie Dinner thrown by some bizarre-sounding organization with a long, Germanic name could be called a personal effect. Laura thought not.

She waited. And waited. Five minutes turned into ten. The longer she waited, the crosser she grew. She swung herself around on her wheelie chair. Then she swung round on her chair again, and the door opened.

"Excuse me," said a voice behind her. "You must be Laura Foster, yes?"

"Oh, my God," said Laura, clutching the side of the desk and turning herself round on the chair. "I'm so sorry—"

A tall, beefy man with an eerily familiar face strode forward. "I'm Marcus Sussman."

She stood up, and held out her hand. "It's you!" she said.

"You're—" said Marcus Sussman, looking at her with a momentarily bewildered expression. "I've seen you before." His brow lifted. "Oh, my God."

"Yes," said Laura.

"You're that girl in the pub, last month. In Norfolk!" He seemed amazed, although he registered no positive emotion, nor issued any further apology.

"You stole my table, then you spilt your drink over me," Laura said in what she hoped was a tone of benevolent amusement.

Marcus Sussman looked at her, nonplussed, as if she were talking Swahili. "Right," he said.

He was a strange man. She remembered him now. His clothes were beautiful; his shirtsleeves were fastened with cuff links and the tailoring of his suit was perfect, even Laura could see that. On him, the effect was odd, though. It was that of harnessing something, hiding something, putting on a costume. He wasn't suave or elegant. He was fleshy, rather large, too tall; his hair was slightly too long, falling in big bracket shapes on either side of his forehead. And he had egg on his plump silk tie. Or something encrusted—she could see it. Why didn't he flick it off, or notice? Hadn't someone told him?

"Real coincidence, that," said Marcus Sussman.

"Yes, what a small world."

Again, Marcus Sussman stared at her rather nervously, as if she had just taken off her top and then thrown a brick through his window. "Will you sit down?" he said eventually. "Do. Here—" He gestured to the chair from which she had just risen, and Laura, trying not to look confused, sat down again. He cleared his throat. "Ah. So—what were you doing there? Holiday?"

"Yes," said Laura.

"Right," said Marcus. "I've got a friend who lives there, bunch of us went down for the weekend. Great stuff. Beautiful part of the world. Isn't it?"

"Yes," said Laura. "It is."

Marcus coughed into his clenched fist. "Did you go to Chartley?" he said politely.

Laura decided he was her nemesis, sent to kill her with socially awkward questions. Why couldn't he just get on with it, get down to business? "Yes," she said. She looked at her notes.

Marcus said, quasi-nonchalantly, "Wonderful place, the George. He owns it, old Nick Ranelagh. The marquis, right?" He tapped a pencil on the glass-topped desk, drumming out a rhythm. "Turned it around, used to be a real dive. Got backing, investment. Mate of mine sorted it for him. Friend of a really good friend of Nick's, actually. He knows him quite well, you know."

He nodded at her eagerly, hair flopping wildly. Laura wished he would be quiet, but she knew the rules of the dance, so instead of leaning forward and saying in a lewd old cackly tart's voice,

"Actually, I know him, too, *in the worst way*," she said, "Right. Wow. Fantastic."

"Yes," said Marcus more enthusiastically, warming to his theme. "Great bloke, actually, old Nick. Only met him once or twice before—you know. He took over the house and stuff. Yah. Good bloke."

"Right," said Laura again. She dug her palm into the hard plastic ridges of the folder. "That's fantastic. It's a lovely pub."

Marcus stood up rather suddenly and frowned, as if she hadn't been given permission to speak. "Okay—it's Laura, isn't it? Let's discuss this, shall we? Look, I'm not going to beat about the bush, I'm pretty pissed off with you guys."

"I know you must be," Laura began, nodding so violently that her neck hurt, to show she agreed. "And I'm really grateful to you for agreeing to meet me."

Marcus ignored her and said, "But we have a commitment to the local community. And I would like to do something about it. Well, I used to want to—until all this." His eyes flickered, impatiently.

"Right," said Laura, opening her folder and taking a deep breath. "Look—Marcus?" She wasn't really sure if she was allowed to call him by his first name, all of a sudden. "I can completely understand why you feel the program hasn't really worked for your company."

"I know why it didn't work for the company," said Marcus, warming to his theme. "Because that school's run like something out of *Lord of the Flies*, it's fucking incredible. When I tried to suggest they were doing things wrong—the kids running riot, all that . . . You know that some little git tried to kill me?"

"Er—" said Laura. "Volunteers aren't really supposed to suggest changes to teaching policy, Marcus. You're only there to help your designated child with his reading—"

"He got me in a fucking headlock and pulled a knife on me!" Marcus yelled, waving his arms in the air, his attempted air of authority completely vanishing. "That's why I rang to complain. I kept ringing you, and you were never there!"

"Oh, God," said Laura. "Right. I am sorry." She put her hand out involuntarily. "Really sorry. Did you . . . report it?"

Marcus subsided in his chair, just a little. "No. I thought about it, but I realized it wasn't ever going to do any good. So I pulled us out of the program instead. It's a shame. I'm on the board here, you know."

"Wow," said Laura, trying to look impressed.

"But that's not the point," he said, looking cross again, almost with himself. "The point is, I wanted to put some money into St. Catherine's. You know, it's the nearest school to Linley. We have a good reputation for that sort of thing. Thought giving money, investing in the school, might be some way of—you know." He looked down between his legs at the floor.

Laura didn't know, but she desperately *wanted* to know; was this all a waste of time, or not? So she said after a pause, "No, sorry. Er, some way of—what?"

"Well," said Marcus. "You know." She looked at him encouragingly. He pulled his top lip over his bottom lip and said quietly, through his teeth, "Uhm. Well, you know. Doing something, making a difference. That sort of thing."

She nodded, suddenly enormously touched by him without understanding why. "Right," she said. "Well, I wanted to be the one to apologize to you personally, it's completely my fault, you know. There's been a—a change in the way we handle the schools, and I assure you this will be dealt with in a different way in the future. I've put some information together to show you. Can you give me five minutes to go through it with you? So I can change your mind, I hope." She smiled at him winningly.

He stared blankly at her, then crossed his arms. "Fine," he said after a pause. "I've got a meeting in fifteen minutes. Let's get on with it."

"Yes," said Laura. So she looked down at the folder and plowed on.

Ten minutes later, sweat was practically pouring off Laura's brow. It wasn't that Marcus was *rude*, exactly, or intimidating, or even unpleasant. He was none of those things—in fact, there was something almost endearingly odd about him. It was more that he was socially incapable. To Laura, who was used to responding and interacting very much on instinct—often to her cost—he was completely frustrating. He showed no interest in what she was saying, it seemed, but it wasn't as if he didn't take her seriously. On the contrary. He gave her a mental workout the like of which she hadn't experienced since pretending to be examiner for Yorky's qualifying exams a few years ago.

She couldn't work out if he was doing it to show her he was top dog, but she thought it was probably that Marcus was just one of those incredibly clever people, and that was all there was to it. His communication skills were zero—but who needed communication skills when you were the kind of person who only had to look at a pound coin for it to multiply itself by ten?

"Here's the last sheet," said Laura, handing it over almost gloomily, for she could not see any way that Marcus was going to come up trumps and write her a blank check. "This is about motivation, communication performance at schools that have been involved with the mentoring scheme. It shows the positive effect it's had on children's performance. And here"—she pointed at the sheet—"a couple of quotes from people about how much they've enjoyed working with the children. Something you know yourself already of course." Too late, she remembered that Marcus's kid had pulled a knife on him, damn, so she hurried on, "Er—but just so people who are looking for a little bit more than their job, who want to put something back—that's a really good page of information to show them."

"If they hate the jobs they're doing and want to do something else, you mean? Harrumph." Marcus exhaled loudly.

"Well, no," said Laura. "But it's a good way of adding something extra to your life. Someone else's, too."

Marcus said nothing for a moment, but peered at her through his floppy hair. "Like you, I mean." He flicked his hand out dismissively. "Why do you do the job you do?"

Laura gazed at the egg on his tie again as he sat there fiddling with his cuff links awkwardly, almost aggressively, legs sprawled out in a V shape.

"Well—er," said Laura uncertainly. "Why?"

"It's just interesting. Don't you think it's interesting, why people do what they do?"

"Sometimes. I fell into my job," said Laura with a wry smile. (She wasn't going to say that she had applied for her job, four years ago, only because she'd snogged an absolutely gorgeous man at a party the week before who'd told her there was a vacancy there; and even though he worked for a totally different business coordination scheme on another council, the old Laura had passionately hoped the two of them would meet regularly and fall in love over literacy initiative brochure language meetings. Alas, she'd never seen him again.) "But I love it, and I want to be good at it, more than anything." She realized she was gazing into space, cleared her throat, and said, "How about you?"

"Not sure, really," said Marcus. "Fell into it, too."

"Do you like it?"

"Not really the kind of job you like or don't like. I just don't think I'd be much good at anything else." He said it without emotion.

"Oh," said Laura, not sure what to say once again.

But then Marcus shifted in his seat, looked at his watch, and said shortly, "I have someone coming in now. The meeting I mentioned. 'Fraid you'll have to go."

"Of course," said Laura, springing up like a jack-in-the-box. "I—er—just let me get my stuff together—er. So." She stood still and breathed in. "Marcus, will you talk to Clare? Consider agreeing to let Linley Munroe rejoin the program, maybe think about the investment choices I mentioned? I know she's keen—"

"Yes," said Marcus. He stood at the door and their eyes met briefly.

Laura looked away and busied herself shoving papers into her folder. She realized, as she stuffed the papers back in in a slightly haphazard fashion, that she was waiting for him to say, "Thanks for coming in," or at least some acknowledgment, even if he loathed her and the whole thing; but she knew he just wasn't the type—probably hadn't ever said thanks for anything in his life, it just wouldn't occur to him. He even . . .

". . . with me to the dinner?"

"I see," Laura said noncommittally, putting the folder under her arm. God, it was cold; she wanted to be back outside again.

"Forget it," Marcus muttered, half to himself. "This way, then." He turned away.

"Sorry," Laura said. "I wasn't really listening. What did you say?"

Marcus straightened up, cleared his throat, and said in his strange, low voice, "Well. There's a dinner—for our banking division. Our clients are having it—they're Germans. It's in a couple of weeks. Would you like to come with me?"

"Why?" said Laura in total astonishment.

Marcus's eyes bulged slightly and he said, "Right, sorry. We have to bring a date. I just thought—well, I'd like to think about what we've discussed today. I think it could work out, you know. Perhaps we could talk about it again. At the dinner. So I—I just thought I'd ask if you'd like to come."

Was this how it was supposed to be? Marcus was asking her out. Her. She who thought no one would ever look at her again. Laura felt weird, disconnected from the situation. She looked at Marcus and felt nothing, no feelings whatsoever other than a strange, misplaced affection; but perhaps that was a *good* thing, rather than rushing in headlong like before.

She crossed the room, then realized it was even more awkward being right opposite him, and stepped back, cross with herself. "Oh, God. I'm so sorry. I didn't realize—sorry, I just didn't get that you were asking me on a date. You see—right. She couldn't feel more stupid.

"No problem," said Marcus abruptly. "No. Problem." Then he did something quite remarkable. He almost smiled. The corners of his eyes crinkled, and it was gone almost as soon as it was there, but she knew she'd seen it.

"I'd love to come." She said frankly, "Sorry to be so stupid, I really didn't realize that's what you meant." She put her hand on his folded arms. "Anyway. Thanks." She said again, like a robot, "I'd love to come."

"Really?" said Marcus. He shook his head as if in disbelief, and grinned at her again, showing his teeth in a big, boyish smile. "Wow!" Then, almost instantly, he snapped his gaze down to the floor and fiddled with his cuff links again. "Yup, great. And the money—I'll think about it."

Laura smiled. This is amazing, she thought, looking at Marcus. For the first time in months and months, a) I'm in danger of actually being good at my job; and b) on a completely unrelated, yet bizarrely linked subject, I've got a date—with someone who actually wants to be seen in public with me.

"Thanks!" she said, her eyes sparkling at him. "For thinking about it. And—you know."

Marcus said stiffly, "No, thank *you.* It will be my pleasure. I'll be in touch. Do I have your mobile number?"

"No," said Laura. "I'll write it—"

"Give it to my assistant," said Marcus, fiddling with his cuff links. "I'm due in a meeting now. I'm glad you came in, thank you. I'll talk to Clare. We'll discuss this again at the dinner? Thanks." He raised his hand in a gesture of farewell and walked off, and Laura, watching him disappear around a corner, knew she was leaving another little bit of her old, stupid self behind. She hugged the folder and looked around Marcus's office.

How strange. She felt totally unemotional about it—her stomach wasn't churning, her heart wasn't thumping in her chest. She hoped it stayed like that, this feeling, that it didn't change. She clung to the cloak of numbness that hung over her. It was her best friend.

chapter thirty-nine

Things may have been going well with Yorky and Becky, but that didn't mean Yorky was any more relaxed as a host. When Saturday came, he was like a cat on a hot tin roof, leaping nervously about the flat all day, so much so that he ended up hitting his hand on the kitchen doorframe fairly hard whilst trying to explain to Laura the best way to make lasagna. His finger swelled up, and Laura took over the cooking, as she had known all along she would.

She loved cooking, more so than ever. It gave her a feeling of control, a sense of purpose. She was in charge, no one else telling her what to do, and she loved mixing, chopping, stirring, crushing flavors together, deciding what to do next. It was funny—she and Yorky used to cook together all the time, but now she preferred to do it alone. Like most things, these days.

As Laura was putting the lasagna into the oven and checking her watch, Jo and Chris arrived.

"Look who's here!" said Yorky, ushering them slightly manically into the kitchen. "Look who's here. Great! Say hello to Laura, and then come and get a drink."

"Is Becky here yet?" said Jo, looking round eagerly.

"No, no," said Yorky, glancing over his shoulder just to make sure she hadn't crept in behind the others without his noticing her. "Er—no."

Laura hugged Jo. "Hello, love! How are you?" she said, squeezing her tightly.

"I'm good. Ohhh," Jo said. "Laura, it's so good to see you."

"You too," said Laura, surprised at her normally restrained friend. "I can't believe it's been three weeks, it seems like—nothing, though. It's flown by."

"I know," said Jo. "And yet we packed so much in, you just wouldn't believe it."

"Sounds like it," said Laura, smiling brightly. "It sounds amazing."

Chris leaped on her enthusiasm, and said eagerly, "We brought the laptop along, in case you want to see the photos. I know they're probably really boring, but we thought you might be interested!"

Laura and Yorky exchanged looks.

"Ooh . . ." said Laura. "Yes. . . . Let's see, after supper, shall we?"

An hour later, they sat down to eat. Simon had talked of little else but Jorgia since his arrival—Jo and Becky clasped their hands, said it was wildly romantic and sweet, and hung on Simon's every word on the subject, while Laura stared suspiciously at them, wondering what on earth they were talking about. Simon then got out a photo of Jorgia to show everyone. He put it on the table, propped against the mustard, and Laura couldn't help feeling even more like Bridget Jones at the Smug Marrieds' dinner party, even if one of the couples was half represented by photo only.

"Jorgia sends her love," said Simon at one end of the table to Laura at the other end. Jo and Yorky and their respective partners were on either side of them. Becky smiled at Laura and made an "ahh" sound. She had brought Laura some flowers, which Laura could tell made Jo think Becky was the nicest person in the whole world. Laura could also tell Jo was gearing up to invite Becky and Yorky round to dinner with her and Chris, so they could talk about mini-breaks together and Jo could show Becky their wedding photos. She could feel it, it was coming, and she knew she wouldn't be invited. Hah, like she wanted to be. She realized Simon was smiling expectantly at her, so she sat up in her chair and looked at her brother.

"That's so nice of her," said Laura politely.

"So, mate. When's she coming over?" said Chris, handing Jo the salad. "When are you going to see her?"

A cloud passed over Simon's face. "I don't know, actually," he said. He looked rather glum. "I hoped she'd come as soon as possible, but she still hasn't got the money, she says." He paused. "I'm going back in about a month's time, though. I haven't spoken to her for a while, that's all." He sighed. "I miss her. You know."

"You really think you might move to Peru?" asked Yorky.

Simon turned to him. "Yeah, you know, I really might. It's a big step and everything, but—it just feels right. I can't explain it."

Laura said nothing. She chewed on her lasagna.

"That's amazing, Simon," Jo said, smiling happily at him. "But—wow, that's a big step."

"I know," said Simon. "It is, but it doesn't feel like it, somehow. I can't explain it. I can really see myself moving there."

"Oh, come on," said Laura suddenly. Yorky looked down at his plate.

Simon stared at her. "What?" he said.

Laura said patiently, "Look, Si. It's really great you've met Jorgia, and everything. And you love her and all that. But—come on." She stretched out her hands in a placating gesture. "You have to wise up slightly. You know? You're not going to move there. You might think you are at the moment, but long term—seriously, no way." Yorky was still looking down at his plate. Laura tried to catch Jo's eye for support, but Jo was staring at Simon. She carried on blindly. "I mean—who is she, this girl? You barely know her. You're completely different! You've got nothing in common! It's never, ever, going to—"

"And what the hell do you know about it?" Simon's expression was ugly. He pointed his finger at her, his voice shaking. "You're amazing, Laura. What business is it of yours in the first place? Eh?"

"It's not that—it's—" Laura said, taken aback by the vitriol in his voice. She tried to reason with him. "Listen, Simon. I'm just saying—"

"No, *you* listen," Simon said. The others were looking distinctly uncomfortable now. He pointed at his sister again. "You listen, for once, instead of sitting there in that smug judgmental way you keep doing since I've got back, when you don't know the first fucking thing about it. You have no right, no right at all!"

"Simon—" Jo began, a look of anguish on her face, but Laura waved her away.

"Oh, really," she snapped back, a flush of anger rising to her cheeks. "It's none of my business when my own brother's leeching off Mum, and Dad, and—and Gran, and lazing around the house doing jack-all just because of some random stranger he thinks he's in love with! Oh, no, none of my business, you're quite right."

"That's what I mean," Simon said, his voice dripping cold disdain. "The hypocrisy of it. You should listen to yourself, Laura. It *is* none of your business, okay? I've been back three weeks, and I know I have to get a job. Mum and Dad don't mind. *You're* the one who minds. It's so fucking hypocritical! You make me laugh! You, all of a sudden judging *me* because you think I'm in some dodgy relationship, when you—you go from one crappy relationship to another, some loser who you think's the answer to your prayers, and you're too fucking stupid to see they're just leading you on! You practically *lose your job* because of it! And when I fall for someone—I know it's hard, I know it's going to be difficult, but I really *love* her, you can't see that, can you, I *love* her—you don't even say 'Great!' or 'Can't wait to meet her, brother!' No, you sit there with your sour-milk expression, like you've got it all sorted, like you're perfect."

He paused and wiped his hand across his mouth, breathing deeply. "I don't understand what's happened to you. You didn't used to be like this."

Jo was staring at her, her eyes huge, shaking her head. Laura looked at her, perplexed, and then at Yorky, who was looking down at his plate. She knew what that meant. It meant he agreed with Simon. A pain stabbed in her side.

She and Simon knew the drill of their arguments, now they were older, well enough not to let them fester. And—Laura bit her lip. He was wrong, he was fucking rude and wrong, and it was never going to work out, but—it *was* none of her business. So as they waited for her response, the silence in the room growing more and more awkward, she took a deep, deep breath, fighting the urge to scream, to burst into tears, to slap her little brother.

"Sorry," she said. "Fine. I just worry about you. Because you're so different. That's all. But you're right. I don't know what it's like, being with someone like that. It's none of my business."

Simon nodded and looked apologetic. "I shouldn't have yelled at you," he said. "But you don't know what it's like, you're right."

Jo looked quickly from Laura to Simon. Then she said slowly, "Well, that's not exactly true, is it? Laura?"

"What?" Laura said, not really paying attention. She put the salad bowl gingerly on top of the pile of plates Yorky had picked up as he staggered into the kitchen, followed closely by a rather shaken-looking Becky.

"It's not exactly true." Jo was playing with her wineglass, sliding it from one hand to the other. She looked from one Foster sibling to the other. "About you being with someone really different from you. Laura does know about that."

"What?" said Laura, bewildered. "What are you talking about?" How could Jo know about it?

Jo nodded at her emphatically. She reached out and took her hand. "Love. We were on the same flight back yesterday as Fran. Your cousin. And Ludo. Had a long chat with them. They'd been in—"

"Singapore," Laura finished for her. Why did she know that? Yes, Annabel had told her. "So?"

"Fran?" said Simon. "You poor things. For the whole flight? What a nightmare."

"I don't understand . . . ," said Laura.

"We had a long chat," said Jo. "Fran and me. She told me all about your granny's birthday party." She looked searchingly at her friend. "About who was there. About who turned up. You know."

Laura went pale. She could actually feel the blood draining from her face; it was the oddest sensation. "Oh, my God. Look," she said, recovering herself, "they don't know what happened—"

"Well, they couldn't wait to tell us all about it," said Chris suddenly, next to his wife.

"I'm sorry, darling," said Jo, her eyes on Laura's. "So . . . it's true, then? Who you met—up there?"

"What are you talking about?" asked Simon, frowning.

"What if I told you your big sister spent her holiday with your parents having some grand affair with the Marquis of Ranelagh?" Jo said.

"Who?" said Simon blankly.

Jo and Laura were sitting by the pile of newspapers that needed to be recycled, and to Laura's immense horror, Jo pulled the supplement with the offending article off the top of the pile. Why hadn't she thrown it away? Why the hell couldn't she bring herself to just chuck it in the bin?

Jo smoothed the newspaper on the table and jabbed at it with her finger. "One of the richest men in England. His house is over three hundred years old. Look!" She gestured at the picture of Nick, standing in front of the house. "Laura. Is that him? It is, isn't it? He's the one Fran told me you were seeing."

"What?" said Yorky, standing in the doorway holding the plates for the cheesecake. He shook his head violently. "Laura? What's going on? *Who*'ve you been seeing?" The spoons atop the plates slid onto the floor with a loud clatter.

"Some millionaire marquis," said Simon, standing behind Jo and peering over the newspaper. "Laura, seriously? My God."

"Oh, God," said Laura. She crouched down, picked up the spoons, and slammed them on the table.

"Is this true?' said Yorky, putting the plates down heavily, sounding like a stern Victorian paterfamilias.

"Er, yes," said Laura.

"You—shagged—*him*?" Yorky pointed at the paper.

"It wasn't like that," Laura said.

"Him?" Becky said timidly. "Seriously?"

"Yes, yes," said Laura. She could feel her ears burning red. "I was on holiday in July," she said, trying to explain it to Becky, who was looking really alarmed. "I met him—at his house, when we went to look round, you know. Me and Mum and Dad. He asked me out, we had a few drinks. Um. And it was great. But I had to come home." She smiled at Becky, as if this were completely normal. "Just a holiday fling."

She avoided the gaze of Jo, whose small, determined face was watching her, eyes narrowed, lips pursed. She turned to Yorky, who was shaking his head at her. He gave her a small smile. "I knew it," he said. "Just knew it. Didn't you?" He turned to Jo.

"Yes," said Jo. "Bloody hell, yes."

"A marquis? You must be over the moon," said Simon slowly, drawing the paper toward him. "Your very own romantic hero. When are we going to meet him?"

"You're not," said Laura. "I'm not seeing him again." She stood up. "You didn't bring in the ice cream, Yorks."

"But—" Yorky said. "Why not?"

"It was a holiday fling, nothing more," said Laura. "You won't believe me, so I can say it till I'm blue in the face, but it's true. He didn't tell me who he was, I thought he was just some ordinary bloke. We were—" She stopped. "I thought we were friends. Yeah, we slept together. Yeah, it's a beautiful house. Oh, the idea of it was all very romantic. But it didn't work out. It's just—well, the reason it was never going to work out with me and Nick is, we're so different. Too much difference. It's a fairy tale. Fairy tales aren't real. And that's why—I worry about you and Jorgia, and I shouldn't. You're right, it's not my business."

"Ah, sis," Simon said, putting his arm around her shoulders and giving her a squeeze. Next to him, Yorky leaned over Jo and Becky to stare at the article. Chris watched them all stoically. Simon said in an undertone, 'I'm sorry, Laura. I mean it. Let's forget it. But I think you're wrong, you know." He paused. "I love Jorgia, that's all I'm sure about. Seriously. You don't fall in love with someone because it's convenient."

Sadness flooded into Laura's heart, a great wave of it, overtaking her so unexpectedly that she was almost knocked out by it. She felt so alone, all of a sudden, and she couldn't understand why, when here were her two best friends and her brother. What if Nick were here, she thought for a second, and she could put her head on his chest, feel him draw her close to his body, feel safe, as safe as she had in his house, in bed. What if she could tell him all of this, how would it be? She wished . . . No, she reminded herself. Forget it.

"Are you sure it wouldn't work?" said Jo urgently, in a quiet voice. "Are you sure you don't want to see him again?"

Laura wanted to laugh. Those were two totally separate things, weren't they? Of course she was sure it wouldn't work. And of course she wanted to see him again. Her eyes filled with tears. Mistake, mistake. She could not let Jo see her cry, could not let them see it meant anything to her.

"Oh, darling," said Jo softly. "You're not very happy at the moment, are you?"

"I am," said Laura. "I've got a date next week,' she added weakly, as a diversionary tactic.

"Well, that's good!" said Jo encouragingly. "Do you like him?"

"Oh, yes," said Laura. "He's—yeah. He's great. Met him through work. He's a financial analyst something. Er—seems really nice."

"What's he called?"

"Marcus," said Laura reluctantly, and the image of Marcus, fiddling with his cuff links, loomed large in her mind's eye.

"Look, there you go, then!" said Jo, trying to seem inordinately pleased. "No more marquises, eh? A nice, normal date with a nice normal bloke, just what you need."

"Er—" said Laura, not sure how to respond. "Well—I suppose so."

chapter forty

"When do you have to meet this man, darling?"

"Not till seven-thirty, don't worry."

"Here, one more glass? And I'll just go and get the necklace."

"Absolutely, thanks, Gran. This is really kind of you."

"Well, it's lovely to see you, my darling girl."

Laura drained her glass, and her grandmother poured some more champagne into it. "There you go," she said, and she padded back into the kitchen to put the bottle in the fridge. "I'll just get the necklace." She disappeared down the corridor.

Laura gazed around the flat, then looked out the window. It was a still, light autumn evening, with just a hint of cold in the air. She was meeting Marcus at a champagne bar near the Royal Courts of Justice, where the dinner was taking place, and since Marcus had rung her up the previous morning to confirm, and mentioned casually that it was very formal black tie and could she please be dressed appropriately ("Classic," Jo had said when Laura told her this. "He obviously thinks you dress like a hooker"), Laura was demure in a black velvet dress falling just below the knee, tied with a pale silver Regency-style ribbon high on the waist. But she needed something else to not feel cheap, so she had rung up her grandmother and, killing two birds with one stone, asked if she could a) come to see her that evening to b) borrow her diamond necklace, which had been Mary's own grandmother's.

From the window in Mary's sitting room, one could see across the rooftops of central London, down south to her beloved Selfridges, toward Mayfair and Hyde Park. The sitting room was light, filled firmly with old, odd pieces of furniture from Mary and Xan's travels. An old Moroccan rug, woven with gold, hung on the wall. A mahogany writing desk, stuffed with letters and housekeeping files, all written in Mary's huge, looping scrawl. There on the wall was the picture of Xan that Laura loved so much. He was standing in the garden at Seavale, the sea in the distance, leaning on a spade and smiling at something past the camera. A rough cloth sun hat was jammed on his head. And there, staring up at him with frank adoration, was a very small (Laura thought four, perhaps) Simon, naked except for a pair of shorts, gazing with his mouth open. Laura smiled as she looked at the picture. It was funny how much Simon resembled his stepgrandfather. He was slow to anger, quick to laugh, just like Xan had been.

After what Simon had said to her the previous Saturday, so cold and harsh, after Laura had seen the open disdain in his eyes, she had taken a long hard look at herself. Was she different now? She knew she wasn't the wide-eyed romantic she'd been a year ago. But had she, in trying to turn over a new leaf, to protect herself, gone too far the other way? She thought of Jo's comforting hand on her arm as she tried not to cry, thought how nice it would be simply to burst into tears and tell her all about it, how much she missed him, how she thought perhaps Mary might have been right all along but she had the feeling it was too late.

It wasn't too late for her, though, she knew that now. She wasn't going to change, again. She was just going to stop being this way or that way and simply be herself, again. Stop hiding. Stop dressing things up in fairy-tale costumes or dressing them down, packing them away and keeping them hidden. Just be herself. Go on dates, work hard, have a laugh. Enjoy herself.

She looked at her watch. "You okay, Gran?" she called. She could hear her grandmother in her bedroom, clinking various boxes open and shut.

"Here it is." Mary appeared, shaking her fist in the air. "It wasn't where I thought it was, I couldn't find it. Silly of me."

She opened her hand. Against the wrinkled, soft palm lay an old link chain and, at the center, a cluster of stars with twirling tails, intricately and beautifully made. One stone caught the light outside and twinkled quickly.

"Let me put it on you," Mary said, and she shuffled past the armchair and slid the necklace around Laura's neck. "Look at yourself."

Laura patted her collarbone, loving the feeling of the scratchy, cold metal on her skin, and stood up to look in the small looking-glass by the balcony door.

"It's lovely," she said. "Just lovely." She was glad her hair was up, twisted loosely into a chignon, so that the necklace could be seen. It was beautiful. Laura felt grown-up. She took Mary's hand. "Thank you so much for letting me wear it tonight," she said. "I'll take good care of it, I promise."

"Of course you will, darling," said Mary, staring at the necklace. "You'd be wise to anyway," she added, turning away. "It'll be yours one day, when I'm dead. Then you can wear it all you like."

"Well," Laura said, slightly briskly. "We don't know that, do we? It should be Annabel's, and anyway, I'm not having this conversation with you, Gran!"

"Not Annabel's," Mary said stubbornly. She picked up her drink, still standing in the middle of the room, and said rather gothically, "You're my blood daughter, not her."

"Mum is, you mean," said Laura, feeling rather uncomfortable.

"Who?"

"My mum. Angela. She is." Laura pointed to the wedding photo of her mother on the wall.

"Yes, yes," said Mary impatiently. She blinked, and said accusingly, "Stupid, stupid, we shouldn't be talking about this, you know."

"Well, thank you so much. I'm so excited."

"More excited about the necklace than this date, am I right?" said Mary, and she gave Laura an appraising stare. Her eyes danced, and Laura laughed, partly with relief.

"Er," she said, picking her glass up again and twisting it round in her hand. "Well, I don't know about that. Marcus—he's . . ."

Marcus had had an invitation for the dinner sent to her, addressed to "Miss Laura Foster," a thick cream card with gold around the edge; and today she had received flowers at work, a huge bouquet with a message that said, "I look forward to tonight. Yours, Marcus," which made Shana and Nasrin almost apoplectic with mirth—only Laura had heard them out in the stairwell laughing about something five minutes later, and she suspected it was that.

She thought it was nice, very, very nice. How many people actually did that? And wasn't it awful that girls spent their whole time complaining about boys and saying they were crap—and then when a boy did something totally lovely and thoughtful, they laughed at him, like it was pathetic and needy and a bit strange? So what if she wasn't madly in love with Marcus? She'd only met him once, properly; he'd asked her on a date, and he seemed nice if a trifle, well, odd. Nothing ventured, nothing gained. The new Laura. She smiled at Mary.

"Yes?" said Mary encouragingly, sinking slowly into a chair.

"Ahm," said Laura, not sure how to start. She caught her grandmother watching her, with her bright, clever eyes that missed nothing, and thought, Actually, it's pointless to try and spin this for you, you miss nothing. It was strange that it was so.

"Heard from that nice young man lately?" said Mary.

"What? Him? No. No," said Laura, giving her grandmother a quelling stare. She took a sip of her drink.

"Nothing?" said Mary.

"Nothing," said Laura, then realized it sounded as if she was expecting to hear something. Of course she wasn't. "No, nothing. You sound like Aunt Annabel."

"What do you mean?"

"She rang me—" Laura began, then noticed the look on Mary's face, the one that brooked no criticism of Aunt Annabel. Laura knew she wouldn't be able to explain it to her grandmother, so she just said, "Oh, nothing."

"She's excited about it," said Mary unexpectedly.

"Oh, good grief," said Laura. "There's nothing to be excited *about.* She's never called me before, why's she suddenly so interested?"

"Perhaps she was glad to have something to call you about," Mary pointed out.

"I doubt that, highly," Laura muttered. "When was the last time she called Mum up, just for a chat?"

"Oh, darling," said Mary firmly. "Your aunt and your mother—they're very different. But they're more alike than you think. You all are. Annabel—she does love you, you know."

"We're not alike," said Laura, thinking of her and Simon, her mum and dad and their normal, easy life, and the Sandersons, so grand, so snobbish, so riddled with strange and foreign customs and ideas about life, and at the head of them, Aunt Annabel herself.

"That's just not true," said Mary softly. "You have far more in common than you realize. Far more." She ran her nail around the edge of the glass, picking up the sheen of condensation that clung to it. "Why do you want the world to be black and white? It's not."

Laura looked down at the rather cheap velvet material of her dress. "I don't," she said, wondering whether they were still talking about Annabel or not.

Her grandmother was silent, and then she cleared her throat. "Do you mind if I say something?" she said suddenly.

"No . . ." said Laura uncertainly, thinking that if yet another person was about to have a go at her—especially Mary, whose good opinion mattered so much to her—she might just throw her hands up and scream.

"I think you have too many people telling you what to do and telling you what you're like," said Mary flatly. "Don't you?"

"Yes," said Laura, nodding fervently, thinking of Jo, Simon, everyone at work, even Nick, telling her she was weak, pathetic.

"I'm not going to tell you how I think you should live your life, or what I think you should do," said Mary. "Now's not the time. But I will say this: Don't try to paper over things that matter, Laura. The cracks will appear. Maybe not immediately, but they will."

"What do you mean?" Laura said quietly, not wanting to know but feeling she had to ask.

Her grandmother said firmly, "Just what I say. Don't paper over cracks, over things you think you can't cope with."

Mary's melodious voice grated on her nerves, and Laura stood up; she had to get out of there. Suddenly the flat was not warm and cozy and full of memories, but crowded and claustrophobic, closing in on her. "I have to go, you know. I'm going to be late." She gathered up her bag and little evening cape. "Sorry."

Mary was unperturbed. "Fine. You look beautiful, Laura," she said, standing up slowly and smiling at her. "I'm—I am proud of you, darling, you do know that?"

"Oh," Laura said. "Thank you, Gran." She kissed her. "Thank you." She went to the front door, Mary behind her. "I'll call you soon," she said. "Thanks again, Gran. Lovely to see you. Sorry it's been . . . so long."

"Don't worry," said her grandmother. "It will always have been too long, darling." And she closed the door.

Laura walked slowly down the stairs, wondering if she should go back up, shake Mary out of her strange mood, then reminded herself nothing would be accomplished by it. Paper over cracks? What was she talking about? Everything was fine; she was going on a date, with no expectations other than a nice evening, and with the hope that she might get some money out of him for the program, too. She was on the way, it was a fresh start! She wasn't papering over anything, and it was silly to say she was.

Pah. Laura shrugged as she reached the bottom of the stairs. The hunter's moon was rising as the sun disappeared. It was huge, golden, so low in the sky and so close she felt as if she could reach out and snatch it. Laura stared at it through the glass-paneled front door of the building, as it hung above the wide boulevard down toward Oxford Street; then she stepped onto the pavement and hailed a cab, following the moon east toward the City.

chapter forty-one

"It's very kind of you to invite me," said Laura, settled at a table with Marcus twenty minutes later, a glass of champagne in her hand.

Marcus gave her an unsmiling smile and looked round the crowded bar, which, on a Friday night in the City, was pretty much wall-to-wall bankers, lawyers, and accountants, male and female, dressed in suits or black tie, throwing money around like it was going out of fashion. He said stiffly, "My pleasure. Why not."

"And—Marcus, thank you so much for the flowers, it was incredibly sweet—er, kind of you. Again. Thank you!" Laura said, feeling completely embarrassed at this, though she couldn't work out why.

"Really, it was my pleasure, as I've said," Marcus said repressively, as if her mentioning the flowers was disgusting.

Laura sighed inwardly and ran her hand lightly along the back of her neck.

"Laura. I'm not being very expansive, I fear. I very much enjoyed meeting you. And it is my pleasure that you've agreed to accompany me this evening. I'm honored."

"Er," said Laura, not sure how to respond. "Well, thank you there. It—it's great."

"I've looked over the material you gave me and Clare," said Marcus. "I *think*"—he touched her arm lightly—"there may be a way we can join your program, give you some money."

"Really?!" said Laura, her face lighting up. "That's wonderful, thank you!"

"Let's see, let's see," Marcus admonished. "Let's talk about it at dinner. We need to discuss it a little further, but—well, all being well—ah." He raised his eyebrows at her.

"Well, thank you for thinking about it, anyway," said Laura. "Wow."

Only a couple of people at work knew Laura was here tonight, but she'd dropped enough hints about Linley Munroe that they were all super-curious about what she was going to pull off. She imagined the scene on Monday, her casually sauntering into the office, Rachel and Nasrin going over some figures again, wondering how they were going to explain to Gareth that the investment still hadn't come through, as Laura nonchalantly said, "Oh, the money? Yeah—I've sorted it. No sweat." Then high-fives all round, Rachel's face lighting up with a smile the way it used to, before Laura started screwing things up. . . . She luxuriated in the image, and then came back down to earth with a bump, to find Marcus staring at her, and realized she had to get through the evening first before this was in the bag.

Silence descended again, unwelcome; but, thankfully, Marcus took the conversational plunge. He took a deep, shuddering breath, adjusted his tie, and said, "So. Let's talk about it later, eh? Tell me. Where do your parents live?"

Laura smiled at the obviousness of the social questioning. “Harrow,” she said.

“Ah,” said Marcus. “Chap in the office next to mine went to Harrow.”

“Not that bit, I bet,” Laura said patiently. “My mum and dad live in deepest suburbia. About ten minutes off the main road. You have to drive for miles to find a shop selling milk, it’s all mock Tudor semidetacheds and cul-de-sacs. But it’s nice. How about you?”

“What?” said Marcus.

“Are you from London?”

“Yes, yes,” said Marcus.

“Where?” said Laura.

“Near Camden,” said Marcus vaguely, and Laura didn’t push the subject further, knowing from experience that when people seem noncommittal about something, they are doing it deliberately. “But, yeah. I live in Vauxhall now. You know those apartments? Over the Thames?”

“Wow,” said Laura. “How great.”

“Yep. It really is. Pretty expensive, but worth it, I can tell you. Very good investment for the future, you know.” Marcus stuck his lips out and nodded, his eyes half closed. “Not sure if I’ll stay there forever, but it’ll definitely work as a rental. Some guy like me in a few years’ time.” His eyes boggled at her, and Laura nodded, pretending to look interested. “I’ll move on and up then, you know.”

“Mm,” Laura said.

Marcus leaned back in his chair and gave a mock yawn. He stretched his arms. “Yep. Probably to Balham—you can buy a good-size family home there, although it’s pretty damn expensive. Still, it’ll be very handy for me. For the City.”

“Yes,” said Laura. “I like Balham.”

Marcus nodded at her, looking pleased, "Plus, it's a nice area for kids on the weekends."

"Right," said Laura, then realized she didn't understand. "Why?"

"Well, there's shops and cafés, and the park nearby, and of course you can drive to Richmond—"

"No," Laura interrupted. "Why do you need a family home?"

"For the family," Marcus said, looking irritated again.

"You're—not—" Laura instinctively grabbed her bag in case she needed to make a hasty exit. "You're not *married*, are you?"

Marcus looked amazed, and for a split second Laura thought, Oh, God! How could I have got this so wrong? Again?

But Marcus said abruptly, "Of course I'm not. Do you think I'd ask you out if I were married? What kind of man—no, of course I'm not."

"Good, good," said Laura, surreptitiously putting her bag back down on the seat. "Sorry. It's just I thought—you were talking about family homes and everything, the cafés and stuff. I assumed you might—er."

"I'm merely expressing—trying to say that—it's of no importance," Marcus said.

"Sorry," said Laura quietly, looking at the table. She felt sad again. "I didn't get it."

"I was just thinking aloud," said Marcus after a pause. "You know. If one were married. Where would one live. Have to think about that kind of thing these days."

"Even if you're not going out with someone?" Laura said, then regretted it.

But her companion said, after another pause, "Well, yes." He smiled, for the first time that evening. "Bit tragic, isn't it."

"What?"

"Planning where I'd live if I were married. With children." He cleared his throat with a long, drawn-out sound like rounds on a firing range. Laura looked at him, smiling self-consciously. She saw his large fingers mechanically clutching his cuff links, his large, normally expressionless face now wearing a rather anxious mask. His beautifully pressed dinner jacket, the studs of his shirt perfectly done up except for one missing, just visible if you looked, hidden by the jacket. Her heart contracted with sadness as she looked at him. He needed a wife; he needed someone to love him and look after him, a nice girl to move to Balham or wherever with him, who would think he was absolutely marvelous. In his way, he was a hopeless romantic, too.

"You look beautiful tonight," Marcus said, as if he were talking about the weather. He leaned forward and kissed her on the lips, rather heavily and clumsily, almost defiantly, and sat back again. "Thank you," he said formally.

"Hey! Ah," said Laura, rather flustered, feeling she should thank him, too, or write him a formal letter.

Now that he had staked his claim, as it were, Marcus seemed to relax visibly. He stood up and offered Laura his arm. "We should be on our way, if that's okay," he said, and picked up her cape and put it round her shoulders.

"What kind of people are going to be there?" asked Laura, as he opened the door for her. He took her arm.

"Oh, all sorts," said Marcus, smiling rather indulgently at her, as if she'd asked an adorable question.

They were opposite the Royal Courts, and Laura could see black ties and evening dresses trickling in through the elaborate stone gates, up the steps. She said, "No, I mean—tell me a bit about it. Are the guests your company's clients or the bank's?"

"Sure. They're our clients. The sponsor is a fairly big German bank—they have investors of their own there, too. They have a lot of very rich private clients, so it's a formal affair and there are often some pretty important people there. But, yeah, they're all good guys. Should be fun."

He took her arm as they crossed the road. "Right," said Laura, thinking that sounded like anything *but* fun, and already so confused by the progress of the date so far, her role therein, and the evening ahead of her that any action on her part would be pointless. She squeezed his arm. "God, Marcus—who's that?"

A tall, blond man, maybe in his late fifties, had got out of a car that had pulled up in front of the building. He was opening the other passenger door, from which emerged a woman so overly made-up, so wholly encrusted with jewelry and sparkle, that she looked like a blow-up doll. She took her companion's arm and looked around impassively, disdain writ large on whatever part of her face still held expression.

"My God," said Marcus, grinding to a halt.

"I know," said Laura. "She looks ridiculous."

"No," said Marcus. "I didn't think they'd come. That's—Lars Thorson."

"Who?" said Laura.

"Lars Thorson. Don't you know who he is? He's—well, he's the richest man in Sweden. Invested in tech stock when it was still geek territory. That's his wife, Tania. Right old slapper," said Marcus with relish, pulling away from Laura to get a better look.

Thorson. She knew that name. She knew that name. Laura looked at Marcus in panic, trying to reassure the inner voice of warning in her head. "Good God, look at her," Marcus continued, his eyes lighting up. He stared openly at the couple in front of them as Tania Thorson rearranged her shawl, then turned to Laura. "God, can't believe it. Tania Thorson. She used to be a bit of all right. Look at her. She looks like a—"

"Right, right," Laura said, steering him toward the revolving doors. "Right. And," she said, not wanting to ask the question, but knowing she was going to, "don't they have a daughter?"

"Yep, they do. Cecilia. Very fit. Used to come to presentations with her daddio. Funny, that," said Marcus, squeezing into the door behind her and practically propelling her round, his hand on her back. "Just remembered."

"What?" said Laura as they emerged on the other side, feeling slightly dizzy.

"She's going out with Nick now, you remember old Nick? Ranelagh. Yeah. She's called Cecilia. Mate told me he was giving her one these days. Hope she doesn't take after her moth— Hey! Hey! There he is!"

"There who—" Laura said, her brain spinning, as the doors behind them kept spinning, spilling out people who pushed past her, swarmed around her. She couldn't see Marcus, he had vanished; she could hear his voice, but where was he?

"Nick! I say!"

The sea of people cleared, the way parted, and there was a newly invigorated Marcus, patting someone on the back, someone who turned to face her as Marcus was saying, "Good one! Good one! Let me introduce you, old chap, this is my gorgeous date for this evening, Laura. Hey, Laura. This is the Marquis of Ranelagh, my dear. You've visited his place, you know. You told me."

"Yes," said Laura, mechanically holding out her hand, looking up into Nick's face. "Hello."

"Hello," said Nick, meeting her gaze. His short dark hair was combed and neat, his evening dress immaculate, his expression remote. His other hand was in his pocket, and he squeezed her hand, then dropped it, looked from one to the other of them. Laura's arm felt numb, as if it were something sewn onto her body. It fell by her side, a deadweight, as she watched him, not knowing what to say.

"Nice to see you, Laura. Marcus—great to catch up. Maybe

later. Excuse me. I should say hello to the Thorsons, they've just arrived."

"Course you had, mate!" Marcus winked at him, hugely gratified at being present for this. He put his arm proprietorially around Laura, as if to say, We're all in the same boat, aren't we? Laura rocked against him, feeling like a deadweight, realizing that, for Marcus, this was shaping up to be a great evening, whereas for her, it was probably one of the all-time lows, down there with her other grandmother, Deidre's, funeral and the time Simon was sick over her brand-new Levi's 501s just before her first date with Sean Phillips when she was fifteen.

"See you later," Nick said politely. He smiled briefly at both of them. "Have a good evening. Good to see you both."

He walked off toward Tania Thorson, who was walking stiffly toward the hall, and Laura watched him put his arm round her fondly, kiss her, make some joke. He hugged Lars and shook hands with a couple of other people who'd arrived, all serious, slick, wealthy-looking. Marcus gazed at them almost hungrily. Laura gazed at them, back at him. Her hand stole up to the necklace, and she stroked it gently.

chapter forty-two

The next two hours were two of the loneliest of Laura's life. The rain began soon after they arrived, and all evening it thudded on the roof of the hall. All through the drinks at the front of the hall, she stood mutely by Marcus's side as he roared with laughter and slapped backs with a succession of identical-looking, identically dressed men. He was happiest, she soon realized, in the company of other men. The blokes, the guys, the chaps he worked with, who moved vast amounts of money from A to B and then made it into C.

She hung back as he networked, tried to do her bit as The Date, a polite smile plastered to her face, tried not to scan the crowd, until they were ushered farther back along the huge, echoing, vaulted hall for supper. The moment they were seated and had each been presented with a laminated cardboard folder describing the achievements of the German bank over the last year and going forward, Marcus turned away from her to the man on his right, with whom he proceeded to have a similarly raucous conversation. He would turn to her occasionally and ask her if she was okay, and then almost immediately turn back with enthusiasm to a long discussion about the rise of the hedge fund.

"Sure you're okay?" he said to her on his third swivel round.

"I'm absolutely fine," Laura said, lying through her teeth. Marcus smiled at her. "Marcus," she began determinedly, "I wondered, by the way—about the donation we discussed—"

"What's that?" said Marcus.

"The sponsorship program," Laura said, putting one finger on his arm.

"Oh, absolutely," said Marcus. "Absolutely."

"Can we—should we talk about it at some point? Firm up the details?"

Suddenly, Marcus's hand shot out and clamped itself around her leg. All at once Laura felt totally like a prostitute touting for business, or some kind of dodgy honeytrap, as Marcus's fingers clumsily patted her skin and he turned toward her, gulping his wine greedily.

"Have you . . ." she faltered, and looked down at his hand, high up on her thigh. He squeezed her leg, and smiled at her amicably.

"Great," said Marcus. "Remind me about it later. Just got to ask this chap—" And he turned away again.

Laura sank back in her chair, dispirited. Apart from the hand on her leg, she might as well have been invisible, she thought wretchedly, and outside the wind whistled along the glass, rattling it as the rain beat down.

Periodically Marcus would squeeze her thigh; and it reminded Laura of when she and Simon were small, on the sofa in the lounge at Heathcote Road watching TV after school, and Simon would suddenly poke her viciously in the ribs. She would poke him back. They would sit there in huge tension, not knowing who would dare to poke next, and when it came each would scream with the recognized shock of it. So Laura felt as she gazed around her table, around the room, trying not to look bored, waiting for Marcus's next hard, crablike squeeze on her thigh. It did not make for a particularly relaxed dining experience.

The man on her left was a kind, polite German banker who tried his best to engage her in conversation; but the rest of the table was fairly loud, his English was not great, Laura's German was nonexistent, and the noise in the rest of the hall grew ever louder, with guffaws and shouts echoing out, a bit like the last day of term at a particularly muscular boarding school, and so it was a little hard to hear what he was saying. Besides which, Laura's knowledge of German banks was not all it might have been; and what with Marcus's hand periodically making her jump, and the nice German man—whose name she had, of course, instantly forgotten—trying his very best but failing to sustain conversation, the first two courses inched by in what seemed to be an eternity, during which the hands on the huge iron clock high up in the vaulted ceiling barely seemed to move, the noise seemed to grow louder, and the food—especially the watercress mousse—felt like slimy slabs of sponge in her mouth.

Was it that Nick was there, over there, past the next table, just visible if she tilted her head very slightly? Was it that? Was it true that she could really look over and see him anytime she liked, after more than two months, remember all those things about him that she'd forgotten, the cast of his jaw, his shoulders, his expression when he smiled? Or was it that she had finally realized she didn't know him, would never know him; that this was the world he lived in, not the one he had pretended to show her over the summer?

She stared at him through the sea of black-jacketed shoulders, and just once allowed herself to wallow a little. To remember dreamily how unreal, how fantastical that time at Chartley had been. Like a favorite film or a childhood holiday that takes on the golden-hued appearance of a fairy tale, every day long and sunny, every event magical. Here he was again, and she could see him out of the corner of her eye, whenever she wanted. She realized now that, during the past two months, she had got so used to *thinking* she saw him everywhere—on the street, in the pub, on the Tube—that she was always turning her head to see if that tall, dark man in the corner was, in fact, Nick, come to find her. And now, that tall, dark man in the corner was, in fact, Nick. But he was with someone else, and she—

As Lars Thorson leaned forward to say something quietly to Nick, and he looked blankly into space as he listened, nodding, she remembered with a stabbing agony the last time she'd seen him, how the holiday had come to an end. She took a deep breath. Could Nick really be enjoying this totally dire evening? Was he really the person who could get satisfaction from smarming up to some rich industrialist and his blow-up doll of a wife? And their thin, bloodless, humorless daughter?

For Cecilia Thorson was there, very much there, sitting up straight next to him; and that was really the only interesting thing about this evening, except Laura wished she could stop staring at the two of them, so poised, so glamorous, so—*grown-up*–looking. They reminded Laura of effigies from medieval tombs she had seen on a school trip to France years ago—side by side, she with straight hair, straight nose, long thin face, elegant pursed lips; he taller, prouder, statesmanlike. Not someone she knew or remembered at all. Laura shook her head.

"Okay there?" came Marcus's voice suddenly, close to her ear. His rather large nose brushed unexpectedly across Laura's neck. She jumped, realizing she was staring at Nick, and she saw him turn instinctively, his gaze meeting hers across the room. She swiveled round to Marcus, who was making a kind of guzzling, gurgling sound in her ear, which surprised her until he said with an effort, "You do look—gorgeous, you know, L-Laura."

"Thanks," said Laura, who was never sure how to respond to compliments like that. "Yes, I know. No, I don't, what are you talking about?"

"I—I just want to . . . grrr." Marcus shook his head, and made a sound like a small bear.

Oh, dear, thought Laura. Please, let this be an upset stomach, rather than a prelude to sex. Because, Marcus, if you seriously think you're getting some tonight, you are Wrong Wrong Wrong.

"Having a good time?" his voice murmured heavily in her ear, sounding rather like an unskilled Barry White impersonator. Laura had to fight back the urge to reply in kind: "I sure am, baby, how you doin'?" She bit her lip, and Marcus, taking this for an encouraging sign, squeezed her thigh again.

"Oh, Marcus—" said Laura feebly. "Don't—don't do that. It's . . . you know."

"Oh," said Marcus, sitting back in his chair suddenly. "Sorry." He looked mortified, his hair flopping sadly on each side of his head like a bunny's ears.

Laura felt mean. "Sorry," she said. "It's just—anyway. Are you having a good time?"

"Yep, absolutely," said Marcus. "Really interesting bloke next to me, used to run the Singapore arm of this startup we invested in couple years ago."

"Oh. Hey. That's so . . . cool. Cool!" said Laura, unsure of the correct response. She was even more aware of the conversational gap between them. "So you—"

"Anyway, how about you?" said Marcus enthusiastically. Laura realized he was a little drunk. His mouth was slacker, his eyes duller. "You having a good time?" He leaned forward again. "Sorry haven't had time to talk," he said. "Very glad you came. But must talk to people. You sit there." He patted her thigh again, as if she were a tiny leprechaun who might hop off her seat and run wildly among the guests throwing gravy around and causing havoc.

"Right," said Laura, picking up her fork to push an uneaten pile of chocolate mousse across her plate. She wanted to hate Marcus, be furiously cross with him, blame him for Nick being there, for how crap a time she was having. Yorky had gone for drinks with Hilary tonight after work in Shepherd Market; she could be there, too, dressed normally, sitting there having a laugh, instead of here, feeling this awful; and she wanted to blame Mareus for it, but she couldn't. No, she had to go through with it.

This was a sort of watershed evening for her, she realized. Perhaps the presence of Nick was a sign from the gods, a symbol of how strong she had to be, of what she had to pull off. She was on a date, and she was going to get Marcus to give the schools sponsorship program a big donation or die trying. She could still do it. She had to. Wasn't this what she'd been at work early trying to sort out during the endless weeks since she'd come back from Norfolk? Building up contacts again, putting together information, cajoling, flattering, skirting around the issue like a gavotte—and nothing, nothing from any of the other companies so far, and Rachel was depending on her. More than that—she *had* to pull it off, or else her job was in jeopardy again. And even more than that, perhaps, she had to do it for herself.

Laura took a deep breath, set her face in a stern expression, and said firmly, "Marcus. Can I get you a coffee? And then can we talk about the sponsorship program, before we have too much to drink and forget?"

"George! Hi! Good to see you, mate. Listen, about the liability claim," said Marcus suddenly, turning his back on her to address a man standing behind him. His left hand shot out and clamped down on her leg again.

Laura snarled to herself, and realized she had to calm down. Time to while away five minutes in the loo, I think, she told herself. She took her bag and made to stand up, but just as she gingerly put her hand on Marcus's to remove it, she noticed Cecilia Thorson standing up with her bag and heading across the room. Laura shrank back in her seat. No, thanks, she thought. I don't want to be loo buddies with her. Cecilia sailed gracefully past, her expression proud, unruffled. Laura watched her from under her eyelashes, her hand clutching Marcus's in a frenzied grip. Damn it.

She looked up at the clock and then around the room. It was nearly ten o'clock; she'd been there for two hours. The rain was still pounding relentlessly on the glass roof. The tables were breaking up; coffee was being served, but people were moving around, men and women nonchalantly leaning against chairs chatting to each other. The polite German man next to her had disappeared. It was getting late. She had to rescue this situation—but how? Perhaps she should just go, she thought hopelessly. Face Rachel's hopeful face on Monday and admit failure.

As if answering her thoughts, she turned to find Marcus's hazy stare fixed on her. He half licked his lips, a tiny, unconscious movement. Laura realized he had passed from being a bit intoxicated to properly drunk.

"Laura," he said. "Witchu. Wouldchu like—what are we doing later?"

"Er—" said Laura uncertainly. "It's not over yet, is it? Oh, no. What a great evening. Perhaps—"

"Come back to mine," Marcus urged, hedging his bets with the optimism of the drunk. "Go on! You'd like it." He patted her arm, his hand sliding heavily down her skin. "Please."

"Well, thanks," said Laura, feeling a bit like she was wrestling with an octopus, only a drunk octopus in a dinner jacket who was head of some important league under the sea. She removed his other hand, which was making its way between her knees. This was silly. Time to admit defeat. "Look, Marcus, I think I'd better head off. We can talk on Monday," she said flatly.

Marcus sat up and said, "C'mon, Laura. You really shouldn't go, you know. Really should stay."

"Why?" said Laura, not looking at him. She picked up her cape.

"You should . . . be being more nice," said Marcus, lolling softly forward so that he was propped up by the table. "Be nice. I've taken you out and everything. Wanted to discuss the—the, erm, the thing—the thing with the schools. Them. And now you're not even being very nice. Are you?"

"Oh, my God," said Laura, freezing with one arm in her cape and one arm out of it. This was what it must have been like to be Michael J. Fox's mum in *Back to the Future*, being forced to make out with the boorish villain in his car at the prom.

Everyone else had left their table, and the majority of the crowd was moving back into the front of the hall. Marcus looked up at her resentfully. "God, Laura. Don't you like me? Am I . . . ugh."

"I'm sorry, Marcus," said Laura, not sure how much of this was drunk Marcus talking and how much was potential date-rape Marcus talking, and not willing to hang around to find out.

"Who the hell do you think you are?" Marcus's voice was slurred. She couldn't see his face; he was staring at the tablecloth. His hand was still on her arm; it slid off onto the table. "You can whistle for it. The money. Bloody sorry I ever asked you."

"Fine," said Laura. "Look—I'm sorry," she said again, and suddenly it made her furious that she was saying sorry, and a sense of impotent anger at her own failures—all of them, all alive and present and jogging into each other in this bloody huge room—made her stand up. She pulled her arm through the cape in one almighty wrench, feeling the lining tear slightly. "I'll . . ." She looked down at Marcus, who was gazing up at her with the vacant, uncertain look she remembered from before, but it wasn't enough to stop her. She turned on her heel—she'd always wanted to know exactly what that was like, and now she knew—and strode toward the door without looking back, not knowing whom she despised more at that moment: herself, for getting all excited about the evening, stupid girl, for trying to mix business with—pleasure, if that's what this was. Or bloody Marcus, for—well, being a fruit loop. Hopefully, just a drunk fruit loop.

As she reached the first set of doors, a voice behind her said, "Hello, Laura, how are you?"

Laura spun round, her heart in her mouth, but standing there was Charles. Lovely, dependable Charles. Relatively normal (relative to the rest of the room, that is). She looked up at him, and he smiled at her with his kindly smile and said, "You have a face like thunder. Is everything okay?"

"Yes," said Laura, nearly laughing. "Charles. It's so nice to see you! How are you? You're here—with . . ." She trailed off.

"Nick's just saying good-bye to Cecilia," said Charles, looking at her carefully. "I'm sure he'd love to know you're here, though, Laura. I should—" He looked around.

"No! No," cried Laura insanely. "I've seen him already, we've said hi! Don't worry."

"Oh," said Charles, and an expression of—what it was, Laura didn't know—crossed his face. He shifted a little. "So, who is he? The chap you were with tonight?" Laura bit her lip. "The one I saw you shaking off? I was about to come over, actually, see if you were okay, but just as I started over, you were up and away."

"Ha," said Laura, feeling exhausted all of a sudden. "Just—oh, some bloke."

"Are you leaving?" said Charles, gesturing toward the main

doors. Laura nodded. "Some bloke, eh?" he said, falling into step beside her.

"Yep. It's a work thing. Oh," Laura said rather brokenly, "never mind."

"Oh, go on," said Charles, his voice warm. "I've spent the evening between one woman moaning about her interior decorator in Chamonix and a really attractive girl from the bank who asked me if I was gay. Can't get worse than that, can it? What's up? Tell me."

They were in a human traffic jam as people clogged the doors, hesitating as the rain lashed the pavements. Laura laughed softly and looked at him, remembering how easy he was to talk to.

"Well," she said, and briefly outlined the reasons for her presence there. It was all rather tangled, and as she finished with "And now I don't know what to do. I said I'd get the money, I promised I'd be better at my job," she realized she was sounding like a five-year-old who isn't allowed a pet rabbit. But she couldn't help it—she felt stupid, standing there all dressed up, having danced out of Mary's flat looking forward to a date and the chance to make things right at work. Why, oh, why? But there was something hugely comforting about Charles, he was so easy to talk to; and as they inched forward in the queue for the exit, she said, "I'm sorry. God, I keep saying that tonight. But I am."

"For what?"

"For being so boring. It's so stupid," said Laura. She shook her head. "Forget about it."

"Forget it. So, what are you going to do? About the money, I mean?" said Charles.

"I have ways and means," said Laura, smiling with a confidence she didn't feel.

"Good for you," said Charles. "I bet you do," and he patted her shoulder reassuringly.

That was almost too much for Laura. She gulped, and said in a wavering tone, "Thanks, Charles. Thanks a lot," and he gave her a quick, slight grin as they stood together in silence.

"Where are you going now?" Charles asked as they finally reached the lobby. He looked out through the doors onto the Strand, staring thoughtfully at the rain as it splashed into puddles.

"Well," said Laura, looking at her watch. "God, it's still early-ish, isn't it? I think I'm going to head into Soho." She took a deep breath and said, "Actually, I want to go home. I'm really tired and I need to—to think it all through." She looked up at him. "I think I'm going to get a—oh."

As if in a dream, Laura saw Nick arriving, patting Charles's shoulder; saw him as he saw her, raised his chin, faced her. She saw all of this as if they were underwater, moving slowly; as if it were someone else instead and she had no control over what she said or did.

Charles said, "I'll go and see where the car is." He nodded politely at Laura, and stepped aside.

"Laura," said Nick. His expression held no emotion whatsoever. "Nice to see you."

He looked at his fingers, flicked something imaginary from one of his nails, and smiled at her. His expression was cold and his dark eyes rested just above her head. It was strange; she remembered his eyes as being so full of warmth, emotion, flashing with anger or amusement, and to see him like this was—it was almost like seeing a corpse, a waxwork of him. This wasn't the Nick she knew.

This is who you are, isn't it? Laura thought in a flash of clarity. You really are this person most of the time. She looked at him, and didn't know what to say. The events of the evening were catching up with her.

"I have to go," she said, starting away.

"Of course," said Nick, his voice slightly raised. "Well. Good-bye, then."

Laura looked back at him. "Say good-bye to Charles for me, will you? Tell him I couldn't stay."

She headed for the door, and felt a hand on her arm.

"It's raining," said Nick's voice in her ear. "Look, Laura, why don't we give you a lift to wherever you're going?"

"No, thanks," said Laura desperately. "I'll get a cab."

She turned to look at the steady column of men and women in evening dress, fluttering and cooing on the pavement outside as the rain came down more heavily and steaming cabs already filled with passengers passed by.

"It's pouring with rain, everyone's leaving, you're wearing virtually nothing. You'll never get a taxi, so just stay here and I'll drop you off."

"I . . ." Laura said, shaking his hand off her arm, very tired. "Oh, please just let me go. . . ."

"Come on, Laura," said Nick. "Let us give you a lift. Please." His jaw was set. He said, not looking at her, "Charles is with me, he can keep the peace."

"Honestly, don't worry," Laura said, her mother's fear of socially awkward situations settling over her like a cloud. "I live in North London, it's miles away."

"Well, that's perfect," said Nick. "We're going that way anyway." He unwrapped his scarf. "Great. There's Charles." He hailed his friend. "What news?"

"Car's outside, Nick," said Charles.

"We're giving Laura a lift back to North London," said Nick. "Because it's on our way."

Charles's expression didn't flicker. "Great," he said. "Let's go."

He opened the door for Laura, and she felt something light drop onto her shoulders, over her thin evening cape. She looked down. It was a scarf.

"Keep the rain off," Nick said. Out on the pavement, a smartly dressed man was rushing forward with an umbrella. Nick put his arm under hers; she felt the slight pressure of his hand guiding her. Her eyelids were heavy; and she felt dizzy all of a sudden. She climbed into the car and straightened her skirt, pulling it over her thighs; he stood looking down at her for a moment, and shut the door with a bang. She heard him throw the umbrella into the back, then have a brief conversation with the driver as Charles slid into the front seat next to the driver, and Nick got in next to her. The car smelled of leather, luxurious, oddly stifling.

"Thanks, Paul." Nick nodded at the driver, and they moved away without noise.

chapter forty-three

She may have been feeling totally drained, and wanting to bang her head on the window, but Laura was a trooper. No matter that the evening had begun badly and ended disastrously—she briefly considered whether there was any chance the Marcus she had left semiconscious at the dinner table could still be the Marcus who would ring up on Monday with a donation to the sponsorship program for twenty thousand pounds, and then realized the answer was no—she wasn't going to behave like a five-year-old. No matter that it was pouring rain. No matter that her date was drunk and a bit weird, and that Nick was here with a beautiful blond millionaire's daughter. She could still make civilized conversation, be polite.

"Thank you for this," Laura said, shifting on the leather. "It's really kind of you."

"Not at all. My pleasure."

Laura fell silent, aware it was just the two of them talking while

Paul, the driver, and Charles in the front pretended not to be listening; Nick seemed to be completely at ease with it, of course. She looked at him, sitting comfortably in the back, his beautiful gray wool coat glistening with raindrops, one arm flung across the back of the seat, one strong brown hand resting lightly on the leather, just a little way from her head.

She wasn't really sure what to do or say next. All the cheerful, socially adept questions she could possibly ask him—"Have you had a nice evening?" "Who was at your table?" "How's the estate?" "Ha-ha, well, isn't it strange, bumping into you like this?"—sounded too loaded to her. And the ones she really wanted to ask—"What's going on with Cecilia?" "Have you missed me, because I've missed you?" "Can I lick your face, or would that be weird in the back of the car?"—were obviously not suitable. So she pulled his scarf around her a little more, and sank down a little farther into her seat.

"So . . ." said Nick. He tapped his fingers on the headrest behind Laura, and she jumped. "Sorry." He touched her shoulder lightly. "Sorry, Laura. I'm—this is weird." He looked at her frankly, and Laura turned to him.

"It is, isn't it?" she agreed, remembering again with a rush of—what?—how nice he was, how easy and straightforward, and wondering how she could ever have thought he was remote, hard to understand.

"Good evening, wasn't it?" Nick said. "Lovely atmosphere. Very relaxing. German bankers are my favorite bankers."

"Good?" said Laura, laughing. "Ooof. What a night. I thought it was never going to end. How can you do it?"

"I don't, that often," said Nick. "But I was in town, and Lars . . ."

Laura was determined to be chipper, upbeat, polite. He had

made the effort; it was up to her to repay him. "Is that Cecilia's dad?" she asked, in a tone of polite interest.

"Yes," said Nick. "Nice bloke. He's really helped me out over the past couple of years, and he invited me. I thought it would be rude not to go."

"Absolutely," said Laura airily. "Yes, these things can go on a bit, can't they."

Nick gave her a strange look. "Go to them a lot, do you?"

"Oh. Well, you know, here and there," said Laura, trying to sound like she knew what she was talking about.

"Go with Marcus, do you?" said Nick.

"Er," said Laura. "Well, tonight I did."

Nick flicked a piece of dust off his coat. "Surprised to see you with him."

Laura thought of Marcus—not the Marcus she'd run away from, the one lying drunk and passed out on the table, but the one who had kissed her rather determinedly at the bar, holding her hand. His old-fashioned courtesy, how he just wanted to meet someone nice. She said defensively, "He's all right. Okay?"

"I'm sure he is." Nick's face was in the dark; she couldn't really see it. "Sure he is."

The car moved steadily along the Strand, the streets glossy and black in the rain. Charles turned to Paul and asked him about directions in a quiet voice. They were alone in the back.

"How's work?" said Nick suddenly.

Laura knitted her hands in her lap. "Um. Okay."

"What does that mean?"

"It means . . ." Laura cast around in her mind for the right response. "Oh," she said wearily, "I'm not sure."

"You've got your job back, though?" he said, and there was concern, interest in his voice.

"Yes, but . . ." She put her palms flat on her lap, not knowing how much to say, wanting to tell him everything, knowing she should keep it all back. Laura turned to him, but she still couldn't see his face, and so she just said rather weakly, "Yes. I did."

"So why—" Nick began, but Laura found herself putting her hand up.

"Do you mind if we don't?" she said. "Talk about it? Bit stressed about it at the moment. I think I've cocked up. I don't want to think about it, not tonight."

"Anything I can do?" said Nick. Laura gave a hollow sigh under her breath, and he said immediately, "Sorry. That's probably the least helpful thing someone can say."

"No," said Laura quietly. "Thank you, though."

"I'm serious," he said, his voice close by. "If there is anything, Laura—"

She nodded. There was a ball of air in her throat, pushing down into her chest, making it hard for her to speak. He watched her as Laura shrugged, trying to look unconcerned; she felt she merely succeeded in looking a bit stupid.

"And how are you?" she asked, pulling herself together. "How is everything at Chartley?" She stopped, realizing she sounded rather like Aunt Annabel.

His voice soft with amusement, Nick replied, "Great, thank you. It's a little quieter since the summer, of course. Since you were there."

"Yes, I can imagine," Laura said, her head on one side, trying to pretend he was just a tour guide, and she was just a tourist. "Um. What are you up to at the moment, then?"

"Well, the crops are all in, and that's gone well—the weather's been fantastic, which made it easier, which is good."

"Ah," said Laura, trying to sound informed. "The harvest."

"Yes," Nick said gravely, but his mouth twitched. "The harvest.

And we've just started a major project, cataloging all the paintings, sculptures, and so on in the house. Going to take a few years, but it's important, needs to be done."

Laura always loved hearing him talk about the estate, what he was doing with it. "Really? For insurance, or . . . ?"

"Insurance, yes, and so we have an idea of what's there."

"Like what?"

Nick shifted closer toward her, half an inch, almost imperceptible. He paused before saying, "Well, when my father died, everything was a total mess. When I went through his study for the first time, I found two paintings, little watercolors. Didn't think anything more of them. Turns out they're sketches by this Victorian artist, worth about ten thousand each. Dad had just shoved them in a cupboard, years ago."

"Blimey," said Laura. "He must have had no idea."

"He did," said Nick, his voice flat. "He bought them for my mother, as a wedding present. We found the paperwork. They were framed. He'd obviously taken them out of their frames and rolled them up, put them out of sight."

"Oh," said Laura. She looked down. Their knees were angled toward each other, almost touching. She said quietly, "That must have been a bit weird for you."

Nick ran a hand through his short hair, and glanced out the window. "Bit weird, yes," he said, turning back and smiling slightly at her. "It's funny."

"What's funny?" said Laura, watching him.

"I haven't said this to anyone. But I keep thinking about her lately."

"Who? Your mother?"

"Yes," he said. "I don't know why. I spent so long training myself not to miss her when I was younger. So sometimes months go by, and I don't really . . . wonder about her. What she's up to, how she is. And then sometimes . . ." He looked at her. "Like lately. Since you left. I keep thinking about how she is."

"Really?"

"Yes. I want to see her again. You know."

"Nick, she's your mother," said Laura simply. "Of course you want to see her again."

"Yes, of course," he said, with a trace of the old impatience. "But you don't understand."

"I know I don't," Laura said, shaking her head.

"Sorry, that's wrong," he said. "You do understand. About some things." His eyes were on hers, with an expression half-sad, half-smiling that she found terribly painful. They said nothing, but looked at each other in the darkness.

"You should get in touch with her," said Laura firmly.

Nick shook his head. "Thank you, no. I don't think that would be a very good idea."

His arm was still behind her on the back of the seat; he flung it next to his thigh, and drummed his fingers on the leather.

"Perhaps you're right," he said eventually.

"But you're the only one who can make that move," said Laura. She wanted to bridge the distance between them, make it all all right for him, but she couldn't. "Trust me. I know."

"And how do you know that?" said Nick, amused.

"Well, I don't know," said Laura frankly. "I know what I think you should do."

"As ever," he said, his voice low. "That's Laura. Rushing in, speaking before she thinks. Bossing people around, setting fire to things. Being hugely rude. And . . . running away, when I don't want her to leave."

His eyes flicked up to the front seat, where Paul and Charles were still engaged in low, desultory conversation, and he looked back at her and down again. She followed his gaze. His hand was inches away from hers, both resting on the seat. She remembered his touch, how warm and strong he was. She closed her eyes briefly, overwhelmed with wanting just once more to hold his hand, to lean against him. Both of them looked down at their hands, neither of them saying anything, though Laura desperately wanted to say something, the right thing, wanted to move her fingers toward his. And then Nick lifted his hand and scratched his cheek, and the spell was broken.

"You didn't reply to my text," he said eventually in a low voice.

She shook her head, not trusting herself to speak.

He smiled and said, "So, here we are. I made up my mind I wasn't going to speak to you when I got into the car."

"That's nice of you," said Laura, recovering herself.

"I mean it."

"Really?" said Laura.

"Yes, Laura. I did. The way you left . . ."

"I know," said Laura. The car reached the end of the Strand; they were at Trafalgar Square, and light flooded across Nick's face as they drove through the square and under Admiralty Arch.

"Do you understand why I had to leave?" she said, hardly breathing, wanting him to give her the answer she didn't dare to hope for.

"I didn't, no," he said. "Absolutely not."

"Really?" said Laura, her heart pounding.

"Not at first, no," said Nick. He nodded to himself. "But now I do."

"Oh," said Laura. "Right."

She knew exactly the reasons why she'd left, why she'd given up on them; but she couldn't, at that exact moment, remember what those reasons were. "It's just—not meant to be, is it, I suppose," she said, scanning his face, but his expression was formal, closed again, and she couldn't read him anymore.

"I don't think it is," he said. "If that's what you think, too."

Laura rubbed her eyes and looked out on the Mall as they drove sedately along the wide, tree-lined boulevard. The rain had stopped. She looked at him suddenly, and caught him staring at her with that old, familiar look, his eyes searching her face, drinking her in. His lower lip was caught between his teeth. He winced, as if he were biting down too hard, and wiped his hand across his mouth, smiling suddenly at her.

"Is that what you think?" she said, looking intently at him. "Really?"

"Yes," said Nick. He gave a half smile, and patted her leg. "Funny, isn't it."

She felt the warmth of his skin on hers. "Nick—" Laura whispered. "I think—"

A mobile phone buzzed angrily in the quiet. Nick pulled his phone out of his pocket as Laura sank back into her seat.

"Hello. . . . Good, thank you. And you. . . . Thank you." His tone was expressionless.

Hearing the break in conversation, Charles turned around in his seat and peered at her. "Oh, hello, Laura!" he said, as if he were surprised to see her there.

"Hello, Charles!" Laura said. "What a shock, how long have you been there?"

"Oh. Ha-ha-ha," said Charles, looking confused. "I'm sorry to disturb you, Laura. I just wondered—"

"No. It's a friend. She was at the party." Nick's voice was quiet, and he had turned to the window, but Laura could hear every word. "I'm giving her a lift home. . . . No. Cecilia, I've told you—"

Charles started talking over him. "Where in North London do you want us to take you? I just wondered."

They were at Buckingham Palace, turning up toward Hyde

Park Corner. Laura pressed her hands to her cheeks, the events of the evening crowding in on her. Marcus kissing her in the bar. His hand on her thigh. The feel of Mary's necklace on her skin. Nick's hand, next to hers, but so far away. She looked down at her lap, saw her bag with the list of points about the investment program she'd planned to give Marcus sticking out of it, and anger and sadness and frustration at her own failure washed over her, this time with such force that it nearly knocked her back against the seat. What was she doing, in this car, with a man who clearly wasn't ever going to be hers? How had she managed to get herself into such a stupid situation again? How was she going to make it right with Rachel, who had put her faith in Laura, only to be disappointed again? She dug her nails into her palms. She had to get out, she had to get out.

"Actually, Charles—I'm meeting some friends just off Piccadilly. Can you drop me at Hyde Park Corner?"

"Really?" said Charles as they swooped past Green Park. "I thought we were—"

"No, it's fine," said Laura, panic in her voice, as Nick lowered the phone, frowning, and shoved it into his pocket almost viciously. "I'll just hop out here. It's only quarter past ten, you know. Still time to meet them." She tapped the handle. "Can I get out?"

"You're going?" said Nick. "What?"

"Yes," Laura gabbled, trying to stay calm. "My flatmate's in a pub just round the corner from here. With some friends. I'm going to meet them." She clutched her bag. "Thank you, Paul," she said as they drew up on Piccadilly. "I'll just hop out here."

"Why on earth do you want to get out here?" said Nick. "We can give you a lift home."

"I want to meet my friends." Laura knew she was sounding slightly shrill. "Please. It's been a . . . weird evening, what with one thing and another, you know, and I have to explain it at work, about Marcus—"

"What do you mean?" Nick interrupted. "What's Marcus got to do with work?"

"Oh, God, nothing, nothing," said Laura, pressing her hands to her cheeks, which were burning red. "Just—just please let me out."

"Laura." Nick took her hand then, curling her fingers up, wrapping his hand around hers. "What's up? Are you okay?"

She couldn't look at him, couldn't bear to let him be kind to her, that was worst of all. She cleared her throat. "I'm fine," she said. "Just . . . need to get out. Please, Nick. Honestly."

"Don't go, Laura," Charles said in a low voice. "Please."

"I think she wants to go," said Nick. She turned to him, but he flashed her half a grin, almost a grimace. "Well, Laura . . ."

"Yes," said Laura, opening the door.

"Take care," he said, and tapped her on the shoulder.

"Nick," said Charles, looking at his friend. "Don't you want to—"

"Laura has to go," said Nick. "Don't you, Laura?"

"Yes," said Laura, suddenly anxious to beat him in the Who Is the Most Nonchalant stakes. "Thanks for the scarf, Nick. Bye. Great to see you again!"

Charles turned away again and sighed.

She squeezed Charles's shoulder, then got out of the car, and as she did she felt Nick clutch her wrist, only for a fleeting, tiny second, and then it was gone. She looked into the dark interior, wanting to see his face once more, but the engine roared up again and they were off.

Laura breathed in deeply, watching them go, and walked up the quiet street, not looking, not caring, and when she opened the door into the steaming pub, full of wet drinkers, happy drinkers, drunk drinkers, she leaned against it for a second, desperately wanting to turn around to see if he was there, in case he'd got the car to turn around, to come back and find her. But she knew he wasn't going to do that. She looked across the tiny pub, and caught sight of Yorky and Hilary sitting in the corner. Her feet hurt. She made her way over to them.

"So," Hilary said, taking a drag of her cigarette. "Yorky tells me you've been sleeping with a duke or something. *And* you had a date tonight. How the hell was it?"

chapter forty-four

By the end of Friday night, curled up against Yorky on the last Tube home after a few more glasses of wine, Laura was of two minds about what had happened that evening. She kept trying to think it all through, and then her brain hurt, and she fell asleep until Yorky had to wake her up by yanking her hair.

But on Saturday, Laura woke up convinced that Marcus would still give them the money, that her job was okay, and, more important, that Nick still felt something for her—she knew it. It was there. It was hard for them both, but there was just something there. She bounded around the house all day feeling chipper, made a cake, cheered Simon up when he rang to complain about how he and Jorgia had had a row, bought some odd-looking crocus bulbs from the corner shop and planted them in her window boxes, then went to Shana's birthday party in Dulwich and had a great time.

On Sunday, however, she woke up absolutely certain that Marcus would wash his hands of the program forthwith, that Rachel would be forced to sack her, and ultimately that Nick had been, very kindly, giving her the brush-off, telling her they couldn't be together, that Cecilia Thorson was his bride-to-be—and hey, fine, whatever, you know. And she couldn't get rid of that feeling of creeping, enervating, horrible Sunday certainty, coupled with despair at herself for mucking it all up, *again.* She couldn't have a proper conversation with Nick—she was emotionally stunted and pathetic. She'd basically led Marcus up the garden path—how totally unprofessional could you get? And she'd led Rachel and Nasrin and the others up the garden path, too—making them think the bad times were over, that she, supergirl Laura, could sort it all out for them. Hah. What a joke.

It ruined her mood. She ate the cake; she shuffled around the flat; she sat on the sofa wrapped in her duvet watching *Countryfile* and the *Coronation Street* omnibus, and ate a whole packet of ginger nuts, dipped in tea. When one of the ginger nuts fell into the tea almost whole, she cried. Yorky and Becky retreated downstairs to Becky's flat, leaving Laura alone in her self-inflicted misery. If Yorky was bad, she was worse. She felt like she was in a boxing ring, being bounced from side to side by a much tougher opponent. Bounce. Bounce. She couldn't decide, couldn't decide if she was going mad or if she'd already got there.

Thankfully, someone else made the decision for her.

When Laura got to work on Monday morning, she was later than usual—which, since her time of the New Leaf, was virtually unheard-of—and Rachel and Nasrin were both there, poring over an Excel spreadsheet, which Laura knew very well had all the figures for the year on it—because they spent most days poring over a version of it, totting things up, taking other things away, desperately trying to save their program, pull more money from a hat like the proverbial rabbit. Her heart sank even further, from somewhere around her stomach right into her pumps. This was it. She squared her shoulders.

"Hey, Laura! I hear Shana's party was good," said Rachel.

"What?" said Laura, looking around her, distracted. "Oh! Yes, yes. Yes. Brill party. Brill-eee-ant. Loved it. *Loved it.*"

"I said it was good," said Nasrin. "I didn't say it was brilliant."

"Right," said Laura. "You're right. Yes. Hey, Rachel. Lovely top."

"Oh, thanks," said Rachel, looking down at her chest as Laura sat down at her desk with a clatter, and switched on her computer. "It's really old, actually. Thanks! So, Laura—"

"Did anyone see the golf?" Laura said loudly, desperately.

"The golf?" said Nasrin. "Why would I see the golf? Why would you, for that matter?"

"It was brill," said Laura. "Brill-eee-a—oh shut up," she muttered to herself under her breath.

Rachel walked toward her with a smile on her face. "So," she said. "So, Laura . . ." She gestured for Nasrin to join her. Nasrin followed her. "Hey!" Rachel caught sight of Shana in the doorway, just arriving. "Come over here, listen to Laura, she's got some good news for us!"

Laura wanted to curl up and die, quite literally just stop existing.

"Is this about the money?" said Shana. "I kept meaning to ask you, but I hardly saw you on Saturday. Go on! What is it?"

"Yeah," said Nasrin. "Come on, Laura!"

Laura looked up at their hopeful faces. She had never felt more wormlike. "Um," she began. "Look, Rachel. I know I said the money was in the bag—"

"What?" said Shana.

"—but," Laura continued, keeping her voice steady, "Friday was a bit of a disappointment. . . ."

"How so?" said Nasrin.

Tim appeared in the doorway. "Hi, you lot!" he called. "Cool! Is this about Laura's windfall? Our ticket out of the doghouse?"

"Hi! Hi!" Rachel said, gesturing to him. "It's great. Get over here!"

Laura wanted to shoot her for being so dense, for making this so very, very much harder than it needed to be. "Oh, God," she said flatly, as Tim stuck his head between Nasrin and Rachel, putting his arms around them, like they were an England football squad singing the national anthem. "Look . . ." She bit her lip. "It's bad news, I'm afraid."

"What?" said Rachel.

"He said we could whistle for it. The money. Marcus did," Laura said incoherently.

"He said what?" said Rachel.

"The money. He's not giving us anything. He said we could whistle for it."

"Whistle for it?" Rachel repeated, like she was new to the English language.

"Yes," said Laura patiently.

"That's really weird," said Rachel.

"Why?" said Laura.

"His assistant rang just before you got in. Said the check was on its way."

"What?" Laura said in disbelief. "Are you sure?"

"Absolutely," said Rachel. She smiled. "Actually, it's not a check, it's a bank transfer—but, you know, it's still cold, hard cash. Thirty thousand pounds! Laura, you're a genius." She bent and kissed Laura on the cheek. "He's not in this week, your friend Marcus. He's on holiday for two weeks."

"Oh," said Laura.

"It was his assistant I spoke to. Marcus rang from the airport to ask them to do it. Isn't that nice of him?"

"Well done, Laura," said Nasrin, nudging her.

"Yeah," said Shana, slapping Laura really hard on the back so that she coughed and spluttered. "Job well done."

"I don't get it," Laura muttered, but she could feel a ray of sunshine stealing over her. She wasn't a screwup. Marcus didn't hate her. She wished he weren't away—it was annoying, but she'd just have to make it up to him when he got back. Oh, she'd misjudged him, and no mistake. He wasn't a slightly overweight drunken lech. He was a misunderstood philanthropist and, in her opinion, a great, understanding man. Who obviously had no memory of what he did when he was drunk.

The office settled down to the Monday routine. Laura could hear Rachel in her office, on the phone to Gareth: "Yes! It's going straight in, today! . . . I know! Well, it was absolutely Laura's doing, we're so proud of her. . . . I know. . . . Yes, of course. I agree. It's fantastic."

Laura opened her e-mails, whistling.

Laura,

I'm sorry about the way I was on Friday. I understand you had a bad evening for other reasons as well. We still have unfinished business, you and me. Don't you agree? I don't really understand what's happened, and I think we're both too proud to admit it. Will you come up to Chartley for the weekend in two weeks' time?

We're having a belated Harvest Festival dance, a charity thing. I think you'd enjoy it. And the house is beautiful in autumn, you should see it at its best once more.

Let me know by return e-mail. Don't call me. My phone isn't working.

Please don't mention this to anyone else, of course.

Nick

part four

chapter forty-five

"Gran? Granny? Are you there? Can I come in?"

Laura shuffled impatiently in the drafty hallway of Crecy Court and checked her watch: about an hour until the train for King's Lynn left. She knew her grandmother was in; she'd seen Cedric on his way out and he'd told her she was.

"Gran?"

Eventually, she heard sounds from inside the flat, creaking on the parquet floor. "Granny," she said again. "It's me, Laura."

The door opened about a foot. Mary's face appeared round it. "Oh," she said. "It's you."

"Gran, hi. I just came to give you the necklace back."

"Come in, come in," said her grandmother, opening the door a little wider. Laura looked at her curiously as she went in. She was as immaculately dressed as ever, with a large, sparkling paste brooch on her white shirt. But she looked tired, very tired. Her eyes, usually alive and sparkling, were devoid of emotion. She nodded at Laura, motioned her to sit down.

"I'm sorry I've had it so long—" Laura began.

"It's fine, darling," Mary said. "Fine." She walked over to the window and looked out at the sky, darkening in the late afternoon.

The general view amongst the family was that Mary had "gone downhill," as Aunt Annabel so annoyingly put it, in the last couple of weeks. Something was worrying her, and the result was as if her brain were short-circuiting. She worried endlessly, didn't know people sometimes when they came to see her. She didn't want to see people when they arrived, and asked them constantly when they were going. Annabel in particular seemed to incur her ire more than others. Mary could barely stand the sight of her, and Annabel, along with Lulu and Fran, had been ejected from Crecy Court by Mary and Jasper and made to wait outside on the pavement for Robert to come and pick them up. (Laura and Simon couldn't help smirking a little when they heard that.)

But Laura thought her grandmother looked okay. She wasn't acting bewildered, or wearing slippers to go to the shops, or shuffling round in her nightie at four-thirty in the afternoon. She just looked tired and not particularly happy, staring out the window, not really looking at anything.

Laura said, "I can't stay long, Gran. Sorry. I thought I should let you have it back, though." She took the necklace out of her pocket, feeling the cold stones clustered in her hand.

"Thank you, darling," said Mary, turning away from the window, shaking her head as if coming alive again. "Very kind of you. Where are you off to?"

"Well," said Laura. "Actually, I'm off to Norfolk for the night."

Mary's eyebrows shot up. "Ye gods and little fishes. Well!" She clapped her hands. "Have a drink."

"I don't have time."

"Just a quick one. I have some wine open, as it happens."

"What a surprise," said Laura cheekily.

"Don't be rude, young lady." Mary pointed at the cabinet; Laura got out two glasses as Mary fetched the bottle from the kitchen. "So. You're off to Chartley, are you?"

"Yes," said Laura, leaning forward and hugging her knees. "Thanks," she said, taking the glass Mary had filled.

"Where's your aunt going tonight?" Mary said suddenly.

"Annabel?" Laura replied. "Good grief, no idea. Why?"

"Nothing. She telephoned me earlier, to tell me some rubbish about some old colleague of Xan's who's been made a commander of the order of the British Empire—as if I care, I'd completely forgotten he even existed, haven't seen him for twenty years. Good grief, she is a dreadful social climber," Mary said blithely, as if she were saying, "Good grief, she is wonderful" or "Good grief, she is the mother of two daughters." "Well, anyway, she said she was going to Norfolk tonight. I could have sworn it."

"Help," said Laura, laughing.

"Well, exactly," said Mary. "Watch out. Dear girl, but she can be so vexing. I'm quite out of patience with her at the moment, you know."

"Why?" asked Laura, wanting to know.

"Nothing in particular," said Mary, brushing her hands together. "So, tell me. Needham. Vivienne's son. What happened, may I ask?"

"I don't know," said Laura. "Actually, I really don't know. I saw him a couple of weeks ago—when I was on that date."

Mary nodded. "Hm, yes. The young banker. What was he called?"

"Marcus," said Laura.

"Yes. What happened with him?"

Laura clapped her hands. "He got drunk, made a pass at me

and passed out. And now he's gone on holiday, and his company's donated a huge sum to the school sponsorship scheme. It's very weird, but I don't care. We've got the money."

"Oh, well done, you," said Mary. "Darling. They should have had you during the Second World War. You're rather like one of those Russian spies who'd get the chaps awfully drunk and then get what they wanted out of them."

"I hadn't thought of it like that," said Laura, rather pleased. "I thought I made a bit of a fool of myself. And him. Poor bloke."

"Oh, no," said Mary. "Marvelous behavior. You used your powers for good. So you haven't thanked him yet, then?"

"No, he's been away," said Laura. "Back on Monday. I will then. I'm really going to thank him, too."

Laura had had a flash of realization about Marcus, since the dinner and in his absence: He'd be perfect for Rachel. She just knew it, and she was going to set them up when he got back. A few weeks ago, organizing a setup would have been anathema to her; now she was excited about it. Rachel hadn't been on a date for ages, and she was so sweet and kind, and just looking for someone who wanted to buy a big house in Balham and fill it with lots of rather stocky, strange children. Enter Marcus. Okay, he was a bit weird; okay, he probably liked being tied up and whipped—Laura's imagination was running on overtime in this department, obviously—but there was something about him, something lovable; and Rachel herself had a really filthy streak and the dirtiest laugh in South London. Laura rubbed her hands together and smiled at the thought of it.

"So tell me . . ." said Mary, sitting down in her chair. She blinked rather heavily, and took a few shallow breaths.

"Gran? Are you okay?" said Laura.

"I'm old, Laura," said Mary. "That's all." She took a sip of wine. "That's better."

Laura frowned at the bottle. "I'm not sure that's medically approved, you know, Gran."

"Rubbish," said Mary. "I'm strong as an ox. Never felt better."

She was silent, and Laura was quiet, too. The clock ticked loudly on the wall, and Laura thought about all the times she had sat in this flat with her grandmother, talking about things, anything, life, love, relationships, work, family. All the important things. The funny thing about Mary was, you could get straight down to it, no meandering around. She could talk to her grandmother about anything that was on her mind, or that involved both of them; and sitting there, taking it all in, she realized how lucky she'd been.

"What time's your train?" said Mary.

"Just under an hour. I had better go, you know."

"Of course," said Mary. "Why are you going?"

Laura was flummoxed by the question. "What?"

"Why are you going, tell me?" Mary stretched out a hand and looked at her wedding ring.

Laura thought about it for a moment. She looked directly at her grandmother. "I don't know," she said. "I want to see him, I suppose."

"Darling," said Mary, and then she stopped.

"What?" said Laura.

"Nothing," said Mary. "You know your own mind. And so does he. You must trust that." She cleared her throat. "It's a formal dinner, is it?"

"Yes," said Laura. She looked at her watch, knowing she was a bit late, but desperately wanting someone's advice and approval for what she was doing. She was nervous, and she didn't want to be; unsure, and she didn't know why. "Can I show you the dress I bought?"

Mary said with real pleasure, "Of course you can," as Laura

fumbled with the zip of her bag, and pulled the dress from its tissue paper.

She loved the dress. She had bought it, rashly, excitedly, in a little shop in Hampstead the previous weekend, biting her nails at the bill, smiling nervously with Jo at the indulgence of it. It was claret-colored, heavy silk, with wide shoulder straps plunging diagonally and twisting over the empire waistline. It hung just below the knee. She had spent ages choosing it—she wanted to look elegant, sophisticated, but she didn't want to look like, well, a tweedy dowager. She had picked out that dress thinking of Nick, wondering if he would like it, hoping he would, wondering why he'd invited her, looking forward so much to seeing him again, being able to tell him how stupid she'd been, how stupid they'd both been. . . . Laura's stomach lurched as she shook it out and held it up to show Mary, who fingered the fabric lovingly.

"Silk, beautiful." Mary nodded her approval. "It's perfect. Really. He's a fool if he doesn't think so." She glanced at her wrist. "You know, darling—"

"I should go." Laura stood up resolutely, suddenly filled with happy, nervous excitement, like a child before its birthday party. "Oh, Gran. Thank you. Bless you. I'm so glad—"

Mary made to stand up, and sat back abruptly. "Oh," she said. "Damn it."

Alarmed, Laura crouched beside her. "Granny?" she said. "Are you all right?"

A small smile crossed Mary's face. "Ha! I'm fine. You'll miss the train, come on now. Just a bit of indigestion—I let Jasper and Cedric take me out to that new steak place for lunch today." She stood up this time, clutching Laura's arm. Laura felt pain with the pressure, but she said nothing. Mary walked to the door. "Go away. I order you," she said.

"Gran—I'm going to get Jasper."

"He's out. I just want a little nap," said Mary. She smiled brightly at Laura, and suddenly Laura felt stupid. Mary looked full of beans, alive, her eyes sparkling again. "Don't treat me like a child, Laura, I'm fine!" she said. She caught Laura's arm at the door. "Darling, have a wonderful time, won't you?"

"I don't know," said Laura. "Are you sure you'll be all right?"

"Yes," said Mary firmly. "Good grief, the fuss. Now, enjoy yourself."

"I hope so," said Laura. "I'll call you tomorrow, come and see you on Sunday, maybe?"

"That," said Mary, "would be heaven."

And she kissed her, and shut the door gently. Laura turned to watch her as the door closed and her face disappeared.

She was late for the train and almost missed it; racing up the platform, Laura flung herself into a first-class carriage, then had to scrabble unhappily, clutching her bag, her knuckles grazing the plastic seats as she passed, through two more first-class carriages, a buffet car, and a goods compartment before she reached a standard-class carriage. It was mercifully thin of fellow passengers. She tucked her suitcase into the luggage bay and curled into a seat, tucking her feet up under her. As the train pulled out of North London into Hertfordshire, she gazed blankly out the window at the gently undulating autumnal landscape, the neat garden cities, the strange, dark sky.

It was autumn now—late autumn. She had failed to notice it, tucked up in the landscape of the city; but here, out in the countryside opening up before her as the train sped on, she could see the seasonal change. The velvety orange and red of the trees, pulsing across the landscape; the empty, churned fields. The thin, pure sun, its rays weaker and weaker in the late October afternoon.

Charles was meeting her at the station. He had rung her to

confirm the time, just as she was leaving the office. She wished it had been Nick calling to confirm, but no; trusty Charles, yet again, to the rescue—Laura shuddered when she remembered all the very many ways in which, over the past couple of months, Charles had seen her at her absolute worst.

And now here she was, on her way to Chartley, trying not to get too excited, but also simply happy that he'd been the one to do something about it, and that she was going to see him again. One part of her said: *It's great, he knows you've both made mistakes, and he wants to start fresh.* The other part, the part she wished didn't keep beating on the door of the first part, said: *This is weird. He hasn't spoken to you, he just sends you abrupt e-mails; he can't even be bothered to come and pick you up at the station. If he does still feel something, why can't he just say so, or invite you down for a normal weekend? Why this dinner-dance thing?*

Laura pulled her jacket closer around her, shivering slightly. She felt uneasy, and she didn't know why. So she picked up her book and tried to read, but she found she couldn't concentrate.

Her mind wandered. How funny that she was here and no one, apart from Mary, knew she was here. She hadn't wanted to explain it to anyone; she'd told Yorky simply that she was going to stay with her parents for the night. What would her mum say if she knew? Or Jo? Jo would worry that Laura hadn't packed the right things, had left something behind. And her mum would say, "That's nice, dear."

The truth was, she knew she was doing the right thing; whatever happened this evening, she was glad to be going, glad he had asked her to come see him. She was also glad it was at Chartley; she loved it, but she feared it, and she had to get over it. Mary's voice echoed in her ear: "You know your own mind. And so does he." Laura smiled to herself.

* * *

"Laura." Charles greeted her at the station, bending forward to kiss her. He took her bag. "It's lovely to have you here. Thank you so much for coming."

Laura always expected to feel awkward in Charles's company, until she was with him and remembered how easygoing and kind he was. He shut her into her seat, then climbed in next to her and said, "I'm glad you came."

Laura wasn't sure how much Charles knew; but then, she wasn't sure what *she* knew either, so it was all really the same thing. She said cautiously, "Well, it's lovely to be here."

Charles pulled out onto the road. His eyes were fixed on the road ahead. In a toneless voice, he said, "Nick's going to be chuffed, too."

"I should bloody hope so, since it was his idea in the first place," Laura wanted to say, but she didn't. She sat in silence for a while as they turned down narrow roads, banked on each side with hedgerows, and above them the huge Norfolk sky opened out above the flat landscape.

She felt nervous; she let the feeling slide through her, enjoying the sensation. She felt as if she had been numb ever since she left Norfolk, and that little by little over the past couple of weeks, that layer of cotton wool was coming away. It wasn't because of Nick, she realized. It was because she'd finally recognized that she needed a balance, the balance between being hopelessly head-in-the-clouds about everything, and being Mrs. Danvers for the rest of her life, dour and dressed in black and frowning on anything enjoyable.

So as they went along, Laura was torn between the desire to clutch Charles's arm and say, "Take me back to the train station," so she could go back to London and spend the evening with Mary, finishing off the wine and talking to her about everything under the sun, and the desire to clutch Charles's arm and say, "Go faster," so that she could be there, at Chartley, see Nick waiting on the huge front staircase for the car, watch his face light up as he saw her in the front seat. She was torn between wanting it to be over, wanting to know the outcome, the resolution to this weekend, and wanting this feeling of excitement and anticipation never to end.

"Who else will be there this evening, then?" she asked Charles.

"Let me see . . . various people from Chartley, and from the village. Some cronies of Lady Rose's, on some committee of hers, something to do with pheasants or game or something. And some bods from London, some of them to do with this ownership scheme we're running for the estate workers. Nick's being given an award for it."

"What?" said Laura.

"Kind of like a right-to-buy scheme," said Charles, steering carefully past another car on the road. "Most of the people who live on the estate and in Chartley village, they don't own. They're Nick's tenants. Their families have been for generations. Nick's started this scheme to help them buy their houses themselves."

"Oh," said Laura, "really? Wow. That's amazing." She looked down at her nails.

"Absolutely," said Charles with enthusiasm. "It's been fantastic. Take-up rate is huge. Very popular. Of course, it's not popular with the trustees and so on. He's had a battle on his hands there."

"Why?" said Laura.

"Well, think about it," said Charles. "He's giving away his property, bit by bit. Breaking up one of the last great estates in the country. They're furious. So's—well."

He paused. "Who else?" asked Laura encouragingly.

"Lady Rose. Very cross with him, I'm afraid. Well, she—there you go, anyway," said Charles, and Laura knew that was all she'd get out of him.

"So, he's getting an award tonight?" said Laura.

"Not really, no," said Charles. "They're coming down, the charity committee, to see the effects of it. They want to give him an award, but of course Nick's said no. Hates that kind of thing. Stupid idiot. He doesn't realize—well, once again, there you go."

"That's amazing," said Laura. "I didn't realize he . . . he could do that."

"Of course he can," said Charles. They reached a T junction. He stopped the car and looked at her. "Laura, I don't mean to pry, but can I ask one thing?"

"Yes," said Laura, not knowing what the question would be, slightly nervous.

"I don't understand something. About you and . . . and Nick. Please—he doesn't know I'm asking you this."

"Yes," said Laura. "Go on, what?"

Charles put the car into gear, but he carried on looking at her. "Did you honestly not realize who he was?"

"When?" said Laura stupidly.

"This summer, Laura. When you met him. And you thought I was Lord Ranelagh, not him. Did you—seriously, did you not think it was him?"

"No!" said Laura. "He told me you were. Why would I think any differently?"

"He didn't," said Charles. "You assumed. He never actually lied, did he?"

"Well, no," Laura conceded. "But why do you find it so weird? I just didn't realize."

"That's what I find so strange," said Charles, starting through the intersection. He was silent for a moment; then he said, "I just—I always think of him as . . . as this person."

"What person?"

"A—a lord, a grand personage. You know. We're friends, have been for most of our lives. I see the real Nick more than most people do. But part of me always sees him as the Marquis of Ranelagh. Can't help it, just do. Owner of this beautiful estate." He waved an arm, encompassing the fields around him. "Descended from generations of Danverses and Needhams. The lord of all he surveys. He's an incredibly important person, not just because he's famous or whatever, but because he's in charge of hundreds of lives, looks after millions of pounds' worth of wealth. It's funny. I can't ever forget that."

"Well," said Laura. She thought of the Nick she'd known that summer, the Nick she still knew who missed his mother, who snored in his sleep. "He wasn't being that when I met him, was he?"

"No," said Charles, and his smile was sad. "That's why you're special."

Charles grew more nervous as they approached the house, Laura could tell, though she didn't know why. Afterward, it made complete sense, of course; but as they drove through the Chartley lands and then onto the estate, turned into the driveway, saw the sign, now freshly painted, Laura had seen all those months ago with her parents, she had no idea what lay ahead.

"Right, right, we're nearly there," said Charles. The car crawled slowly up the driveway. The autumn sunset had begun, and the light filtered through the leaves. The view was carpeted with trees of all different colors, red, gold, orange, green. A light mist sat in the valley sloping away to the left; the park itself was ablaze with color. Laura craned her neck eagerly for that first glimpse of the house, to see what it would look like in this light, at this time of year.

Gradually, the hall slid into view, section by monumental section, as the drive curved toward it. Laura had forgotten how huge it was, just how imposing. She looked up to the East Wing, to make out Nick's room. It gave her a context, a sense of familiarity in this bewildering, vast landscape that she knew, yet felt so alien in.

"Look," said Charles as they reached the house. He turned off the engine. "I'll go in. I may be a minute or two. Stay here, okay?"

"In the car?" said Laura.

"Yes," said Charles. "I have to—to check something. And I'll—I'll find Nick. Don't want you wandering around the house getting lost, and all that."

"Er," said Laura, confused. "Okay, of course."

"Great," said Charles. He opened his door and got out, then looked back in at her. "I really won't be long, honestly. I just have to find Nick and explain something to him, and find out—er, what your room is, yes, that's it, what your—"

"Charles?" came a voice from behind him, and Charles spun around. Appearing through the fast-falling dusk was an unmistakable figure.

"Nick!" Charles said, his voice rather high. "My God, hello."

Laura sat still, not knowing what to do. Something wasn't right; she couldn't make it out.

"Hello," said Nick. "Where have you been? I've been looking for you. You've been ages. You said you were—hello. Is that someone in there? Have you got someone in the car, Charles? Well, I never. Hello?"

He bent down, his arm on the roof of the car, and looked in. His expression froze. "Laura?" he said, his voice soft, hoarse almost.

"Hello," said Laura, suddenly shy. She clambered out of the car and stood across the bonnet from him and Charles.

Nick stared blankly at her. "Sorry. What on earth are you doing here?"

"Er . . ." Laura said, not sure if he was joking or not. "Am I early?"

"Nick," said Charles, putting his hand on Nick's shoulder.

Nick turned to Charles. "Laura—here. You're here," he said, turning back to her. He looked at her almost desperately. "Why have you come back? Why now?"

"You invited me!" said Laura, half laughing, trying to keep her voice light. "You can't change your mind."

"Nick, listen," said Charles more loudly.

"What?" said Nick. "What are you talking about?"

A kaleidoscope of images and words started rushing through Laura's mind. The e-mail. The broken phone. Charles's nerves. Nick's expression.

"Oh, God," said Laura. She looked at Charles. "Charles—?"

"I invited her," said Charles, standing straight and looking at Nick. "I invited her down. Pretended to be you. I thought you should see her again. I thought you two should—sort it out. There are things you need to tell her, Nick."

"You did *what*?" said Nick, advancing toward him.

"Oh, shit," said Laura. "Oh, no. No, no. You sent that e-mail, didn't you?"

"Yes," said Charles. His expression was defiant, aggressive, as with those who know they are wrong but feel they have just cause to be. Laura and Nick stared at him as he stood between them. "I'm sorry," he said. "Well, I'm not sorry. She's here now, Nick. She can't go back till tomorrow. I know you both hate me, but—but I did the right thing."

Laura swallowed, and shifted on both feet. She didn't know what to say. The gravel crunched under her shoes. She wished she were anywhere. Anywhere but here.

"The right thing—" Nick swore under his breath. He took a step toward Charles. "Charles, you—oh, God. What have you done?"

He grabbed the shoulder of his friend's jacket. Charles stared at him impassively. They were still for a few tense seconds; then Nick released him and stepped back.

From behind them, through the vast wooden entrance doors, came a lilting voice: "Nick! Nick, darling! Come inside! I can't find the drinks. I'm thirsty!"

As if she were a housewife ordering her husband around through the patio doors at a barbecue, there at the stop of the stairs was Cecilia Thorson, in a headscarf, wide print skirt, pretty little pumps. She fluttered, birdlike, halfway down the stairs. "Nick? Nicky," she said across the driveway. "Are you coming?"

"What's she doing here?" said Charles sharply, under his breath.

"Rose invited her," said Nick. His lips were thin, his voice expressionless. "She turned up about fifteen minutes ago. Now do you see what I mean?"

He turned back toward Cecilia. He didn't even look at Laura, or Charles. He took a deep, ragged breath. "Yes," he said, looking up at her. "I'm coming, Cecilia."

His back was still turned to Laura. "Find her a room," he said in a low voice to Charles. "She can be your date tonight. I'll talk to you about this tomorrow, Charles."

And without another word, he strode away toward the steps. He took them three at a time, took the outstretched hand Cecilia offered him, and led her inside. Laura watched him as if it were a scene from a film, not her life. She put her hands to her throat, trying not to retch. She couldn't breathe.

chapter forty-six

Any additional worry that Laura might have had about being an uninvited guest for whom there was no room was swiftly put aside. Charles, mortified, ushered her in—through the front doors, that was something; she thought in a daze that if she'd been swept in by the back door, like a call girl on hire for the evening, she would actually have *walked* all the way back to London—and she was met by Mrs. Hillyard who, with calm professionalism, treated Laura's arrival as if it were entirely part of a plan, as if she were a deeply welcome guest. Within two minutes, Laura had been shown to a pretty little room, decorated in toile de Jouy and replete with flowery porcelain, on the side of the house toward the sea.

"Drinks are in the great hall at seven o'clock," she said with a smile. "Do let me know if there is anything you need, Miss Foster."

Let's see, thought Laura as she sat on the edge of her bed. A revolver with three bullets, one for me, one for Nick, and one for bloody Charles? A helicopter out of here? And a memory wipe so

I never remember this? Look on the bright side, she told herself, as a tear rolled down her cheek and she sniffed loudly. At least the slight question I had in my mind about whether or not this was going to work out is gone. At the ridiculousness of that thought, she gave a watery chuckle. "Oh," she said, turning round and opening her suitcase, trying not to give in to it all, "this is completely absurd!"

She opened the case. There, lovingly packed at the top, hastily rewrapped in its paper, was the claret-colored dress she had bought to wear that evening; and at the sight of it, the memory of buying it, the memory of showing it to Mary a few hours ago when she had been so full of excitement and anticipation, Laura's resolve crumpled, and she cried. She bit her lip, hard, walked over to the wardrobe, and hung it up. It swayed in the old teak case in solitary splendor.

The matching bag and shoes, which she could also ill afford, she put at the foot of the bed, and then she looked around the room. The old, gun-colored radiator was on the other side, miles away from the bed. Was it even on? She suspected not. She suspected she would freeze tonight. She took out her underwear, and shuddered. Unpacking was becoming like a horror film with lots of flashbacks, each item invoking a new memory of the pathetic hope with which she had packed it, and a corresponding moan from her at how stupid she had been, how completely embarrassing all this was. The jaunty little cardigan and jeans that she'd packed for Saturday, not knowing what they'd be doing, hoping it would be something as wonderful as the summer . . . ugh. She threw the suitcase on the floor, and kicked it under the bed. The room was cold, she realized; she went over to shut the window.

Outside on the terrace below, a man in a long white apron was polishing an array of silverware: candlesticks, plates, platters, trays. The doors to what Laura thought were the kitchen were flung open, and he was chatting away to someone invisible inside. Next to him stood a rather recalcitrant, awkward-looking teenager, polishing with a distinct lack of enthusiasm. Around them was a buzz of activity, although always dignified. People kept emerging, shaking out various things, consulting with the polisher. Two gardeners trundled past, each pushing a wheelbarrow. They stopped at a respectful distance from the silver-polishing, made a few inquiries, went on. In the distance, the pine forest was black against the early evening sky. Around Laura in the great shell of the house, lights were coming on, illuminating the façade as she looked out of it.

She had never felt more alone, more out of place, more unwanted. It was an odd sensation, the numbness before the real pain kicked in. She didn't know which was worse.

There was a knock at the door. She opened it, and there was Charles.

"Hello," said Laura, slightly coldly. She turned away, drew her suitcase out from under the bed, and resumed unpacking.

"Laura," said Charles. He bent his head formally, as if abasing himself before her. "I came to tell you I'm so sorry for this bloody awful situation. I'm a total idiot. Should never have tried to pull something like this." He couldn't meet her eyes.

"I know," said Laura, trying to be understanding, he looked so desolate. "Never mind."

"No," said Charles, flexing his fingers in agitation. "Listen, Laura. You know I had no idea Cecilia'd be here."

"Obviously you didn't," said Laura wryly.

"You know Nick didn't either. He's furious with Lady Rose for inviting her."

"Bully for him," Laura murmured.

"Laura, there's nothing going on between them, you do realize that?"

"Are you serious?" said Laura. "Don't be ridiculous."

Charles hopped from one foot to the other. "Well, of course there's something going on, but it's not what everyone thinks."

"Well, I think they've had sex, and I also think he only met her because her parents are incredibly rich and on the lookout for a nice catch for their millionairess daughter and his sister wants them to get married," Laura said. She was biting her lip, trying not to let him see she'd been crying.

"Right," said Charles. "Well, you're right about that—but—I was only trying to help." He sank onto the bed and rubbed his eyes. "And of course it's all messed up. He's furious with me. Never seen him so cross."

"Well," said Laura. "Oh, Charles, don't look like that." She wiped her nose on her forearm rather inelegantly, sniffed loudly, and sat down next to him. "You were honestly trying to do him a favor. He can't really be that cross with you, can he? Why?"

"Don't you know why?" said Charles. "You really don't know why he's furious, that you're here? And she's here?"

"No, why?" said Laura.

"Think about it," said Charles. He got up and stood there, looking down at her. Laura's face was blank.

"God, the two of you," he said eventually. "You're each as bad as the other. You're both just too bloody stupid to see it."

"What do you mean?" said Laura. She shook her head, staring up at him blankly. Her pupils felt dilated, her limbs heavy; she was tired with the shock of it.

"Work it out for yourself, Laura," said Charles. He flicked her cheek with his finger, an oddly touching gesture. Laura smiled. "I'll pick you up at seven, then," he said, heading for the door.

"Do I really have to go tonight? Face all those people?"

"Nobody knows, do they?" Charles pointed out.

"You're right," said Laura. "It's hardly like the girls in my sixth form are waiting downstairs to laugh at my shame."

"Exactly. Get dressed, you'll feel better, smile that lovely smile of yours, and you'll be fine. I promise."

Laura smiled at him gratefully. "Thank you."

"See you later."

It was five-thirty. She was suddenly exhausted. She looked at the pretty little bed covered with old lace cushions, the bedstead she knew was real old cast iron, not bought on sale from a bed warehouse in Dalston, and lay down on it, closed her eyes, and fell asleep. She thought she heard the door open, but she said, "Shoo," and turned over and carried on dozing.

Laura woke up to a loud knocking on her door. Without looking at her watch, she knew instinctively that it was Charles, and that she was late. She jumped out of bed, trying to ignore the head rush it gave her, and hopped to the door.

"Shit," said Charles, gazing down at her. He was in a smart suit, his short hair carefully wetted and combed back. Laura followed his gaze, from the creased jacket she hadn't taken off since leaving the train to her rumpled skirt; she could feel her hair was standing up in odd places all over her head. She rubbed her eyes, and put her hands to her hair experimentally. Hm.

"It's seven o'clock," said Charles desperately. "Laura, did you—"

"I fell asleep," said Laura. "I was tired. Shit. Sorry."

"You've got five minutes," he said helpfully. "I'll wait outside."

"No, no," said Laura. She didn't know Charles hugely well, but she knew him enough to know his idea of hell was tardiness of any kind. She patted his arm. "Go down, Charles. I'll see you down there. I'll be ten minutes at the very most, and I mean that."

"Are you sure?" said Charles. "I can hold the fort. Explain you're on your way."

"Oh, Charles," said Laura, leaning wearily against the doorframe. "You are totally perplexing to me. Who's going to care if I'm late or not? No one even cares that I'm there in the first place."

"I do," said Charles kindly. He looked her up and down, sucked his lips in, and smiled. "And Nick does, even if he might not show it."

"Charles," said Laura gently, "please don't." She coughed. "Look, it's going to be hard enough to get through this evening as it is. If you keep being jaunty and optimistic, I might actually lose what remaining cool I have and belt you. So"—she tried to sound mock-scary, when in reality she wasn't angry, simply tired, dead tired, wanting to fall asleep and never wake up again—"we'll go, have some nice food and wine and chats, and tomorrow first thing you drive me to the station. Okay?"

"Well," said Charles doubtfully, "maybe not first thing. This Harvest Festival dance—it goes on pretty much all night, you know. You don't want to miss out."

"God, you really don't get it, do you, Charles?" said Laura, and she made to shut the door. "See you down there."

"Now, hurry and get ready, and I'll be waiting for you downstairs by the door. Hurry up!" He shut the door behind him.

Laura stood up straight. Right, she thought. Right, then. If this is as bad as it gets—bring it on. I'm going to do it. It's going to be okay.

Twenty minutes later (it would never have been ten minutes, never), Laura nervously clutched the huge newel post at the top of the Grinling Gibbons staircase and began her descent. It had taken her a good few minutes to find the grand staircase in the first place. She had got lost, gone down and up various corridors and into various alcoves, feeling totally insignificant and lost, like a dormouse. She peered down into the great hall at the bottom, where the guests were all congregated, drinking champagne. Laura clambered down the stairs as quietly as she could, trying not to draw attention to herself. It was a hard staircase to navigate in high heels—the railing had clumps of terribly intricate grapes and apricots and what looked alarmingly like a real-life rat but she thought must be a squirrel, and she didn't know what to hold on to and what might fall off. Halfway down, she looked across at the wall and saw a normal, everyday railing attached to it. She clicked her tongue, but it was too late to stagger across the wide steps and use that instead. Typical. So she carried on, negotiating the steps and the carved fruits of the world with the utmost care, taking in the scene below her as best she might.

It was as if the stage were set for something. There was a sense of expectation in the air. A long night was ahead of them; all those present clearly knew that. It wasn't the terrifying set of people Laura had thought it might be—posh, ghastly, noisy, superior—certainly nothing like last time. That was something. There were a few Colonel Mustard types, but there were also lots of quite nice, ordinary-looking people. Everyone was in suits and smart dresses, Laura was relieved to see. She hadn't been sure of the dress code when she bought the dress; looking down, she knew she wasn't going to look out of place, sartorially at least.

A little farther down, the vast staircase curved gently and revealed the full mass of guests. There he was. In the corner of the room by the fireplace, talking quietly to someone, smiling and looking amused, as Cecilia Thorson, decked out in what looked like a peach chiffon tutu, complete with matching bag and shoes and—good God, thought Laura, is that a silk *parasol*?—stood attentively by his side. Laura looked at him, then at the view around her, the old sensation of her last night in Norfolk assailing her again. She thought of what Charles had been saying in the car that afternoon about Nick. All of this was his. This vast, airy hall, its great tapestry hanging along the north wall, the rest of the room lit with paintings and armor hanging on the walls. Out across the floodlit, smooth terrace, all the way to the folly at the top of the distant hill, and far beyond that. And these people in this room—most of them owed their living to him. To that one man.

As if she had called his name, Nick turned abruptly and looked up as she came down the stairs. He looked at her briefly, as if to say, "Are you okay?" and when Laura nodded, he raised his glass, still unsmiling, gave her one more look, a strange cold look, then turned away. Laura stood still, not knowing how to move. She could see Charles waiting by the stairs for her, so she made her way down, slowly, as he pushed through the crowd to greet her. He ran up the last few steps.

"Laura," said Charles. He kissed her hand. "My dear girl. You look sensational."

"Pff," said Laura articulately.

"Oh," said Charles. He came up so he was level with her, and they were both standing on the same step. "One more thing, Laura. I thought you'd want to know. I nearly forgot. There *is* someone else here you know." He assumed an innocent expression. "That's nice, isn't it?"

"Me? Who?" said Laura suspiciously, her eyes scanning the crowd.

"Your aunt. Annabel, is it?"

"What?" said Laura blankly.

"Annabel Sanderson. She's your aunt, isn't she?"

"Yes," said Laura slowly. "Of course. Oh, God."

Lady Rose's cronies. Charles had said they were coming. Aunt Annabel was one of them, she knew it. They were on some committee together; she'd said so in the summer. Several times. Mary had known as much this evening, Laura knew it, but she hadn't wanted to say anything. Oh, dear, oh, dear. This evening was presumably the zenith of Annabel's social-climbing aspirations—being invited to a private dinner and dance at Chartley Hall. With the Marquis of Ranelagh—and her own niece, who Annabel was convinced was his One True Love. . . .

Laura looked wildly around her. Aunt Annabel was in the crowd somewhere. She was there. It made complete sense—but why, Laura thought, clenching her fists and casting a baleful look heavenward. Why, Lord?

Charles adjusted his tie. "Anyway . . ."

"Good God." Laura realized she had to say something. "She's a—" She was about to say "dreadful social climber," in unconscious echo of her grandmother. She smiled to herself. "Hell. She's quite something. Have you met her?"

"Oh, yes," said Charles politely. "She's charming. Very pleased you're here. Look—she's waving at you." He pointed into the crowd.

Laura didn't look. "She knows I'm here?" she said in some alarm.

"I was introduced to her, and she saw me adding your name on the seating plan for the dinner. She was—very excited." Charles coughed. "As well she might be. I told her you were my date for the evening, by the way. Just so she knows."

"Thank you," said Laura. She knew what he was getting at.

"Anyway. Come and say hello."

He took her by the hand and led her through the heaving crowd to the center of the room; and there, a determined expression on her face, was Aunt Annabel, wearing what Laura immediately categorized as Posh Lady's Formal Attire # 1—a black velvet cocktail dress, with a jaunty red silk bolero jacket. There was a lot of corseting going on; Laura could tell from the rather stiff way the usually rather stout Aunt Annabel was standing.

Lady Rose was a little way away, immaculately attired in a beautifully tailored raw silk suit, talking expressively to Lady Lavinia, who was decked out in a kind of long, flowing tepee of a dress. Next to her stood a nervous-looking youth. Sean, Laura remembered with clarity. Sean from the village. Laura was surprised to feel a strange stab of familial relief to see her aunt, waiting for her alone in a strange sea of faces, someone wholly familiar.

"Hello, Aunt Annabel," she said, putting her hand on her aunt's starchy silk arm. The whole situation was suddenly too much for her; Laura felt as if she were in a scene from one of her old romance novels, and was overcome with the urge to snort most unedifyingly with laughter. She wished she had a fan she could hide behind and say, "La! Sir, you are too kind!"

"Laura, well!" said Aunt Annabel, grasping her shoulders and looking at her appraisingly with a fond, almost girlish glint in her eyes. She kissed her. "What a lovely surprise to see you here. Charles was just explaining how kind it was of you to accompany him tonight." There was a faint but audible tone of surprise in her voice; Laura knew it for what it was, a classic Aunt Annabel maneuver. Translation: "What's going on? I thought you were with the marquis, dear? I hope I haven't misrepresented the situation to all and sundry? Well. I say."

"Well, dear, it's lovely to see you," Annabel went on. "We are *so lucky*, aren't we?"

She gave the word "aren't" about five syllables; Laura gave Charles a look, but he smiled back impassively.

"Lady *Rose*," said Aunt Annabel, practically bowing her head at the name, "was *delighted* to hear you were coming tonight, Laura dear. I must take you over to say hello to her."

"No," said Laura, panic rising within her. "It's really—it's okay. I've met her."

"Nonsense," said Aunt Annabel. She waved over toward Lady Rose, who turned with a fixed smile on her face and saw Annabel and Laura together. Her smile grew cold; she touched her palm with the pads of her fingers in the most cursory wave, and turned back to her conversation.

"Oh," said Annabel slowly. "She must be busy." Laura almost felt sorry for her aunt, though not quite. Annabel smiled brightly at her. "Isn't this lovely?"

It was strange, but Laura suddenly found herself thinking Annabel sounded almost like Laura's own mother, who was constantly trying to smooth things over, make everything socially acceptable. Angela was often flustered, nervous about things. Laura had never seen her aunt behave the same way. It was funny how people were all the same in different contexts. Annabel looked brave, and shrugged her shoulders. Laura said, in an effort to be sociable, "So, Aunt Annabel—who else is here from your committee?"

"Oh," said Aunt Annabel, looking around, "not that many people. She mentioned that we were all invited at the last committee meeting, a few weeks ago. We're on the same pro-hunting lobby group, you know," she said to Charles. "The Backboners, we're called."

"Ah," said Charles. "Right."

"You're a total fraud! You don't go hunting!" Laura wanted to yell at her. "The nearest you've ever got to tweed is the Austin Reed sample sale!" Instead, she nodded politely at her aunt, who said blithely, "Well, yes. But the invitation was all rather vague, Lady Rose is so busy. I had to really track her down, call her secretary a couple of times to be sure of the details. And most couldn't make it. Such a shame. So wonderful, though. To be *here.*"

"Hm," said Laura.

"Yes," said Charles politely. "Well, wonderful that you could be with us, Mrs. Sanderson. Ah, here's some more champagne. Would you like a new glass?"

"Thank you," said Aunt Annabel, smiling at him with what Laura could only assume was an attempt at a coquettish flutter of the eyelashes, which she found most off-putting.

Charles handed Annabel another glass from the tray and, as the waiter had already vanished, put the old glass down on a sideboard.

"I do hope it's all right to leave glasses on the side here!" said Aunt Annabel, regaining her composure. "Can you imagine the havoc a ring mark would cause! Wonderful. Oh, look. There's the marquis." She flicked a glance at Laura. Laura followed her stare across the room, and saw Nick watching them across the crowd. She stared back at him, not knowing what to say.

"Oh, Charles," said Annabel, who had obviously performed a formal ceremony in her room of throwing caution to the winds and was now being as embarrassing as possible, "who's that girl standing next to him?"

Laura watched as Lady Rose appeared beside Cecilia Thorson, took her elbow, and smiled charmingly at her. She said something to Cecilia, who laughed loudly. Nick said nothing. He carried on looking at Laura.

"That's Cecilia Thorson," said Charles. "Um. She's a friend of Nick's."

"Right," said Aunt Annabel. "Well." She looked at Laura, obviously rather confused. Cecilia put her hand on Nick's arm; Laura stared at them, and he stared back at her, his eyes eventually flicking to Annabel and Charles, too. Then he smiled across the room, just at her, and she didn't know what to do.

Annabel saw this. She said nothing for a moment; then she looked at her niece. "So, Charles," she persevered, "you know Laura, too, then?"

"Yes," Charles said, intervening gracefully. "She knows us both. Very lucky we are." He patted his stomach. "Ah, here's a tray of delicious canapés. Mrs. Sanderson, may I tempt you?"

"Yes, please," said Annabel, plucking a tiny vegetable roll off a tray. "So, can you tell me *what* that idiotic young man is doing with her, then, when he should be over here with my niece?"

"Oh, God," said Laura, trying to hide behind her champagne glass.

"No, I can't tell you that," said Charles, trying not to smile. "Can't tell you that at all."

"Harrumph," said Annabel almost grumpily, and Laura stole at glance at her aunt, trying not to want to . . . like her.

chapter forty-seven

Apart from the twin social demons of Annabel and Lady Rose Balmore, and apart from the constant jabbing pain in the side she got every time she saw Nick with Cecilia Thorson, Laura had to admit the Harvest Festival looked like a good party, if only she'd been able to throw herself into it. By eight o'clock the great hall was crammed with people, all sorts of people, mostly from the village and the estate; there were children running around, hiding under tables, playing catch in the entrance hall. Charles pointed out to Laura the London housing committee who were so impressed with Nick's innovative scheme, four or five of them all huddled together in black, looking worried, nervous, and highly out of place. They clearly felt out of their depth. Laura wished they wouldn't; even she could see, after a couple of glasses of champagne, that it just wasn't that kind of party. It wasn't, funnily enough, an Annabel/Rose party, rather stiff and formal and posh. It was nice. Relaxed. When someone stood on the table, a short, fat man with a florid face, and shouted that everyone should go through, she found herself smiling and laughing with people, total strangers, as she filed into the ballroom, where two hundred people were sitting down to dinner.

The atmosphere couldn't have been more different from her last dinner at Chartley; even the ballroom looked different. Suspended high above them, two huge chandeliers sparkled gently, giving out a soft light. The crystals reflected the light from the hundreds of candles on the tables, in sconces on the walls. The huge polished wooden floor gleamed warmly; at one end of the vast room, a great fire leaped in the hearth. There were four long tables, each banked high with sparkling crystal glassware, some of which also caught the light and twinkled. The scent of lilies and roses filled the room; flowers were everywhere, on the table, on the windowsills. Laura stood in the doorway and looked up and down the room, giving a small gasp as she took it all in. It was beautiful.

To her pleasure, she was next to Charles on one side. He was opposite Lady Lavinia and Sean—and this seemed to flummox him somewhat. Especially since Sean seemed to be suffering from some kind of physical complaint throughout dinner; he kept jerking unexpectedly, and Lavinia would look up and around her demurely. Laura watched her. She didn't know if Nick's sister was really manipulative or just in a world of her own. On Laura's other side was a nice man from the village, Freddie, who owned the butcher's and had just started using only locally sourced and produced meat. He had supplied the sausages that evening. They were having bangers and mash, piles and piles of it.

The food was delicious; Laura realized she was absolutely starving. The sausages were incredible, properly meaty, seasoned, tasting of real, good things. The potatoes came from the estate, earthy, velvety, creamy. The tables were groaning with food; the waiters never stopped going round with wine. The noise in the ballroom grew and grew with the sound of people chatting, drinking, laughing—having a good time. Laura couldn't see where Nick was, and after looking for a few minutes, she gave up. She turned to Freddie.

"Who drew the short straws and had to work tonight?" Laura said, indicating one of the waiters as he passed. "Bit unfair that they're on and they have to wait on their colleagues."

"No," said Freddie, putting a huge dollop of mustard on his plate. "Waiters are all hired for the evening. No one at Chartley works the night of the Harvest Festival."

"Really?" said Laura. "Blimey."

"Oh, yes," said Freddie. "His lordship's most particular about it, you know. Won't hear of it. He says, if you're having a party for the estate, it's a party for everyone. So everyone comes. But you know, that's the marquis for you. He really is—"

Laura couldn't really bear another long exposition from yet another person about why Nick was just the greatest person in the world ever, since landlords, lords, and even land were invented. So she said, because she was genuinely interested, apart from anything else, "Can you tell me something then? What's the difference between a proper sausage and—you know, a horrible one, that looks like whipped pink cream?"

"Well," Freddie began.

Opposite her, Sean jerked suddenly again, and said urgently, "Lav—oi, don't *do* that, okay?"

Lavinia looked at him innocently. "What do you mean?" she said primly. Her eyes danced. Laura looked at her. She really was beautiful, not at all like her sister. She looked very like the photo of her mother that had been in that newspaper article about them all. Very 1960s, ethereal and pale, with lots of eyeliner and piled-up auburn hair—and the unconvincingly ethnic outfit, which annoyed Laura. She wanted to take it off her and pop her into a nice, simple Audrey Hepburn–style gown. Then she realized she was sounding awfully like her mother, and smiled.

As Freddie described cuts and prime hunks of pork and seasonings, Laura turned to smile at Charles, to find him staring helplessly at Lavinia. Like a card file in her brain, various nuggets of information started racing through her head, collating themselves. She didn't need the confirmation—the look on poor Charles's face said it all.

Lavinia looked across the table at Charles, a mischievous expression on her face. "Freddie!" Freddie ground to a halt. "Charles, darling. Sean says I'm being naughty. I'm not, am I?"

"Yes, you are, Lavinia," said Charles, and he sounded rather stern. "Stop it. It's not right. Leave him alone."

"Thanks, mate," said Sean, looking wildly around him, then back to Lavinia, who looked solemn for a second and then slid her hand into his lap again.

"Lavinia!" Charles said sharply. "I won't tell you again. You will not behave like this. Not tonight. Okay?"

He grasped her wrist, clutched it for a second, then released it. Lavinia looked up at him, rather surprised.

"Charles!" she said. Charles met her gaze impassively. "Oh, right," Lavinia said, and she leaned back in her chair, accepting defeat. She yawned. "I'm so bored, so bored. . . ."

Laura found herself wanting to reach across the table and slap her face repeatedly, and also to tell her to wake up and smell the coffee in the shape of lovely, kind Charles, so obviously head over heels in love with her. She didn't think Lavinia deserved for anyone to point things out to her, though. She was too self-centered. Yes, thought Laura. She gave her a brief glare, and said brightly to Charles, "It all seems to be going really well, doesn't it?"

Charles was gazing again. She kicked him. "Charles!"

He turned to her and widened his eyes, as if trying to bring himself back to reality.

"My God," said Laura. "You really have got it bad, haven't you?"

"I don't know what you mean," said Charles, clearing his throat and delicately arranging the cutlery. The noise in the ballroom seemed to grow a little louder.

"Lavinia," Laura whispered. "You're in love with her!"

"I am not," said Charles indignantly.

"Yes, you are," said Laura firmly. She smiled, and clapped her hands softly under the table. "Oh, this is wonderful! It's like something out of a Victorian novel."

Charles looked down and cleared his throat again. He said stiffly, "Do be quiet."

"No," said Laura. "I'm your date for the evening, remember? So you have to put up with me. And my ghastly relations. No, Charles, I know exactly what it's about. You're in love with Lavinia."

"I'm not enjoying this," said Charles, looking briefly across at Lavinia, who was nibbling Sean's ear. His face was puce.

"Sorry," said Laura, feeling momentarily contrite. "Golly, you must really regret having asked me tonight."

"Pretty much, yes," said Charles frankly. "Now, be quiet."

Laura stole a glance at him. "I think you should do something about it," she said after a pause. "I'm telling you, she needs someone like you. To bring her into line. And you need to look after someone."

"I assure you—" Charles said, trying to keep his voice low.

"Shh," said Laura, paying no attention. "You love Lavinia. You have a complex about being in love with your best friend's sister."

The tips of Charles's ears grew pink and he sank farther down in his chair.

"You also have an even bigger complex about not being good enough for her, because you're only a simple maiden from the village. And all that."

"I'm not a maiden, Laura, that's not—well, I suppose—"

"And just when, after years of building up to it, you've finally plucked up the courage to ask her out, probably, she starts screwing some teenager who can't say 'please' and 'hello' without getting confused. Oh, Charles."

"Look who's talking," said Charles, sitting up crossly.

"What?"

"You're a fine one to start lecturing me about having a complex about being the simple maiden from the village," said Charles. "Do you not *listen* to yourself?"

Laura had been so caught up in the romance of Charles's situation that she wasn't really paying attention. "Oh," she said.

"Exactly," said Charles. "It's not that simple." He looked across at Lavinia and Sean, who were whispering to each other, and blinked, very slowly. "Now," he said, opening his eyes, "tell me. The Chartley satellite dish is on the blink. Have you seen the new series of *Curb Your Enthusiasm*?"

The band had started setting up at one end of the room; people were clearing the tables; guests were starting to move around. The lights were low. Between the din of the room and the softness of Charles's voice, Laura had to lean toward him to hear what he was saying. She patted him on the shoulder consolingly, and looked up to find the Marquis of Ranelagh crouched down, having a conversation with Lavinia opposite. His eyes flicked over to Laura and Charles, who sprang apart.

"Hello," said Nick, standing up. "I was just making sure everything's okay at this end. How are you all?"

He addressed the question to the table at large, and nodded

easily as some people raised their glasses to him, others carried on eating, still others called out thanks or rude jokes.

"Great bangers, Freddie," Nick said, nodding at Freddie. His hands were in his pockets; he took one out and shook Freddie's. "Thanks a lot. Remind me to come down tomorrow and we'll settle."

"Of course, my lord," said Freddie. Laura was watching Nick; she saw a tiny muscle flex in his cheek involuntarily, and she realized how much he hated the title. She smiled at him, in what she hoped was an amicable, grateful way.

"Having a good time?" Nick asked her.

"Yes, thank you," said Laura. She was, she realized, much better than she'd expected. "It's wonderful. Charles is—"

But she got no further. He nodded, just like his elder sister, and turned to talk to Charles, leaving her addressing thin air.

Laura sat there for a moment, as Charles shifted around in his seat and asked some technical question about the remote control on the gates so that people could leave through the main entrance, no matter how late. Nick replied shortly. Tears she could not control filled Laura's eyes; she murmured to Freddie, "Excuse me," and, pushing her chair back, stumbled toward the hall. People were standing, sitting, talking, laughing; no one noticed her as she crept out of the huge room and clattered across the great hall, suddenly silent and dark, long moonlit shadows falling across the gray stone floor.

From behind the staircase, deep within the bowels of the house, Laura could hear the clatter of feet, growing louder. She looked around wildly—she didn't want anyone to see her. There was another door leading off from the hall, and she ran through it, and found herself in a gloomy, long room.

chapter forty-eight

As her eyes grew accustomed to the darkness, Laura jumped. She looked around her and realized she was in the picture gallery. Sculptures were scattered the length of the room, cupids, Graces, sleeping fauns, dying centurions, all in bone-colored marble. The floodlights outside gave the unlit room and the figures within a ghostly, ethereal quality.

Lining the walls were portraits, all in the same ebony frames, rows of Needhams and Danverses, rows of marquises, all watching her, their eyes following her around the room. Laura shivered and hugged herself, stroking the silk of her shoulder straps. It was eerie—she felt as if she had stumbled into another world. She stared around her in wonder. So, this is what I missed when I left the tour early, she thought, and gave a tiny laugh in the silence of the room. There was a dimmer switch on the wall; how incongruous, she thought. She took a step to go turn it on, then thought better of it; she shouldn't really be here, she ought to go back, only—

Suddenly a voice behind her said, "Laura?"

She turned, and there was Nick, leaning against the open door. He came into the room; walking toward her, he said, "What are you doing in here? Catching up on your sightseeing?" His face fell into shadow as he stood beside her.

Laura said, "I—I wanted some fresh air."

"It's rather hot in there, isn't it," he agreed.

"Yes," said Laura, although she was actually quite cold. "Yes, it is."

"You seem to be enjoying yourself," he said pleasantly.

"It's a beautiful room," said Laura, all at once perfectly calm. "I hadn't seen it before."

He began to walk slowly down the length of the room; she fell into step beside him, and they were silent for a moment. He looked sideways at her and cleared his throat. Indicating one of the black-framed portraits, he said in a conversational tone, "Very beautiful. Yes. Let me give you the guided tour."

"Don't you have to . . ." Laura made a helpless gesture with her hands.

"Have to what?"

"Do something? Look after the guests?"

Nick put his hands in his pockets and turned toward her. "I don't suppose anyone will miss us for a few minutes, Laura."

She blushed, feeling like a silly schoolgirl; but before she could say anything, he pointed to the painting nearest to them. "So. Have you seen this, here? It's supposed to be a Holbein. Unsigned."

Laura recovered herself. "Really? My goodness."

They walked a little farther, and she noticed they were perfectly in step, his tread firm against the light clatter of her heels, almost like a dance.

"One of the jewels of our collection, this painting. Can you see?" He put his hand lightly on her shoulder and turned her slightly away from him.

"Yes," said Laura, trying not to relax into his touch. "Who is this?" She noted, almost with detached amusement, that her nails were digging into her palms, as if she were nervous, but she didn't feel it—did she?

Nick said, "Lady Ranelagh, Restoration period. She may have slept with Charles I—but then, who didn't."

"Well, who didn't," Laura echoed. She stared at the subject, a woman with tumbling golden curls, a confident expression, almost pursing her lips, in love with life. "It's lovely. She looks nice, doesn't she?"

"I always think she must have been fun to have around," said Nick. "Her husband raised the money for Chartley. Got it off Charles I, I think, basically for prostituting out his wife. It was her idea."

"Families!" said Laura. "My dad's mum used to get me and my brother to wash her neighbor's car, and in return he'd mend her garden fence. It's very much the same thing."

She was joking, but Nick stopped and stared at Lady Ranelagh again. "You know, it kind of is the same thing, actually."

Laura laughed. "No, it's not."

"People are more alike than you think, Laura." He moved off smartly without saying any more. "Right. Let's go a little farther. Here, Lady Charlotte Needham. She married Lord Hastings. It's by Reynolds."

"I love that," said Laura, admiring the girl with black ribbons in her dark hair and a grave, rather serious expression. "She's sweet. She looks like . . ." She was going to say "your sister Rose," but didn't think it would be proper; yet there was a look of Rose about the girl's dark, candid eyes, her rather purposeful features.

Nick carried on, and she fell into step with him, down the long, dappled gallery, where faces caught the moonlight and smiled at her.

"And here is the seventh marquis, after whom I am named," he said, and Laura looked up to find the real portrait of her old friend, the one who had started it all. The seventh marquis smiled benevolently down at them, and Laura's heart stopped again as she remembered how she had felt that funny, romantic, silly evening when she found the postcard on the bus home.

"He looks . . . just like you," she said.

Nick bowed slightly. "I'm honored," he said. He started walking again, his face impassive.

"Who's that?" said Laura, stopping again. She pointed up to a portrait of a woman in a long black dress. Her face was in profile, her hand resting lightly on her breastbone. Beside her lay a photo, and a vase with blossoms in it. It was a stark, spare painting, the only decoration the woman herself, and Laura stared, transfixed, because she was so lovely. Nick said nothing.

"It's your mother, isn't it?" said Laura, suddenly realizing.

"Yes," said Nick. "This is when she got married, in 1959. She was only twenty-three. She'd already been acting for about six years by then; she was pretty young."

"She's beautiful," said Laura honestly.

"She was," said Nick. "I don't know, I haven't seen her for years."

"How long's it been?" Laura asked softly.

"Since I was eleven, 1981. I was eleven when she . . . left."

"And you've *never* seen her again?" said Laura.

"No," said Nick. His voice was bleak. "We weren't allowed to."

"Have you thought about it any more?" Laura mimicked writing with a pencil and paper. "I mean—getting in touch with her?"

"Oh, Laura." His hand was on his forehead; he was himself suddenly. "God, I just don't know how to go about it. It's easier to just think you'll do something about it one day, to save yourself actually doing something about it now. You know?"

"I know," said Laura. "I do know. Oh, Nick. You have to see her again. You really do. If only for yourself, you have to . . . ."

He looked so dreadfully alone in his black jacket, the hollows of his cheekbones dark in the moonlit room, his eyes unreadable. She stared at him, drinking in the sight of him, her heart clenching as she thought how vulnerable he was, despite everything he had.

She went over to him. "Not my business," she said, and shivered. "I'm sorry."

He looked down at her. "What for, Laura?" he said, smiling. "What on earth for?" and he took her left hand in his right hand and put it in his jacket pocket, then did the same with her right hand, his fingers closing around hers, so that she was facing him. He said quietly, "So. I thought we weren't speaking to each other."

"You were quite horrible to me last time I saw you, in London," said Laura.

"Laura, shame on you." His hands, in their pockets, tightened around hers. "You were the last person I was expecting to see there. That was a good day, that day, and you came along and ruined it."

"Charming!" said Laura.

"I mean," he said, his mouth close to her ear, "that was the first day I hadn't thought about you. Constantly. And then there you were. Having a really bad day. And I was trying to make it better, but I didn't know what to do—what to say . . ." He trailed off. "How's work, by the way?"

"Work?" said Laura, momentarily wrong-footed. "It's fine. Great, actually. Much better than when I last saw you."

"Really?" he said. "Why?"

"Oh . . ." Laura looked around her, weighing up whether to

go into Marcus's about-turn, and found the eyes of an Elizabethan lady in a ruff on her. She looked down. It wasn't important, not here; she shouldn't bother him with it all, even though she really wanted to. "Nothing. Don't worry about it. But thanks, though."

"Really?"

"Absolutely," she said, wishing she could talk to him, tell him everything, but not feeling able to here, under the collective gaze of his family, alive and dead. "I'm sorry about that night. It was—weird."

"You ran off," said Nick. "Again."

"Well . . ." Laura shifted on her feet. "I'd had a bad evening. And I felt completely out of place. And then Cecilia phoned you, and—I just thought you were being polite, and trying to get rid of me."

"She was checking up on me," said Nick. "I should have told her to go away. I'm sorry."

"And yet here she is again," Laura pointed out.

He sighed. "Oh, God. I promise you, there's nothing going on between me and Cecilia. My sister invited her tonight. Nothing to do with me."

"Where is she?" Laura said curiously.

He jerked his head up. "Actually, she gave up. Told me I was pathetic and went to bed about fifteen minutes ago. Her bed, obviously. She's got her own room. She has, Laura. Believe me."

"Nick," said Laura, putting her hands up, "really—it's none of my business."

"Isn't it?" he said, his voice reverberating in her ear, his lips close to her hair. "It's nothing to do with you, is it?"

"No," said Laura, shaking her head and looking up at him, bemused. "Nick—you're the Marquis of Ranelagh. I'm nothing. Well, not nothing, but . . . You can do what you want, I don't—"

"You still don't see it, do you?" said Nick. "Seriously, you still can't see it?"

"What?" said Laura.

He ran his hands through his hair and, not looking at her, said, "What if being with you was the first proper conversation I'd had with someone for years? That I felt like the person I really was, for once?" He backed away and gripped his tie, loosening it. "God, Laura. Don't say that, not you, especially not you."

"What do you mean?"

"You can't see it, even now?" he said tiredly. "I'm not the Marquis of Ranelagh, that's not me. That's the thing I inherited, just like you inherited your total stupidity from some family member of yours, I don't know who."

Laura gasped in outrage, and he smiled wickedly at her in the darkness. She shivered.

"Silly girl. I'm sorry. You're cold." He looked at her appraisingly, then took off his jacket and put it around her shoulders.

"Thank you," she said.

"My pleasure," he replied, mock-formally. He took a quick breath, and said, "We seem to have been going around in circles, haven't we? But let me just say this." His voice was softer. "I'm not the marquis. I am sometimes, of course. But I'm still the person you met this summer, before it all got confusing, bogged down with all that other crap." Laura made to say something; he held up his hand. "Listen to me, Laura. I'm Nick. My mum ran off with someone when I was eleven, I haven't seen her for more than twenty years, and my dad and I didn't get on. He was a bully. I liked geography at school, I hated French. I like *The Sopranos.* I don't like Arsenal. When I was in America for the summer when I was nineteen, I slept with a stripper."

"Really?" said Laura, interested despite herself. "Where?"

He shook his head, trying not to smile. "Tell you later. Let me finish. All of that stuff I told you, I could talk to you about. About how much I love the house. About the way to run things, how it all means so much to me. Just like any other job, without all this other crap getting in the way."

"What crap?"

"You know," he said impatiently. "Fawning. Ceremony. Old ladies in car parks. Insane men with tour guides. People bowing, asking the same questions all the time. It's my responsibility. I have to deal with it, and I don't mind, in fact I'm proud of it; but you—you made me feel like a real person for once. And I—I wanted to do the same for you. I wanted you to feel better about yourself, to realize how completely, totally wonderful you are, Laura."

He took her hand and kissed her palm gently, his forehead touching hers; and out of the corner of her vision Laura saw the portrait of his beautiful, smiling mother, her dark eyes watching them. She gave a ragged, deep sigh, as Nick pulled her toward him. He bent his head and whispered, "Oh, Laura . . ."

"No," Laura heard herself say. She looked up. There, on the opposite wall, the seventh marquis stared down at her, clutching his book. "I can't, Nick. Not here." She stepped back a little from him.

"What do you mean?" said Nick, his brow furrowed, his face instantly closing up.

"Not here," Laura said softly, making a tiny gesture with her hand. "These—all of them. I can't."

"I don't understand," he said, releasing her other hand and shaking his head slowly. "Don't—don't do this, Laura."

"Nick," said Laura. She had to make him see why it was so important. "They're the reason we can't be together. All of these people, here." She gestured the length of the room. "You and me—when I'm with you, it doesn't matter. And I can see you in my flat," she added rather inarticulately.

"What on earth are you talking about?" said Nick. "I've never been to your flat."

She took his hand. "I mean, I can see you talking to my friends, lying on my sofa." She squeezed his hand; he had to see what she meant, had to. "Us, together, normal. That's why I—I thought I was falling in love with you. Not because of any of this stuff. The fairy-tale romance bit of it, Nick—I don't want that. I just want you, do you understand?"

His jaw was set. "Laura. But all of this—this *is* me."

"Oh, I know it is," said Laura impatiently. "But you just said yourself, there's a big part of you that's you, just yourself, and *that's* the bit you need someone to share with you." His eyes searched her face; she looked at him, imploring him to understand. "And here—this room, all these people. *They're* the bit that complicates everything. They're the reason we can't be together."

She lapsed into silence, still holding his hand, not knowing what to say next.

Nick laughed suddenly in the gloom of the room, a warm, comforting laugh. "Laura, oh, Laura." He stroked her collarbone, and she shivered at his touch.

"What?" she said.

"You're right, you know, but I think you're taking it too seriously."

"I—"

"Look," said Nick, with the air of one trying to be reasonable. "I want to talk to you. Properly, about all of this. But I want to kiss you first. You're right, this room's a bit daunting. So. Let's go somewhere else."

"Just like that?" said Laura. "It's as simple as that, is it?"

"Absolutely," he said. "The trouble with you is, you overthink everything. I like you, you like me. Let's go and sit on the steps and talk. Without great-grandmothers A, B, and C watching us."

He bent his head and kissed her, quickly, hard on the lips, and then said, "Okay?"

"Okay," said Laura. "Okay."

"Come on," he said, holding her hand again, and they walked back up the length of the room and paused near the doorway. Laura could see Charles, circling in the background of the great hall. She was sure he was looking for Nick, and she didn't want him to come, didn't want them to have to separate, wanted to stay like this forever.

"Well, I'm glad I've seen this room, anyway," she said. "I don't want you to think I didn't like it. It's—er, it's lovely."

"What a polite guest. My pleasure," said Nick. "All mine."

"All yours," she said, laughing at the absurdity of it all. "I'm glad you found me here."

"I was looking for you, Laura," he said. "And now let's go."

The gallery doors were flung wide open; Charles strode into the room, his phone in his hand. "There you are."

"Hey," said Nick, but Charles wasn't looking at him, he was walking toward Laura.

"Laura, my dear," he said, with the same kind face he always had. Laura smiled at him, but her blood froze as she looked into his eyes, saw their expression. "Your aunt's looking for you. You're going to have to go. It's—it's your grandmother, Laura. She's had a massive heart attack. She's in the hospital. It's not good. She's asking for you. Laura, your mother needs you to go back to London. Tonight."

chapter forty-nine

As long as Laura lived, she would never forget that journey. Bizarre details. The mints Aunt Annabel had in her car. The travel atlas; half the cover was torn off, so unlike the Sandersons. The way Annabel drove, wildly, hunched over the steering wheel, her face pale in the darkness, her makeup like a mask. Those things that Laura had unpacked so carefully, painfully, a few short hours ago, now flung randomly into the suitcase. They should have just left, should have asked the others to send things on, Laura realized afterward as the journey went on, deeper into night, as Annabel drove in silence and they both had time to think.

Yes, Laura had time to think; hours of time. It was over three hours from Chartley Hall to the hospital in town; but what could she think about? Nothing. Her mind couldn't concentrate, couldn't consider what she might find there, what might not be there. She didn't understand, couldn't process it all. When she tried to think about it, it was as if her brain had short-circuited.

Nick had offered to drive; Annabel had practically pushed him away, racing to the car, roaring away from the house in a frenzy that Laura had never seen before.

They tried to talk at the beginning of the journey, but both of them were so overwrought and worried that conversation was hard.

"Where are they?" Annabel asked, as Laura finished a call to her mother. They had been driving for over half an hour. Laura glanced at a sign; they were still in Norfolk. Oh, hurry, hurry, she thought, please hurry.

"Still at the hospital. They're all there."

"Who?"

"Mum, Dad, Simon. Cedric and Jasper. And Fran and Robert."

"Where's Lulu?" said Annabel instantly.

"I don't know. . . . I didn't ask."

"Why isn't she there?" Annabel said. Since she had no way of knowing or finding out, Laura said nothing. "What did they say?"

"They said she's unconscious now. But she has been talking. I think—" Laura's voice faltered; she wasn't used to saying things like this, didn't know the language. It was too easy to default to clichés from hospital television shows or books. "I think she's worse."

"What's she been saying?" said Annabel sharply.

"I don't know," said Laura. "Mum didn't say. Except—she was—except she was asking for me. She wanted to see me and Simon. She recognized him."

"Just Simon?" Annabel hunched over the steering wheel even higher, peering at the road ahead as if willing the car to take flight and soar across the countryside, take them back to Mary.

"I don't know," Laura said again, feeling helpless. "I don't know."

"Well, you're her grandchildren, not Fran, I suppose." Annabel cleared her throat. "And if Lulu's not there—perhaps she's waiting for her to get there."

"I'm not sure," said Laura. "Aunt Annabel—I don't think she knows what's going on."

There was a dull stabbing pain behind her eyes, like something crawling, scratching them. This was all wrong. Mary wasn't someone in a hospital, dying! She was the most alive person Laura knew. Her place in the world was so sure. She knew what she knew, was so certain of everyone and everything, which was why she was the most reassuring grandmother one could possibly have.

"Come on, come on," Annabel muttered. She bit her lip. Laura looked at her. She looked awful; it was as if she had aged about twenty years, but there was something more than that. Her composure was the first thing that struck one about Annabel; it was her most noticeable quality, more than her glossy brown hair, her perfect makeup, her glamorous, determined air, her rather braying voice. It was the quiet certainty that her world was right, that she was right. Now, looking at her aunt, Laura felt she was seeing a tiny bit of the other Annabel she might be for the first time, and it was a strange experience.

They were on a main road finally, thankfully, and the electric strip lighting overhead bathed their faces in a ghostly green light. It was one of those endless, featureless roads, its only characteristics of interest blue signs, chevrons, traffic cones. Nothing else was visible from the road. They could have been anywhere in the country. Laura blinked, trying to remember where she'd been; but already the memory of Chartley, of Nick and what he had said, what it had all meant—it was racing far into her mind, already framed and deposited in a memory bank, a lovely pure snapshot of something in the past. She couldn't connect it with this.

Laura shunted down in her seat, wrapping her slightly-too-big-for-her jacket around her for warmth. She looked down. She was still wearing Nick's jacket, the one he had put around her in the picture gallery—that was this same evening, wasn't it? Her mind scrabbled to remember, and the creatures pinching behind her eyes grew more frantic.

"Are you cold, Laura dear?" said Annabel, her voice quiet and hoarse. "Perhaps we should stop here and get some coffee."

"No, no," said Laura, feeling a wave of panic at the suggestion. "No, please, Aunt Annabel, please—just keep driving."

"Of course," said Annabel. She flicked a look at her niece, very briefly. "Darling. You mustn't get too upset, you know."

Don't say it, thought Laura. I'll be fine if you don't say it.

"She's eighty-five, you know. She's had a good life. A very good life."

"Shut up," said Laura quietly, ferociously. "Don't, Aunt Annabel. I mean it, don't."

"Laura!" said Aunt Annabel, but her voice was still soft. "Listen to me. It's not a cliché with your grandmother, you know. She has had a good life. One of the best. Wonderful times she had with—with Xan, and everyone. She's been everywhere. She knows everyone. She hasn't had a moment's illness."

"That's not the point!" Laura cried. "She wasn't ready! It's not her time, it's not. Why couldn't she—"

"Laura, Laura," said Annabel. She reached across blindly for Laura's hand, took it with her own, and squeezed it. "Do you really think that's true? That she wasn't ready to go? Because I don't."

"How can you . . ." Laura began, and her voice trailed away as she remembered Mary only that day, wincing with pain and then her face clearing, as if she wasn't in pain anymore.

"I love your grandmother very much," said Annabel. "She's like my mother. I don't remember my mother at all. So Mary brought me up when she married my father." She spoke as if she were talking to herself. "She was so in love with Xan. Always. He was the love of her life. When he died, she wasn't the same. Of course, she's been fine these last few years. But she misses him. And lately—oh, I don't know . . ." She shook her head, arched her back, as if trying to stretch herself, shake herself out in the confined space. "I think lately, the last couple of months, she's—changed. Well, we know she has. She's wanted to go. I think she knew it was time."

"Time?" said Laura, not believing her. "How can she have known it was time? How can she have given herself a heart attack, Aunt Annabel? It's not possible."

"It is, if you just give up," said Annabel, "and, darling—I think it's time you called me Annabel, you know. You're not fourteen anymore."

Not knowing what to say to the twin points of this last sentence, Laura lapsed into silence, counting the miles again, willing the journey away. And then she remembered saying good-bye to Mary—was it only a few hours ago, in the hallway of her flat?—and she knew that her grandmother had known it was the last time, and the blood in her veins froze.

It was around four in the morning when they reached the hospital. Neither of them said anything, but jumped out of the car, hurrying, almost running, trying to find their family, looking for the signs to lead them through the glass and concrete building. The wards were deserted. Laura and Annabel raced in step, following the directions they'd been given.

"Here," said Annabel, clutching Laura's arm in a viselike grip. "It's this one. They said, down this one. At the end."

There was Angela, walking down the corridor toward them, Laura could see her, was nearly there; she could see her mother's face, the tears running down it. Angela was holding something in her hand, and she was shaking her head, shaking her head and crying out loud.

"Laura, oh, Laura," she said, as Laura reached her and enfolded her in her arms, surprised to find that her mother was smaller than she, shocked at how vulnerable she felt.

"Is she—" Laura said, not able to finish the question.

"Yes," said Angela, sobbing into her shoulder. "She's down there. Just a while ago. Too late, you're too late. And she—oh . . ."

She buried her head even deeper into her daughter's neck and made a sound almost like a howl, while Laura stroked her hair, not knowing what to do. Suddenly, holding her mother tight, Laura felt closer to her than she ever had, and it was as powerful a feeling as anything she'd ever known. There was a brief moment's calm, and Laura breathed out, not knowing what to say, as her mother blinked into Laura's jacket, and stepped back. She wasn't looking at Laura, though. She was looking past her. At Annabel, standing behind them.

"You knew, didn't you?" Angela said.

"What?" said Annabel.

"You knew she was ready to go."

"Yes," said Annabel briefly. "Angela. I'm so sorry, darling."

Laura had never heard them talk to each other like this. Like they were sisters, rather than polite acquaintances in the same book group, which was how they usually addressed each other. She looked down the corridor, all the way down. She could just see some figures standing there; they were men. Simon was one, she was sure. Dad and Uncle Robert. They were facing them, watching. She couldn't see their expressions. Annabel stood there, turning her car keys over and over in her hand. Again, Laura didn't recognize her. She looked like a little girl. Annabel reached out and patted her stepsister's hand, awkwardly.

The figures were advancing toward them. Simon was first, his hair standing on end, his face hollow. As he approached, he opened his eyes wide, as if he didn't know what to do. He hugged Laura, and George, behind him, threw his arms around them both.

"Hello, love," he said, and kissed his daughter's ear. "Glad you're here. Glad you're here." He went up to his wife and put his arm around her, as Laura turned to Simon.

"When did it happen?" she asked him.

"About an hour ago." Simon spoke quietly. "Her breathing was shallow, they knew it was going to happen." He pressed his thumb and forefinger to the bridge of his nose and breathed in, a hissing sound, and then went on, "Yeah. It was another heart attack, Laura. After it happened, she wouldn't have felt anything. She just—slipped away."

"Did you see her? Did you—talk to her?"

"Yes, but she couldn't say much," said Simon, and his lip curled in on itself, like he was trying not to cry. "When Cedric found her, she was . . . pretty much gone anyway." He wiped his face on his sleeve, and pulled Laura toward him.

"Let's go home," said Laura. She touched Robert's arm briefly; he was on the outskirts, mutely watching the scene before him. "Robert, I think you should take Annabel home," she said. "She's been driving for hours, she must be exhausted."

Annabel, who had been looking quietly at Angela, turned at this. "Fine," she said blankly. "Fine. Where's Fran?"

"On the phone to Lulu, outside. Come on," said Simon, taking his cue. "Mum—Dad? We're going home."

"We can't just—leave her," Angela said.

"Yes, we can," said Simon. "The doctor said so herself. You can come back tomorrow to arrange everything then. Cedric and

Jasper are still here, they're going to stay." He looked at Laura. "Do you want to see her?"

"Yes," said Laura quietly. "Just a minute, Mum. Annabel—you coming too?"

She walked to the end of the corridor. Jasper and Cedric were sitting there, even more incongruous in this setting than any of the rest of them. They stood up, rather creakily, as Laura and Annabel approached.

"Dear girl," Cedric whispered. He kissed her. "She's just in there. Wouldn't have felt a thing. Smile on her face when I found her, you know."

Laura only half heard him. She was opening the door to the tiny room, not at all afraid of what she might see. She knew it was her grandmother; she knew she had been ready to go; and Laura knew she had to see her again, that death was not frightening when it looked like this. Mary was lying under the sheet, one ringed hand resting on her chest. Her eyes, so full of life, were closed. Without its usual animation, her face was solemn in repose. She was not there anymore. Laura kissed her forehead. Mary's skin was cool and smooth, sweet-smelling as always, that old-fashioned powder she used; and Laura turned away feeling as if her heart was breaking. A tear dropped onto the sheet, onto Mary's hand. This was the last time she would see her. But she was not there anymore; Laura had to keep remembering that.

Her parents were waiting for her in the doorway. George put his arm around his daughter. "Let's go home, love," he said. "Time for bed."

chapter fifty

"Of course I'm coming tomorrow," said Yorky.

"But, Yorky—it's a Thursday. How will you get the time off?"

"I've cleared it with my head of department," said Yorky, standing up rather straight. "I explained it to them. Said I had to go to a funeral. They're going to have my classes covered. It's only the afternoon, isn't it. No problem."

They were in their kitchen. It was Wednesday, the day before Mary's funeral. Laura had just got off the phone to her mum, and was drying plates in a rather desultory way, staring out the window. Yorky put his arm round her and squeezed her. "Want to be there, to make sure you and Simon are okay," he said rather stiffly.

Laura buried her head in his armpit gratefully, trying not to let him see how very touched she was. She and Yorky didn't do excessive displays of emotion. "Right," she said. "Oh, Yorks. Thanks a lot."

"Not at all," said Yorky. "Jo's coming, she's got the afternoon off, too. She's coming here, she'll drive me."

"Wow," said Laura. "I didn't know that." You know times are serious when your friends are making arrangements about you without telling you about it, she thought. She put down the tea towel and turned around.

"Thanks," she said, taking the glass Yorky proffered.

"How's your mum?" said Yorky.

"She's fine."

"Really?"

"Yes," said Laura. "You know, she really is. We all are."

That evening, Laura went to her parents' for supper. When she arrived, her mother was on the phone to Annabel in the hallway. She raised her eyes at Laura and blew her a kiss.

"How're you?" Laura said to her brother, as they were making drinks in the kitchen.

"I'm okay." Simon was slicing a lemon; he didn't look up. "How about you?"

"I'm okay." Laura flicked through the stately homes calendar on the kitchen counter, and looked round the kitchen, cozy and warm in the chill October evening.

"Wish tomorrow was over," said Simon. "I hate funerals."

"No, really?" said Laura. "Actually, though, you know, I'm almost looking forward to it."

"Really?" Simon handed her a drink. "Why?"

"You know, it's Gran. It'll be great. You know everyone loved her. Everyone thought she was the greatest person in the room."

"True," said Simon. "Still . . ." He looked sadly at the photo on the fridge of Mary sitting in her deck chair at Seavale. "Wish she was here instead."

Laura shook her head, her eyes filling with tears, because of course that was what she wished, too, more than anything else; but she felt this very strong feeling of calm about her grandmother, and kept remembering what Annabel had said.

"Burr," she said, sniffing. "Stupid."

Simon hugged her. "Ah, sis. Don't cry."

" 'Mnot.' Laura wiped her eyes.

"So—what happened, then?" Simon shoveled some crisps into his mouth. "You went back up to that bloke's house, didn't you?"

Laura nodded. "Yes. Well. No. Yes, I did, I—actually? Let's forget it."

"No, tell me," said Simon. "What's going on? You like him, I mean you really like him. I can tell." He ate some more crisps, but looked at her sideways.

"You know what?" said Laura frankly. "I actually have no idea what's going on. But I think he needs to sort himself out a bit. And so do I."

"Right."

"And till then, let's forget it. Tell me what's going on with you and Jorgia. How is she?"

Simon said casually, "I've got a job, you know."

"What?" said Laura, peering down the corridor to where Angela was nodding silently, still on the phone to Annabel. "What can they still be talking about? What? You've got a *job*? Doing what?"

Simon shrugged. "Working in a garden center."

"What?" said Laura, not quite able to process the information her brother was giving her. She stared. "A garden center? Why?"

"I love gardening," said Simon. "I want to be a gardener."

"No, you don't," said Laura, bewildered. "Who are you? What are you talking about? What about Jorgia, about going back to Peru?"

"I do want to be a gardener," said Simon stubbornly. "I love gardening, you know I do."

It was true—Simon did love gardening, always had done.

"Where?" said Laura, trying to get a grasp of it all.

"Out toward Windsor, quite near here, actually. It's that house, Myddleton Manor. You remember, Mum and Dad used to take us when we were little. It's got the boating lake, and the ponies. Just off the M4 motorway."

"Oh, my God, yes!" said Laura.

Simon said, "It's what I want to do, you know."

Laura was confused; lots of things were going through her head. "I know you do, but—Simon, what about Jorgia, what's happened?"

Simon said, "It's over with me and Jorgia."

"Oh," said Laura, looking at him in distress. His face was impassive. "Why? Oh, I'm sorry."

Simon said, "We were too different, Laura. She—well. It's not going to happen. We had a big argument last week. And we talked yesterday—we both kind of agreed. You know? So. Yeah." He shrugged, a completely boyish gesture. It said, "I'm not fussed." It meant, "I'm really upset but I'm a man, so no chance I'm going to talk about it."

"Oh, Simon." Laura looked at her brother.

"It's weird," Simon said. "I really thought we'd make it work, you know?"

"I know," said Laura. "I'm so sorry."

Simon coughed. "I'm okay, honestly. Well, kind of. It's weird, though. I was talking to Jo the other day, and we were saying how different our lives are, all of that. And I looked at her and thought, Yes, but I still know you. I *know* you. Who you are and all of that. What kind of person you are. I don't really know that with Jorgia.

I loved her. She's beautiful. I loved her family, their lifestyle. But I didn't really know her."

"But you would have done, with time," said Laura, feeling panicked all of a sudden. "It's not important, that stuff. You'd have worked it all out. Don't you think?"

"No," said Simon impatiently. "You don't understand. I don't mean all of that. Of course I would have done, I'd have got to know her better. I just mean, I *know* Jo. I know who she is, really well. And that's not because she's been our friend for years and years. I mean that, even if she lived on the other side of the world and all of that, it's comfortable, she's from our group, she does the same things we do, she thinks the same way. Jorgia and me—" He made a helpless gesture with his hands. "I don't really know her. Does that make sense?"

Laura looked at him. After a minute, she said, "It makes a lot of sense. A lot of sense. But . . ."

"I know I was harsh to you, that night at supper," Simon said. He handed her the crisps. "I'm really sorry. I've felt really bad about it—"

"Simon, don't, seriously," said Laura. "I'm the one who should feel bad about it. I was too judgmental, too hard on you. I just—I thought I knew it all. I was wrong, I'm sorry."

"Maybe you were a bit," said Simon. "But actually, the point you were making—you were right, you know."

"What do you mean?"

Simon shifted in his seat so he was facing her. "You jumped down my throat, but you were right. We're too different, me and Jorgia, and there's no way to overcome those differences. Two different worlds."

She said, "But you said, Simon, you said that people don't fall in love with each other because it's convenient. They fall in love because they fall in love, and that's it."

"Well, yeah. I suppose that's still right. You don't choose who you fall in love with. But that doesn't mean it can work out. That doesn't mean it can last. Seriously, Laura. You and the marquis, I mean. You knew what you were talking about. It'd never work, you're from two completely different worlds and, like you said . . ." He shook his head.

"But, Simon—" Laura put her hand out and patted his arm. "Si, I think I've been completely wrong about it. I think you can make it work. Differences don't matter. Honestly."

Simon wasn't really listening. He said glumly, "It's like me and Jorgia, man. I've been so convinced that it wasn't going to work. I really thought she was The One. I still think she is." Simon rubbed his chest, as if he was in pain. "I got a bit scared, I think, that she might be. I think I wanted it to self-destruct, so—hey! Why are you laughing?"

Laura caught his hand. "Oh, I don't know," she said, leaning forward and helping herself to the crisps too. "We're each as bad as the other, you know. Terrible."

Angela came into the kitchen. "Sorry about that, darlings," she said, rubbing her hands. "Your aunt's convinced herself she's organizing a state funeral. She keeps telling me about all these wonderfully glamorous people who've rung and said they're going to be there." She picked up a lid on a pot on the stove. "I've no idea who any of them are, but they sound terrifying." George appeared from the conservatory, holding a hammer. "Put that away, dear. Right. Let's have supper."

All four Fosters ate quietly together, with no one saying much, but nothing really needing to be said; and after Simon and George had cleared away and gone off to do some man-style thing in the conservatory, Angela and Laura were left sitting next to each other on the sofa.

Angela said, "Do you mind if Simon stays in Mum's flat for a while? Just a while?"

"Course not," said Laura. "What a great idea."

"Well," said Angela, "it needs someone there while we decide what to do with it. I was there today, and there's such a lot of stuff. What will we do with it all?"

"I don't know," said Laura, tentatively patting her mother's hand. She looked at her. Angela's eyes were bright with unshed tears, but she was composed.

Angela took the embroidered floral cloth left from the tea tray, smoothed it out on her lap, and looked at her daughter. "I don't know what she'd want me to do with it, either," she said. "Whatever I do, I'm sure I'll get it wrong, you know. Ha." She smiled. "Which reminds me." She reached into her handbag, which was by her feet. "I found these. In her bureau drawer."

She handed Laura a letter in Mary's writing, addressed to her. It was clunky, heavy.

"What is it?" said Laura.

"No idea," said Angela. "I got one, too. So did Simon."

"But," said Laura, slightly alarmed, "what does it mean?"

"I think it means she knew she wanted to write to you," said Angela.

Laura clutched the letter in her hand; she wanted to open it, and at the same time she didn't want to know. "Don't you wish you could have one conversation with her about it instead?" she asked. "With Granny, here?"

"Of course," said Angela firmly, folding the cloth neatly into quarters. She pressed it down with her hand. "But it's funny. It makes me realize, all these years . . ." She stared into space.

"What, Mum?" said Laura gently.

"Well, it makes me see. I was in the flat today, looking around, thinking, Is there anything we need to take now? and your aunt was being so dreadfully bossy, and instead of being cross and saying nothing, it made me feel"—she looked up to the ceiling—"so happy. And it's funny. I look back, down the years. And I realize how happy I've been. How lucky we all are. What a lucky family we are, to have each other. To have this house. Oh, I know, it's not an interesting life, it's not full of glamour and drama, but it's the life I wanted. I've never wanted anything more, you see."

George was coming through from the kitchen. There was a scuffle as the tray of drinks hit something. "Oh, dear," they heard him say, and there was a bit of muttering. Laura looked back at her mother.

"Honestly, darling. Never wanted more than your father. It's strange, isn't it? I thought I'd miss the life I had, the traveling, the rather posh girls and boys I met, the excitement of it. I never did, not once. Since the day I married him and we settled down—I honestly don't think I would have changed a thing."

A tear dropped from her cheek onto the folded cloth; Angela brushed her eyes.

"I've been happy. I never really thought about it like that, before Mum died. I've been happy."

The door opened; George came in, carrying a whisky bottle and four glasses.

"I thought a little toast was in order, ahead of tomorrow's events," he said.

"Oh, George," said Angela, putting her head on one side.

Simon followed his father in. He took the drinks off the tray George set down, and gave one each to his mother and sister, then handed one to his father.

George cleared his throat, still standing, and said, "Well. A toast. Stand please."

Laura and Angela stood. He raised his glass, met his wife's eyes.

"To Mary," he said. "In loving memory."

"To Mary," they said in unison. Laura looked around the room at her family. She would be glad, she thought. Yes.

Simon dropped her home, and Laura climbed the stairs to the flat, tired and confused, the letter clutched in her hand. She had to remind herself it was Wednesday, and normal life was carrying on. It was strange, to have been at work this week, to speak to people on the phone, to do normal things. She wanted to say, "My grandmother died on Saturday. I'm very upset. So's my mum. But actually we're fine." A grandmother dying—it wasn't a big deal. It was sad; people were kind. Rachel had bought her some tulips, had been lovely, because she knew how close they were. But it wasn't a life-changing thing. Yes, they said, you'll be sad, oh, when's the funeral, right. Oh, that'll be nice. Lovely. It was the kind of grief people were able to talk about, console each other about. Whereas Laura knew it was something different; it was really strange. She felt like a new person, as if her life had undergone a seismic shift. She knew who she was, whether she was at home with her parents, or back at her own flat, or sitting at work. She knew who she was.

She saw herself for once without pretense, not as a girl from some book in a crinoline, dipping low in a curtsey at a ball, or as an evangelical new person who was going to sort her life out, who brooked no argument, who let no one into her life, who did not suffer weakness or fools. She was just—herself. She looked at the letter, there in her hand, and carefully tore it open. A velvet pouch slid out, and two sheets of paper.

chapter fifty-one

Darling Laura,

I am writing this letter to you in the full expectation that you may not read it for a few years, although I suspect and hope it may be sooner than that. It is a beautiful September day as I sit here at my desk. Cedric is upstairs on his balcony; he is singing something rather jolly, Puccini, I think. He is watering his plants. I can see the very tips of the trees in Hyde Park. It is sunny and dusty. The leaves are rather crispy. Summer is over; everyone is waiting for autumn. I love this time of year. The summer fatigue. I am alone in loving it, I think. But it reminds me of Cairo.

I want to tell you something, Laura. I have always tried to hold back from telling you what to do, because I have always felt you had enough people around you, directing you, and perhaps you needed someone with whom you could just talk. But now I think it may be time, time for me to be honest with you. As honest as I can be. I do this because I want you to be happy. More than anything,

I want you to be happy, for you have great happiness and love within you, Laura darling.

You will find enclosed the necklace I lent you, which you have always loved. I would like you to have it, please. It gives me great pleasure to know that after I am gone, you will be the one to wear it. It is valuable; more valuable than you realize, for Xan gave it to me, bought it for me in Cairo, when we first met.

We were both married to other people, you knew that. I was still married when we met. When we fell in love. You did not know that. My first husband, James Dearden, was the man I married when I was eighteen, and it is because of him that I moved out there. I was so young; I had never left England before. To be in Cairo—oh, Laura, the heat, dusty, pervasive heat, when you have lived through endless British winters with no such thing as central heating, no money for fires, the constant heat was like a drug to me. I was so happy. At first.

But James was not a good husband. I tried, Laura, but I was too young, too selfish. He and I—we should never have married. He was not a bad man, but I believe he became one. He could be vicious. Boorish, unpleasant, dull—and stupid. I could forgive him most things, but not that. Hated Egypt, the people, the life. He only liked the club. And drinking. I look back and try to remember, and I don't know that we were ever happy. When I had your mother, it got worse. He didn't care, wasn't interested. He wanted a son. Your mother was a beautiful baby, so good, contented. She was perfect, and he didn't care. He couldn't see it, and I hated him for that.

When the war came, people were evacuated, mostly to South Africa. But we stayed there. I was still only twenty-four when I met Xan. He had just arrived in Cairo; I felt as if I had been there for decades, in a living tomb. James and I were barely speaking. There was danger everywhere, nothing was certain. Xan knew no one. He was entirely alone; he was working for the army as a translator, a sort of traveler, someone to smooth relations out with the Egyptians. He had been everywhere, traveled to so many places already. He made me laugh. I understood him, even though we were very different. He was my age. James was forty, darling, to me he was an old man; he was drinking more and more. He beat me. The first time he beat me, I ran to the club, and Xan was there. We began an affair, I suppose you would call it, but that sounds so tawdry, so implicitly temporary. This—it was true love, I knew it from the start. Do you remember that story I used to tell you, about the trip to the desert, to the pyramids, to see the sun rise? Darling, it was true, I promise; but that was when it all began, when I was still married. But I simply knew, so well that I did not stop to analyze it. He was the love of my life. Still is.

Xan had been married, darling. Lucy, his wife, had died in England, and they had had a little girl. That was Annabel. And after the war was over, she came out to join him. I always remember the first time I saw her, at a party at the club. In the garden, it was, shaded and green. One of the few green places there. I remember how I smiled and said hello to her. She was a pretty little thing. I watched Xan with her, this funny little toddler clutching his leg, and I hated myself with all my heart and soul, every part of me, because I was glad his wife was dead, glad I had never known her, and I wished my husband were dead, wished we could be together. Yes, I did. I remember going to the English church, and taking Communion that next day. I remember how I felt, how much pleasure it gave me to kneel at the altar with a heart full of black things, full of adultery and jealousy and murderous rage, and spite. Daring God to throw at me anything more that he could. Knowing I was untouchable, that nothing could hurt me anymore. I remember the feeling; I remember so much of it all.

Not to be with the one you love, Laura, the one person you should be spending your life with—it's like a kind of living death. To wake up every morning and know you are still here. To have that brief, sweet moment of blankness, before your mind reminds you who you are, and why you are unhappy. It was like hell. A living hell of the heart's own making.

You know that James died. He had a heart attack, brought on by years of drinking, years of unhappiness. Almost six months later, I could barely believe it. And I hated myself for it, too. Xan and I were married a year later; everyone said how lucky we were to have found each other, and no one ever knew, no one knew I had lied, that I had prayed for this to happen, not even Xan. We had forty-five years together, Laura. We brought the girls up together, we traveled the world. We were never apart. And no one could have been happier than us, except for one small thing: We lied. And, oh, it doesn't matter! It doesn't matter!

I have always thought Annabel knew there was something between her father and me, before James died. I think she would remember . . . seeing things. Perhaps not, but I have always felt she knew. And I have always felt guilty about Annabel ever since. We both did. She never mentioned it, all those years. She has never seemed to mind. But I do, and I don't know why. Lately I do.

My mind is wandering. It is hot, out here on the balcony. I have the photo of Xan in my locket; I am looking at it now, as I write these words to you, Laura. I am very tired these days. Very tired, and cross. I worry, I feel myself starting to worry. I am old, Laura, and my life has been wonderful. This is what I wanted to say to you: You think of me as so resolute, and so proud, and so confident, think I always have been. And what terrifies me is, forty-five years ago, I nearly made a dreadful mistake. I would have stayed with James, I know, because I was afraid to leave. Afraid to leave a man I didn't love, who beat me, who was a drunk, who didn't want me or my daughter in his life. That is what terrifies me in the night—that if James hadn't died, I wouldn't have had the courage to seize happiness for myself, for Angela, for Annabel. For Xan and me. I took the coward's way out, and did nothing.

Don't be the same, Laura. When I think about what you might be missing, it terrifies me on your behalf. I think you might have missed the right person, your true love, because you have spent your life looking too hard for him. You have a great capacity to love, Laura. Don't run away from it. Use it. Stop wasting it. Throw yourself into it, and don't be scared. I promise you, with all my heart, that you will never live a day when you regret it.

Don't be afraid, my darling. I am so proud of you. Remember, I love you. That will never go away.

Granny

A postscript: Did I ever tell you about the summer Xan and I lived in the south of France, in the early eighties? Most interesting. We lived next door to a fascinating couple, Frederick Needham and his wife, Vivienne. I think you know who they are. She left her husband, his own brother, and her three children, and the greatest house in the country to be with him. Oh, you would have thought they were a golden pair, in their lovely house. Flowers everywhere, a riot of bougainvillea, a simply beautiful view of the sea. They could sit there together and look out at it all day, every day.

But they weren't happy. They were miserable. She ran away rather than face her unhappiness, and she was paying for it. Their love wasn't strong enough to withstand it. She missed that lovely boy of hers; we often talked of him. She should never have let him go. Vivienne followed her heart, without thinking of the consequences. I think you used to be rather like her, Laura. Not anymore. Now I worry that you think too much about the consequences of things. They are not important, as she had discovered. A society scandal—what is that, compared to a mother's love for her son? She lost far more than she gained, simply by caring too much about the proprieties, by listening to the outside world's chatter and clamor. So she never went back to see her children. Never. She decided to be unhappy instead. That is the penance Vivienne decided to pay.

She was so proud of him. I liked her very much. I think she would like you.

Good-bye, my darling.

chapter fifty-two

On Thursday at lunchtime, Jo arrived to pick up Laura and Yorky, to take them to the church. Laura was going to meet the rest of the family there. It was a gray day, the sky a uniform blanket of cloud, and Laura was in her room, hunting for her scarf.

"She's in the car, outside," Yorky called through the door. "I'll go down—see you in a minute?"

"Sure," Laura yelled. "I won't be long, sorry."

The scarf usually hung at the end of her shelf. It had fallen on the floor. As she bent to pick it up, she noticed, hanging on the back of the door, Nick's dinner jacket, the one he had put around her shoulders—was it only six days ago? She had put it on a hanger; she didn't quite know what to do with it. She stroked the fabric softly. Holding the scarf, she stood up, and realized that Mary's letter had fallen out of the bag on her shoulder. She scooped it up and stared at it, at the sloping, scratchy writing, the black ink on the cream paper. She patted the necklace around her neck. Jo's horn beeped tentatively outside, and Laura realized she had been standing there for a minute or so in front of the bookshelf, looking at this letter in her hand. Something clicked inside her and she pulled out one of her old hardbacks and put the letter between the pages. Shutting the book and sliding it back onto the shelf, Laura put her bag over her shoulder and left the room, closing the door behind her. She never read it again.

Angela had said quite firmly that they should meet at the church, which was around the corner from Crecy Court. It was as if they were merely meeting at Mary's flat, she said. She didn't want them turning up in a grave, solemn column. Laura agreed to her request, rather surprised; but she was glad of it, glad to have Jo and Yorky to walk down the aisle with, through the light, airy church crammed full with people. Mary had many friends, and it seemed they had all turned out—of course. Laura scanned the crowd.

"I don't know who half these people are," she muttered to Jo as they made their way down the aisle.

"Well, they obviously wanted to come, didn't they?" Jo patted her arm. "They loved her. I think that's really nice."

Jo and Yorky escorted her to her seat at the front of the church, then found seats themselves farther back. Laura sat down next to Simon, and leaned over to kiss her parents. George patted her knee. Across the aisle sat the Sandersons. Annabel was rigid, dressed entirely in black, wearing a small black hat with—

"Is that a *veil* Annabel's wearing?" Laura whispered to Simon.

"Yes," said Simon. "She's got gloves on, too—look."

Sure enough, Annabel was decked out in white kid gloves, completing the impression that she was, in fact, a schoolmistress from the 1930s. Or, Laura thought with a smile, a living, breathing version of Mrs. Danvers. She sat there, expressionless; and then, as if aware of Laura's eyes on her, turned slowly and gave her niece a smile of great sweetness. Laura looked at her, and thought how like Angela she was; and an idea took root in her head, a small idea, but one that, when she thought about it, made perfect sense. And then they stood up, because the coffin was arriving.

The service was short, only two hymns and one reading. Jasper gave the address. He said, looking down at Mary's extended family, that she had been all things to all people, and so he didn't have much to say, because they should not be sad, they should be happy. "That is why we do this today—to celebrate someone's life. In Mary's case, it truly is a celebration. We will not be sad," he said, rather theatrically wiping a tear from his cheek. "Rather, we will celebrate and imagine her welcoming us at her flat, or at Seavale, or before that, for those many of you who knew her when Xan was alive. The way she would say hello, with that sparkling look in her eyes that we all knew so well. The way you knew when she was enjoying herself or, alas, when she was terribly bored by what you were saying." The congregation laughed. "I shall miss her," he said simply. "That's why I'm sad. But I think she's happy, now she's with Xan."

Cedric, magnificently attired in a purple floral cravat, did the reading. Laura was amused to note, even through her distress, that his appearance caused a frisson of excitement in the church. This was exactly his crowd, she thought. If, at my funeral in fifty years' time, Jude Law got up and gave a reading, there'd be the same reaction. Half the congregation going, "Oh, my goodness! Is that Jude Law? My Lord! My dear, isn't he handsome?" and the other half going, "Who's that bloke?"

He read John Donne's "A Valediction: Forbidding Mourning," and he wasn't theatrical—for once. He was quiet and dignified, and as his voice rang through the church, the thick cloud outside seemed to lighten just a little, and it was bright inside; and as Laura looked up and down at her family, all of them, she thought about things that had gone before, things that were happening now, and about her grandmother's letter, how life was for the taking.

It was not sad, she knew it wasn't, and yet she kept crying throughout. But it didn't matter. She knew she was crying for the right reasons; looking at her mother and her brother, she knew they were thinking the same. She wished she could see Mary one more time, just once, to tell her all the things she wanted to, to ask her so many more things. But she couldn't. Mary had known it was her time to go. She wanted to be with Xan, not with them, and now she was.

As they filed out of the church, toward the cold white London light, Annabel took her niece's arm. "How are you, Laura dear?" she said.

"I'm okay," said Laura. "How are you, Annabel? That was a beautiful service, thank you."

"Well, I think we did her proud," said Annabel. "I know your mother was worried it'd be like a Russian Orthodox Easter service—about five hours long. But, in the end, I thought about what your grandmother would have wanted. I think she would have wanted that."

"You're right," said Laura, smiling at her.

"Very hard woman to really know that well," said Annabel. "And I knew her almost as long as your mother." She frowned, and they stopped in the porch of the church as the coffin was loaded into the hearse. Angela and George were the only ones going on to the crematorium; the rest of the party was gathering back at Crecy Court for refreshments. Angela stepped back a little and stood next to her stepsister, and Laura saw them look at each other and smile, so very alike.

"Everyone can walk to Mum's flat while we're at the crematorium, that's okay isn't it, Annabel?" said Angela, appealing to her to organize things. Annabel seized the mantle of team leader.

"Cedric and Jasper will lead you all to Mary's flat, where there are refreshments," she boomed in a loud voice. Laura turned around, only to find Fran and Lulu cringing behind her. She smiled at them, recognizing their embarrassment.

"Walk with us," said Fran solemnly.

Laura hadn't seen Fran since her flight back from Singapore with Jo, when she'd spilled the beans about her seeing Nick. Funny, how bothered Laura had been by that, how she had cursed the universe for letting it happen.

"Yes, of course," said Laura. "I wanted to ask you, anyway—"

She was casting about in her mind for something else to ask Lulu and Fran, something easy and conversational, when Cedric appeared beside her.

"Hello, old girl," he said, squeezing her waist. He shot Lulu and Fran a blank look; they shrank back, darted out of the way, and hurried on.

The other mourners followed them, led by Jasper and Annabel, and Laura took one last look inside the church as the doors were closing.

"Walk you back to your grandmother's, eh?" said Cedric, and they set off, Laura's arm through his, bringing up the rear.

"You read beautifully, Cedric," Laura said. She leaned against him.

"What? Oh, thank you. Thank you," said Cedric, batting his eyelashes. "Well, you know. I loved her, your grandmother."

"I know," said Laura.

"Asked her to marry me about four times," said Cedric conversationally. He looked up at the sky, around at the narrow town houses lining the road down to Baker Street.

"Really?" Laura wasn't that surprised; she knew Cedric worshipped Mary.

"Yes, but she always turned me down flat. Said she would never marry anyone after Xan, and I should go away and find someone else. Quite rude sometimes, actually." He ruffled his own hair. "Women."

"I can imagine." Laura smiled. "She was quite . . . scary sometimes, wasn't she?"

"Oh-ho, yes," said Cedric. "Very much so. Did I ever tell you about the time—"

Jasper appeared. "Come on, old boy. You've got the keys. Stop messing around and hurry up."

"Well," said Cedric crossly, "I . . . excuse me, Laura," and he strode off, leaving Laura smiling after him, watching the procession disappear down the road.

"Excuse me?" came a tentative voice behind her.

She turned round. There on the pavement was a woman in a headscarf, an ancient Burberry tightly belted around her tiny waist, holding a long black umbrella in her tiny gloved hands. She looked about seventy, possibly younger. She looked at Laura expectantly, her huge dark eyes full of concern.

"Have I missed Mary Fielding's funeral?" she asked. "I only flew in this morning, and then my train was late, I . . ."

Laura gazed at her, and then at the others, disappearing down the road. Suddenly she recognized her, and she knew who she was talking to. "I'm afraid so," she said. "I'm so sorry."

"Oh, dear," said the woman. She caught Laura's hand impulsively. "I did want to say good-bye. She was so wonderful, you know, so wonderful. I haven't seen her for—golly, it must be twenty years."

Laura couldn't stop looking at her, fascinated not just by her extreme beauty but because of who she was. "You're—Vivienne Lash, aren't you?" she said.

"Yes, yes," said the woman, a lovely smile breaking out over her face. "How did you know that? Most of the people who recognize me these days are extremely decrepit."

"I just do," said Laura, smiling at her.

Vivienne Lash glanced at her, then up and down the road. "Oh, I'm so cross with myself for being late. I wanted to say goodbye to her." Her eyes were sparkling with tears, but she blinked rapidly, looked around. "Goodness," she said, her eyes flitting ahead of her, "isn't that Cedric Forsythe ahead of us?"

Cedric had stopped to marshal his flock across a street, his walking stick waving in the air. Laura said, "Yes, it is."

"What a small world, how funny. He was so kind to me. I should go and—" She dug her hands into her pockets, a curiously familiar gesture, then shook her head. "No," she said after a minute. "I'll let you all get on, darling." She looked at Laura curiously. "Were you her granddaughter? Are you . . . Laura?"

"Yes," said Laura, amazed.

"She used to talk about you all so fondly. Ah, and here you are."

"Come and have a drink with us," said Laura. "Come and say hello to my parents, and . . . the others. I'm sure they'd love to meet you."

"No, no," said Vivienne Lash, still smiling but backing away. "I won't intrude. I wanted to come to the funeral, that was all. No fuss. Now I must get going, darling. Oh, it's so nice to have met you at last." She kissed Laura on the cheek and darted away, ballerinalike.

"Can I get you a cab?" Laura called. "Are you sure you don't want to come back?"

"No, darling." Vivienne Lash stopped still in the middle of the road and turned around. "I'll go straight to the station, thank you. Thank you!" She waved.

"Where are you going?" said Laura.

"I'm going to see my son," said Vivienne Lash. A huge smile curled around her face, and she caught her hands together. "I'm going to see Nick, my son."

Laura nodded numbly, and Vivienne Lash said in a low voice, "Yes. My son."

Her voice broke, and one little hand flew to her mouth. She cleared her throat, breathing in rapidly through her nostrils.

"I'm sorry," she said, looking back up at Laura, with an expression so like her son's, yet so poignantly maternal that Laura was overwhelmed by the force of it. "It's rather important to me," she said simply. "I haven't seen him for—for a long time."

"Yes," said Laura.

"I've been very stupid. For far too long." She tightened the belt around her waist. "Far too long. Waste of time. All that time." Laura watched her shyly underneath her lashes, not sure what to say. "So, then," said Vivienne Lash. "I really must go."

She waved to Laura again, and turned away. Laura stood still and watched her; suddenly she called out, "Mrs. Needham?"

Vivienne Lash turned around. "Yes, darling?"

A car drove past; she was on the other side of the street. Laura crossed hurriedly, fearing she might have vanished by the time she reached her.

"Can you do me a favor?" she said.

"Of course," said Vivienne. "What is it?"

"It's a long story," said Laura. "But I know your son." She put her hand on some railings; she felt suddenly light-headed, the shock of the day's various events catching up with her.

"Do you?" Vivienne's face lit up. "How wonderful. Nick? How do you know him?"

Laura said, smiling, "It really is a very long story. Can you just tell him something from me? Can you tell him—tell him—"

She paused, not knowing what to say, and Vivienne Lash watched her expectantly.

"Tell him," Laura said eventually, "that you saw Laura. And that she still has his dinner jacket, and she thinks he ought to come to her flat and collect it, since he wears it such an awful lot."

Vivienne mouthed the words to herself. She nodded, and looked at Laura thoughtfully. "Mary's granddaughter," she said quietly. "Well, well."

"Is that all right?" said Laura.

"Of course, darling. I'm an actress, I can remember my lines, you know." She kissed Laura again. "I am very glad to have met you, my dear. I'll see you soon, I think. Now"—she threw her umbrella lightly from one hand to the other—"I must go." And she flew down the street, one hand on her hair, looking about fourteen.

Laura leaned against the railings, lost in a world of her own. After a few moments, she realized Cedric was calling her name, and she ran toward him, toward the others, turning once to see if Vivienne was still there, but she had vanished like a puff of smoke.

chapter fifty-three

Autumn had come and gone in a flash, and now winter was here. It whistled through the bare branches outside Laura's window, clacking on the glass in the night and causing her to wake up with a start. It crept in through the gap under the front door, through the sash windows of their sitting room. It glittered and sparkled on the frost on the cars in the morning. It coughed and wheezed on the Tube, randomly spreading seasonal malaise. Suddenly it was dark, all the time. Through the streets, on her way to the Tube station each morning, Laura stomped her feet in her boots, hugging herself and shivering in the bitter cold. Yorky had bought a ridiculous, loudly patterned tweed coat, which he said made him look like Sherlock Holmes, but which Laura felt privately made him look like a down-and-out. They would walk together, swooshing the leaves out of the way, chatting about the day ahead of them.

One day, when winter had fully set in, Yorky and Laura were

walking down the road together, and Laura was trying to look interested while Yorky agonized about what he should buy Becky for a Christmas present.

It was nearly December, a month after Mary's funeral. Laura's parents were, astonishingly, on a really rather adventurous holiday. George had booked a trip to the Galápagos Islands for them, asserting his role as head of the family so boldly that Laura and Simon had spontaneously broken into a round of applause when their parents announced it to them. Annabel, of course, was a little sniffy, calling it a ridiculous waste of money; it was a sign that perhaps things were starting to settle down, that Annabel felt able to start being a disagreeable old cow again, as Simon had put it to his sister afterward.

Simon was living in Mary's flat for the time being, sorting out things, keeping the place occupied. He was going to see Jorgia in the New Year; Laura didn't know what would come of it, but she was glad he wasn't giving up just yet. His job at the upmarket garden center was going really well; he obviously had a flair for it. Laura suspected he rather liked being the young man in amongst a lot of rather older men (with trim mustaches and creased slacks) and women (wearing those sweatshirts that said things like LONDON * PARIS * WINDSOR!). She also worried that he was turning into an old man, since he seemed to spend most of his evenings with Cedric and Jasper at Crecy Court, smoking panatelas and drinking whisky, listening to Jasper's tales of love and betrayal among the artistic community in postwar Cornwall and Cedric's increasingly fantastical ramblings amongst the film sets, theaters, dressing rooms, and premieres of the British film industry during its 1950s peak.

Laura missed her grandmother much more than she had expected. She knew why, she knew it would pass; but as the weeks went by and she carried on in her own life, she realized she had so many questions she'd never asked her grandmother. About her life, about how much she had loved Xan, about all of that. She felt as if a light had gone out of her life, someone who understood her had gone; and she felt that she had never really tried to talk to her own grandmother, otherwise she would have found all this out. Now it was too late.

A month had passed since Mary's funeral, and she had heard nothing from Nick. What had happened when his mother arrived? How had they been together? Was it awful for him or wonderful, was he glad? She wanted to know if he'd got her message, but she realized that was a slender thread to hang a relationship on. The two of them were better off apart, perhaps, and as her life settled back to normal, it grew easier to persuade herself of that.

Laura hugged herself as she walked next to Yorky and, realizing her thoughts had drifted, as they did more than she would like these days, she nodded intelligently and tried to pretend she had been listening all along.

"Anyway, Becky says she doesn't want an expensive handbag, but does that mean that's actually what she *does* want?"

"I don't know," said Laura, trying to concentrate. "I think, knowing Becky, that means she doesn't want one."

"Do you think?" said Yorky.

"Absolutely," said Laura. "She's a sensible girl, you know. She's not like—like . . ." She was going to say "Amy," but stopped herself.

"Were you going to say Amy?" said Yorky, smiling at her.

"Well, yes," said Laura. "God."

"They're getting married, you know," Yorky said suddenly.

"Seriously?" said Laura. "When?"

"After the baby's born. Chris told me. I didn't know if you'd want to know or not."

"Oh, Yorks," said Laura. She patted his Sherlock Holmes–like sleeve. "Bless you. I think that's great. Good for them."

"Well, I hope so," said Yorky. "You okay?"

"Honestly, I am," said Laura. "I can't believe it was a year ago, you know. Almost exactly a year, that it all started up. Gosh, I was stupid."

"He was stupid, too," Yorky said loyally; as Laura made to protest, he added, "Yes, but you were pretty dim about it all."

"Hah," said Laura. "Oh, well."

There was a pause; they both kept on walking.

"Laura," said Yorky after a while. "I've been—want to ask you something."

"What?" said Laura.

"Well . . ." Yorky appeared to be in the early stage of a nervous tic. His face was twitching solemnly. They stood by the curb. "Look. The thing is . . . I want to ask Becky to move in with me."

"Oh," said Laura, and nearly walked out in front of a car.

Yorky grabbed her arm and pulled her back. "I'm sorry to spring it on you like this. I haven't asked her yet, you know. Wanted to see what you thought."

"Hm," said Laura, nodding.

"I know it's a bit soon," said Yorky. "It's only five months. But, you know something? I know it's right."

Laura nodded again. Yorky stood up straight.

"I keep thinking, all these years I've been mooning around after girls, hoping to get them to notice me, and Becky's been downstairs for the past two years, right under my nose, and I almost didn't do anything about it. And that's ridiculous. I'm sorry, it's awful to be kicking your best friend out into the street, but—can you see what I mean?"

"It's a bit of a shocker," she said eventually. "But that's great! Just great." She hugged Yorky. "I'm really pleased for you, man."

"It's not going to be for a couple of months," Yorky said. "She could say no, too—so don't pack your bags just yet."

"I won't," said Laura. "But I'm pretty sure she's not going to say no, Yorks."

He kissed her on the cheek. "You're the best, Laura. Thank you. I'm sorry, this is a bit of a crap time to spring this on you, but—" His face brightened suddenly. "Hey! Simon's going to Peru in February, isn't he?" Laura nodded. "Couldn't you stay in your grandmother's flat for a bit?"

"I could," said Laura. They crossed the road. "But you know, I think it's time I moved on somewhere else. Grew up a bit. Bought a place of my own, maybe."

"Well," said Yorky.

"Or I could just move into Becky's flat," said Laura, half joking, but Yorky thought it was a great idea, the simplest solution to the problem, and Laura spent the rest of the walk to the station persuading him that if she needed a change, moving downstairs wasn't necessarily it.

When they reached the Tube, they went their separate ways. "Thanks again," said Yorky, patting her arm. "Just for being pleased for me, even if you're not."

"I am pleased for you," Laura said honestly. "I really am." She took her book out of her bag. "Right. You'd better go, isn't that your train?"

"What's this?" said Yorky, holding up her copy of *Regency Buck*. "Back on the Georgette Heyers again, Laura? Oh, no. . . ." His face paled, and Laura snatched the book back.

"I know what I'm doing this time," she said, nodding wisely. "Seriously! Everything in moderation."

Yorky nodded, unconvinced.

"I'm reading *Trainspotting* next, for a bit of balance," said Laura, pushing him away. "Now, go! You'll be late!"

She watched him run down the tunnel, and smiled as she walked to her own platform, shivering in the cold. She thought of Dan and Amy, engaged. Dan, on this platform months ago, waiting for her, and it could have been for another person. It was, really. She was older. Not necessarily wiser, not necessarily fundamentally different. But . . . she'd changed, she knew that. Whether for the better or not, she wasn't sure. She wasn't necessarily happier than she had been, she thought, as she sat down on the bench she and Dan used to share. Then she considered it again. Yes, she *was* happier, she realized. Happy by herself, happy not to depend on the heady rush of a new crush to buoy her up. She laughed a little to herself—how boring that sounded for a girl who'd loved and lost one of the most eligible men in the country—and picked up *Regency Buck*. Sometimes fantasy was better than reality. In moderation, as she'd assured Yorky. Obviously.

It was a Friday. All through the day, as Laura fielded calls and tapped away at her computer, she kept thinking about Yorky, about leaving the flat. It made her feel sad, but at the same time she knew it was time to move on, for both of them. To have thought, a year ago, Yorky would be about to ask a girl to move in with him—and she might say yes. Laura couldn't wait to discuss it with Jo. It was wonderful—but weird at the same time.

Laura left work on the dot of five-thirty. She poked her head into Rachel's office on the way out. "I'm off," she said, waving. "Have a lovely weekend. I e-mailed you next year's school term dates."

Rachel looked up from her desk, where she was applying some lipstick. "Are you going, already?" she said, astonished.

Laura came farther into the office. "Yes. I'm sorry—I hope that's okay?"

"Of course it is!" Rachel said, pleased. She smacked her lips together, and smoothed down her dark mulberry-colored shirt. "Laura, you haven't left before seven for weeks. This is great!"

"Oh," said Laura. "Phew." She eyed her boss curiously. "What are you–oh, my God. You've got a date, haven't you?"

"Yes . . ." Rachel said, blushing rosily. "Maybe . . . not sure."

"It's with Marcus!" said Laura. "It is! Oh, my God! Is it tonight? Second date?"

Rachel and Marcus had been on a date the week before. Laura had not had particularly high hopes, given her previous experience with him, but she'd encouraged Rachel to go. She clapped her hands in excitement. "Oh, my God. Wow! You never said, you just said it went okay and you weren't sure!"

"Well," said Rachel crossly. "It was okay. It was really nice, actually. I just didn't want to go around yelling about it. Now, shush, stop getting overexcited."

"No!" yelled Laura again. She collected herself. "Sorry. Wow. Where are you going?"

"Some corporate thing at the Opera House," said Rachel uncertainly. "It's through his work, some German bank. We're meeting for a glass of something beforehand."

Laura's heart sank, recognizing the signs. "Oh," she said.

"Yes," said Rachel. She looked solemn. "I can't believe he's asked me. Lucky me."

"Lucky you," echoed Laura, smiling, and she felt her throat constrict with emotion, though she didn't really understand why. "Well, we—er, we love Marcus. I'm sorry, by the way," she said. "Can you tell him I'm sorry I haven't been in touch? Since he got back? You know, Granny's funeral and everything. I hope he got my letter, saying thank you for the money."

"I don't know," said Rachel. "That's the funny thing. I mentioned the donation last time. Tried to say something about it. You know what he said?"

"No," said Laura.

"He said he didn't know anything about it."

"What?"

"Yeah." Rachel brushed some bronzer onto her cheek. "I keep meaning to ask someone about it, actually. Haven't done. I mean, the money's there, it's all fine. So I just never thought . . ."

"That's weird," said Laura.

"It is weird, isn't it?" said Rachel, her face clouding momentarily. "But I think Clare must have sorted it out, off her own bat. Not Marcus. Which means . . ."

Which means my date with him actually was a total waste of time, thought Laura, smiling to herself. It seemed like a long time ago now. Funny.

"Have a lovely weekend," Rachel called as she left.

Laura walked out onto the street, into the cold December air, and caught a bus, which she didn't usually, but she wanted to see the Christmas lights across town. Yorky was staying the night with Becky, and she was having Jo and Hilary over for supper. So, Marcus Sussman and Rachel. Yorky moving in with Becky. Well, well, well. She sat on the bus as it bumped slowly up Tottenham Court Road and looked out the window, drinking in the bustling, energetic, aggravating sea of humanity below her, people on their way home, people on their way out. She was happy just to gaze and plan the menu for tonight in her head, happy to let the week's events, the day at work wash over her.

When she got back to her dark, cold flat, Laura turned on all the lights, unpacked the food, put on a CD, and started cooking. Soon the kitchen was filled with a warm, spicy fug, as Laura absorbed herself in what she was doing, chopped and fried and sautéed and mixed in complete happiness. She was just finishing off and thinking she should start to set the table, when she dropped a spoon into the casseroled sauce of the lamb shanks by mistake; it splashed everywhere, and Laura cursed, feeling some of it hit her face.

"Ouch," she said, licking her cheek experimentally and grabbing a tea towel. "Bollocks," she said, as she looked at the clock and realized it was seven-thirty and they'd be here soon. Jo was always, always bang on time. The downstairs doorbell rang. "Shit!" she said, dabbing her face with the towel and walking toward the intercom; this wasn't working out and she'd wanted it to, just for once.

"Hello," she said, licking her lips as she spoke into the intercom.

There was a crackle, then silence. Then a low, familiar voice said, "Laura. It's Nick. Can I come up?"

chapter fifty-four

"What?" said Laura, her hand flying to her cheek. "Who?"

"It's me, Nick. I'm coming up."

"You—"

"Thanks," came Nick's voice more indistinctly, and she heard someone in the background say, "You want come in, boy? Come in."

"Mr. Kenzo!" Laura said loudly into the speaker. She dropped the phone so it hung off the wall, and opened the door. She stood there for what seemed like hours, but of course it was only a few seconds, hearing voices growing louder as they approached; and eventually, Mr. Kenzo and Nick appeared together on Laura's landing.

"Hello, Laura!" said Mr. Kenzo happily. "Your friend, he was outside, I've let him in! Good evening, sir."

"Good evening," said Nick. "Thank you for the recommendation."

"What?" said Laura, standing aside to usher him into the flat, as Mr. Kenzo unlocked his door.

"I want to go to Marmaris, and your neighbor was kindly explaining when is the best time to go," said Nick imperturbably.

"You want to go to . . . ?" Laura said helplessly. "Get in."

"Bye," said Mr. Kenzo loudly as she shut the door. "Goodbye!"

"Hello," said Nick, as Laura shut the door and leaned against it, staring at him.

"You're in my flat," said Laura, not knowing what else to say.

"Well spotted," said Nick. "Is this the sitting room?"

"No," said Laura. "Oh. I—yes. I mean, yes."

"It's really nice," said Nick.

"I'm moving out, actually," said Laura. "I'm being kicked out."

"Well, it's not that nice, then," he said. "Right. Aren't you going to offer me a drink or anything?"

Laura said nothing, just carried on looking at him, leaning against the door. "What are you doing here?" she said after a while.

"You told me to come and collect my dinner jacket, Laura."

"That was over a month ago," said Laura. "And I didn't tell you. I told your mother to tell you."

"Well, I had to discuss it with her. Think about it for a while." His eyes were warm, full of laughter. "Can I have a drink? Just water, if you don't have anything else? It's been a long drive."

She didn't know what to say, was unable to process the request. She said stupidly, "Why are you here?"

"Well, this isn't quite the way I wanted to say it, but—I wanted to talk to you." He was looking at her, determined.

"About what?" said Laura, and then she remembered the lamb

shanks, bubbling on the stove. "Argh," she cried, and ran into the kitchen. "Oh, dear. Open the door again, would you?"

The meat was caramelizing somewhat, a little crusty and fried around the edges. A moment later and it would have burned. Laura turned it off, and sat down at the kitchen table. Nick was in the doorway.

"You're here," she said again, helplessly.

"Oh, God, Laura," said Nick slightly impatiently. "If you're going to act like someone with learning difficulties, I'm going to wait outside."

"Okay, okay," said Laura. "Tell me, then. Tell me why you're here."

There was a pile of tea towels on the table; Yorky had taken them out of the washing machine and dumped them there. She started smoothing them out, folding them over and over.

Nick watched her and said nothing for a moment; then he walked toward her and leaned against the counter. He cleared his throat.

"I'm here to tell you I love you," he said matter-of-factly.

"What?" said Laura.

"Yep," Nick said. He nodded. "I wish I didn't, most of the time. But I do."

"You—"

"Yes," said Nick calmly. "It's a real pain." He pulled her to her feet and wrapped his arms around her. "You are a thorn in my side, Laura." He bent his head and kissed her. After a few seconds he lifted his head, still holding her tightly. "An annoying, gorgeous thorn in my side. And I can't seem to get rid of you, of feeling like this. So that's why I'm here. I'm in love with you, and I know whatever you say, I always will be."

He kissed her again.

"I thought you should know," he said, his voice a little hoarse.

"My God," said Laura, struggling to know what to say. "We're in the kitchen."

Nick laughed, and held her tighter. He looked down at her and kissed her gently. "Oh, Laura."

She lolled against him, pressing her body against his, feeling as if she was coming alive as she touched him. Nick, here, in front of her, holding her.

"Laura, I know you think us together is going to be hard. I know you think we're too different, that it's all too odd. But it's not. There was something my mother said to me when I saw her: If you find someone you love, you have to do something about it. I tried to do something about it before, you know. To help you, to make things better for you. But it wasn't the right thing to do. I should have come down here straight after you left me."

"Why?" said Laura, intrigued. "What did you do?"

"It doesn't matter." Nick kissed her again. "Does not matter at all."

She pressed her hands on his chest and stepped back. "You," she said, nodding. "You gave the money. Didn't you? You gave the money to the program at work!"

"No," said Nick.

"Yes, you did," said Laura, staring up at him. He grimaced, then inclined his head slightly, looking uncomfortable. "Oh, Nick. I knew it wasn't Marcus! It was you! Why did you do it?"

"I wanted . . ." he said, shaking his head. "Laura, you were so upset, that night in the car. I just wanted everything to be better for you. I thought I couldn't have you, that we were never going to work out, and it really got to me, seeing you like that. You were so mysterious about work and everything—and then when you left, Charles explained what had happened with Marcus. So"—he bent his head—"I thought, Well, if we can't be together, I can still do something to make her life better. And other people's, too," he added disingenuously. "But yours most of all.

"This is what my mother said to me," he went on. "She said I was a fool if I let you get away. She told me to stop making odd gestures like bailing you out at work anonymously. She told me to get down here and tell you I love you. Myself. In person. Because if you love someone, you have to be brave and tell them. Don't let them go."

"That's what someone said to me," said Laura, thinking of Mary and her letter.

"And if you say no, I'm going to spend the rest of my life trying to convince you I'm right. I promise. I won't leave you alone. Because it's not about who's what or where or anything. We should be together. The other stuff doesn't matter. That's all."

"We should," Laura echoed. She was feeling faint. She never felt faint. Her head was spinning; she felt light-headed, weightless in Nick's arms. She leaned against him again. "Yes," she said. "We should. And you're right, God! You're right. Who cares about the other stuff?"

"You mean it?" he said.

"I do," Laura said, looking up into his face. "You know something?"

"What?"

"I've always seen us at Chartley. Not here. I tried to picture it, but I always thought this"—she gestured around the kitchen—"might be weird, having you here."

"And?"

"And it's not," said Laura, smiling up at him. "It makes perfect sense. I like your house better, though."

"Shall I take you up there tomorrow?" he said. "For the weekend? Would you like that?"

"I can't think of anything I'd like more," she said. "Is—there anyone there?"

"No," he said. "Mum left last week, but she's coming back for Christmas. No sisters, either. Just you, me, and Chartley."

"And all the ghosts of relatives past," said Laura.

"Yes," said Nick. "But they don't matter, do they?"

"No, they don't," said Laura. "They just don't. You and me. That's what matters."

Then he kissed her again, her head in his hands, just the two of them, wrapped around each other, clinging desperately to each other; and Laura gave herself up to the sheer enjoyment of it for several minutes, or it could have been hours, days, she had no idea, for once it was just the two of them, alone in time and space, nothing else to bother them, no geological layers of mistrust and anger and exes and stupid things like class and money—

"Er . . . Laura?"

Laura and Nick sprang apart, and looked into the hallway. There in the corridor, looking completely shell-shocked, were Jo and Hilary, each clutching her handbag and a bottle of wine. They said simultaneously:

"The front door was open. . . ."

"The entry phone was off the hook. . . ."

Then both trailed off into silence as Laura looked at them, not sure what to say.

Nick coughed, and stood up straight. "Er, hello," he said.

"Hi," said Jo and Hilary in unison. Hilary raised her hand weakly. Jo's mouth was wide open.

Laura looked at them, then back to Nick. She smiled at him, a small, definite smile. He looked down at her and smiled back, his eyes full of understanding and warmth and the amusement she knew they shared, which was why she loved him and knew him, better than anyone else. She stepped forward, holding his hand.

"Jo, Hilary," she said. "I'd like you to meet Nick. The Marquis of Ranelagh. Er . . . he's staying for supper. Aren't you?"

"Yes, if that's all right with you two," said Nick. Hilary and Jo nodded mutely, and Nick looked around the kitchen. "Right," he said, taking off his jacket. "Why don't I set the table?"